Mist
iver
N
W
E
S
97
19
Painted Hills
Mitchell
verland Trek
6
John Day Fossil Bed
National Monument
D0209676

INTO THE MIST

Also available by P. C. Cast

Sisters of Salem,
with Kristin Cast

Spells Trouble
Omens Bite

House of Night,
with Kristin Cast

Marked
Betrayed
Chosen
Untamed
Hunted
Tempted
Burned
Awakened
Dragon's Oath
Destined
Lenobia's Vow
Hidden
Neferet's Curse
Revealed
Kalona's Fall
Redeemed

House of Night Other World

Loved
Lost
Forgotten
Found

House of Night:
Legacy The Graphic

Novel

Goddess Summoning

Goddess of the Sea
Goddess of Spring
Goddess of Light
Goddess of the Rose
Goddess of Love
Warrior Rising/Goddess of Troy

Partholon

Divine Beginnings
Divine by Mistake
Divine by Choice
Divine By Blood
Elphame's Choice
Brighid's Quest

Mysteria, with Maryjanice
Davidson, Susan Grant, and
Gena Showalter

Mysteria Nights
Mysteria Lane
Mysteria

Tales of A New World

Moon Chosen
Sun Warrior
Wind Rider

INTO THE MIST

A NOVEL

P. C. CAST

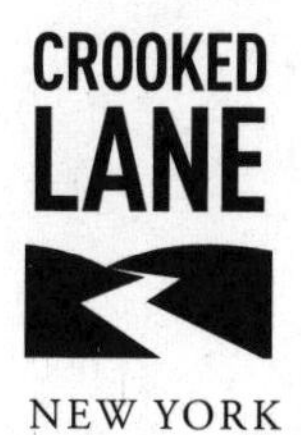

NEW YORK

Published in the United States by Crooked Lane Books, an imprint of The Quick Brown Fox & Company LLC.

Crooked Lane Books and its logo are trademarks of The Quick Brown Fox & Company LLC.

Library of Congress Catalog-in-Publication data available upon request.

ISBN (hardcover): 978-1-64385-918-7
ISBN (ebook): 978-1-64385-919-4

Cover design by Peter Strain
Map design by Sabine Stangenberg
Interior illustrations by Kim Doner

Printed in the United States.

www.crookedlanebooks.com

Crooked Lane Books
34 West 27th St., 10th Floor
New York, NY 10001

First Edition: July 2022

10 9 8 7 6 5 4 3 2 1

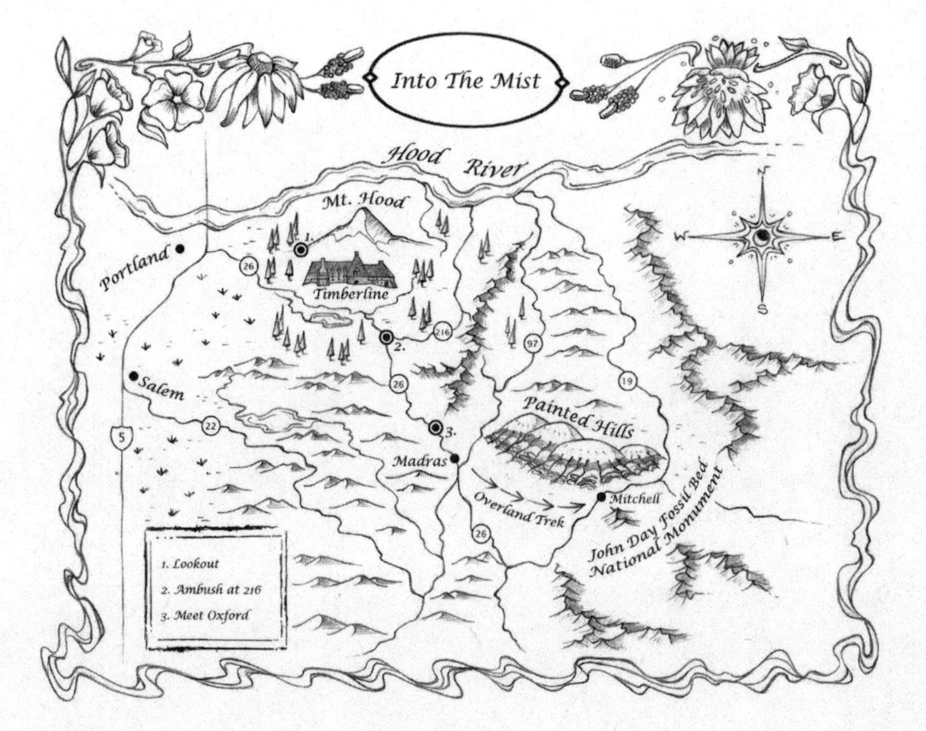
Into The Mist
Hood River
Mt. Hood
Portland
Timberline
Salem
Madras
Painted Hills
Mitchell
Overland Trek
John Day Fossil Bed
National Monument
N
S
W
E
26
216
97
19
22
5
1.
2.
3.
1. Lookout
2. Ambush at 216
3. Meet Oxford

To Lola Palazzo—the Stella to
my Mercury, the Thelma to my Louise.
Let's go on holiday—hello!

MERCURY RHODES

CHAPTER

1

"HOLY SHIT! BRIGHT *and* cold is so confusing." Mercury Rhodes dug in her purse for her sunglasses, which she found—predictably—at the very bottom of the bag. She fished them out, frowning at the lint from balled-up, unused tissues that always lurked in her purse, and blew across the lenses before she shoved them on her face.

She was joined by her best friend, Stella Carver, who—also predictably—had her shades perched perfectly on her nose. Stella pulled up the faux fur collar on her 1920s flapper-style car coat and took a sip of her mimosa. "Oh please, Acorn. We've been at Timberline for five days, and this is what—your third conference here?"

Mercury raised a brow. "Fourth. And don't call me Acorn."

"Fourth. Whatever. You're not used to the bright mixed with cold yet? And by the by, I like your dad's nickname for you, *and* ten plus years of best friendship allows me Acorn privileges."

"Fine. Call me Acorn. And, no, I think it'll always be weird to me that I can get a sunburn *and* frostbite at the same time. More importantly, where'd you get the mimosa?"

"Ram's Head Bar made me a to-go flute. Aren't they sweet?" Stella tilted her mirrored sunglasses down. Her glacier-blue eyes sparkled mischievously as she batted her eyelashes in mock innocence.

Mercury snorted. "You're an Oklahoma public schoolteacher, so I know *they're*"—Mercury air-quoted the word—"not being sweet because you're an over-tipper."

"You know I always tip a solid twenty percent. Bad tippers have no soul." Stella's full lips curled up into a cat-licking-cream grin. "But there are more ways to show appreciation than with money."

"So, you hooked up with that infant last night?"

Stella clutched her fake pearls. "Dusty is thirty and a half. An absolutely legal adult."

"You're forty-five and a half. That's a fifteen-year difference."

Stella shrugged. "Numbers. Mere numbers."

Mercury rolled her hazel eyes. "*Fifteen years.* And please. His name couldn't actually be Dusty Rose. With all that long hair and those tattoos, he's textbook romance hero cliché."

Stella tossed back her mane of blonde and silver-streaked curls. "Oh, honey, who cares about a decade or so? Look at this fabulous ass." She wiggled her shapely butt. "Does it say I'm too old? Not hardly. And with his skills, who the hell cares what his name is?"

"You're not talking about his ability to mix a perfect cocktail, are you?"

"Huh? Did you say *cock*?"

A man rushed past them, jostling Stella's arm so that she spilled half of her mimosa on the wide concrete stairs that stretched from the entrance of Timberline Lodge to the parking lot of the Oregon ski resort. "Come on!" he blustered. "Get that SUV pulled around so we can load the luggage! We need to get going so we're at the Portland airport an hour and a half before flight time!"

"Jesus H. Christ!" Stella glared at the man. "Watch where you're going, Mr. Hale!"

Richard Hale glanced over his shoulder at the two women. "Ladies, fun and games are over. The rest of the teachers are already waiting with the luggage around the side of the lodge." He gestured dramatically at the driver of the nearby Escalade, who began to swing the vehicle past them to follow the side road that led to the bellhop station. Then Richard Hale faced the two women, his look of disapproval focused on Stella's half-empty mimosa. "Ms. Carver, is that really necessary?"

"Yes. Completely."

His sigh was long suffering. "Well, you're waiting at the wrong place. No wonder Coach Davis was confused and pulled up here." Hale paused, and when neither woman responded, he ran his hand through his short, thinning blond hair. "Well, come on. Follow me to where you're *supposed* to be." He marched down the stairs after the rental SUV.

"Principals make my ass hurt," said Mercury as she combed her fingers through her wavy hair.

Stella chugged the last of her mimosa and threw the plastic flute into a nearby waste can. "Preaching to the choir, my friend. Better follow him before he has a stroke." She hooked her arm through Mercury's and whispered, "And you know he has high blood pressure, soooo . . ." She let the last word linger and waggled her eyebrows.

Mercury barked a laugh. "Ha! Don't *all* principals have high blood pressure?"

"Probably." Stella shrugged. "Most of 'em can't even handle a classroom, yet they're promoted." She rolled her eyes. "Mediocrity is so much easier to control than free-thinking excellence, but they put mediocrity in charge of those of us who are free-thinking and excellent—hence the high blood pressure issue."

"Preach, sister!" Mercury lowered her voice. "Too bad his fave, Deena, doesn't have her National Certification and wasn't eligible to attend the spring conference. She *really* gets his blood pressure up."

Stella's laughter was full, loud, and contagious. "Hey, they're platonic. Remember?"

"Uh, nope. But I do remember that he's married and so is dear little Deena. I also remember seeing her leave his office last month, very disheveled—with her appliqued sweater on *inside out.* And then Dicky Hale named her head of the English Department at the next faculty meeting. Coincidence? I think not."

"I love faculty scandals," said Stella. "Especially when the participants are too inept to even attempt a decent cover-up. I mean, Deena is the youngest, least experienced teacher in the English department. Like it's not obvious how she got named head?"

"Right? Clearly it's the correct job title, though."

Giggling like girls, the friends joined the small group waiting beside the black Escalade. A young, harried bellhop nodded automatically as the principal explained to him how to load the luggage into the rear of the big SUV. Beside the SUV three women watched the luggage loading with silent semi-interest. When they saw Mercury and Stella, two of the three grinned and waved. The third pursed her lips in an expression so familiar that deep crevices framed her thin lips—pursed or not.

"There you two are!" The tall brunette, whose skinny jeans and cropped top made her look more student than teacher, lifted a cardboard drink carrier that had two paper cups in it. Puppy-ish, she bounced up on her toes as she offered the drinks to Mercury and Stella. "Got you guys your fave."

"Coffee and Kahlúa?" Mercury asked as she reached for one of the cups.

"Yep. With no sugar for both of you, right?"

Mercury grinned as she took one of the cups from the cardboard holder. "Jenny, you were the best intern I've ever had."

"I'm the only intern you've ever had," Jenny quipped.

"Well, you're the best new nationally certified teacher I know," said Stella before she took her own cup and sipped it with a satisfied smile.

Mercury lifted one brow. "You've never even watched her teach."

Stella shrugged. "I don't have to. She knows how we like our booze coffee. Her attention to detail is clearly excellent, which makes for good teaching."

Mercury laughed. "Point well made, girlfriend."

"Do you really think having your ex-intern fetch spiked coffee is the proper way to mentor her as a young teacher?"

Stella curled a lip. "Absolutely. Acorn and I live by the motto: start as you mean to finish. So take your dark, judgmental cloud elsewhere, Karen."

Karen sniffed disapprovingly. "I don't know why you insist on calling Ms. Rhodes by that nickname. It really isn't professional."

"She's my best friend. There's nothing professional about that, which you'd know if you had a best friend," quipped Stella. "Plus, her dad wasn't wrong when he nicknamed her. Her hair really is a perfect acorn shade." Stella reached out to pat Mercury's wavy, nut-colored hair.

Mercury sidestepped Stella's hand and muttered, "Stop antagonizing her!" under her breath at her friend, then stifled a sigh and forced herself to smile at the pinched-face teacher. "Good morning, Mrs. Gay." Mercury always called the history teacher by her last name. She realized it was childish, but she thought it was hilarious that someone so uptight and homophobic had that particular name. "Did you sleep well?"

Karen Gay nodded jerkily. "Of course. Sleeplessness is a sign of a troubled conscience."

"Or fun, Karen. You do remember fun, don't you?" added Stella—who *always* called her by her first name because, as she put it, Karen *is such a Karen.*

Karen's only response was a disapproving glance as she straightened her cardigan and smoothed her strictly starched and ironed khaki slacks.

"Oh, look you guys." Amelia Watson, the last member of their little group representing Tulsa Public Schools, called their attention to the sign "Timberline Lodge Welcomes Nationally Certified Teachers Spring Conference Members" that another bellhop was changing to "Welcome Portland Nike Executives."

"That's kinda sad," she said.

"I don't know," Mercury said. "All of this bright cold is wearing on me. It's pretty, but snow year-round is just not right."

Stella shook her head. "Please don't be such an Okie."

"But I am an Okie!" Mercury loaded the sentence with a lazy twang that sounded like Tulsa on a hot summer day.

"Well, I think it's nice here. I like the snow and—" Amelia paused, winced, and rubbed her protruding belly.

"You okay?" Mercury stepped closer to the pregnant teacher.

Amelia sighed and nodded as she continued to massage her middle. "I'm fine. He's just agreeing with me by kicking my ribs."

Stella studied her. "Are you sure you're only seven months along? You look big enough to pop any second."

"Thanks." Amelia laced her words heavily with sarcasm. "That's exactly what every pregnant woman wants to hear."

"Sorry!" Stella held up her hands in mock surrender. "Your pregnant dress is real pretty. I love that shade of yellow. Truce?"

Amelia laughed. "Truce. But it's called a *maternity* dress. I'm the one who's preggers—not my dress."

Richard Hale, principal of Will Rogers High School, undertipped the bellhop and then made a shooing motion at the little group. "Let's go! Load up."

"I'm sitting in the back with Mercury and Stella," said Jenny as she climbed up into the rear bench seat of the rented SUV.

The principal frowned disapprovingly while the three women slid into the seat before he offered Karen Gay his hand and helped her into the center bucket seat.

"Why, thank you, Mr. Hale. I do appreciate a true gentleman," Karen said primly.

Then the principal turned his frown on the pregnant teacher. "I suppose you still have to ride in the front seat."

Amelia's cheeks went pink. "I really can't help it. I'm always travel sick when I'm pregnant. It's better in the front seat."

"Amelia can sit back here with us," Mercury called. "But she'll probably puke."

"We don't mind, though," Jenny said.

"Fuckin' A we don't! Come on back here with the cool kids!" added Stella.

Predictably, Stella's language made Mr. Hale wince. "No, it's fine. Ride up front. Coach Davis! Move back. I'm driving."

"No problem. You're our boss," said the coach. He climbed from the driver's seat to the empty bucket seat behind it and nodded politely to Karen before he winked at the women behind him.

Mercury hated that Coach Davis referred to Hale as their "boss." The truth was that a principal is an administrator—not an employer. The school board actually did the hiring and firing—of principals as well as teachers—but she winked back at him and Stella blew him a kiss, which made the amiable coach grin. Then Mercury startled as someone rapped on the SUV's window, but as soon as she focused on the person—an athletically attractive woman whose tawny beige skin radiated health and whose thick, raven curls perfectly framed her smile—she quickly lowered her window.

"Imani! I missed you at breakfast," Mercury grinned back at her.

"And I missed you at the bar," added Stella.

Imani's laugh was deep and filled with joy. "Oh, honey, you know sleeping with the bartender doesn't mean you were actually *at the bar*, right?"

Stella smoothed back her hair. "We stopped by the bar. Afterward. So he could make me a goodbye mimosa."

"You're nasty," said Imani. "Which is why I like you."

Mercury cleared her throat expectantly.

Imani laughed again. "You're nasty too, even if you aren't the cradle robber your bestie is."

"That's only because she's older." Mercury paused. "But I do aspire to be her when I grow up."

Stella spoke around her friend. "You want to squish in here? We're heading to the Portland airport."

"Nah, but thanks. I booked an afternoon flight back to San Diego so that I'd have time for a little hike before I had to leave." She gazed up at Mount Hood, stretching white and majestic behind them. "I do love me some San Diego, but sometimes I crave snow and mountains and all this raw nature."

Mercury shivered. "Ugh. Snow. Ugh. Nature. You can have both. Hey, don't forget to email me your botany lesson plan for that cool photosynthesis lab."

"I won't forget," Imani said. "And you two remember you promised to take a road trip to San Diego this summer and stay with me."

Stella flipped her hair. "Are you kidding? No way we're forgetting. *Lots* of military men stationed there, and my summer mission is to find Mr. Right Now—hello!"

"We are leaving!" Mr. Hale shouted from the driver's seat as he put the SUV in gear.

Imani jumped back as Mercury and Stella waved.

"I hate it when Dicky acts douchey in front of other teachers," Mercury muttered to Stella, who nodded as she sipped her coffee and Kahlúa.

"Don't worry," Stella whispered back. "Teachers expect principal douchery."

Jenny snorted a laugh and almost spewed coffee out her nose.

"It's always great to see Imani, though," said Mercury. "I'm so glad our combined love of weird science stuff brought us together."

"Right?" Stella's thick blonde and silver hair bounced around her face as she nodded. "I'll never forget meeting her in that pottery and brickmaking workshop. How many years ago was it?"

"Four," said Mercury. "Jenny, didn't Imani also take that workshop on radio wave experiments with you this year?"

"Yep, and afterward we met y'all for margaritas at the bar. Remember?"

"I definitely recall the margaritas," said Stella. "And that's the night I met Dusty." She waggled her brows.

Richard Hale's watery blue eyes snapped up to the rearview mirror. "You know, this conference is for academic enhancement, not partying."

"Yeah, we know. Together, over the past four days we attended"—Mercury paused as she counted—"six workshops, five curriculum and development meetings, a massive teacher roundtable, *and* we also had a great time. Women are wonderful multitaskers," said Mercury. "At least that's what you say every semester when you want us to take on extra duties for no extra pay, remember?"

"I definitely remember," said Stella.

Jenny chimed in, "Me too."

Coach Davis covered his laugh with a cough while Karen Gay pursed her lips and opened the *Guideposts Magazine* she always kept in her briefcase.

Hale grunted and flicked on the radio.

Stella used her coat as a pillow, propping it against Mercury's shoulder. She drained her coffee cup, grinned sleepily at her friend, and said, "Night-night."

"Night, nasty." Mercury settled back with her Kindle. She scrolled through her library and tried to decide between something fae by Holly Black or something fae by Karen Marie Moening, but then ended up not reading either—the tall pines that filled the forest on both sides of Oregon's highway 26 west kept pulling at her attention.

Oregon was so green—even in the snow. A born and raised Okie, Mercury was used to green fading to olive, then sage, and finally brown. This was her fourth trip to Timberline Lodge, and she was still amazed at seeing the multiple shades of green along with the snow. She looked forward to getting closer to Portland, where the snow would be replaced by ferns and thick, spongy-looking moss. As they drove, the verdant landscape worked like a white noise machine. Her eyelids grew heavy and had just begun to flutter closed when Amelia's tentative voice broke the spell.

"Um, sorry, but I need to stop."

Mr. Hale glanced at her. His lips pressed into tight disapproval.

Amelia shrugged and patted her basketball-sized belly. "He decided to quit kicking my ribs and is now jumping up and down on my bladder. Or at least that's what it feels like."

Hale's voice was as tight as his lips. "We've only passed Government Camp a few minutes ago. We are not even twenty miles from the lodge."

"I really can't help it." Amelia's voice sounded small, and that pissed Mercury off.

Mercury leaned forward, which caused Stella to wake up and blink blearily. "Hey, she's pregnant. Just stop and let her pee. Jesus."

"I'm awake because Amelia has to pee?" Stella grumped.

"No, you're awake because Mr. Hale is being a misogynist bully," said Mercury as she caught the principal's gaze in the rearview mirror. She shook her head at him like he was an errant student, and he quickly looked away.

"It's just that there's no rest stop near," he muttered.

"I don't need a rest stop," Amelia blurted out as she patted her purse. "I brought toilet paper. I'm cool with peeing in the woods."

Coach Davis stretched and said, "Hey, don't I remember one of those scenic lookout places not far from here?"

"Yep," said Stella around a yawn. "We stopped there two years ago on the way to the lodge."

Mercury raised a brow at her friend. "Oh yeah, that's where you puked, right?"

Stella shuddered. "Yes. It's also the last time I ate prosciutto. Never. Again."

"Doesn't that brown sign say 'scenic turnout'?" Amelia pointed off to the left of highway 26.

The principal sighed and began to slow the SUV. "We'll stop. But this isn't a joy ride. Get out. Do your business. Then let's get going again."

"Hey, we didn't take our annual selfie," said Stella.

"Perfect opportunity! *With* an amazing background." Mercury nodded as Hale guided the SUV into the turn lane and then crossed over to the gravelly scenic turnout spot. As he parked and Amelia lumbered from the passenger seat, the women poured from the SUV.

"Hey! I said we need to get going!" Hale said.

"Oh, come on, Mr. Hale," Jenny said, dimpling at him. "Let's all take a picture."

Coach Davis clapped the principal on the shoulder. "It's just a picture, and we did leave in plenty of time to make it to the airport."

Mrs. Gay closed her magazine and sighed. "Mr. Hale, if you wouldn't mind terribly, I would like to take a picture of the scenery for my classroom. The history of this pass is as rich as it is tragic."

"See?" Coach Davis said. "It's unanimous."

"Okay, I suppose we do have some extra time," the principal grumbled as he reluctantly followed the teachers. "But let's make it quick."

CHAPTER

2

THE SCENIC TURNOUT was really not much more than a gravel parking lot and two wooden benches positioned in the middle of a well-tended grassy area. But it was surrounded by huge, old pines framing a breathtaking drop-off that allowed viewers a gorgeous vantage point to gaze southwest. From the scenic perch on the side of Mount Hood, travelers could look out on a view so spectacular that they could see almost to the coast.

Mercury bypassed the benches and went to the edge of the grass. She stretched and then rubbed her sweater-swathed arms in a failed attempt to warm them while she drank in gulps of cold mountain air enriched with birdsong, and stared. She loved Tulsa. Oklahoma's red dirt was in her soul, and she only felt truly at peace in her hometown, but Mercury appreciated the magnificence of the land before her. It seemed she stood on a magic mountain as the view unfolded in turquoise, cerulean, and shades of emerald that were many layered and brilliant.

"It's something, isn't it?" Stella said around a yawn as she joined her.

"I never get tired of all the green. I think I could live here, or at least down there"—she jerked her chin in the direction of Portland—"where it's not so cold."

Stella snorted. "Leave Tulsa? You? Girl, you bleed red dirt."

"Well, someday when I'm rich I'll buy a second house here," Mercury said wistfully.

Stella raised a perfectly plucked brow. "So, you changing jobs?"

"Nope. Winning the lottery. I have it all planned." Mercury smoothed her loose knit sweater over her generous curves and cleared her throat like she was preparing to lecture her AP biology class.

Stella tossed back her thick hair. "Ooh, I like this game. Will you buy me a car? Something red and sporty with a ragtop?"

"Absolutely. You have my word on it. *And* I'll take you on a spa vacay with me to somewhere warm and beachy." Mercury spoke without moving her gaze from the view.

"Did someone say beach vacay?" Jenny hurried up to them, with Amelia waddling in tow.

"If we're going to a beach vacay, could we please wait until I'm unpregnant?"

Mercury grinned, but kept her focus on the horizon. "Absolutely. I'm not even going to make any clichéd beached-whale jokes."

Amelia rubbed her protruding belly and sighed. "As the sole representative of our English Department, I thank you for that."

Coach Davis straightened his school sweatshirt as he emerged from the trees to their right. "Whew, had to see a man about a horse! Ready for our selfie?"

"What does that even mean?" Mercury asked Stella.

"Manspeak for peeing," whispered Amelia.

"Well, I know that, but *why*?" said Mercury.

"Come on, ladies!" The coach's enthusiasm was contagious. "This is a great spot." He took in the view and pointed to the northwest. "That's Portland over there. And you can even see Salem." Davis gestured to the south. "Wow! It's just amazing."

"I forget you grew up in Oregon," Jenny said.

"Yep! Born in Bend, which isn't very far south of Timberline. OSU recruited me to play college football and, well, after that I just stayed."

"Oklahoma grew on you." Jenny grinned.

"Seems like it," Coach Davis agreed, then he looked over his shoulder at the second of the two benches where Karen Gay was seated as she snapped several pictures with her phone. "Karen—Mr. Hale, join us!" Coach Davis gestured magnanimously.

Mrs. Gay stood and buttoned the top of her thick cardigan. "It really is a lovely view," she said as she joined the group.

Everyone looked expectantly at their principal.

Richard Hale waved dismissively from his bench. "No, you go ahead. I'll just take in the scenery."

Mercury walked quickly to him. "While you do that, how about helping us out?" She handed him her phone. "It'd be great if you took the picture. That way we can be sure we'll all be in it."

"Yeah, unlike last year when *someone's* head got cut off," called Stella as she pointed to herself.

Hale squinted at the phone. "What do I press?"

Mercury showed him and then jogged the few yards back to the little group. She stepped between Stella and Jenny and put her arms around their waists. "Squish together!" she said.

"Are y'all ready?" asked their principal.

"Yep," Mercury said. "Say *summer break!*"

"Summer break!" they shouted.

"Hang on," said Hale. "Don't move yet. I'll take a few more just to be sure I got a good one." He stood and tapped the phone several more times while the group grinned at him. When he appeared satisfied, he went to Mercury and gave back her phone, his gaze focused over her shoulder. "It is an amazing view. I'm glad we stopped."

"It's always good to appreciate the beauty of our God's creation," said Karen Gay.

Mercury considered reminding Mrs. Gay, for the zillionth time, that not everyone was a member of Church on the Move, nor an evangelical Christian—nor, for that matter, a Christian at all. But she chose not to waste her breath. As a Pagan living in the Bible Belt, Mercury was more than aware that people like Karen Gay believed anyone who didn't worship like they did was not just going to hell in a handbasket, but was also a bad person. And that Pagans in particular weren't just going to hell, but were Satan's minions—or some such nonsense. Sadly, experience had taught her that no amount of logic would change a mind that was closed. Instead of wasting her breath on Mrs. Gay's narrow mind, Mercury turned back to the view, but her attention was pulled to the parking lot by the crunch of gravel as a faded blue Chevy pickup pulled off the highway and parked. Two men climbed out, stretched, and headed for the tree line.

"Looks like they have to see a man about a horse too," said Coach Davis.

"That truck!" Stella said. "I swear it looks exactly like the old pickup my dad taught me to drive on." She laughed softly. "It had a stick shift on the floor, and whenever I put it into third gear, I had to keep my hand on it because if I didn't, the damn thing would fall off the column and plop on the floorboard."

"That's crazy," Mercury said.

"Absolutely." Stella grinned and her voice turned nostalgic. "But I can drive anything with a stick shift."

"Is there anything still drivable with a stick? I mean, except for an eighteen-wheeler or whatever." Jenny squinted at the truck like it was an exotic insect.

"Barely," Coach Davis spoke up. "What's the year on that old Chevy, 1960-something?"

"Dad's was a 1959, and that one looks pretty similar," said Stella.

"Wow, they don't make 'em like—" Coach Davis began, but his words were interrupted by a bizarre humming that filled the air around them.

"What the—" Richard Hale spoke over the vibrating sound. He'd returned to his bench, but stood and stared, slack-jawed, out at the view.

The little group stared too, while the humming intensified. Mercury cringed—whatever it was seemed to reverberate through her body. The hair on her forearms lifted and pain knifed through her head. Beside her, Stella put her hands over her ears and staggered against Mercury.

"Look!" Coach Davis pointed up at the western sky.

Mercury saw something that appeared to be a contrail, like an airplane would leave in its wake, far above the area Davis had said was the city of Portland. It was heading straight down in an arrow-like trajectory.

"And there!" Amelia pointed southwest to a similar contrail.

"Oh my God, they're everywhere!" Jenny cried.

Mercury's gaze scanned the sky as she turned in a stationary circle. Jenny was right. In the distance all around them tails of cloudy white shot down from the sky, so many that she couldn't count them all. The humming intensified as a huge mass of birds that had been perched in the trees surrounding them took wing in unison—each screeching horrible, soul-shaking cries that echoed eerily around the clearing. From the tree line the two men dashed out to stand a few yards from them as everyone studied the sky.

Stella grabbed Mercury's hand as the contrail over Portland disappeared into the city. She leaned into her best friend and spoke for her ears alone. "I think this is bad. Really bad. We need to get out of here."

Mercury opened her mouth to respond just as the first blast hit Portland. It created an enormous rising burst of fire that was almost perfectly round, like a gigantic crystal ball filled with flame.

"There too! In Salem!" Coach Davis shouted as another fire circle lifted from the southwest. From all around them, the outlook allowed a front-row seat to watch brilliant balls of fire explode everywhere, with such force they seemed to eclipse the sun.

Then a wall of sound echoed from the many balls of flame, followed immediately by bizarre flashes of green that jetted from the center of each fireball. Mercury was looking directly at the Portland ball when the explosion of sound met the green geyser—it changed shape, expanded, and became a wall of emerald that catapulted out, out, out. Like an impossibly swift tsunami of color, the glow rushed from the core of fire to cover the city and the surrounding land, and raced toward them.

Mercury stared at the green tide and was filled with the strangest feeling of panic mixed with fascination. There was something about the green—something that evoked the Wizard of Oz and concealed mysteries—something as intriguing as it was terrifying.

"Get the fuck down!" Stella screamed and pulled Mercury to the grassy ground with her. Jenny and Amelia did the same, but she could see that Coach Davis, Mr. Hale, and Mrs. Gay were frozen as they stared at the advancing wall of roiling green.

The emerald cloud hit them with sonic boom intensity. Had Mercury not already dropped to the ground, she would have been knocked off her feet. She clung to Stella with one hand and covered her head with the other as sound, debris, and a wave of green mist engulfed them. Around them thick pines snapped, filling the air with the sounds of gunshots. She could hear someone screaming, though she couldn't even see Stella through the soupy jade air.

Mercury panted with fear and shock—and inhaled the moist shamrock-colored air. It felt like breathing in the forest: the scent of growing things filled her nose with the sharp tang of cut grass, the rich, loamy aroma of tilled earth, and the unique sweetness of wildflowers. Her battered body was overwhelmed with an agonizing pinprick sensation, like she'd sat on her foot too long and it was tingling awake, only this sensation was a flood of pain that broke against her skin from the inside. It felt like hot razorblades filled her blood, her lungs, her skin with agony.

Mercury knew she screamed and screamed, but the blast of sound that was the harbinger of the green wave still reverberated around her, drowning everything but the internal thunder of her heartbeat echoing in her ears. She and Stella pressed themselves against the earth as their bodies writhed in pain. Mercury felt Jenny shaking beside her as the young teacher sobbed in terror.

Mercury tried to turn her head, to reach out for Jenny, but the earth suddenly mirrored Mercury's tremors. The ground beneath her cheek shuddered and shook. Forest debris rained shards of bark and pine against her body while another emerald tsunami pummeled them from Salem in the southwest.

Mercury tried to hold her breath, but it was impossible. She gasped with pain and panic, and the green surrounded her and filled her completely. Something struck the side of her head and her face, already wet with tears, became warm with blood.

Then the world went from green to black and she knew no more.

CHAPTER

3

CONSCIOUSNESS RETURNED LIKE the flip of a light switch, though Mercury's thoughts didn't catch up with her body for several breaths. She lay on the ground with her face in the grass. *What the hell? Why am I on the ground?* Her mind was sluggish, like she'd washed down a Xanax with a glass of wine. Something slid across her temple and cheek and down her nose. She wiped at it and then stared at the splash of scarlet on her hand—and memory rushed back, chasing away her confusion.

She sat up and then gasped and held her head in her hands while pain spiked through her temples. Her body felt strange—tingly—and bruised. Her joints ached like the last time she'd had the flu, and blood seeped from a cut over her left temple, down her face. Mercury brushed it away with her sleeve and crawled the short distance to Stella. Her friend was curled on her side in a fetal position, facing away from her. Something had torn through the faux fur of her car coat and turned the sleeve of her ripped sweater red.

"Stella! Oh Goddess! Stella!" Mercury touched her. Stella's skin felt cool—unnaturally cool—but her eyelids fluttered and then opened.

"Mercury? Wha—" She tried to sit up, but Mercury gently held her in place.

"No! Don't move. We have to make sure you're not broken anywhere."

"Mercury!" On her right Jenny sobbed her name.

"Stay still, 'kay?" Mercury said quickly. "Gotta check on Jenny." Her focus was tight. It included Stella and Jenny, though from her periphery she could see that mounds of debris were scattered around them, but her brain couldn't seem to process more. Still on her hands and knees, she crawled to the younger teacher. Jenny sat up. She rubbed her wrist as she stared at Mercury, who asked, "Are you okay? Is anything bleeding or broken?"

"You're bleeding." Jenny's voice sounded bizarrely normal, like she'd just commented on a new haircut or outfit.

"Yeah." Mercury wiped at her face again. "I think I'm okay, though." She felt Jenny's shoulders, arms, legs—as she checked for breaks and tears.

"My wrist is sprained, but not too bad. I—I don't understand. What could have—"

A moan sounded from the other side of Jenny, and Mercury felt a terrible foreboding. "Amelia!" She and Jenny crawled to their pregnant friend, who was bent over at the waist, on her knees with her forehead pressed into the grass and her arms wrapped around her bulging belly.

"He's coming!" Amelia's tear-soaked face looked up at them. Her skin was almost colorless except for her cheeks, which were bright spots of flushed pink—drops of blood in a pail of milk. "It's wrong. Something's wrong."

She panted between words and then another contraction took control of her and she made an inhuman growling noise deep in her throat.

"Nothing's wrong!" Mercury spoke automatically. "He's just coming a little early, that's all."

"Yeah, you're going to be okay." Jenny's voice was calm, but her eyes were dark saucers in her face.

"Press your hands into her lower back," Mercury told Jenny, who nodded and shakily complied. Mercury bent so that her face was near Amelia's. "Breathe with me. You remember! You know how to do this!"

Amelia turned her head so that she could meet Mercury's gaze. Her pale skin was shiny with sweat, and her eyes were wide and glassy. "No," she moaned. "It's never been like this. And he's too early. It's too early! Something's wrong—something feels broken inside me."

Panic made Mercury's legs so weak that she was glad she was already on her knees. This was Amelia's third child. The other two had been born at home uneventfully with a midwife and a doula. *She does know how to do this, but that also means she knows if it feels wrong.* The thought flitted through Mercury's mind, and with it her brain finally caught up with her body. "Just breathe! Everything will be okay. You're a pro at this," Mercury insisted. She panted with Amelia while her focus expanded. She looked around frantically for Coach Davis, who worked as an EMT at his second job for the Broken Arrow Fire Department. Mercury ignored the broken trees and crevasse-like gaps that had appeared in the ripped earth around them. "Where the hell is the coach?" she hissed under her breath when Amelia's body relaxed momentarily between contractions.

"He was standing just over there, on the other side of Amelia when—" Jenny began, but her words broke off as her gaze rested on something on the ground not far from Amelia.

Mercury recognized the coach's sweatshirt by Will Rogers High's bold royal-blue, gold, and white colors, but it looked strange. Before she could think herself out of it, she lurched to her feet and staggered to the coach.

Mercury saw what was wrong and the sight made her body freeze in place. Coach Davis had . . . flattened. Blood and body fluids squished under her feet as a pool of liquid expanded from him. He lay on his back. His mouth and eyes were open as if in surprise. His eyeballs had turned red. Congealed blood leaked slowly from them, and as Mercury stood there with the back of her hand pressed against her mouth to hold in her screams, the coach's body dissolved into a pancake of clothes, skin, bones, teeth, and hair.

The next contraction consumed Amelia, and her scream was a feral thing that tore from between her panting lips. The sound of it thawed Mercury, and she rushed back to the laboring woman.

Stella was there, crouched beside Amelia. Mercury joined them as Jenny shifted to allow her near, which gave Mercury a view of the back of Amelia's maternity dress. The bright, happy butter color was now soaked with red, like a terrible rose that bloomed larger and more brilliantly scarlet with each contraction. Stella met her gaze and shook her head. Mercury swallowed bile.

"I have to push!" The words burst from Amelia. "Help me up!"

Mercury, Jenny, and Stella supported her torso as Amelia half squatted, half knelt. Her dress was hiked up around her waist. Her fingers scrabbled at her panties, which Mercury slid down her blood-slick thighs just as her body tensed and wetness gushed from between her legs.

Amelia slumped back in Jenny's arms as she gave birth with a torrent of blood. Mercury caught the baby. Its tiny body was viscous and began to disintegrate immediately. It seeped through her fingers while the placenta poured from Amelia, followed by more and more blood that continued to pump from the young mother—a new tide of red with every beat of her heart.

Mercury bit the inside of her cheek and positioned herself so that Amelia could not see what was left of her son as she placed the little body on the grass between his mother's thighs. She glanced over her shoulder at Jenny, who was sobbing as she cradled Amelia in her arms, and shook her head slightly. She saw in Jenny's gaze that she knew—she understood—and the young woman held Amelia more tightly. Stella moved up beside Mercury.

"No! Oh no," Stella whispered and then tore off her coat so that she could pull her sweater over her head and hand it to Mercury.

Mercury took the sweater and pressed it between Amelia's legs to try to stop the flood. It only took moments for scarlet to soak through the sweater and slick over Mercury's hands.

"Why isn't he crying? Is he okay?" Amelia's voice was barely a whisper. The spots of red had faded from her cheeks, leaving only chalky, damp skin. Her lips were tinged blue and her gaze was unfocused.

Mercury forced herself to sound normal—happy even—as she would have had the baby been alive and thriving. "He's fine. He's just small. I'm going to keep the umbilical cord attached for a little while yet, but you can hold him in, in a—" her words hitched to a stop as her voice faltered.

Stella touched her shoulder before she moved to help Jenny hold Amelia. "Yeah, just let Mercury dry him off and wrap him up, then you can hold him."

"C-cold. Y-you're right. It—it's s-so cold," Amelia's teeth chattered and her body convulsed with shudders.

Stella wrapped her coat over her dying friend. Tears seeped down her face, but her voice was steady and her touch was strong as she held Amelia's hands. "Right? It is really cold out here. That's why Mercury has to be sure he's warm. What's his name?"

Amelia's blue lips tilted up at the corners. "Daniel. After his father." Her teeth had stopped chattering, and her body had gone very still. She drew a breath that rattled strangely. "He's our first boy. I can't wait for Dan to meet . . ." Amelia released a long exhale and her body relaxed. No inhale followed. Her open, empty gaze looked surprised.

"Amelia!" Jenny shook her. "Amelia!"

Stella placed Amelia's hands together over her deflated stomach, and then she touched Jenny's shoulder gently. "She's gone. There's nothing we can do."

Jenny stared at her. "The baby?"

Mercury shook her head and wiped her bloody hands on the grass. "He—he didn't make it either."

"Oh God! Jesus help us!"

The three women looked up to see Karen Gay standing just a few feet from them. Her face was bruised and her cardigan torn. Her hands were clasped in front of her, and she was panting as she repeated over and over the same words.

"Oh God! Jesus help us! Oh God! Jesus help us! Oh God!"

Mercury collected herself as she hurried to the history teacher.

"Jesus! Oh Jesus!"

"Are you hurt?" Mercury tried to touch her, but Mrs. Gay cringed away from her bloody hands.

"Oh Lord! Oh God!" she shrieked.

Mercury grabbed her shoulders and shook her. "Stop it! Get yourself together and tell me if you're hurt!"

Mrs. Gay's thin, pale lips pressed into a line. She blinked several times, as if trying to clear her vision, and drew a shaky breath before she replied. "I—I don't think I'm hurt." Mrs. Gay didn't meet her eyes. Instead, she stared at the gelatinous mound of red between Amelia's thighs. "She—she's dead."

It wasn't a question, but Mercury answered it. "Yes. Amelia and her baby." Mercury was trying to sift through the horror that threatened to numb her mind. Her gaze went from Mrs. Gay to sweep around the turnout. The rich scent of earth filled the area from several places where the ground had split open. Their rented Escalade had been tossed on its side like a child's discarded toy. The faded pickup was still upright on all four tires, though it looked as if a giant's hand had pushed it back to the middle of the gravel lot, which reminded Mercury suddenly of the other men. Her eyes scanned past the broken pines surrounding them—some with trunks so thick she and Stella couldn't have touched hands around them. They'd been snapped in half like number-two pencils. She looked to where the men had been standing when the bombs—*Were they really bombs? Are we at war?*—had begun to explode, but her gaze was caught by a person who sat on the closest bench, the only bench still intact.

Mrs. Gay must have seen Mercury's start of surprise, because she spun around. "Mr. Hale!" she shouted and rushed to the man on the bench.

Mercury wanted to warn her, but the history teacher moved too fast. She reached out and touched the principal's shoulder—and her touch set off a grisly reaction, like he had been held together by a string of wet dominos. His body quivered. Then, with a horrible, sloshing sound, it fell apart. His arm slid from his shoulder to the bench beside him and continued to seep down into the earth. The movement caused his head to detach from his neck so that it dropped behind the bench to hit the ground with the sound of a melon splitting open. His headless torso slumped forward and quivered as it dribbled onto the grass like a macabre Jell-O mold left out in the summer heat.

"Lord! Jesus! Lord!" Mrs. Gay scrambled back. Over and over she wiped her bloody hand on her khaki pants as she stumbled into Mercury, who grabbed her and held her while she sobbed and called to Jesus to save her.

Stella was there, beside Mercury. "The men. The two from the truck. That's them over there." She pointed.

Mercury released Mrs. Gay, whose legs collapsed. The history teacher dropped to her knees and began to pray softly as Mercury followed Stella's pointing finger to two mounds that just minutes before had been living men. Then her gaze continued beyond them, and she looked out at the view.

At first her brain didn't register what her eyes saw. How could it? Everything had been altered so utterly that her mind kept telling her that it couldn't be real—this couldn't be happening.

Nothing looked the same. It was like one of the old gods had grabbed an edge of the earth and then lifted and shook it like a dirty rug. The land was ripped and gouged and utterly alien. Portland was gone. In its place was flame and smoke and green-tinged darkness.

"They finally did it. They finally destroyed the world." Stella spoke with no emotion, but she wrapped her arms around her torso while tears dripped from her eyes down her cheeks to soak the long-sleeved shirt she'd layered under her sweater.

Mercury could only manage one word. "They?"

"Men. Politicians. *Them*. The greedy, corrupt people in charge whose job it was to keep us safe." Stella's voice cut like a knife.

Mercury's gaze swept to the left—to where Coach Davis had said Salem was. It was the same as Portland: flames and darkness. The land between was a ruin—torn, broken, and on fire. Spots that weren't on fire glowed with the strange green fog that had spewed from the blasts.

Like a zombie, Mercury ambled around, turning in one spot. Above the broken trees and torn earth, smoke and debris spread like a deadly contagion to cover the day with darkness that had already begun to blot out the brilliant blue morning sky.

"It's everywhere." The words slipped from Mercury's numb lips. Terror seared through her as she tried to comprehend what her eyes reported. *I want to go home. I want to go home. I want to go home.* Her brain replayed the words again and again until Stella's voice broke through.

"Mercury! Look at me!"

Mercury turned to face her best friend. Stella brushed the hair back from her blood-slicked cheek. Mercury had to draw several shaky breaths before she could speak. "I—I don't know what to do."

"Of course you do. You're smart, capable, tough. Both of us are. Think!"

"We need shelter." Mercury forced back the alluring fog of panic. *I can freak out later. Now we need to act.* She glanced up and then gestured at the growing line of smoke that had begun to shroud the sun. "We have no clue what's in that, but we're still alive. Jenny and Karen are still alive."

"That's more like it, Acorn."

"Okay, yeah. We can do this. So, let's get our asses in gear and see if we can all stay alive." Mercury turned her back to the view that had become a nightmare, and the old Chevy caught her gaze. "You can drive that truck."

Stella almost smiled. "I can."

"We need to get back to Timberline. Fast."

"Agreed," said Stella, who took Mercury's hands and squeezed them—hard. "Remember—together we can do this. We *have to* do this."

Mercury allowed herself a moment to hold onto Stella and stare into the blue lifeline of her familiar eyes. Then she dropped her hands; drew a deep, cleansing breath; and raised her voice as if she was projecting to the rear of a noisy classroom. "Jenny, Mrs. Gay—we have to get out of here."

Jenny was still holding Amelia's body. Mercury watched her lay the dead woman's torso gently on the ground. The young teacher lifted Stella's coat off the body before she went to what was left of the dead infant. She scooped up the tiny, partially disintegrated corpse and placed it on Amelia's chest. Jenny gently brushed her fingers though Amelia's sweat-matted hair before she walked to them.

"Here." Jenny handed Stella her coat. "Amelia can't feel the cold anymore." She wiped tears on her sleeve and turned to Mercury. "What do you need me to do?"

"Give the dead a Christian burial, of course!" Karen was still on her knees just a few feet from the three women.

Mercury responded with the first thing that came to her mind. "Do you have a shovel?"

Mrs. Gay frowned. "Well, no. That's a silly question."

"It's a practical question, Karen," said Stella. "You say you want to bury everyone. How are you going to do that with no shovel?"

While Karen opened and closed her mouth soundlessly, Mercury turned to her two friends. "The Escalade is trashed. We need to find the keys to that truck and see if we can get a door to the Escalade open so we can pull out the suitcases."

Jenny's gaze slid to the semi-smashed SUV that lay on its side. "Shouldn't we just leave them?"

"Sure, if you want to wear only what you have on for the foreseeable future," said Mercury.

"Oh, I get it. You're right," Jenny said. "Sorry, I'm not thinking very clearly."

"You're doing great," Mercury assured her.

"I'll check out the truck." Stella headed to the pickup.

"Let's get as much of our stuff out of the SUV as possible," Mercury said to Jenny. "We can toss the suitcases in the back of the truck, and the four of us can squeeze into the cab." She looked down at Mrs. Gay, who was still on her knees. "Come on, Mrs. Gay. We're all in this together, and we need your help."

"I just—I think we must do something about the dead." The history teacher's gaze kept flitting from the mound of rust-colored goo that had once been their principal to Amelia and her dead infant.

"Mrs. Gay," Mercury said gently, "there is nothing we can do for them. What we need to focus on right now is *our* survival. We don't know what's in that mess up there." She pointed above at the expanding wall of smoky darkness. "We have to get out of here and to a shelter. We're not from here. We don't know the area at all. Our best bet is to return to Timberline, but it could very easily have been destroyed too, so we need to get moving or we'll chance being stuck outside at night in the cold and snow and whatever else might be coming for us." Mercury offered her hand. Karen hesitated and then took it and stood.

"Mercury Rhodes," Karen said primly, "at the very least we need to pray over these poor people."

"You pray. I'm way more concerned about the living," Stella said as she rejoined them. She held up a keychain that had a green and yellow "Go Ducks" logo on it. "Keys were in the ignition, and there's almost a full tank of gas. The men musta been painters. There're a bunch of old paint cans and tarp in the bed. I'll toss out the paint."

"We'll get the suitcases," Mercury said.

"We need to hurry," Stella's gaze kept retuning to the nightmare view. "I have a bad feeling."

Mercury rubbed her arms. "Me too, and it's freezing out here." She headed to the wrecked SUV with Stella and Jenny in tow—and then stopped when she realized Karen was still standing there—beside the bench—staring at what was left of Principal Richard Hale.

"She's going to be a giant pain in the ass," murmured Stella.

Silently, Mercury agreed, but she was used to managing pain-in-the-ass students. She knew how to get kids everyone else thought were nothing but trouble on her side and even coax them to perform for her—or at the very least stop being annoying. Automatically, she used her classroom management skills, honed by more than a decade of teaching teenagers Richard Hale used to call "the bottom of the barrel," on Mrs. Gay.

"Karen, how about you pray over each of them"—Mercury made a sweeping gesture that took in Hale, Amelia, Coach Davis, and the two dead strangers—"while we get the truck loaded."

Karen nodded solemnly and rubbed the gold crucifix she always wore around her neck between her thumb and forefinger. "Yes. Yes, I can do that."

"That was smart," Jenny said as they approached the SUV.

"Give 'em a task to keep 'em too busy to cause trouble," Stella muttered.

Mercury rounded the back of the big Escalade and breathed a sigh of relief. As the vehicle had been thrown on its side, the rear hatch had popped opened. "Here, y'all! It's unlatched. I think we can force it the rest of the way up."

The three women wrenched open the hatch. Stella went to the pickup, started it, and backed it to the rear of the SUV so that the front of the truck was pointed out at the silent highway. She kept the engine idling as she jumped out of the cab, opened the tailgate, climbed into the bed, and began tossing paint cans onto the parking lot.

"Wait—don't throw out those tarps." Mercury struggled to roll two big suitcases over the gravel. "We can cover our stuff with them. Plus we might need them. Later."

Stella met her gaze. "You hate camping."

"I hate dying even more."

"I'm a good camper," said Jenny, who hauled two more suitcases behind her.

"You can pitch a tent?" Mercury asked Jenny as she handed Stella the first of the luggage.

"Yep. I can even start a fire with sticks, but it's a lot harder than the movies make it look. Basically, it takes a lot of time."

Stella lifted another suitcase, grunted, and then replied. "No need to worry about stick rubbing. I bought a new lighter at the Portland airport."

Mercury raised a brow at her best friend. "Before or after you bought those pre-rolled joints?"

"During." Stella said, and Mercury lifted another suitcase up to her, which her friend didn't grab because she was staring over her head toward the once scenic view.

Before Mercury could ask what was going on, she heard a weird rustle that came from somewhere behind her. It was like a group of kids were wading through piles of fall leaves. She turned just as the first deer ran past her. The doe's brown eyes were huge and panicked as it raced by. Behind the doe, squirrels, rabbits, several more deer, a fox and a whole cluster of chipmunks poured up over the lip of the mountain, as well as from the tree line on either side of them. The creatures darted past the vehicles, completely ignoring the humans.

"What level of Jumanji are we on?" As each moment unfolded, Mercury felt more and more like she'd been trapped in a video game where everyone dies over and over again.

"Get the rest of the suitcases and grab Karen. We need to go—now!" Stella said.

Mercury and Jenny sprinted back to the SUV. Jenny grabbed the last two suitcases while Mercury climbed up on the side of the vehicle and pulled open the back door. Immensely relieved, she snagged her giant purse, Stella's Louis Vuitton knockoff, and Jenny's backpack before she jumped to the ground, dodged a panicked raccoon, and raced to the pickup. They tossed everything to Stella, who hastily tucked tarps over their things before she jumped from the bed and got behind the wheel. Jenny slid quickly in beside Stella.

Before Mercury joined them, she spotted Karen Gay. The history teacher stood over what was left of Coach Davis's body. Her hands were folded and her head bowed. She seemed utterly oblivious to the woodland creatures who fled past her and through mounds of strangely overgrown grass. Mercury rubbed her eyes, sure her vision was messed up. She blinked and refocused on the weird grass not far from Mrs. Gay, and with a jolt she realized two things. One—her eyes weren't messed up. The grass was taller and brighter green than it had been just moments ago. And two—the clumps where the long grass had grown were in the same spots where she and Stella had been knocked to the ground, unconscious and bleeding.

"Mercury Elizabeth Rhodes! Pull your head out of your ass and get in this truck!" Stella's voice cut through her focus.

"Sorry, yeah, okay." Mercury cupped her hands around her mouth and called, "Mrs. Gay! We need to go—now!"

Karen turned her head to glance over her shoulder at Mercury. Her brow was furrowed in irritation. She opened her mouth, clearly to shout back at Mercury that she wasn't done, but before she could speak, the ground began to shudder like a horse trying to rid itself of flies.

Stella pushed in the clutch and wrestled the old gearshift into first. She shouted, "Mercury! If Karen wants to stay, *leave her!*"

"Mrs. Gay!" Mercury shouted as she moved to the passenger side of the truck, holding onto the hood to stay on her feet while the ground pitched and rolled and the trees that still stood swayed ominously and made sounds like gunshots as more of them splintered and broke. "Now or we leave you!"

"Coming! I'm coming!" Karen called while she jogged toward them, but the earth quaked too hard. She stumbled—fell—struggled to her feet and started forward again only to get knocked to her knees once more. Behind her the mountainside began to crumble.

Fuck! She's not going to make it!

Mercury couldn't bear to lose any more of them—not even someone who was a major pain in the ass. She bent at the waist and put out her arms to try and help her balance, then sprinted toward the history teacher.

"Shit, Mercury! No!" Stella shouted behind her.

Mercury ignored her friend. *I can save her. I have to save her.* She reached Mrs. Gay, who had fallen to the grass again. Mercury yanked on her hand, lifted her to her feet, wrapped her arm around the older woman's round waist and propelled both of them forward.

"Hurry! *Shit! Shit! Shit!* Hurry!" Stella screamed.

Mercury didn't look behind them, but she could hear the horrendous ripping sound the earth made as it shook apart and became an avalanche of dirt and trees and snow and rocks. Jenny had the passenger door open, and Mercury half threw, half pushed Mrs. Gay into the cab and then leaped in behind her. Before she'd even closed the door, Stella floored the truck and they fishtailed, throwing gravel everywhere. Mercury stared through the rectangular rear window as they shot out of the turnout and onto the highway in time to see the bench that held what was left of the congealed corpse of their principal get swallowed into nothingness.

STELLA CARVER

CHAPTER

4

STELLA HANDLED THE old truck like a Hollywood stunt driver. The earth convulsed under them while more of the mountainside disintegrated, taking the westbound two-lane highway with it. The Chevy's engine roared as they raced across the interstate divide to the opposite lane. Stella yanked the wheel to the right and headed the wrong way down the highway while she dodged around fallen trees and gaps in the asphalt. The four women held onto the dash, the back of the bench seat, and each other while they were tossed about the cab.

It reminds me of the old Star Trek—with The Shat—and how the crew used to get thrown around the bridge of the Enterprise. The bizarre comparison flashed through Mercury's mind, which almost caused her to giggle. *This is hysteria and shock. Get it together, woman!* she told herself sternly as the earth continued to shudder and more and more of the mountain—and highway—on their right sloughed off.

Mercury noticed one car stalled in the left lane, facing them, but Stella sped by too fast for her to see if anyone was inside. A little farther down the interstate, they whizzed past an SUV that had rear-ended a car. Both were fully engulfed in flames.

"Shit! Shit! Shit! Shit!" Stella repeated as she steered the old truck past the fireball and around an abrupt curve in the highway, where she almost ran headlong into a jackknifed eighteen-wheeler that was being sucked into a raw crevasse newly torn in the asphalt.

Mercury felt more than saw Jenny cover her eyes with her hands. Beside her Mrs. Gay panted like she was sprinting next to the pickup.

A deer darted in front of them. Stella cursed again and somehow managed to miss it.

"Lord save us!" Mrs. Gay cried and grabbed onto Mercury's hand like she was Jesus.

Mercury couldn't make her voice work. She squeezed Mrs. Gay's hand and tried to keep from flying into the windshield as Stella continued to race the truck down the highway until finally the earth stilled its horrible shuddering.

Silently, Stella pulled the truck to the side of the broken highway. She shifted into neutral, stepped on the emergency break, burst from the cab, bent, and puked.

Mercury was beside her in moments. She gathered her best friend's thick hair and held it back while Stella heaved and heaved.

"Jenny! I have a bottle of water in my purse—get it!" she called over her shoulder. Mercury kept holding Stella's hair while she rubbed her back gently. Jenny ran up to her and handed her the open bottle of water. "Here, honey. Can you rinse your mouth out and drink some of this?"

"Not—done—yet," Stella said between retches. Eventually, the puke turned to dry heaves, and then Stella staggered several steps away from the steaming pile of bile and breakfast. Mercury went with her and offered the bottled water again, which she finally took. Stella rinsed her mouth, spit, rinsed again, and then took several long swallows before she shakily handed the bottle back to Mercury. "Th-thanks."

"Keep it. Finish it. You puked a lot."

"I was a lot freaked." Stella sounded more like herself as she finished the bottle of water.

"You did good, though! You got us out of there," Jenny said.

"I might have shit myself," said Stella.

Mercury glanced at the back of her friend's jeans. "Doesn't look like it." She sniffed at Stella. "Doesn't smell like it either."

"But we wouldn't blame you if you had," Jenny said quickly. "That was so damn scary."

"The highway is gone." The three women looked at Karen, who stood by the rear of the truck. She pointed and they followed her finger.

Stella had pulled off the highway at the top of a rise. Mercury remembered the area clearly. Heading from Timberline to Portland, this part of highway 26 wound to the highest part of the pass—which culminated at the scenic turnout nightmare they'd just sped away from. From where they stood, they could look down this side of the mountain. Not far from there they would turn north onto Timberline Highway and climb up to the lodge, which was on the upper slopes of Mt. Hood.

The view was so altered it was unrecognizable. Mrs. Gay was correct. The entire eastward two-lane part of highway 26 was gone. Had there not been a generous section of grassy, tree-filled easement between the east and west lanes of the four-lane, they, too, would have fallen down the side of the mountain.

Automatically, Mercury grabbed Stella's arm and pulled her back from the easement so that they stood firmly on the cracked asphalt beside the truck. She looked up at the prematurely darkening sky. It wasn't even noon, but the day had turned to dusk.

"This is hell. The world has become hell." There was terror in Karen Gay's voice. Her restless fingers worried the hem of her torn and bloody cardigan. Her face was devoid of color.

"Nope. This isn't hell." Mercury heard herself respond, and then her thoughts caught up with her mouth. "We don't know *what* this is, but I do know what it is not. We're not dead. We survived. And this is *not* hell." She caught Jenny's gaze. "Do you have any water in that backpack of yours?"

"I—I think I do."

"Get it. Let's all drink some. It'll make us feel better. Does anyone have to pee? If so, squat by the side of the road. We'll be leaving in just a few minutes."

"Will do!" Jenny's long brunette curls bounced wildly as she climbed into the bed of the truck and lifted the tarp to search for her backpack.

"You going to be okay to drive?" Mercury asked Stella.

Stella was rubbing her arms as she paced back and forth behind the truck. "Yeah, I'll be fine. Just need a minute or two to be sure I'm not going to puke again."

"Good." Mercury headed back to the cab to check the old pickup's glove box and behind the bench seat. She wasn't sure what she wanted to find, but it gave her something to do besides having an anxiety attack.

"You mean we're still going back to Timberline?" Karen was on her heels.

Mercury glanced at her. "Well, yeah. We definitely can't go to Portland, and none of us know this area. Timberline is our best shot at shelter and information."

"If anyone's left alive there," said Mrs. Gay.

"Yeah, here's hoping."

"Don't you think we should stop at that little town that's at the turnoff before we take the Timberline road?"

"You mean Government Camp? Um, maybe." Mercury popped open the glove box. Nestled there in a black leather holster was a pistol. "Huh! I thought only Okies and Texans carried guns around in their glove boxes." Carefully, Mercury pulled the pistol from its holster and opened the cylinder. "Fully loaded too." Mercury expertly snapped the cylinder closed, checked that the safety was on, and then put it back in the glove box.

"Did I hear you say *gun*?" Stella head popped into view through the open driver door.

"Yep. It's a .38." Mercury squinted as she looked through the rest of the glove box. "It's loaded and there's a box of shells for it. There's also a big pile of napkins and"—she paused and then held up a clear plastic bag full of little oblong balls of color—"jelly beans."

"Gross," said Stella. "I hate jelly beans."

"Ditto." Mercury put the bag back in the glove box. *But it is sugar and energy, and we may need to eat those damn things.*

"Here, y'all. I had two bottles of water in my backpack." Jenny lifted the bottles as she joined them.

"Let's split one of the bottles and then get out of here," said Mercury.

Jenny opened the water and handed it to Mercury—and her eyes went huge as she spotted the .38. "OMG, you found a gun!"

Mercury closed the glove box and gulped the water, then gave the half-empty bottle back to Jenny before she answered. "Yeah. I know Stella's proficient with firearms."

"Fuckin' A, I am." The color was returning to Stella's cheeks. She stopped before she drained the rest of her bottle of water, pulled an old balled-up tissue from her jeans, wetted it, and told Mercury, "Hold still. I can't look at the dried blood that's smeared all over the side of your face anymore." Stella gently wiped the blood from Mercury's forehead, nose, cheeks, and neck while she continued. "But let me be clear. I'm proficient with firearms, *and* I'm for sensible gun laws."

"Yes, as am I, which is why I have never fired a gun in my life," said Mrs. Gay.

"What about you, Jenny?" Mercury asked.

Jenny shrugged. "I'm for sensible gun laws too."

"No. Well, yes. We all are, but I meant do you know how to use this .38?"

"Oh yeah. My dad taught me before I went away to college. One of my high school graduation presents was a little bitty Glock 43X. I also shot a .38 when Daddy took me to the range at Zink Ranch," Jenny said as she handed the rest of the water bottle to Mrs. Gay.

"Okay, good to know."

"There," said Stella as she studied Mercury's head. "How are you feeling? Any headache or weird vision?"

"Nope," Mercury responded automatically, and then she realized she'd also responded correctly. Her head didn't hurt at all, and it had completely stopped bleeding. She felt a wave of relief. When it had been bleeding all over her face, she'd thought she was going to keel over any second—when she'd had time to think about herself at all. "I'm fine. It musta just been superficial."

Stella snorted. "I don't know about that. It looked pretty scary just a few minutes ago, but you do seem okay now." She lifted her hand to touch the wound on her arm and then stared down at it. "Thought mine was worse too, but it's just a scratch." Stella shook her head. "Guess my mind was really rattled back there 'cause I thought it was pretty deep—as in it probably needed stitches. Glad I was wrong."

"Well, my wrist still hurts." Jenny rubbed it and grimaced.

"Do you think it's broken?" Mercury asked.

"Nah, just a sprain. Karen, looks like you're going to have a black eye," Jenny said. "Are you hurt anywhere else?"

"I don't believe so." Karen touched her bruised and swollen cheek gingerly.

"Well, I'm glad we're basically okay." Mercury returned to going through the cab of the truck. She lifted the old-fashioned lever that allowed the bench seat back to tilt forward. There was a black duffle bag stuffed behind the seat. She unzipped it and looked through an assortment of tools and zip ties. "Huh, these guys even had duct tape in here."

"All that stuff's good in case we need to MacGyver something." Stella peered over the seat at the open bag. "Any more ammunition in there?"

"I don't see any."

"I really don't like that the gun is loaded. I–I'm just not comfortable with violence," said Karen after she drained the water bottle.

"Karen, someone bombed America. Comfortable or not, it looks like we're in the middle of violence," Stella said

"We don't know what happened!" Karen snapped back at her.

"No, we don't," Mercury said. "But, like my dad says, let's prepare for the worst and hope for the best." Those few words, *like my dad says,* left Mercury's mouth, and with them her memory easily replayed her father's gruff, loving voice—and her knees went rubbery. Mercury grabbed the open passenger door and pressed her forehead against its faded blue metal. She blinked hard, over and over, as she tried to stop her panicked panting.

Dad! Is he okay? Mercury had always been a daddy's girl—from day one—but she was also close to her mom, who—*Oh God! Mom! And my brothers—their wives and kids! They have to be alive. They have to be alive. Please, oh please, they have to be alive!*

Stella's hand on her shoulder pulled her from the quicksand that was sucking her into panic.

"Hey, you're okay. We're okay," Mercury turned her head to meet Stella's gaze as she continued softly. "Tulsa might not have been hit. This could just be a West Coast thing."

"Tulsa . . ." Jenny whispered the word like a prayer.

"My husband. Our sons." Mrs. Gay's fingers found the hem of her cardigan again, and she picked relentlessly at the threads she'd already loosened.

Mercury wiped her cheeks before she straightened. "We can't know for sure what's going on back home—at least not yet we can't. So, let's get to some shelter, whether that's Timberline or Government Camp, and see if we can find out what the hell has happened."

"Hey, has anyone checked their phones for service?" Jenny asked.

"Mine's in my purse—back there." Stella motioned to the truck bed.

"I—I don't know where mine is," said Mrs. Gay.

"Well, shit. I totally forgot mine is in my pocket." Mercury reached into the front pocket of her jeans and retrieved her cell phone.

"Mine's here!" Jenny lifted it out of the backpack and held it up like a trophy. Then she tapped the cover of it and frowned. "Zero bars."

"Yeah, ditto," said Mercury. "Keep it out, Jenny," Mercury shoved hers back in her pocket and motioned for Stella to get behind the wheel. "Check it while we're driving. Maybe we'll get lucky and there'll be a cell tower still working."

"Okay, will do," Jenny said solemnly.

Stella climbed back in the pickup, and Mercury slid in next to her while Jenny stared at the face of her phone. If this was the apocalypse, she was going to head into it sandwiched between two friends.

Jenny got in beside her and then held her hand out to Karen. "Here, Mrs. Gay, I'll help ya."

Karen Gay smoothed her short, graying blonde bob with fingers that trembled noticeably. The lines that framed her lips looked deeper, and her skin appeared almost brittle. Mercury tried to remember how old she was, but realized she'd never known the history teacher's age. She was a fixture at Will Rogers High School and had seemed late middle aged when Mercury had started teaching a little over a decade ago. She made a mental note to keep an eye on her. Stella was in her mid-forties—but youthful, in shape, and vibrant. Karen Gay was a good thirty or so pounds too heavy and probably hadn't really sweated since her twenties. They weren't friends. They'd never be friends, but Mercury damn sure didn't want to watch one more person die. Ever.

"Th-thank you Jenny," Karen said shakily and took the young teacher's hand before squeezing into the cab and closing the door tightly.

Before Stella put the truck in gear, she felt around the bench seat under her butt. "Sometimes these old trucks actually have seat belts. Does anyone feel any?" The women searched the seat and found none. "Well, okay, no seat belts." She reached to her left and pressed down the lock. "Karen, lock your door." Karen did so without comment. "Here we go."

Much more slowly than before, Stella started down the only half of the highway left. She wove the truck around fallen trees and guided it past slashes in the asphalt. The first car they came to was stalled in the middle of the two lanes, heading the correct way, toward them. There didn't appear to be anyone in the vehicle. As they drove by it, Karen, who had the best view of the car, gasped and turned her face away.

"What it is?" Mercury asked quickly.

Mrs. Gay shook her head. "Another man. Just outside the car. Dead. Like poor Mr. Hale."

"I wonder what the hell is going on with that," Stella murmured softly so that her words only carried over the engine noise to Mercury.

Mercury shrugged. She had no answer. Everything that had happened since the first explosion was beyond anything she'd ever imagined. She didn't even like apocalypse movies. They creeped her out too much, so she never watched them—well, except for an occasional zombie flick. *Great, and now I'm living a fucking apocalypse. If zombies show up, I'm going to . . .* Mercury's thoughts trailed off because the truth was, if zombies showed up, she wouldn't give up. She'd fight to keep herself—and her group—alive. She squeezed her eyes closed and sent a quick prayer, which would've seemed utterly ridiculous just an hour before, to her patron goddess. *Please, Gaia, no zombies.*

They rounded another turn, and a long section of highway unfolded in front of them—though here, too, there was only the two westbound lanes still intact. The cliffside lanes were mostly gone. Mercury didn't let herself look over the earth-torn edge. It wouldn't do any good. She couldn't save the people who had been swept down the mountainside, so she focused on what was ahead of them instead—clusters of stalled cars and trucks—as well as more wrecks. She thought she could make out people around some of the vehicles, though they weren't close enough to tell if they were alive or dead. What was for sure was that their truck was the only one moving within sight.

Understanding jolted through Mercury. "The bombs caused an EMP. That's why none of those cars are running."

"Oh shit." Jenny stiffened beside her. "Then *that* is going to be nuclear fallout." She jerked her chin up at the unnaturally dark sky.

"Nuclear weapons?" Stella's voice went up several octaves. "That's so, so bad. What's an EMP?"

"Electromagnetic pulse," Mercury said.

"Oh Lord Jesus! Then we're all going to die!" Karen wrapped her arms around her torso and rocked back and forth.

Stella met Mercury's gaze. "Was that what the green fog stuff was—nuclear fallout?"

Mercury shrugged. "Honestly, I don't know. I've never read or seen anything about fallout, or even bombs, that are green. Jenny, you just got out of college. Have you?"

The young teacher shook her head. "Nope. Never."

"It's nuclear. That's what causes an EMP," insisted Mrs. Gay.

"Not necessarily," said Mercury. "Other bombs can cause an electromagnetic pulse." She looked up at the sky and her stomach tightened. "But let's hurry and get to cover."

"Sounds like a plan." Stella shifted into third. She held onto the wheel with both hands and didn't take her gaze off the road. "Why is this truck still running when all the rest aren't?"

"One reason is that it's pre-electric and pre-computerized," Mercury explained. "I would think the pulse would've still fried the battery, but my guess is it didn't because it was off when the blast hit. All these cars and trucks we've been passing—none look like they're old enough to be pre-electric, and they were all running when the blast hit, so they're fried. My guess is if the Escalade hadn't been wrecked, we could've driven it out of there because it wasn't running when the bomb hit."

"Hey, are those people?" Jenny squinted at a clump of cars and trucks in the distance, easily visible because they were situated on a rise in the highway.

"I think so," said Stella. "We can put some of them back there in the bed of the truck. They can hunker down under the tarp. It'll be windy and cold, but better than walking, especially if they're injured."

"We're not stopping, are we?" Mrs. Gay's voice had lost its trembling fearfulness and returned to its familiar sharpness.

Mercury looked around Jenny and at her. "Of course we're stopping. We're not driving by people who need help."

"But you can't know what kind of people they are," Karen said. "They could be dangerous."

"What just happened is *dangerous*." Mercury frowned at her.

"We're going to help anybody we can," said Stella.

"We can't just leave people out here to die," added Jenny.

Mercury cleared her throat and finished with, "It's the Christian thing to do."

Karen's gaze snapped to hers. "You're not a Christian."

"Correct." Mercury's answer was immediate. "But you are." She held the history teacher's gaze until Karen looked away.

CHAPTER

5

"SHIT. SOME OF them look like they're hurt," Stella said as the old truck slowed, and they reached the first of the vehicles.

From a distance it had appeared as if the cluster of cars and trucks had been a massive pileup, but as they got closer, it became clear that only one car had rear-ended a huge Winnebago. A few of the other vehicles had skidded around the accident and were partially on the side of the road before the EMP brought them all to a standstill. There were several people lying on the mountain side of the westbound lanes, as far as was possible away from the easement of broken and bent pine trees and the nonexistent west lane. Two people stood over them. A mile or so farther down the highway, Mercury could just make out what looked like a small group of people walking down the middle of the road, away from them.

"I'm going to stop, but I'm not getting out," said Stella.

"No one is. Or at least we aren't at first," Mercury said quickly. "Just roll down your window and let's see how we can help."

Stella nodded, pulled the truck beside the group, and rolled down her window.

"Hey there," she said. "Do y'all need help?" Stella sounded completely normal, but her Okie accent had thickened, a sure sign that she was stressed.

The two people who were standing were women—one was middle aged and the other, considerably younger. Their resemblance made it seem as though they could be mother and daughter. The older of the two wiped her sleeve across her dirty face wearily and nodded as she motioned for the girl to stay where she was. She walked to the truck.

"Hi. Thanks for stopping. It's, uh, crazy that your truck works. All these other vehicles quit when the explosions started." The woman's eyes darted around like she expected someone to leap at her from out of the back of the truck.

Mercury leaned forward and smiled. "I'm Mercury. This is Stella—and Jenny and Karen." She ignored the woman's comment about the truck and nodded at the people lying on the ground behind her. "We're heading back toward Timberline. Do you folks need a ride?"

"Oh yes! I'm Sadie Jenkins and this is my daughter, Gemma. We were on our way home from brunch at Glacier Pub when all hell broke loose. We're okay, but the others—well, they're dead." She finished in a rush and wiped her sleeve across her face again. "Gemma and I helped these people. We don't know them, but they can't walk, and when that group left," she jerked her chin at the people in the distance, "we just didn't feel right abandoning them."

Stella asked. "Do you know those other people?"

Sadie nodded. "Yeah, there's a guy in charge named Alvin Rutland. He's a hops farmer with a big place east of Government Camp. The men with him are his workers, and there are a few women with them I didn't recognize. Al said he'd send back help once they get to town."

"And he's okay, this, um, hops farmer?" Mercury asked.

"Well, I don't *really* know him. He's more of an acquaintance."

"No, I meant does he *feel* okay. Is he wounded?" clarified Mercury.

"He seemed to be fine. He and his men were in that Range Rover." She pointed to a big black vehicle that had skidded to a stop on the near side of the Winnebago. "When the green stuff hit and all that debris came with it, their group was shielded by that thing. Rutland had a bloody nose, but besides that he was walking and talking, so . . ." She shrugged.

"And the other men walking with him? They're not, uh, wounded?" Stella said.

"Nah. They all hunkered down against the Winnebago, which saved them from the worst of it. Some bloody noses and scrapes, but not bad enough to stop them walking away." She lowered her voice and added. "More than half of the people died, though. It's really awful. The men just—just dissolved. My daughter and I, we left them where they fell. We didn't know what else to do."

"There's really nothing else you can do," said Stella. "We need to focus on the people who are alive."

"Speaking of which, how about we get those wounded people in the bed of our truck," Mercury said. "If you don't mind the wind, you can ride back there with them too."

Sadie's shoulders slumped with relief. "We don't mind at all, but we'll need some help getting them into the truck. We have one with a broken leg, and I think another has some cracked ribs. And the others—two men from the Winnebago—are unconscious but seem to be breathing just fine." She paused. "You came from the other side of the pass?"

"No, we weren't through the mountain when the explosions happened," Mercury said. "We were only a little farther down the highway, at the scenic turnout."

Sadie's eyes lit. "So, you could see a ways?"

Mercury nodded. "Yeah, all the way to Portland and even Salem."

"Between here and Portland—did bombs or whatever this is—hit that area too?"

Mercury moved her shoulders. "It was hard to tell, especially because we're from Oklahoma and don't know the area, but it looked like most everything there"—she jerked her thumb over her shoulder to point behind them—"is either on fire or torn up by the earthquakes."

Sadie looked down and didn't appear to be able to speak. When she finally met Mercury's gaze again, her eyes were filled with unshed tears. "Our home—it's just this side of Portland in Gresham. My husband always stays home on Sunday mornings so Gemma and I can have a mother–daughter brunch."

"I'm so sorry," Stella said.

Sadie nodded and wiped her eyes. "He could be okay. We do have a basement. I'm—I'm just going to believe he's okay. He has to be. He just has to be."

"I hope he is. I, uh, think we should get going," Mercury said gently. "An aftershock could happen any time."

"You're right. Yeah, we need to get out of here." Sadie drew a deep breath and wiped her face again. "Can you help Gemma and me get them into your truck?"

"Absolutely," said Mercury. "Mrs. Gay, Jenny and I will work with Sadie and her daughter to move the wounded while you lift the tarps and push the luggage out of the way."

"And I'll stay behind the wheel in case we need to get out of here quick," added Stella.

Mrs. Gay narrowed her eyes and pursed her lips, but she unlocked her door and lumbered to the rear of the truck so Mercury and Jenny could slide out. Mercury put down the heavy old tailgate, and then she and Jenny boosted Mrs. Gay up into the bed.

"We should hurry," Mrs. Gay grumbled.

"Yeah, that's what we're doing," said Mercury before she turned to Sadie. "Okay, let's get these people out of here."

Together Jenny and Mercury went to the roadside with Sadie. There were four adults on the ground—one woman and three men. Mercury went to the woman, whose jeans were ripped open down one leg, exposing a nasty break. Someone had placed two long sticks on either side of the leg in an attempt to stabilize it and tied them together with what looked like torn-up strips of a T-shirt.

Mercury glanced at Sadie. "Did you make that splint?"

"No, the teenager did," said the woman with the broken leg. Her face was sallow, and a film of sweat beaded her upper lip.

Mercury's gaze went to Gemma. "Good job with that."

Gemma shrugged. "During school breaks I volunteer at OHSU."

"OHSU?" Mercury asked.

"Oregon Health and Science University. I wanna be a doctor—actually an orthopedic surgeon." The teenager put her long, cocoa-colored hair behind her ears. Her green eyes were bright and intelligent, and she looked way older than her years.

"Impressive!" Jenny said.

"She's always loved science," said her mom.

"Huh! Me too!" Jenny smiled at Gemma. "And now I teach science."

"And I teach biology." Mercury nodded at the teenager. "You definitely did a good job with this splint." She squatted beside the injured woman. "This is going to hurt, and I'm sorry for that, but we need to get you—"

"You don't have to explain it to me. I get it. It's hurts like hell anyway. I'm just thankful you stopped." She paused and smiled weakly at Sadie. "And thankful Sadie and her daughter didn't leave us here like those jackasses did. By the way, I'm Marge Jackson, and this is my partner, Nathan Long."

"Mercury and Jenny," Mercury said quickly.

Nathan, who was lying beside Marge, turned his head and blinked his vision clear. "Nice to meet you ladies. Feels like my ribs are broken, but like Marge here, I'll be damn glad to get into that old truck."

"Do either of you know those two?" Mercury asked, nodding at the unconscious men beside them. Their faces were bloody, though someone—Mercury guessed Gemma—had tried to wipe them clean. Another makeshift bandage was wrapped around one of the men's heads. Blood had seeped through it, and his nose was bleeding sluggishly. The other man's forehead looked like raw hamburger with glass mixed in it.

"Nope. Sadie and Gemma pulled them outta that Winnebago over there. The one rear-ended," said Marge.

"Neither of them were wearing seat belts," said Sadie.

"Well, let's lift the unconscious men in first, if y'all don't mind," said Mercury.

"We can wait our turn," said Marge, and Nathan nodded in agreement.

"The bed's as ready as it's going to be," Mrs. Gay called from the back of the truck.

"The four of us can lift them together," Mercury said as she moved to the first of the two unconscious men. She bent and felt for the pulse in his throat—not because she could tell whether it was fast or slow or anything in between, but because she wanted to check that it was there at all. The man was so still and pale, he looked dead, but there was a heartbeat under her fingers, though it felt like the fluttering wings of a very small bird. "Sadie and Gemma, y'all get on his left. Jenny and I will be on the other side of him. Let's grab wrists under him and lift on three." The four women linked wrists. "One, two, three!" The man was young and slight and more awkward to carry than heavy. They moved together and slowly lifted him to the bed of the truck, where Mrs. Gay put her arms under the man's shoulders and helped pull him to the rear of the bed.

They returned for the second man, the one whose forehead looked like raw meat. He was older than the first guy, though not by much. He was also heavier. Just as they linked wrists beneath him, the man's eyelids fluttered and then opened.

"Where am I?" He looked around frantically. "Jason? Where's Jason?"

Mercury touched his shoulder gently. "You've been in an accident. We're going to take you to find help. Your friend is already in the back of our truck."

"He's—he's my cousin." The man started to sit up, moaned painfully, then reached up to touch his forehead. He flinched and began to pant with panic.

"My face! What's wrong with my face?"

"Don't touch it." Mercury tried to keep her voice calm, but she was utterly out of her comfort zone. Unlike Gemma, she had definitely never wanted to be a doctor.

"It's not your whole face," Gemma said kindly. "Your forehead's been cut up some, but don't touch it 'cause there's still glass in your skin. You're gonna be fine. What's your name?"

"T-Todd," his voice shook. "Todd Wilson."

"Hi, Todd, I'm Gemma. Don't worry, okay? We're gonna get you out of here now."

"Todd, can you slide one arm around my neck and the other around Sadie's?" Mercury asked, cutting her eyes to the woman whose wrist she'd grasped.

"Who are you?" asked Todd, whose eyes didn't seem to be able to focus, but looked glassy and blank. "Where am I?"

"I'm Mercury and you've been in an accident, remember? We're here to help, but we have to get you into the—"

"Something's wrong!" Todd's body began to tremble. "I feel wrong. Inside. Like, like I'm broken. I don't think I can—" His words ended as he began to cough so violently that Mercury lost her grip on Sadie's wrists, and she had to catch Todd's torso before it smacked against the ground.

"Hey, it's okay. We can wait for you to catch your breath," Gemma said.

Todd reached wildly out and snagged Mercury's hand. She was shocked at the strength in his grip. "It's okay," she said, repeating Gemma's words, careful to keep her voice soothing. "Like Gemma said, we can wait for you to—"

Todd made a horrible noise—a cross between a scream and a retching sound—more animal than human. Then he flopped to his side and began to vomit something that looked like red Jell-O. It was pouring from his gasping mouth, his nose and even his eyes. It spread around them in a sickening, sluggish pool of scarlet.

Mercury's mind whirred. *It's like what Hale turned into and what hemorrhaged from Amelia.* She wanted to fling Todd's hand away and run, but she couldn't. She wouldn't. Instead, she gripped the dying man's hand tighter and murmured, "I'm here, I've got you," over and over as Todd vomited his life onto the snowy grass.

It didn't take long. Todd was dead in minutes. Mercury pried her hand free and placed Todd's gently on his chest, folded with his other one.

"Here's what's left of the T-shirt I used for the splint and the other man's bandage."

Mercury looked up to see Gemma offering her an old T-shirt that had about half of the bottom of it ripped away. She smiled shakily and placed the shirt over Todd's face. "Thanks, Gemma." She touched the dead man's hands once more and spoke to him softly. "I'm sorry we couldn't save you. Blessed be."

"D-do you think that's going to happen to us?" Gemma blurted.

Mercury stood and faced the girl. She didn't lie or prevaricate. Teenagers could spot an adult lie in a heartbeat. And Mercury preferred sticking with the truth. "How do you feel?"

"Alright, I guess. My stomach is upset, but I've never seen so much blood and stuff before."

"But besides that, you feel normal?" Mercury pressed her.

The girl nodded. Her dark hair was long and straight, and it fluttered around her with the movement. "Yeah."

Mercury's gaze went from Gemma to her mom, and then to Marge and Nathan. "How about y'all? Besides queasy stomachs and your obvious injuries, how do you feel?"

The three adults muttered various versions of okay.

"Well, one thing I've noticed is that whatever is killing people makes them feel *wrong* first. We lost a good friend back at the turnout after the bombs hit. Right before she died." Mercury paused and then decided it would be better for morale not to mention the dead infant. "She said the same thing Todd did—that she felt wrong, broken inside. So let's not worry unless any of us starts feeling like that."

"That actually makes sense," said the teenager.

Mercury smiled at the kid and then walked to the woman with the broken leg. "So, Marge, you ready to be carried to the truck?"

"More than ready," she said.

Lifting a conscious person was harder *and* easier. Marge could wrap her arms around their shoulders, but she could also cry out in pain—which was awful. Thankfully, she was a petite woman, and they were able to get her to the truck quickly, though Mercury didn't like to think about the pain every bump in the torn and rubble-covered highway would cause her.

Nathan was a lot bigger and heavier than his partner. The broken ribs were agony—so much so that almost as soon as they lifted him, Nathan passed out.

"'kay—fast." Mercury grunted under the effort. "Get him in the truck before he comes to."

The women struggled but managed to heft the big man into the bed. Jenny had to climb in to help Mrs. Gay slide him the rest of the way, but once he was loaded, Sadie and Gemma joined them and made quick work of rearranging the tarps so that they covered most of Marge and Nathan and Jason. The mother and daughter squeezed in on either side of the wounded people, ready to give them help and support. They pulled the tarp up around their shoulders and nodded that they were ready.

"There's not much more room back there without dumping the suitcases," Jenny said after she helped Mrs. Gay from the truck bed.

Mercury nodded at the young teacher and then turned to the crowded truck bed. "This is going to be a hellish ride for you." She closed the tailgate securely. "Stella will try to avoid holes and such, but—"

"We know," said Marge. She lay beside Nathan, half propped up by Jenny's backpack. Her hand rested on his shoulder, though he was still unconscious. "It's a fucking disaster. Nothing you can do about it. Tell Stella we'd rather get to shelter fast than have her pussyfoot around."

"I hear ya!" Stella called from the half-open window.

"All right, if you need something, bang on that rear window and we'll stop," Mercury slid back in the cab beside Stella, with Jenny and Mrs. Gay close behind her.

"Glad to get outta here," said Stella as she put the truck in gear and gave it some gas. "I will try to be as careful as possible, but I agree with that woman."

"Marge," Jenny said.

"Yeah, I agree with Marge. We need shelter. Fast."

"Is that what your gut's telling you?" Mercury studied her friend's profile. Stella's intuition was epic. It was one of the things she appreciated about the older woman—that she'd lived long enough and was self-aware enough to trust her gut—and to follow it.

"Yes."

Mercury nodded and squeezed Stella's leg. Her friend navigated through the pack of vehicles. Several of them had shattered windows and slumped figures inside. Mercury kept her gaze averted, but she noticed that Mrs. Gay stared at every one of them. Her lips moved as she clutched her crucifix and prayed soundlessly.

Once they were clear of the vehicles, Stella increased their speed, though she was definitely not going as fast as she had before there were wounded people in the bed of the truck. Mercury glanced back through the rectangular window. Sadie and Gemma were hunkered down with Marge and Nathan, who had regained consciousness, and Jason, who had not. No one looked up at her.

"How are they doing?" Stella asked, not taking her eyes from the road before them.

"They look alive," said Mercury.

"I hope they stay that way," said Jenny. "It was horrible the way Todd died."

Stella's hands gripped the steering wheel so tightly her knuckles were colorless. "The whole fucking thing is horrible."

"Language!" said Mrs. Gay.

"Uh-uh!" Stella snapped, still not taking her eyes from the road. "Here's the deal, Karen. I won't tell you how to talk or think or act—and you will show me the same respect."

"Well, I don't like—" Karen began, but Stella cut her off.

"No. This isn't up for discussion. I'm not pandering to your provincial bullshit during a fucking apocalypse. If you can't be more tolerant, I will stop this truck right now and leave you by the side of the road."

Karen sucked air. "The—the others wouldn't let you."

"Sure we would," Mercury said.

Jenny snorted a laugh that she covered with a cough. Mrs. Gay's lips pressed into their familiar narrow line, and she shifted so that her back was mostly to the three of them. For a moment Mercury felt incredibly light. What Stella had said to Karen Gay was something the narrow-minded woman had needed to hear for decades. *Maybe some good things will come out of this mess . . .*

"That group is not far ahead."

Stella's words pulled Mercury out of her head, and she focused on the highway. Probably a little over a mile in front of the truck, the group of people had stopped and turned to face them.

"I see 'em. Well, we know that none of them are so badly hurt that they can't walk," Mercury said.

"Or help others," Jenny added.

"Someone had to go get assistance," Mrs. Gay said without looking at them.

Jenny and Mercury shared an eye roll. "Either way, the fact that they're all moving means we don't need to clear out our suitcases to make room for them. Stella, stop long enough to let them know that we'll send back help, 'kay?"

"Okay." Stella's voice sounded tight, like she had to force the word through sealed lips.

"Mrs. Gay, lock your door," Mercury said.

"Already done," Mrs. Gay replied.

As they drew beside the people, Stella steered the truck so that the group was closest to her side of the vehicle. She braked gently and rolled her window about halfway down as a tall, muscular man strode up to them. His jaw was strong, his shoulders wide, and his eyes were a bright, stunning cornflower blue. He held a scarlet-spattered rag in one hand, which he kept blotting against his nose. He grinned at the truck with relief. There was blood in the creases between his straight, white teeth, which bizarrely made him look like he was wearing poorly applied lipstick.

"I don't like this," Stella said under her breath. "He reminds me of someone."

"Who?" Mercury asked as she studied the man, who looked confident and in charge as he strode toward them.

"My fucking last ex-husband."

Mercury's stomach roiled. "He was a handsome, narcissistic bully."

"Exactly," said Stella.

"Shit," said Mercury.

CHAPTER

6

"It's sure nice to see a vehicle that's still moving." The man extended his hand to Stella. "Name's Alvin Rutland, but you can call me Al. Good to meet you girls."

Stella ignored the offered hand, keeping both of hers on the wheel, and nodded instead. "I'm Stella Carver and I haven't been a *girl* for several decades." She smiled to soften the bite of her words. "Nice to meet you. We just wanted to stop and let you know that—"

"Well, good." He sniffed and blotted his nose. "You got Sadie and the kid and the hurt folks. Good." Alan nodded his head and lifted the hand he'd offered to Stella to wave at the bed of the truck. He raised his voice so it would carry over the idling engine to Sadie. "See, told you that everything would be fine!" Without waiting for Sadie to respond, he returned his attention to Stella, though his gaze kept skipping appraisingly from her to the rest of the women in the cab. "Now then, *ladies*"—he enunciated the word carefully and grinned—"I've got five folks with me, and I make six. It'll be a tight squeeze, but we can unload some of that junk from the bed and climb in." He spoke with confidence, as if no one ever challenged his words, then half turned away from them and started to motion for the others to join him.

"No." Stella spoke clearly, her voice loud enough so that the group behind him could hear her. "Everything in the bed is precious. Like I was explaining before you interrupted, we just stopped long enough to let you know we'll send help back for you as soon as we get to shelter."

When Rutland faced the truck again, the amiable smile had slid from his handsome face. "You can't mean to leave us out here."

Mercury leaned forward. "Isn't that exactly what you just did to them?" She jerked her thumb over her shoulder.

Al's piercing blue eyes narrowed, and he forgot to wipe at the blood that dripped sluggishly from his nose. "That was different. Irregardless, we aren't staying out here when we can get in the back of that truck and ride to safety."

"*Irregardless* isn't a word," Stella said. "Believe me. I'm a teacher. I know words and how to use them. I tell you that so you understand when I say *no*, I mean *no*."

"And, FYI"—Jenny spoke up with a little wave—"most women do mean *no* when they say it."

"Ladies, be reasonable." Alvin's voice was steeped in charm. "It's unproductive to argue semantics. Plus, I totally get it—I'm a feminist. I love women and I'm all for equal whatever. But we're in the middle of some gnarly shit here—pardon my language. I don't usually curse around ladies."

"No need to apologize," Stella said. "Gnarly shit *has* happened, which is why we're going to get the wounded people to shelter ASAP. Like I said, we'll send back someone to get y'all."

Al's charming expression hardened to anger. "We're getting in the truck. All you need to do is drive us about five miles up the highway to Government Camp." As he spoke, he motioned again for the group of people to join him. Quickly, the two other men swarmed the truck with Rutland while the three women moved more slowly, holding back to watch what would happen.

"Hey, Al, there's no room for—" Sadie began as the truck dipped to the side with the weight of the men.

"Stop it! You'll hurt them!" Gemma scooted from her mother's side to put herself between the wounded people and the men climbing on the truck.

"Get back!" Nathan shouted. He clutched his chest and tried to sit up, but instead fell back, gasping with pain.

Mercury didn't hesitate. She popped open the glove box, pulled the .38 from its holder, and snapped off the safety. "Roll that fucking window all the way down," she told Stella, who quickly complied. Then Mercury twisted her body and leaned across her best friend so that her arm and part of her torso were out of the window. She pointed the revolver at Alvin and cocked the trigger.

Halfway over the side of the truck, Al froze. His head snapped up and he stared into the barrel of Mercury's gun.

"Whoa! There's no need for that."

"Sure there is. Get off our truck. Now." Mercury was shocked at how calm she felt and how absolutely clear everything around her seemed—like the world had turned to crystal.

Al slid slowly down the truck to stand on the asphalt. He lifted one hand, as if in surrender, but he kept the other clamped on the side of the bed.

Mercury continued to aim the gun steadily at Rutland. "Tell your friends to get off too."

"Boys, you heard her." Al's voice sounded like he was speaking through gravel.

"No problem, boss man," said one of the men as he and the other guy got off the side of the truck.

Al turned his most charming smile on Mercury. "See? Everything's fine and dandy. Let's talk this out."

"We're done talking," said Mercury. "Move away from our truck."

Instead of moving back, Al's grip on the truck tightened, and his smile turned mocking. "Calm down. No need to get so emotional. You know you're not going to shoot me, so let's come to an agreement. How about—"

"How about *this*, Al. You don't know me, so let me clue you in real fast." Her Okie twang rang around them. "I'm from Oklahoma. I *will* shoot you. I won't kill you, but I'll blow out your knee." She lowered the barrel of the gun so that it was pointed at his left kneecap. "You might want to know that my dad taught me to shoot so that I could hunt with him, which I've been doin' since I was a kid. I can kill a pheasant in flight. I can kill a rabbit running for its burrow. I've even shot a squirrel scrambling up a great big ol' oak. So, I can damn sure hit your knee from a few feet away. Now, you and your boys need to back the fuck away from our truck, or I will happily give you tangible proof that I am indeed an excellent shot."

Rutland's handsome face flushed red so that it matched the color of the blood trickling from his nose. His hand slid from the side of the truck, and he took several slow steps back. The men with him followed suit.

Stella put the truck into gear, and without so much as a glance at Rutland, she pulled away from the men.

"I won't forget this!" Rutland shouted after them.

Stella rolled up her window and muttered, "Neither will we."

"We need to watch out for Al," said Mercury. She turned so that she could catch Sadie's eye as she mouthed, "Everyone okay?" Sadie nodded. Gemma gave her a thumbs-up as she retucked the tarp around Nathan. Mercury breathed a relieved sigh and reached forward to open the glove box, but Mrs. Gay beat her to it.

"You did well back there," said the history teacher.

Mercury switched on the safety and slid the .38 into its holster before she gave Mrs. Gay a surprised smile. "Well, thanks." She smoothed her hand through her hair, noticed that she was visibly trembling, and folded her hands together in her lap, to stop their shaking.

"Karen's right," said Stella.

"Yeah." Jenny put one hand over the two Mercury had clasped in her lap. "You kicked ass."

"I do not hold with violence," said Mrs. Gay, "but it's pretty easy to identify a bully, and bullies need to be confronted. That is exactly what you did."

"Thank you," Mercury repeated. "I appreciate you saying that, Mrs. Gay."

The older teacher turned to meet Mercury's gaze. "I would like you to call me Karen."

"I can do that, Karen," Mercury said.

For the next few miles their side of highway 26 had only half a dozen stalled vehicles. At each one Stella slowed so that they could check for survivors. Four of the cars held dead people. The other two were empty. The asphalt was less broken, and Stella was able to speed up. Still, she kept both hands on the wheel and her eyes on the road as she spoke. "I have a real strong feeling that we should pause at Government Camp and let someone know that there are people on highway 26 who need help, but that we should keep going on to Timberline."

"That sounds wise," Mercury said. "From the beginning I thought that was the best plan."

"I agree," said Jenny.

"After meeting Mr. Rutland, I've changed my mind about Government Camp," said Karen. "If he lives nearby, that means I don't want to stop there."

"Good, so we're all agreed," Mercury said. "When we pause there, we can see if Sadie and the rest of them want to get out or go on with us to Timberline."

"There's the sign for Government Camp." Stella nodded at a green and white road sign that listed hard and barely clung to what remained of the easement. It announced the exit for the town was in one mile.

They rounded a gentle curve, directly after which they were supposed to exit off the highway onto a loop that would take them through the small town of Government Camp. Instead, Stella had to brake quickly to avoid a maw-like crevasse that opened the asphalt in front of them.

"Shit! That was close!" Stella wiped stress sweat from her forehead with the back of her arm.

Mercury turned to see if their passengers were alright. Marge was grimacing in pain, and Nathan's face was colorless, but Gemma gave her a thumbs-up again.

Stella spoke softly. "Are you guys seeing this?"

"Holy crap!" said Mercury. Her stomach tightened as her shifting gaze took in the left side of the highway. There was no quaint little town—not even the outskirts visible from the road remained. Everything had been engulfed by the mountain. Enormous pines were splintered and upside down among mounds of muddy snow and boulders the size of houses. She could make out cars that had been swept up in the avalanche. A few bumpers were visible, as well as the broken roof of a house that was completely detached from the structure it used to shield so that it sat atop a mound of dirty snow like an ill-fitting hat.

"Wh-where is it? Where's the town?" Karen sat forward. She gripped the dash and stared.

"Gone," said Stella. She rolled down her window and called to the bed of the truck. "Y'all hold tight. This next stretch will be rough."

Mercury turned again so that she could watch Sadie and Gemma as they shifted suitcases and tarps to make Marge and Nathan—and the still unconscious Jason—more secure. Then Gemma shouted at the cab. "Ready!"

Stella blew out a long breath, wiped her palms on her jeans, and gripped the steering wheel again. "Okay, here we go."

She shifted into first and the truck crawled forward. Stella navigated their way around the crevasse in front of them by steering the truck off the road and onto what remained of the center easement. Mercury internally cringed every time the old pickup pitched and rolled over the broken ground—and tilted precariously toward the torn side of the mountain.

They made their way slowly past the buried town. It seemed Government Camp had contained the avalanche. Only a few boulders and mounds of snow and debris had reached the road, but the earthquake that had started the sloughing of the mountain had shifted so much of the land that several times Mercury thought Stella wouldn't be able to keep driving and they'd have to abandon the truck. She felt weak with relief when they were able to veer left off the road and onto the two-lane Timberline Highway. This stretch of the smaller highway was littered with huge rocks and fallen trees, but the asphalt itself wasn't as torn up as highway 26 had been.

As if reading her mind, Stella said, "I know this road looks like it's in better shape than that other highway, but I still have to go slow and be careful unless we want to bounce Sadie and the rest of them out of the bed."

"Go as slow as you need to," Mercury reassured her. "You're doing a great job."

"And we need this truck to stay in one piece," said Karen.

"Good point," Stella said. She had to leave the two-lane again and bump up the side of the road to avoid a big black Dodge Ram diesel truck that had flipped onto its back like a helpless turtle. The cab was crushed, and a dead man had projected through the windshield and come to an awkward final rest on the pavement. "Y'all see anyone else around that wreck?"

"No, no one," Karen said. She shivered as they passed the truck. Her voice was soft and filled with despair. "So many dead people. I just—I don't know how we'll go on."

"One step at a time—one minute and then the next," Mercury said. "We're alive, Karen. That's what's most important right now. Let's just concentrate on staying that way."

Timberline Highway was only a little over five miles long, but it took them almost an hour to navigate it and finally get to the lodge. As they pulled from the highway onto the property, Mercury at first breathed a long sigh of relief. Past the mounds of snow that had been plowed from the parking lot, she could see the central spire of the hotel—and then Stella drove around an especially large pile of muddy snow to see that the parking lot looked like a giant puzzle someone had upended. Huge cracks in the asphalt had swallowed vehicles whole.

Others had been thrown together to form strange piles of metal, some of which were still smoldering. There were bloody bodies everywhere.

"Are any of them moving?" Mercury asked.

"I don't think so." Karen's voice was raw.

"Yeah, all those dead people are men. They're, um, like Mr. Hale and Coach Davis," added Jenny. She'd gone pale and gripped Mercury's hand.

The truck crawled slowly forward, past one of the smoking piles, and finally the entire lodge came into view.

"What the—?" Mercury began.

Stella braked. "At least part of it's still standing."

Jenny's voice was thick with tears she was trying not to shed. "And there are people. Living people."

Karen bowed her head, clasped her hands, and began to whisper a prayer of thanks.

Stella put the truck into reverse and tucked it behind the last mound of snow so that their view of the lodge was blocked. Then she turned to Mercury. "The three of you should get the wounded people out of the bed of the truck right away. Then I'll park at the far side of the lot, out of sight behind those wrecks."

"But it's going to be really hard to get Marge and Nathan and Jason to the lodge," Jenny said. "They can't walk."

Mercury shook her head. "No, Stella's right. As far as we know this truck is the only working vehicle for miles and miles. If we want to be sure we keep it, we need to hide it."

Karen took a break in her praying to say, "But that doesn't seem honest."

Mercury met her gaze. "Remember Al? Do you really think he's the only man left alive who thinks he's entitled to take whatever he wants from us?"

Karen sighed and looked away, but didn't answer.

"I'm not willing to chance some asshole bullying us out of this truck," said Stella firmly. "We have no idea if what's left of the lodge is even habitable. It's cold up here. There's fucking snow everywhere. If we can't shelter inside, I'm damn sure not going to freeze because our only option is to try to hike off this mountain." She shifted in her seat so she could face the three women. "Did y'all see those pockets of green smoke or fog or mist or what-the-hell-ever it is as we drove here?"

"I saw it," Karen said. "Most of it drifted with the avalanche debris."

"Yeah, I caught glimpses of it," Mercury said.

"Me too," said Jenny.

"So, real talk here—we know the green stuff came with the bombs. We know that after it swept over us, people died. Horribly. Most of those people seem to be men. And they keep dying—like Todd," Stella continued. "What we don't know is what it is or what it can do to us. So, if we have to get out of here, I'd feel a whole lot better if I knew we could drive out and *not* have to walk through any patches of green crap."

"You're right." Mercury nodded. "Let's unload Sadie and the rest of the group here. We can put Marge, Nathan, and Jason on top of the tarps and drag them the rest of the way to the lodge while you hide the truck."

Karen put her hand on the door latch, but Stella's voice made her pause. "I don't think we should say anything about Rutland and his group—and I'm pretty sure they'll agree with us." Stella gestured over her shoulder at the bed of the truck.

Karen nodded slowly. "That man is local. He'll know how to find shelter."

"Sadie said his farm wasn't far from Government Camp," Jenny added.

"I agree. Definitely. Let's get this done. I'll bet they're freezing back there," said Mercury.

It was a lot easier to get the wounded from the truck than it had been to heft them up into the bed, though obviously not any less painful for them. The conscious passengers all agreed to say nothing about the truck or about Alvin Rutland and his group.

"He's a jerk. He didn't care about helping us." Gemma narrowed her green eyes and tossed back her long hair. "Neither did anyone in that group. They just walked away and left us there. I hope we never see them again."

"As my grandma would say, *'From your lips to God's ears,'*" said Jenny.

Each woman grabbed an edge of the tarp, and while Stella backed the truck away and then headed for the far corner of the parking lot, they trudged toward what remained standing of Timberline Lodge.

CHAPTER 7

SWEAT SLID DOWN Mercury's face, into her eyes, and pooled between her breasts as she wrestled with her edge of the tarp. She was too focused on dragging the wounded people around the cracks in the parking lot, the bodies, and the wrecked vehicles that she didn't get a good view of the lodge until they were at the edge of the parking lot that used to lead to the grand front stairs and stone facade of the charming lodge-like hotel.

"Hang on a sec, y'all." Mercury halted and wiped her hand across her face. All of the women were breathing hard, and she could see Stella jogging as she hurried to rejoin them. "Let's wait here for Stella to—" Her gaze, finally clear of sweat, swept over the lodge, and her words stumbled to a stop.

The view was a shock—and not just because the lodge had been torn apart, with half of it lost within a huge fissure in the earth. The biggest shock was the bizarre change in what was left of the summit of Mt. Hood behind Timberline. Just hours before it had been a majestic, snow-covered crown on the lovely ski resort, with a series of lifts and slopes running like arteries from the heart of the mountain. Half of that summit had crumbled and sloughed off—and carried with it part of the lodge as it avalanched down to fill the impossibly large mouth that had opened in the earth.

"It looks worse than I thought," Stella said between panting breaths as she caught up with them.

"It's like those re-creations of the sinking of the *Titanic*," Mercury said. "How half of it broke off and went under before the other part joined it."

"I guess we should be glad some of it is still standing," said Jenny.

"I wonder if it's actually safe to go inside, though," Karen added.

"Well, we can't stay out here," said Stella grimly. She gestured overhead at the dark clouds. "It's hard to tell because of smoke and crap up there, but that line of gray says snow to me. Getting caught outside during snow mixed with"—she paused and grimaced—"*whatever* is not an option."

"I don't know," Marge said from the makeshift stretcher. Her face had no color and was covered with sweat, but she bared her teeth in an attempt at a smile as the women turned to her. "I'm having a great time out here."

Gemma went to her and retucked part of the tarp around her. "You're in shock," she said.

Marge closed her eyes and patted Gemma's hand. "And you're a very good girl."

"Hey! Do you folks need help?" A voice from the lodge startled them all. A man was standing in front of the right section of the building—the part that hadn't been swept into the fissure with the avalanche.

"Yes! We have wounded people with us!" Stella cupped her hands around her mouth and shouted back. Then she turned quickly to Mercury. "Take this. The .38 is in it and I made sure the safety is on." She handed Mercury the big, fringed purse she usually carried with her everywhere.

Mercury nodded tightly and hefted the purse over her shoulder as the noise of an engine had all of them turning in surprise. One of the many ATVs the hotel staff used to shuttle people back and forth roared around a pile of snow. The man who had called to them was driving. Beside him was another, younger guy. Their clothes were torn, dirty, and blood spattered, but both men appeared to be unharmed and healthy.

The ATV slid to a stop on the snowy asphalt in front of them. It looked like a golf cart on steroids. There was room for two people up front, two behind, and it had a mini pickup bed in the rear. The little vehicle idled and the two men jumped out and hurried to them.

"If your wounded can squeeze together, we can fit all three in the back there," said the older man. He had a round face, soft belly, and a kind smile. His glasses were broken, and hung precariously on his nose so that he kept pushing at them.

Mercury stepped forward with her hand out. "Hi, I'm Mercury Rhodes. My friends and I were staying at the lodge the past four nights and—"

"Hey! You're teachers! I remember you," said the younger guy. Mercury recognized him as the bellhop their principal had been bossing around earlier that morning.

Goddess! Was that just this morning? It seems like a lifetime ago.

Mercury nodded and smiled as she turned her attention to the younger man. "Yeah, that's right. The four of us were here for the conference."

"*Oh my God*! Mercury! Stella!" The group looked up to see a woman waving at them from the broken steps of the lodge.

"Imani!" Mercury shouted, and their friend began to sprint to them. She slid down a mound of snow and raced around bodies, debris, and cracks in the parking lot until she reached them and hurled herself into Mercury's arms.

"You're alive! Thank God! You're alive!" Imani clung to her for a moment before she stepped back. "Where were you? Did you see what happened?"

Mercury felt Imani's gaze like it was a lead weight. "We were on highway 26," she began slowly. "We'd, uh, stopped so Amelia could pee." Mercury had to pause then as Amelia's death rushed back and overwhelmed her.

Imani looked around. "Where is Amelia?"

"Dead," said Stella. "Along with our principal and the coach who was with us."

"And a whole lot more people," added Jenny.

"How about here?" Mercury asked quickly. "Did the blasts kill people?"

"Blasts? So it was a bomb? I was in the basement when it happened, with Tyler here, who was helping me with my regular check of our fuse boxes," said the older man. "Oh, sorry. I'm Ken Sampson—the mechanic in charge of the lifts and basically anything electrical—and this is Tyler Anderson, a bellhop and my unofficial apprentice."

"I recognize Tyler." Mercury nodded at both men. "Yes, it was a bomb. Actually, many bombs. So, y'all couldn't see anything from here?"

"Like I said, we were in the basement when it happened," answered Ken.

"I wasn't." Imani held Mercury's gaze steadily. "I was hiking and it was just lucky I went that way." She gestured behind her at the side of the mountain that hadn't slid into the fissure that had swallowed half the lodge. "But I was surrounded by huge trees and couldn't see. Whatever happened—the bombs—knocked me off my feet. I think I lost consciousness. Next thing I knew, I opened my eyes and there was green fog everywhere, and then everything started to shake. But you were on the highway. What did you see?"

"Bombs. All around us," Mercury said. "I'll tell you everything, but we have people who are hurt with us. Can we get them inside the lodge? Are there any doctors here?"

Imani started to speak, but Ken cut him off. "Portland. Could you see Portland?"

Mercury met Ken's gaze: the fear within his eyes said that he was probably from Portland. She tried to form the words that would shatter his life forever, but she couldn't seem to make any sound.

Stella stepped up beside her. "Ken, are you from Portland?"

"I am!" said young Tyler. "But I work up here during spring and summer breaks."

"Yeah, me too, originally," said Ken. "My parents and two sisters and their families still live in Portland. I moved to Government Camp with my wife and daughters when I took this job a couple years ago." His eyes widened. "Wait, you were on highway 26 at the lookout! How's Government Camp?"

Stella's gaze went from Ken to Tyler and then back to Ken. Her voice was kind, but she didn't prevaricate. "There isn't any more Government Camp or Portland. An avalanche buried Government Camp—all of it. A bomb hit Portland directly. Salem too. They hit all over. We saw dozens and dozens of the smoke trails. Everywhere."

Imani gasped and covered her mouth as her eyes filled with tears.

Ken didn't speak. He didn't even seem to breathe. A small, strangled sound came from Tyler's bloodless lips, and his body crumpled to the broken asphalt.

"Hey, guys! Nathan passed out again. We really need to get him some help." Gemma's voice came from the makeshift litter where she was crouched between Nathan and Marge. "And I think Jason just died. There's, uh, blood everywhere."

"We're coming!" Stella called over her shoulder before she turned to Mercury. "Stay with Tyler while we get them inside." She glanced at Ken. "I'm assuming we can go into that section of the lodge, right?"

Ken blinked like he was waking from a dream. "I . . . uh . . . I can't—" His voice broke and he turned his head away.

Imani touched his arm gently. "It's okay. Just breathe." She turned to Stella and Mercury. "The lodge is in bad shape, but we've been bringing the wounded inside to the first floor and trying to stay as far away from there as possible." She pointed to the missing half of the hotel. "But since there aren't many wounded so far, that hasn't been too difficult."

Stella's brow went up. "Not many wounded?"

"No." Tyler shook his head. The teenager wiped the tears from his smooth cheeks. Moving slowly like an old man, he got to his feet. "Almost everyone is dead."

Mercury felt his words like a punch in her gut. She cleared her throat and asked, "Tyler, can you help load the wounded into your golf cart thing?"

"Y-yes, ma'am."

"I'll help too," said Ken. His face was gray and his hands trembled, but together they loaded Marge and Nathan into the rear of the little vehicle. Gemma had been right. Jason had bled out without regaining consciousness. They carried him to the side of the parking lot and covered him with the tarp.

"Tyler, you go ahead and drive the Polaris back," said Ken. "I'm going to check the bodies out here and be sure none of them are still alive."

"Sir, I'll help you. I'm not afraid of blood or anything like that," said Gemma.

Ken shook his head slightly. His lips twitched like they wanted to smile but couldn't remember how. "No, young lady. If you aren't scared of blood, you'll be busy up there." His gaze flicked to what was left of the lodge. "I need the time alone anyway."

"There's only room for four," said Mercury. "Gemma, Sadie, and Karen, you should ride back with Tyler to get Marge and Nathan situated. "Stella, Imani, and I will walk." No one argued. Every so often Tyler wiped an escaping tear from his face, but he got behind the wheel and gave a hand up to Karen. Gemma and Sadie crawled in behind them, and the Polaris slowly began a careful trek back to the lodge.

"Ken, are you sure we can't help you?" Mercury asked.

The older man shook his head slightly. "No one can help me. Go ahead and get warm. They've at least got a fire going up there, as well as shelter and food. I'll be along as soon as I check for wounded."

"Hey, I looked on the way across the lot, and I didn't see anyone who could've been—" Stella's words stopped as Ken turned and began to walk to the first of many dead bodies.

"Let him go," said Mercury. "His family is gone. He's got to try to deal with that."

"Give it to me straight." Imani faced the two women. "How bad do you think it is?"

Mercury and Stella exchanged a quick look before Mercury began, "Let's talk as we walk back."

"I need to hear exactly what you know. Don't sugarcoat it and don't try to distract me," Imani said immovably.

"Okay then." Stella drew a long breath. "We could see the bombs hit Portland. It's gone. Seriously."

"Salem is the same, as well as a lot of the surrounding area—basically everywhere we could see was either destroyed or damaged badly," continued Mercury. "And I think . . ." Her words trailed off as she did think. Mercury knew, somewhere in the back of her mind, which she hadn't allowed herself to fully confront yet, that Tulsa was probably as gone as Portland. The Air National Guard's 138th Fighter Squadron was stationed there with their F-16s. If a foreign country wanted to take out military installations, Tulsa would definitely be on the list, as would Imani's home, San Diego, where her family had been waiting for their wife and mother to fly home. She cleared her throat. "I think it's bad. Really bad."

Imani's head shook back and forth. "Maybe it's just here. Maybe it's just Oregon that was attacked."

Mercury didn't know what to say. So she reached out and took Imani's hand in hers. "I hope you're right."

"But you don't think I am." Imani's voice was emotionless, yet her eyes begged Mercury to disagree—to give her hope.

Mercury's words didn't come. She had no hope to give her friend.

Imani gripped Mercury's hand as her gaze went to Stella. "Tell me. Just say it."

"Why would anyone just attack Oregon? And what we witnessed was more than that," said Stella. "There were smoke trails from bombs for as far as we could see."

Mercury nodded somberly in agreement. "What Stella said. Truthfully, I believe the world as we knew it came to an end today."

"M-my daughter, Jasmine—she's five." Imani's body began to tremble as she spoke. "Austin, that's my s-son. He just turned three."

Mercury put her arm around Imani's shoulders and held her friend as she sobbed. "I'm here," she said. "I'm here."

Stella moved to Imani's other side and wrapped an arm around her waist. "I'm here too. We're in this together. All of us. We'll stay together."

Imani lifted her gaze to meet Mercury's. "They're babies. J-just babies. They w-wanted to come with me this year, and I almost let them, but Curtis took off work to stay home with them. Said I deserved a mommy break." Her almond-colored eyes filled with tears that spilled over and flowed down her cheeks. "Are you telling me my family is dead?"

"I don't know, Imani. None of us knows for sure." Mercury wanted to throw up as she thought about the two adorable, chubby-faced kids she'd watched Imani FaceTime with the day before. They'd been excited to tell their mommy that they'd used sidewalk chalk to draw and color in big hearts on their driveway as a welcome-home surprise.

"Honey, let's get back to the lodge. You're shivering. And you're soaking wet. You need to—"

"I need my babies!" Imani's legs folded beneath her.

Mercury and Stella caught her and gently guided her to the snowy ground. As Imani rocked back and forth and keened over and over, Mercury and Stella wrapped their arms around her and held her while all three women sobbed.

CHAPTER

8

THE HALF OF Timberline lodge that hadn't been swept into the crevasse by the avalanche was in a lot better shape than Mercury had expected. The Polaris the others had ridden in was parked under the roof that protected the baggage load and unload area and was still very much intact. The sign that had been changed a few hours before from welcoming the nationally certified teachers to greeting Nike executives had fallen from its easel, but it was still in one piece. All someone would have to do would be to right the easel and reposition the sign, and everything would almost appear normal. If you ignored the shattered glass doors behind it and the blood that speckled the snowy sidewalk.

"Shit," Mercury said under her breath. "Shit. I really hate blood and such. Ugh, I don't want to go inside."

"Most of the people have broken bones and cuts, and the doc has been working on cleaning them up," said Imani. She'd stopped crying and instead, all the way from the parking lot to the lodge, she'd fired questions at Stella and Mercury about what all they'd observed on their drive from the lookout spot back to the lodge. "What I said before wasn't an exaggeration. There aren't many wounded. There *are* a lot of dead people, though."

"Where are they?" Mercury asked.

"You'll have to ask Tyler and Ken. They were taking care of the bodies." She drew in a long, shuddering breath and then continued. "The five teachers and three administrators I came here with are dead. All of them."

"Were they men or women?" Stella asked.

"Weird that you asked. My group and I laughed that this was the Year of the Coach. Four of the five teachers were men—and coaches. All three administrators were men. Teri and me—we were the only women to come to the spring conference this year. She's dead." Imani shook her head and grimaced like she might get sick. Then she cleared her throat and said, "It was horrible. Absolutely horrible. She died just over there." Imani gestured at the tree line. "I limped back after the earthquake stopped, and Teri had come looking for me. She met me where the trail begins. She was okay. We hugged and cried—and then a limb fell from one of those big pines just as we were leaving the trail. She was only a foot or so in front of me, and it crashed down on her. It flattened the bottom half of her body. I held what was left of her while she died." Imani shook her head as tears leaked slowly down her cheeks.

"What about the coaches and your administrators?" Stella asked quickly.

Imani wiped her eyes. "They were drinking coffee on those benches in front of the lodge. I remember that they all waved at me when I headed for my hiking trail. They were leaving earlier than me, so the guys were waiting together until the shuttle for the airport came." She paused and swallowed several times before she continued. "After Teri died, I went there first." Imani's eyes were haunted by the memory she replayed. "They were dead. Every one of them. Worse than Teri. Way worse. It was like the insides of their bodies dissolved." She swayed a little, like she might fall. "All of my people—all of them are dead."

Mercury took Imani's elbow and steadied her. "Now we're your people. We're very much alive—and we're going to stay that way."

"You said you limped out of the woods," Stella said. "Are you okay?"

Imani stopped swaying and squeezed Mercury's hand before she let her go. "Yeah, I'm fine. I thought I'd broken my ankle, but I musta just needed to walk it out because it's not bothering me now."

"And the green fog was here?" Stella said.

Imani nodded. "Right."

Stella fired another question. "When it surrounded you, did you feel anything?"

Imani opened her mouth and then closed it as she considered. Finally, she said, "Yeah, even though I haven't really thought about it until now. It was like fire inside my body."

"Hot pins and needles." Mercury nodded in understanding.

"That's a good way to describe it," said Imani.

"Something's up with that fog," said Stella. "Something that kills people. Mostly male people."

"But it didn't kill us. *Yet.*" said Imani.

Stella's response was instant. "How do you feel? Really think about it. Not your emotions—we're all upset and freaked out—I mean your body."

Imani rounded her shoulders with a shrug. "Okay. Actually, pretty good. Physically, that is."

Stella reached up to touch her left shoulder—the one that had been cut when the blast had hurled them to the ground. She met Mercury's gaze. "It's scabbed over. Not sore at all. Like it happened days and not hours ago."

Automatically Mercury touched the gash above her temple. It had stopped bleeding some time ago. Except for the itchiness of the dried blood in her scalp, Mercury had completely forgotten about the injury.

"Yours is healed too, isn't it?" Stella asked.

Mercury nodded.

"What about the aches in your joints?" Stella said.

Imani answered before Mercury could. "I still feel sore. Kinda like a mild flu. Definitely not as bad as before."

"Same with me. What are you thinking?" Mercury asked Stella.

"It's more a feeling than a thought. Let's go inside. I'll tell you when I know more, but I can say that I think we can be pretty sure that we're not going to suddenly bleed out like Amelia or those two men we found by the roadside, but pay attention if someone says they feel *wrong* or *broken*."

"Death words," Mercury whispered.

Stella looked grim. "Yep. Definitely. There's probably nothing we can do to help someone if they start feeling broken, but we can be there with them until the end."

"No one should die alone," said Mercury.

Imani stared past the two women and spoke softly. "At least they were together—my babies and their daddy. Curtis would've held them and been with them and told them everything would be alright." Imani pressed the back of her hand against her mouth to stop her sob.

Mercury touched her arm. "I'm here. I don't know what the hell to say, but I'm here."

"Me too," Stella said. "We've got you."

Imani drew a deep breath and straightened her back. "Let's go in and see how we can help."

Mercury and Stella nodded, and then the three women picked their way around the broken glass and entered the lodge. There was a big foyer inside, where the bellboys and the valet parkers had stations. A huge hearth, so big a person could practically stand inside, was burning with ironic cheer in the middle of the room. Mounds of firewood were stacked neatly beside it. Little shops that carried what Mercury thought of as rustic chic stuff—everything from fleece-lined coats to dream catchers and turquoise jewelry—lined one side of a wide hallway that led from the foyer deeper into the lodge. On the other was the entrance to the Cascade Dining Room. Past that, all they could see through the fading gray day were fallen timbers and debris littering everything. Another, narrower hallway veered from the foyer where they glimpsed the beginning of guest suites. But none of that held their attention because the foyer was humming with activity.

Women Mercury didn't recognize were struggling to drag mattresses from the direction of the first-floor rooms to join the several already spread out and occupied around the blazing fireplace. Wounded people lay on the mattresses as a tall, ballerina-lithe woman with long wheaten hair that draped in waves almost to her waist carried a potted candle with her and moved gracefully among them.

More wounded huddled in the wide hallway as they waited for their mattresses. Gemma was there with several pots of candles, crouched beside one man whose nose wouldn't stop dripping blood.

"Oh, good! Stella—Mercury, I need your help!" Gemma called.

"How are you with blood?" Mercury asked Imani.

"Fine, as long as it's not mine."

"Let's go help the kid," said Stella, and they headed to Gemma.

Even before they reached Gemma, she was firing orders at them. "Doctor Hilary needs as many candles as you can find—and those clean sheets and towels to be ripped into long strips for bandages." The teenager didn't look up from the man's face. She was holding a blood-soaked washcloth against it, but she jerked her chin in the direction of the entrance to the nearest boutique. Just inside, Jenny and Karen tore sheets and towels into strips. "Also, do you remember the store that sells, like, toothbrushes and other stuff people forget when they go on vacay?"

Imani nodded. "The one that's farther down the hallway there?" She pointed past the restaurant, where timbers had fallen from the ceiling and walls of the lodge.

"That's it. Can you go down there and grab all the candles you can find and anything that we can use for the wounded? Bandages, Tylenol—*anything*. Doctor Hilary got some stuff from there earlier, but she's too busy with hurt people to go back, and everyone not hurt except you guys is already getting the mattresses in here and making bandages."

"I'll go," said Imani.

"I'll go with you," Mercury said. "We should stay in pairs and not wander around alone." She looked up at the cracked ceiling. "How stable is this place?"

"This section is sound, but don't explore too far away from the main foyer." The man Gemma was helping spoke through the bloody washcloth. "'Specially not close to the west wing of the lodge that got sucked into that avalanche. You ladies be careful."

"This is Bob. He's the lodge's handyman. He's worked here for a million or so years and knows everything about Timberline," said Gemma quickly. "Bob, keep your head back. They'll be careful—don't worry."

"Imani and I are on it," said Mercury.

"And I'll go help Karen and Jenny," said Stella. Then she added. "Hey, so, good thing we have a doctor here."

Gemma nodded. "She works for the lodge. Uh, guys, we really need that stuff."

"Okay, right!" Stella said, and the three women hurried off.

"Who is that kid?" Imani asked quietly.

"Gemma Jenkins," said Stella. "We picked her and her mother up on the highway. They were with some wounded people."

"She's intense," said Imani.

"She volunteers at Portland's teaching hospital," explained Stella. "Wants to be a surgeon."

Imani's brows lifted like the wings of an onyx butterfly. "Smart girl."

Stella nodded agreement before she ducked into the boutique to join Jenny and Karen as they ripped bandages.

"Y'all be quick if you're going down there," said Jenny. "Stuff has been fallin'."

Karen nodded at the women. "Yes, something fell from the roof not long ago." Pots of candles were lit around her and Jenny to aid the wan light trickling in through the cracked outside windows.

Mercury caught the oddly nostalgic Christmas scents of pine and cinnamon from the candles. "We'll be fast."

Side by side, Mercury and Imani hurried down the wide hallway. When they got to the entrance to the restaurant, Mercury peeked inside and shivered as the cold air from outside swirled in through a wall of broken windows. "Hey, help me close these doors. Later we can come back and find something to block those open windows."

The two women struggled with the thick, wooden double restaurant doors that hung off-kilter, but managed to close them before they continued down the hallway. The farther they got from the foyer, the more debris cluttered the floor. They stayed close together as they picked their way quickly around fallen timbers and broken drywall.

"This is it," said Imani. "I forgot my toothbrush and had to buy one here the first night." She paused and wiped a hand across her face. "It seems like forever ago." Shoulders bowed, Imani led the way into the little convenience store.

"Hey, here are some baskets and more pots of candles." Mercury headed to a stack of red and white checkered baskets that had been stacked beside the opening to the store but had spilled across the wooden floor. "Can you see if there are any lighters by the register?"

"Got 'em," said Imani as she grabbed a handful and brought them to Mercury. They each lit one and put the rest in a basket. Then, working quickly, Imani and Mercury piled everything they thought could be of use in the baskets.

"It's like we're in one of those zombie movies," said Mercury. "You know, where the people go into empty stores and just take whatever they want. I'd imagined it to be a lot more satisfying than it is."

"Probably would be if this was a jewelry store," said Imani.

"Or a lovely, chic little clothing boutique."

Imani swept a whole row of Advil bottles into a basket. "Girl, please. Did you see those clothes in that store that they call a boutique down the hall?"

"I think it's called lumberjack chic." Mercury tiptoed carefully around the shattered glass door of a dark cooler and loaded a basket full of bottled water and Gatorade.

Imani snorted. "*I* think it's called ugly."

Mercury barked a little laugh. Imani met her eyes, a smile perched on the corners of her full lips—and then her smile collapsed. "How can I be making jokes? My babies could be dead!"

Mercury went to her and pulled her into a tight hug. "You made a joke because you're alive. That's it. That's the only answer I have. I don't fucking know what else to say—or do—except that we have to keep on going. Keep on living. And there's no point to that if we can't joke or smile or eventually find some semblance of happiness."

"But how?" Imani asked brokenly.

"I don't know, but I'm going to try, and if I figure it out, you'll be the first person I tell."

IMANI
ANDREWS

CHAPTER 9

IMANI AND MERCURY half dragged, half carried six laden baskets each back to the foyer. Karen was standing beside the willow-like woman Gemma had called Doctor Hilary. She held a candle for light as the doc bandaged a woman's bloody arm with long strips of torn sheets that Karen handed to her. The doctor looked up at the sound the baskets made, and nodded in relief.

"Yes, good. Ladies, light those candles and put them around the mattresses, then pull out all the bottles of analgesics you found and start administrating them to the patients. When you do give the patients the medicine, note on the paper I've tucked under the head of each mattress the time, what you've given them, and the amount—which should be double the dosage on the bottle. Be sure you ask each person if they have any known allergies first. If they do, let me know."

"How do we know which people should get the pills?" asked Mercury.

"If they're conscious and not hooked up to an IV, that means I haven't given them morphine and they need pain relief. Gemma can help you if you need it. Oh, I'm Dr. Hilary, and you are?"

"Mercury Rhodes."

"Imani Andrews."

"Do either of you have medical training or experience?"

"We're high school biology and science teachers," said Imani.

"That's better than nothing. Oh, bring me any antibiotic salve you found—like Neosporin. Did you come across any rubbing alcohol or hydrogen peroxide?" Dr. Hilary asked.

"No peroxide, but there were a few bottles of rubbing alcohol and some tubes of Neosporin," said Mercury.

"Excellent, bring those to me, please," the doctor asked before she returned focus to her patient. Karen smiled nervously at Mercury and Imani but followed Dr. Hilary closely and continued handing her strips of cloth for bandages.

"Here are a couple pens I got from that gift shop." Gemma seemed to materialize beside them. "Come on. I'll help you guys." She was already squatting beside the baskets filled with a hodgepodge of items from the convenience store. The teenager had no trouble finding the bottles of analgesics. She lifted one and called across the room to Dr. Hilary. "Hey, Doc, we should start with acetaminophen before ibuprofen, right?"

Dr. Hilary didn't look up from the woman's head she was bandaging, but nodded and said, "Yes, of course."

"Okay, that means we need to find all the bottles of Tylenol," said Gemma as she uncovered the bottles of alcohol they'd loaded into the baskets.

"Because ibuprofen treats pain and inflammation, and acetaminophen only treats pain," said Imani as she crouched and began going through her baskets.

"You two are practically mini-doctors." Mercury said as she went through her own baskets.

"I read a lot," said Gemma with a shrug.

Imani spoke automatically. "And I'm a mom. We know things." Her hands stilled and she whispered, "Or I *was* a mom."

Gemma touched her shoulder gently. "You'll always be a mom."

Imani squeezed Gemma's hand and nodded before she returned to picking through the baskets.

"Need help?" asked Stella.

"Always," said Mercury. "We're looking for alcohol, Neosporin, and acetaminophen. Where's Jenny?"

Stella squatted beside her. "She went to the utility room with that Bob guy—the lodge's handyman, who has a bloody nose. He thinks he can get the generator to work. Says there's one on this side of the lodge."

"I thought the EMP fried everything," said Mercury.

"Apparently, if it wasn't in use when the blast happened, and if the generator wasn't damaged, we should be able to have power as long as the natural gas lines weren't torn up."

Imani's head snapped up. "Wait, shit! Did you say EMP? You mean those bombs are nuclear?"

"That's real bad," said Gemma softly.

"There are other bombs that cause an EMP that aren't nuclear," said Mercury. "I was looking directly at Portland when the bomb exploded there, and I'm definitely not blind. If it was a nuclear detonation, I believe it would've damaged my retinas."

Gemma met her gaze. "Don't say that just to make us feel better."

"I'm not. But the truth is I don't actually know what they were. No one really does. This—all of these bombs—have never happened before."

"Nuclear fallout isn't green," said Imani. "And it certainly isn't a green fog that expands and covers everything after the initial blast."

"It was something biological," said Gemma.

"Why do you say that?" asked Stella as she tore the plastic from jars of Motrin and Advil and poked through their protective coverings.

"Common sense," said Gemma with another shrug. "The green fog stuff covered us too. Right after that, most people exposed to it started to die." She stood and wiped her hands on her jeans. "Okay, we have enough bottles. Let's start administering them and lighting these candles. Do you guys need me to help you?"

"We can handle it." Mercury squinted in the shadowy candlelight at the dosage instructions on the bottles she held. "We ask if they're allergic, and if they aren't, we double the regular dosage and write in on the piece of paper tucked under their mattress, right?"

"Right." Gemma nodded as she spilled a basket out on the floor and piled the alcohol, pots of candles, and several Tylenol bottles in it. "Let's get to work." The teenager strode away toward the doctor.

"Damn, Gemma is like what would happen if Florence Nightingale and a Roomba had a baby," said Stella. "I like her."

"Me too," said Mercury as she straightened with her own loaded basket. She paused before heading out to the wounded. "I thought there would be more people." Mercury took a quick count. "Thirty wounded people—plus the doc, Bob, Tyler, Ken, and those women dragging the mattresses in. That's still less than forty. It seemed like the lodge was full this weekend."

"It was," said Imani. "A few checked out, but most people were having breakfast and waiting for their shuttles when the bombs hit. They died. I swear more than a hundred of them."

"I heard Bob tell Jenny that there were a little over two hundred guests here and thirty-ish lodge staff," said Stella.

Mercury swallowed several times before she could form her next question. "Are there no other people alive?"

"I don't think so—unless Ken actually found some survivors in the parking lot," said Imani as she hefted her own basket.

Stella shook her head. "He won't. I looked while I jogged back to you guys. The bodies I saw were like Coach Davis and Mr. Hale."

Mercury met her friend's gaze. "The green fog is bad news."

"At least for most men. For us?" Stella shrugged. "I guess time will tell."

"I can't think about that right now. Let's go help people," said Imani.

It wasn't as terrible as Mercury had expected. The majority of the survivors had breaks and cuts—which Dr. Hilary, with Gemma's steady-handed assistance, was splinting and stitching. Nathan's broken ribs and Marge's open leg wound were among the worst injuries, though both were resting peacefully thanks to Dr. Hilary's administration of morphine.

"Hey! I need help!" Jenny stumbled into the foyer with Bob leaning heavily on her. Blood flowed freely from his nose and dripped from his chin to make a Jackson Pollock painting of his shirt.

Mercury sprinted to Jenny with Stella and Imani on her heels.

"There's an empty mattress over there on the other side of the fireplace," said Mercury as she put her arm around Bob's waist. "Let's get him to it."

"Gemma," Bob's words sounded wet. "Need Gemma."

The four women helped him down to the empty mattress as Gemma and Dr. Hilary rushed up.

"I need a towel! Someone go to the kitchen of the Cascade and see if there's still ice. If there isn't, go out and fill a bag or basket or whatever with snow," Dr. Hilary shot orders.

"Here's what's left of a towel." Karen handed Dr. Hilary frayed strips of terrycloth as she averted her gaze from Bob and his blood. "I'll get ice or snow."

"G-Gemma," Bob gasped.

The teenager went to her knees beside him and took his hand as Dr. Hilary applied pressure to his nose. "It's okay, Bob. I'm right here."

"Stack something under his legs so that they're elevated," said the doctor.

"Got it!" said Stella as she sprinted back to the boutique and then emerged with a cowhide-covered stool, which she and Imani gently propped Bob's legs up on.

"Bob, breathe out of your mouth with me," said Dr. Hilary.

"I'm—I'm better now." He turned his head and brushed part of the towel aside so that he could see Gemma. "Feel better now. Your hand is so warm. Better now." His eyelids started to flutter shut, but then he rallied and continued, "Generator is on. Gas lines must be intact. Means stoves will work and limited electricity. D-don't try to run too much. Only meant to fuel part of the lodge."

"Shh, Bob. Let's just get your bleeding under control. Then you can update us," said Dr. Hilary.

Bob's smile showed reddened teeth, which suddenly reminded Mercury of douchey Alvin Rutland. "Not gonna be around much longer to help you. Just remembered there's an old CB radio in one of the outbuildings. Tyler can find it. Used to use it to contact the Silcox Hut before we got cell service up here." Bob's voice got weaker and weaker, though his grip was so tight on Gemma's hand that his knuckles were as white as his face. "I gotta go now. It's okay, though. Gonna be with my wife and kids. They got caught in the avalanche. Don't let go of my hand, Gemma. I feel better when you hold my . . ." His eyes rolled to show white, and blood poured from Bob's nose, mouth, and ears.

Imani bowed her head and began to cry quietly.

Hilary started chest compressions, but Gemma gently released Bob's hand and touched her shoulder. "He's not coming back. He's broken inside."

The doctor turned to meet the teenager's gaze. She nodded. Her shoulders deflated and she stopped performing CPR.

Karen jogged up, breathing heavily and holding a wet plastic sack full of ice. “There was ice! Got a whole—” She looked at Bob and her words broke off. “Oh. Oh no.” She bowed her head and began to pray.

Gemma placed Bob’s hand on his chest and closed his eyes. “I hope you find your wife and kids, Bob.”

Hilary sighed wearily and wiped her sweat-beaded forehead with the back of her hand. “I can use the ice to pack around some of the breaks and sprains. Karen, could you find more plastic bags and fill them?”

“Yes, of course.” Karen hurried away.

Mercury felt numb. She’d been with her grandma when she’d died, but that had been a natural, easy passing. She’d never seen this side of death—one that was random and pernicious and horribly bloody—much less seen it over and over again. For a moment she thought she might puke. She swallowed the saliva that flooded her mouth and wiped at spatters of Bob’s blood on her filthy jeans. Then Mercury drew a deep breath. She needed to keep busy. They all did. If they stopped—if they thought too much—they might never move again.

“Where are you putting the people who die?” Mercury asked.

“I told Tyler and Ken to place them in one of the outbuildings,” said Hilary.

“Ken hasn’t come back from the parking lot yet, has he?” Stella asked.

“I haven’t seen him,” said Imani as she wiped her face and stood beside Mercury.

“’Kay,” Mercury said. “Does anyone know where Tyler is?”

Jenny nodded shakily. “Uh, yeah. He was in the generator shed with us. He stayed behind to—well, I’m not sure why, but he seemed to know what he was doing, and Bob trusted him.”

“Would you go get him?” Mercury asked as she took a length of torn towel Karen had dropped and covered Bob’s face with it. “Then we can help him move Bob.”

“Sure.” Jenny left quickly and retraced the blood-spattered trail Bob had left behind.

The doctor stood and rolled her shoulders.

“Hey, um, Dr. Hilary?” The voice came from a woman who lay on the mattress closest to Bob. She had a bandage around her thigh, but other than that she appeared uninjured.

Hilary drew a deep breath and raised her chin before she responded. "Yes, Nicole."

"Are we all going to die like that?"

Gemma spoke before the doctor could. "No. You're not bleeding out. Look at your bandage. After Dr. Hilary sewed your cut closed, it stopped bleeding. Your nose isn't bloody, right?"

"Right," Nicole said as she stared at the clean bandage that swathed her right thigh.

"And you haven't coughed any blood, right?" Gemma asked.

"Right again." This time Nicole looked at the teenager and smiled. "I actually don't feel too awful. Well, my leg hurts and I'm hungry, but that's it."

"Then I'm going to agree with Gemma," said the doctor. "As long as we keep your wound clean, my prognosis is that you will recover." Hilary raised her voice so that it carried to the other patients spread out on mattresses circling the blazing hearth. "No one else has been bleeding like Bob. So, I do not believe any of your injuries are life threatening, but the truth is we don't know how the green fog works on any of us. Bob walked around for most of the day with a bloody nose before that escalated and cost him his life. So, please don't panic, but do let Gemma or me know if you start feeling odd or begin bleeding."

"And I can help with the hungry part," Stella spoke up. "I'm one hell of a cook, and Bob said that the gas is working. I'll go see what I can make to feed us—unless the Cascade chef is in here somewhere—and then I'll be an excellent sous chef."

Hilary cleared her throat and then under her breath said, "The chef is dead. So is his staff."

Stella nodded grimly then smiled at the room. "Let me see what I can do."

"That sounds really good," said Nicole.

"You be the chef. I'll be your sous chef," said Mercury.

"And I can bake biscuits from scratch," said Imani.

"Sounds great—unless the doc needs you; then I can manage."

Hilary waved them away. "Go ahead. We can handle it out here. Food's pretty important right now."

Gemma stood and wiped her bloody hands on the towel she'd tied around her waist like an apron. "What's next, Doc?"

Hilary smiled at the teenager, which changed the doctor's face from pleasant to beautiful. "Clean up the blood. Finish dosing our patients and placing ice packs. I have two more breaks to splint, and I believe only one more laceration that needs to be sewn—for all three I could use your help."

Jenny returned with Tyler, whose eyes were red and cheeks blotchy from crying.

"Darn it. I really liked Bob," he said sadly and crossed himself as he gazed down at the dead man. Then his eyes found Gemma. "Your mom told me to tell you that she's outside with Ken. He, um, didn't find anyone alive and was pretty broken up about it."

Gemma nodded. "Thanks, Tyler. Mom's a good listener. I hope she can help Ken, but I also hope she doesn't stay outside too long." Her gaze went to a window from which the ashen light of an unnaturally dark sky stained the foyer gray. Then the girl sighed and headed to the mattress that held a middle-aged woman whose arm jutted out at an awkward angle from her body.

"She's one tough kid," said Imani.

Mercury brushed her hair from her face. "I was just thinking the same."

"Everyone underestimates teenagers," said Stella.

"You mean everyone who doesn't teach them for a living," corrected Mercury.

"Agreed. Let's go cook," said Stella.

CHAPTER 10

KAREN HAD LEFT the double wooden doors ajar, so the three women easily slipped inside to the Cascade Dining Room. Thick timbers had fallen from the ceiling and crashed into tables, splintering them like snapped matchsticks. Debris and glass littered the area that led to outdoor seating, letting in wisps of cold air.

Mercury put her hands on her hips and studied the broken windows. "We need to close this mess up. Nuclear or not, something deadly was released with those bombs, and we need to make it more difficult for it to get inside here."

"I have an idea," said Stella as she hurried to the bar, which was mostly still intact. She hunted behind the counter as the scent of spilled booze drifted like an enticing dream around them. "Ha! I knew they'd be here." Victoriously she hefted two big rectangular boxes that held industrial-sized rolls of plastic cling wrap and aluminum foil. "If you help me, we can cover what's left of the windows and then pile those broken wooden tables against them. It'll be dark in here, but it looks like it's gonna be dark soon anyway."

"Bob said we have electricity, but any lights that were turned on during the surge would be fried." Mercury found the light switch on the wall and flipped it on. "Nothing."

"Hey, I saw floor lamps out there in the foyer. It was pretty bright before all that mess happened, so I don't think they were on. I'll go grab a couple," said Imani before she retraced their path out of the restaurant.

Imani came back dragging two floor lamps that worked just fine, and the women got busy blocking the windows. They stacked the wooden tables that hadn't been completely splintered against the wrapped windows, and were pretty satisfied with the results before they picked their way to the kitchen.

Stella paused in front of the mahogany bar and sighed happily. "Look at all those bottles that aren't busted. Minor miracle—but still a miracle."

"I can't believe there are any still intact," said Imani.

"Don't question it. Just be glad about it," said Stella as she detoured around a fallen timber and headed to hallway that led to the kitchen. But she stopped abruptly and gasped.

"What is it?" Mercury hurried around the timber to catch up with her friend, followed her gaze, and mirrored her gasp. "Holy shit. This is better than a minor miracle."

The long wall that led to the kitchen was lined, floor to ceiling, with bottles of wine.

Imani joined them. "Wow. I do love vino, but until now I never noticed what a great wine collection Timberline has."

"And most of those bottles are unbroken. Call the Vatican—we are looking at a full-fledged miracle," said Stella. "But we're not idiots, so let's ignore this bounty until everyone is fed and put to bed."

"Then we get drunk?" asked Mercury, only half kidding.

"No. Then we share a couple bottles. Getting drunk on the first night of an apocalypse sounds like what would happen in one of those zombie movies where everyone dies," said Stella.

"Imani and I were just talking about those movies," Mercury said as they entered the kitchen. "How living the plot of one—minus the actual zombies—isn't as satisfying as one might think it would be."

"I gotta agree with you two on that," said Stella. "Hey, the kitchen looks like it's in surprisingly good shape."

"Probably because it doesn't have any windows. Windows are hell during an apocalypse, but it's also completely dark in here," said Imani. "Try the lights. Maybe we'll get lucky and they weren't on when the blast hit."

Stella ran her hand over the inside wall of the kitchen and flipped up a row of lights. "Nah, nothing. It figures. Look at the stove and the grill—there's still food out. They were cooking when it happened."

"Let's drag the lamps in here," said Mercury. While she and Imani felt for sockets to plug the floor lamps into, Stella moved around the kitchen like it was her second home.

"I'll bet I can find something that will help." Stella took her phone from her pocket and flipped on its flashlight. She shone it around the kitchen. "Ha! I knew it." She pulled a heavy-duty flashlight from its wall mount and pressed the "On" button. White light flooded the kitchen. "The coolers are back here. Let's check out what we have to work with."

"Hang on. Here we go. Let there be light!" Mercury said dramatically as the floor lamps bloomed, washing the kitchen in yellow. "Oh fuck! That's disgusting." The light illuminated pools of congealed blood in front of the stove and grill.

"Well, at least someone got the bodies out of here. Step around the blood. There'll be something back here to clean it. All decent commercial kitchens have a great cleanup system."

Grimacing, Mercury and Imani tiptoed around the rust-colored puddles as they followed Stella into the bowels of the kitchen. "Are you ever sorry you didn't stay in culinary school?" asked Mercury as she picked up pots from the floor and helped Imani lift a toppled metal shelf out of their way.

"Only after a conference with an especially ignorant parent or when I check my bank account." She glanced back at Mercury and shrugged. "Weird that I'll probably never have to deal with either from here on out. Ooh, here they are! We have two cold storage units and what looks like"—Stella paused and opened a door to an enormous closet—"a fucking fantastic pantry." Dried goods had fallen from some of the shelves, but the room was loaded with supplies. "Which means the cold storage units are probably filled too." Stella rushed to open the metal doors to the two refrigerated units and clapped her hands happily. "Yep! This is excellent, though we're going to need to pack snow in here so that the temp in the frozen storage stays cold enough."

"Wouldn't it be easier to just put the frozen stuff outside in the snow?" Mercury asked.

"Yes, if you want to take a chance on bears and whatever-the-hell else they have up here eating it before we can," said Imani.

"Exactly," said Stella.

"I keep forgetting how wilderness-y it is out there." Mercury shuddered.

"I'll go find Jenny and Karen. They can use those baskets we dragged from the convenience store and start bringing in snow," said Imani.

"While you do that, Mercury and I will clean up the blood and then get busy using up the unfrozen perishables first." Stella stuck her head out of the cold storage cooler. "Yeah, there's lots of shaved meat in here and fresh veggies. That'll go bad first, so let's make a shitload of sandwiches. I'll also start on the biggest pot of stew I've ever made, which'll be ready tomorrow."

Imani nodded. "And when I come back, I'll start on a giant batch of biscuits."

"Perfect. They'll go great with tomorrow's stew," said Stella.

Imani returned to the foyer as Stella began giving Mercury orders like a drill sergeant—not that Mercury minded. She'd spent many happy evenings following Stella's instructions as they prepared delicious meals for their tribe of girlfriends at the gorgeous, mission-style stucco house Stella maintained meticulously.

Under Stella's confident direction, the two of them had the kitchen pretty much set to rights and the bloody floor cleaned quickly and efficiently, so they started cooking as Jenny and Karen began to haul baskets of snow to the freezer.

There was a sense of calm that settled over the three women while they worked together in the kitchen. It felt normal to make sandwiches, deep-fry thick sliced potatoes for fries, and cut up meat and veggies for a simmering stew. Stella even hummed happily while she plated the sandwiches and waited for the fries to be ready.

"It feels good," said Imani softly. "Working together like this. Like balm to my soul."

Mercury grabbed another potato and began peeling it. She smiled at her friend. "Yep, it does."

"My babies could still be alive." Imani wiped flour from her chin with the back of her wrist as she turned from kneading dough to face Mercury. "Right?"

Mercury met her friend's gaze and answered with the truth. "Right now we know Portland and Salem and Government Camp are gone. That's all we know for sure."

"There's nothing wrong with hoping," added Stella without turning from the sandwich preparation.

"I'm going to try to hold on to hope," said Imani. "Mercury, I've never asked, but did you ever want kids?"

Mercury nodded her head. "Well, yeah. I always thought I'd have kids. I mean, it seemed like I had plenty of time."

"If dickhead Duane hadn't been such a dickhead, you woulda had babies with him," Stella said as she spread mustard across fat slices of bread.

"Hey, we agreed to call him by his formal name," said Mercury.

"I stand corrected—Duane the Dickhead. Tell Imani why you didn't have babies with him."

Mercury sighed as she cut potatoes into wedges for fries. "It was about five years ago. I'd been dating Duane for almost a year, and we were getting pretty serious. Then he announced that he wanted a child so he could—and I quote—'have a normal kid.'"

Stella shook her head. "Such a dick."

Imani sprinkled more flour on her counter. "He had a disabled child?"

"No," Mercury said. "He had a son he and his ex-wife used as a pawn to mess with each other—something it took me almost a year to figure out because I have a don't-meet-the-kid-unless-you-know-you're-truly-serious-about-the-man policy. Anyway, there was nothing wrong with his son that decent parenting wouldn't have fixed."

"But Duane the Dickhead wanted Mercury to have a kid or two for him so he could just start over instead of taking care of the son he already had," finished Stella.

"Yep. I broke up with him the day I realized that's what he was about. It was a damn good thing I figured out what was up before I got pregnant." Mercury shuddered. "Can you imagine being shackled to that dickhead via kids? Ugh."

"You and this Duane weren't engaged?" asked Imani.

"Oh Goddess no. I don't believe in marriage," said Mercury. "I'm not Christian, so I don't think it's any kind of a sin to cohabitate without being married. And anyway, I know too many couples where the wives are really glorified housekeepers, cooks, and mommies to adult manbabies. That's not for me—though I firmly believe each to their own."

Imani nodded contemplatively. "I get what you're saying, but you don't need to be married to have babies. It's the 21st Century."

"Very true," said Mercury. "And I planned on having kids, and then just—I don't know—ran out of time. It's like I turned twenty, blinked my eyes, and I was all of a sudden turning thirty-five."

"Thirty-five isn't too late to have a baby," said Stella over her shoulder. "But ever since Duane the Dickhead, Mercury has given up on men."

"Well, I haven't technically given up. I just haven't met anyone in the past five years who doesn't seem to have major dickhead tendencies," said Mercury.

"What about you, Stella?" Imani asked.

Stella went to the deep fryer as she spoke. She dumped the cooked fries onto a big flat, baking sheet, salted them, and then dropped more of Mercury's newly cut potato wedges into the sizzling grease. "I'm with Mercury on marriage not being for me either. I tried it. More than once. Didn't like it. After my miscarriages and divorces, I meant to adopt, and then a few years ago when I turned forty, I realized I had a hundred plus kids who counted on me every semester." She moved her shoulders. "They were enough."

"I didn't know you'd had miscarriages. I'm sorry," said Imani softly.

"It was a long time ago," said Stella briskly.

Imani's gaze went to Mercury, who shook her head quickly and telegraphed a "let it go" look to her—and as she did, pain sliced through Mercury's finger when the razor-sharp chef's knife slid off the side of the spud and into her flesh.

"Damn! Damn! Damn!" Mercury dropped the knife and shook her hand. Droplets of blood dotted the area around her before she grabbed her finger and squeezed.

"What? What happened?" Stella and Imani rushed to her.

"It's nothing. Just wasn't watching what I was doing, and I cut myself a little." Mercury frowned at the red oozing through her clenched fingers.

"Oh shit! Do you need stiches? Should I get the doctor?" Imani peered at Mercury's finger.

"No! Don't bother the doc. I don't think it's bad; you know how fingers bleed."

"Just keep pressure on it." Stella yanked the industrial strength flashlight from its wall mount beside the metal rack of shelves and disappeared into the pantry. "They're required to have a first aid kit. Aha!" She returned with a large plastic case emblazoned with a red cross. "Come over here to the sink." Stella rinsed the cut as Mercury cussed and looked away. "You were right. It's not bad, and fingers do bleed a lot." She quickly wrapped two Band-Aids around the finger. "Okay, there ya go! I'll bet I can find some gloves back in that pantry. The bandages will be easier to keep dry if you wear them while you cook." Stella went back to the pantry, and when she emerged, she tossed a pair of latex gloves at Mercury.

"Thanks." She pulled on the gloves. "Good as new!" Mercury flexed her hand and only grimaced a little at the pain in her finger. "Where'd you put those Clorox wipes? I bled everywhere."

"Here ya go." Imani handed her the container of wipes before she returned to her section of the counter and the bowls of flour and baking powder and whatever else went into making biscuits.

Mercury wiped the blood from her counter. "I'm not usually so damn clumsy." She bent to follow the trail of her blood spatter. "Oh great. Some of my blood got on the bag of potatoes waiting for me to peel. Hey, you guys remember that scene in *True Grit* where baby sister refuses to eat the corn dodgers because Rooster Cogburn won't light a match so she can see if there's blood on them?"

"That's disgusting," said Imani. "And no, I do not know that scene because John Wayne was a racist asshat and my mama refused to let us watch any of his movies."

"We're Okies. I think mandatory viewing of John Wayne movies comes with the red dirt we were born on," said Stella.

"I seriously didn't know he was a racist until recently," said Mercury as she crouched beside the netting bag that held a shitload of big, golden potatoes.

"White people," Imani said with a sigh.

"Right? We're admittedly stupid about—" Mercury's hands stilled, and her words broke off.

"About?" Imani said without looking at her. "Want me to fill the next word in for you? About *racism*, about *entitlement*, about—"

"Y'all come look at this."

The flat tone of Mercury's voice had both women hurrying to her.

"Where's that really bright flashlight?" Mercury asked Stella.

"I never put it back. Here ya go." Stella handed it to her, but then moved several feet back. "What'd you find? I really hope it's not a rat. I hate rats."

Mercury turned on the flashlight and aimed it at the sack of potatoes. A few of them had green sprouts pushing up through the plastic netting.

"Huh. Weird that there are some old potatoes in that bushel, but whatever," Stella shrugged. "We can't be that picky. Unless they feel mushy, just cut the sprouts off and go ahead and use them. Jesus—I was sure it was a rat."

"But that's the thing. There *weren't* any sprouts on them when we dragged them from the pantry. I know. I've peeled and cut half of the bag," said Mercury as she squatted and lifted out one of the sprouted spuds. "You can still see some of my blood on it." She reached for another potato. "This one too." She held it up so Stella could take it from her.

"Lemme see one," said Imani.

Mercury handed her a potato. She fished three more sprouted spuds from the bag, along with two that had nothing growing from them. "Look, these two are like all the rest in the bag." She put the two perfect potatoes on the counter. "And these three, plus the two you're holding all came in contact with my blood."

Stella studied the potatoes. "The sprouted ones are as firm as the rest." She shined the flashlight on the bag. "None of the others are sprouted." Stella hefted them in her hands. "This is weird. They don't feel different—older or anything—than the others."

"Wait, you're not thinking that your *blood* caused the potatoes to sprout, are you?" Imani peered from the potatoes to her two friends. "That is fucking crazy."

Mercury faced the women as something that had been niggling at her mind since they roared away from the scenic turnout fell into place. "I saw something back at the turnout, but I haven't said anything because I thought it was fucking crazy too."

"Tell us. We're in an apocalypse. Nothing could be crazier than that," said Stella.

"Remember how before you pulled out of the parking lot and floored the truck across the highway, I was yelling at Karen?" Mercury began.

"Wait—I thought you got a ride from someone," interrupted Imani.

"No, that was a lie," said Stella.

"What was a lie?" asked Jenny as she and Karen stumbled into the kitchen under the weight of a snow-laden basket.

"That we got a ride here," said Stella.

"Oh yeah. Total lie," said Jenny.

"But a necessary one," added Karen.

"There was an old truck at the turnout that was drivable after the bomb. I hid it in the back of the parking lot," Stella explained quickly. "Some asshole bully tried to take it from us on the way here, so we thought it would be better for us to lie and have wheels than to tell the truth and chance another asshole bully stealing the truck. Sorry—we forgot to clue you in."

Imani nodded. "Makes sense. Go on."

"Wait, what are we talking about?" Jenny asked as she and Karen lowered the basket to the floor and wiped sweat from their faces.

Imani pointed at the potatoes on the counter. "Mercury cut her finger. Her blood got on the potatoes."

"And they sprouted," Mercury added. "But I swear they *weren't* sprouted before my blood got on them."

"Okay, what?" Jenny shook her head. "I don't get it."

"You think your blood made the potatoes grow?" Karen asked.

"That's what I'm trying to figure out," said Mercury. "Before everything fell down the side of the mountain, I saw something strange about the section of the grass Stella and I had fallen *and bled on*. I only got a glimpse because, well, you know—the damn mountain was breaking apart—but it looked like that grass was taller than it had been before."

"Like, before you bled on it?" Jenny said.

"Yeah," said Mercury. "That's what I mean."

Karen smoothed her tattered cardigan. "Mercury's right about that. I saw it too. I just didn't know what I was looking at. I walked through the spots of tall grass when I went to pray over Amelia and her baby, and then poor Coach Davis. I remember it clearly because it seemed odd and out of place. The rest of the clearing was so neatly tended that it caught my attention, but then, what with everything else that happened, I didn't think of it again. Until now." Karen went to the counter and picked up one of the sprouted potatoes. "This doesn't feel like an old potato."

"Right? Because it's not old," said Mercury.

"It just has your magic blood on it." Imani rolled her eyes. "Guys, *really*? It's insane."

"Well, there's only one way to find out." Mercury took off her glove and unwrapped the Band-Aids Stella had so recently put around her wounded finger. "Hand me a bowl."

Jenny took a small mixing bowl off the metal pot rack beside her and gave it to Mercury. With a little cringe of pain, Mercury squeezed the fresh cut until it beaded with scarlet. She kept squeezing until the red drops rained reluctantly on the two unsprouted potatoes she'd placed on the counter. Then she put them in the bowl and pushed it to the rear of the counter.

"What now?" Jenny stared at the bowl.

"We finish making dinner and the stew for tomorrow," said Stella. "And keep an eye on that bowl."

"I need another Band-Aid and another pair of gloves," Mercury said.

Jenny and Karen dragged the weeping basket back to the freezer while the other three women resumed meal preparations. Mercury forced herself to ignore the bowl as she peeled and cut mounds of carrots and potatoes, and the familiar, comforting scent of simmering stew suffused the kitchen.

"I think we need to fill one of those giant metal bowls with greens for salad," Stella said as she turned the enormous pot of stew to simmer. "They're not going to last, and I can made a quick dressing for it, plus greens equal healthy."

"I'm going to look at the potatoes," said Mercury. "I can't wait any longer."

"Well, it only took a few minutes before—if that's what happened," said Stella.

"We'll all look," said Imani. Jenny and Karen, who had been putting plates of sandwiches and fries on trays for the people in the foyer, quit what they were doing and joined Mercury at the counter.

Mercury hadn't realized she'd held her breath until it escaped from her in a gasp as she lifted the bowl and stared down into it.

"Fuck me," said Stella.

Imani shook her head from side to side. "It's completely insane."

"I'm glad I was here when it happened. I'd never believe it if I hadn't seen it myself, and I have a goddamn master's in botany." Jenny spoke breathlessly.

"It's a miracle," said Karen in a hushed church voice.

Mercury lifted the two potatoes. Through the spots of her dried blood, big green sprouts burst from the skin of both as if they reached up toward an imaginary sun.

CHAPTER

11

NONE OF THE five spoke of it. They continued as they had begun—finished making sandwiches, fries, and salad for dinner. They helped Stella put everything together for tomorrow's stew, then served the food to the wounded along with Dr. Hilary, Gemma, Sadie, Ken, Tyler, and three of the lodge's housekeepers, who made up the only Timberline staff who were still alive. By that time it was only a little after six o'clock in the evening, but outside it was fully dark.

Inside the lodge the enormous hearth was burning brightly. Pots of candles merged with the flicking firelight and perfumed the big foyer-turned-infirmary with a cheerful, piney scent. Tyler and Ken had taken a page out of Stella's book of experience and used plastic cling wrap and aluminum foil to cover broken windows—and then they'd nailed blankets and strips of whatever flat wood they could scavenge over them. One of the wounded guests had produced a pretty good-sized stash of marijuana-infused edibles—all Indica—which Dr. Hilary, an open-minded naturopath, had happily administered to her patients. Now that everyone was post-dinner and post-pot, the lodge felt warm and surprisingly safe.

Mercury and Stella had pulled a coffee table over to a corner of the room, which is where they, plus Imani, Jenny and Karen, sat on the floor and used the squat piece of rustic furniture as a dinner table.

They shared looks. All five women were mulling in their minds what they had just discovered about Mercury—but no one said anything about it. Not yet. Not in public. Mercury had just stood to begin gathering the dinner dishes when Dr. Hilary and Gemma joined them.

"Dinner was delicious. Thank you for that," said Hilary.

"These fries are freaking fantastic!" Gemma sounded like a teenager, even though she'd worked beside Dr. Hilary with a maturity well beyond her years.

"I do love me a good thick-cut fry," said Stella. "Wait until tomorrow. Imani's making biscuits to go with the stew."

"Yum!" said Gemma.

Imani's lips tilted up slightly. "I hope you like them. They're my great auntie's recipe. No one for generations has been able to resist them."

"Well, I'm not gonna even try." Gemma grinned at her.

The doctor cleared her throat. "Ladies, Gemma tells me you saw the explosions."

Stella nodded. "Bombs. Yeah, we saw them."

"It was quite horrible." Karen shook her head sadly. "And all the dead people." She shuddered. "I will remember it as long as I draw breath."

"Me too," said Jenny softly.

Hilary lowered her voice so that it didn't carry to the patients or the staff who were sitting together talking quietly across the room. "*Bombs.* I can hardly think the word. Saying it sounds like something out of a horror movie."

Mercury snorted. "That's what we've been saying too."

"The truth—is Portland gone?" Hilary asked.

"We can't know for certain, but from what we saw . . . completely," said Stella. "Is that where you're from?"

Hilary brushed a thick strand of long hair from her face with a shaky hand. "Yes. I have a practice in the city. I only come up here and work during busy weekends, like this one." She looked down at her hands, which she'd folded together in front of her. My wife, she—" Emotion closed her throat.

Mercury reached out and touched her shoulder. "She was in Portland?"

Hilary looked up and through unshed tears met Mercury's gaze. "No. She joined me this weekend. It was our fifth anniversary. She didn't make it through the initial blast."

"Ah, damn. I'm so sorry," said Stella.

"She was waiting for me in the hot tub by the pool. It was the pool area that fell into the crevasse before the avalanche covered it and that half of the lodge. I should have been with her. I . . ." Hilary wiped her eyes, drew a deep breath, and straightened her bowed shoulders. "She's at peace, beyond whatever the rest of us will still have to live with here. What I want to know is how bad is it? How many bombs? Gemma said a lot. What did you see?"

There was a thoughtful stretch of silence, and then Stella took the healer's hands in hers. "There were bombs everywhere. The world as we knew it is over."

Hilary paled but nodded. "I thought as much. I wonder—my parents are in Manzanita. It's on the coast. Could anything there have survived?"

"It's impossible to say," Mercury spoke slowly. "The sky was filled with smoke trails from the bombs—all over. All around us as far as we could see, and what we could see became fire and rubble. I wouldn't try to get to the coast, if that's what you're asking."

"No. I won't leave my patients. My mother and father wouldn't expect me to. I just needed to know. Almost all of the wounded were guests from out of state, but the staff is either from Portland, Government Camp, or somewhere in between. They're staying right now because they're terrified or too kind to leave before we get the wounded tended to and settled. After what you said, I'll encourage them to stay indefinitely."

Karen picked at her cardigan. "Don't let them leave. It is terrible out there."

"You really believe everyone between the mountain and Portland is dead?" Gemma stared at them with eyes much older than those of a sixteen-year-old.

Stella held the girl's gaze steadily and spoke compassionately. "I'm only going to tell you the truth. I really believe it. And I also believe it's worse than we can imagine. The bombs changed things. There was something biological about them."

Gemma nodded sadly. "That's what I think too."

"It kills men," said Stella.

Hilary's sharp gaze caught Stella's. "That's the observation that I've made. Not one woman has bled out."

"But there are some men here, like Ken and Tyler, who seem fine," said Mercury.

The doctor nodded. "Yes, and they back my hypothesis. Ken and Tyler were in the basement when the blast of green hit us. The other men who are still alive—and there are only a few of them—were in the spa's sauna, which is on the basement level in a room with no windows or access to outside. Their injuries happened trying to get out of the rubble. None of them breathed in the green stuff."

"Bob must have," said Gemma.

"He did. He wasn't outside when it hit, but he was in the hallway that leads to the side of the lodge consumed by the avalanche. When the building broke, some of the green reached him."

"So it seems if men were hit by the initial blast, they died, like our principal and coach," Mercury reasoned aloud. "For lack of a better word, they *jellified*."

Stella chimed in. "But if a man was somewhat protected, like Bob, and still breathed in the green crap, he dies. Just not right away."

"And he doesn't turn into a Jell-O mold," said Mercury.

"Gross," said Gemma. "But true."

"We must keep an eye on everyone and be sure we all stay away from any lingering green fog," said Doc Hilary.

"Absolutely. We're fortunate here," continued Stella. "The kitchen is well stocked. Tomorrow I'll take inventory and figure out exactly how long the supplies will last." She blinked as a new thought came to her. "Wait, there was a bar—Ram's Head." Then, before anyone could respond, she turned to Mercury. "I totally forgot about Dusty."

"You've been busy with the whole end-of-the-world apocalypse thing," said Mercury.

"Dusty the bartender? The one with the hair and the muscles?" Hilary asked.

"That's him."

"His body is beneath the avalanche with my Kate's."

"Well. Shit." Stella sighed heavily. "The bar was on the second floor."

"Nothing on that side of the hotel survived," said Hilary.

"Well, at least the Cascade Dining Room is well stocked," said Stella. "That's something. Let's get these dishes cleared up, and I'll check out the egg situation for breakfast."

"You ladies should choose a few of the ground floor rooms as your own," Hilary said. "The housekeepers went around and unlocked everything that's habitable. The family suites have fireplaces. I'll ask the staff to help me clean up the dishes if you'd like to do that now."

"No," Karen said as she stood and brushed off her dirty khaki slacks. "Taking care of hurt people is a lot like taking care of an infant. I know. My father broke his hip last summer, and I was his caregiver. You should sleep when your patients sleep. The ladies and I will clear up the dishes and then choose rooms."

Hilary nodded wearily. "Thank you. I'll be in room 101, the first of the suites. I'll sleep with the door open. Gemma, you should rest too."

"I will," said the teenager as she took the doctor's arm and began to lead her through the foyer. "I'm not tired yet, so I'll keep an eye on everyone and come get you if I need you."

"Thank you. You've been a lifesaver—all of you have been." Hilary smiled over her shoulder at them and then trudged away with Gemma, her grace temporarily cast out by exhaustion and grief.

"Let's get these dishes knocked out, grab a couple stupid-expensive bottles of wine, and find a room. Then we can talk," said Mercury.

"Sounds like a plan," said Stella.

The women used luggage trollies to collect the dishes. They moved quickly but quietly, so as not to disturb the sleeping patients, and pushed everything into the dining room. Tyler and Ken had cleared a path for them, so it was easy to get back to the sinks. With assembly-line efficiency, they washed, dried, and put away the dishes.

"Hey, while y'all finish up with this, should I take that big-ass flashlight and go out to the truck and grab some clothes for us?" Jenny looked down at her blood- and dirt-spattered jeans and sweater. "I'm disgusting."

"No damn way any of us are going outside tonight. Not when we can't see patches of that green crap," said Mercury. "But you can go to that boutique. I believe I saw some flannel PJs against the far wall."

"And the convenience store has toothbrushes and toothpaste," said Imani. "I'll grab the flashlight and come with you to get supplies."

"Go ahead. Karen, Stella, and I will finish up." Mercury put the bowl she'd just dried on the metal shelf. "I'm going to bring a potato for each of you to our rooms—and a knife."

They stared at her.

"We need to know," Mercury said. "Is it just me, or has all of our blood changed?"

"I need to know," said Imani.

"Ditto," said Jenny.

"I think we must," agreed Karen.

Stella's gaze went to the sprouted potatoes resting in the innocent-looking metal mixing bowl. The green shoots had grown several inches while they were gone. "Yeah. We need to know."

CHAPTER

12

THEY DECIDED TO share one suite. It had two queen beds and a sofa bed, as well as a decent-sized trundle. The fireplace was in the bedroom, so that's where they dragged the mattress from the couch and squeezed in the trundle bed too. One small bedside lamp worked, but the roaring fireplace provided most of the light as well as all of the heat. After they covered the broken windows, stacked blankets across them, and closed the heavy blackout drapes, the room was warm and cozy.

"You think we should stay here?" asked Mercury as Stella opened the first of two bottles of French Bordeaux that would've cost them upward of one hundred dollars each.

Karen jolted like she'd been pinched. "Where else would we go? You know how horrible it is out there."

Stella remained silent, though Mercury noticed she hunched her shoulders and looked suddenly very tired.

"I wish I knew what was going on in the rest of the world," said Imani.

"Same," said Jenny as Stella filled her wineglass.

"Oh, no thank you," Karen said when Stella handed her the next red wine balloon.

"Do you have an alcohol problem?" Stella asked her.

"Well, no. Of course not."

"Then have a few sips. It's the fucking apocalypse, Karen."

Karen looked from Stella to Mercury, who sipped from her own glass, shrugged, and told her, "I'm gonna cut your finger here in a sec, so you might want to have a drink."

"Plus, what was Jesus's first reported miracle?" said Jenny with a grin.

"Our Lord did turn water into wine . . ." Karen lifted her chin and took the glass from Stella. "Just a little, please. I'm not used to it."

Stella poured Karen and herself a glass as Mercury stood and opened her big suitcase-like purse. The women watched silently while she pulled out four steak knives and four small, round new potatoes. She passed the knives and the potatoes out.

"I didn't sanitize them, but I did bring some antiseptic from the kitchen first aid kit, along with Band-Aids. Though if you're anything like me, you won't need the Band-Aids long." Mercury lifted her hand so that they could see her finger—the one she'd cut just a few hours before. The only evidence left to show that it had been injured was a small pink line.

"It's unbelievable," said Imani.

"Well, I hope I have the magic blood," said Stella firmly as she sat on the edge of one of the beds and pressed the knife against her thumb. She sucked in air as scarlet beaded the small wound, and then squeezed until the beading dripped onto her potato.

Mercury took the potato and handed her the antiseptic and a Band-Aid. "'Kay, I'm going to put these on the bedside table under the lamp. First one on the left is Stella's."

"Ouch, fuck!" said Jenny as she cut herself. "I hate knives." Then she exchanged her blood-spattered potato for a Band-Aid and some salve.

"Jenny's is beside Stella's. Who's next?"

"Well, shit. I'll do it," said Imani. She bit her bottom lip as she quickly cut her finger and bled on the spud while she averted her gaze. She still kept her head turned when she handed Mercury the potato. "I really hate seeing my own blood."

Jenny smiled and scooted over nearer Imani. "Here, I'll put on the salve and the Band-Aid. You don't have to look."

"Thanks, I'll drink."

"Karen?" Mercury asked.

The older woman held her breath and pressed the blade to her finger. "Ooh! Stings!" Then she wiped her blood on the potato and gave it to Mercury.

Mercury placed them on the nightstand and pointed as she called out. "From left to right—Stella, Jenny, Imani, and Karen. I'll take more wine."

"I'll gawk at the potatoes," said Jenny. "Oh, and take more wine too."

Stella refreshed wineglasses and put more wood on the fire. With everyone curled up in the middle of heaps of blankets and pillows wearing entirely too big pajamas in bold red and black plaid flannel, it almost seemed as if they'd closed the door on the apocalypse. Then Mercury cleared her throat and broke the interlude.

"So, I'm just gonna say it. I agree with what the doc was saying. That green stuff kills men."

Stella sat cross-legged beside her on one of the queen beds. She nodded contemplatively as she swirled the bold red wine around her crystal balloon. "Fucking A right it does."

Karen had chosen the trundle bed, and she perched primly on its edge, where the group had dragged it to warm near the hearth. She swallowed a sip of wine and looked up at Stella, brow furrowed. "Does that mean you think it's a good thing?"

Stella shrugged. "Not necessarily. But if I could choose, I'd sure as hell have it kill more men than, say, *us*."

Jenny had her legs pulled to her chest as she rested against the headboard of the other queen bed she shared with Imani. She picked at her lip. "It killed Amelia."

"Did it?" Mercury said. "Or did it kill her baby boy in a way that caused her to hemorrhage to death?"

"We don't even know what *it* is," said Imani. She held a glass of wine, but had barely touched it.

"That green stuff," said Mercury. "The fog, whatever—that's what *it* is. I think it's a biological agent that breaks something inside men and makes them bleed out."

"And it also did something to your blood, and now you make potatoes grow." Jenny fluttered her fingers a little tipsily at Mercury.

"Doesn't mean I know shit, though," said Mercury.

Karen suddenly raised her half-empty wineglass. "To not knowing shit!"

The group stared at Karen, and then as one they raised their glasses and toasted together: "To not knowing shit!" And then they dissolved into giggles, which even Imani briefly joined.

Karen blotted her flushed face with the end of her too long pajama sleeve and then fanned herself. "Whew, I'd forgotten what it's like to have friends like you."

Stella raised her brow. "Like us?"

Imani's dark eyes narrowed "Yeah, what's that supposed to mean?"

Karen made a gesture that took in all four women. "You're unapologetic about who you are. It makes you seem somehow lighter than the women I spend time with." She paused, sipped her wine, and continued. "I used to be like you when I was a girl. I wanted to be a dancer, but that would've led to a sinful life, plus he said that I wasn't pretty or talented enough."

"He?" Stella asked.

"My father."

Mercury met Karen's gaze. "I'm sorry."

"Me too," said Stella.

"That's a horrible thing to say to a little girl." Imani shook her head in disgust.

"Legit monstrous," said Jenny.

Stella refreshed Karen's glass, which Karen sipped contemplatively before saying, "It's not really godly, is it? To judge and steal dreams."

Mercury leaned forward. "Well, I think that depends on whether you're talking about the Old or New Testament God."

Stella nudged Mercury with her slippered foot. "Stop. Karen is having a moment."

"No, I'm interested in Mercury's point," said Karen as she fanned herself. "Also, I'm curious about something. You're not a Christian, correct?"

"Very correct," Mercury said.

"Then why do you know the Bible?" Karen asked.

"That's a good question, Karen," Mercury responded. "When I was a little girl I went to church with my friends—and my mom sometimes went to a Presbyterian church a few of her girlfriends attended, and she took my brothers and me with her. It never felt right for me. I had so, so many questions—even back then. Like, why are men automatically in charge? Why is God supposed to 'be love'"—Mercury air-quoted—"but Christians show so much hate for anyone not exactly like them. And the one that really baffled me—why are there so many segregated churches? Especially as Jesus Christ was definitely not the blond-haired, blue-eyed white guy I saw so many pictures of."

"Amen, sis!" Imani said.

"I was raised to believe in education—especially self-education," Mercury continued. "So, I started educating myself about religion. I read the Bible—more than once. I studied the Gnostic Gospels. And the more I learned, especially about Christianity, the more it just didn't fit with me, but when I began exploring different Pagan traditions, I felt like I'd come home." She smiled at Karen. "That's why I know the Bible. It would've been disingenuous of me to reject something without researching it thoroughly."

"That's interesting, and I'm glad you shared it with me," said Karen as she nodded. "Why did you ask which God we were talking about—the Old or New Testament God?"

"Oh, that's simple," Mercury said. "The Old Testament God tested his prophets by telling them to do horrible things—like commanding a father kill his son. Murdering all the firstborn, even the innocent ones who weren't actually keeping his people as slaves. He'd slaughter a man's whole fam and then give him a new one to prove his fidelity. That God sucks."

Karen met her gaze. "I can't say that I disagree with you, but the God I was referring to is Jesus Christ."

"He's a much different God," said Imani.

Mercury snorted. "Yeah, and they killed him."

"Oh. My. God!" said Jenny.

"Which God?" asked Stella.

"No, not literally. Look!" Jenny pointed at the nightstand, where two of the four potatoes had green sprouts shooting through smudges of rust.

"Whose are those?" Imani got to her knees so she could look around Jenny.

Mercury pointed at the first sprouting potato—the one on the left. "That's you, Stella."

"Holy shit," said Stella. "My blood's magic!"

"The next one is yours, Jenny," said Mercury.

"Crap. No sprouts."

"So the next one is mine?" Imani stared at the sprouted spud.

Mercury nodded. "Yep. You can grow stuff. Well, potatoes for sure."

"Huh," she said. "I guess it is a handy ability to have during an apocalypse." Then she drained her glass and looked at Stella. "Sis, I think you'd better open that other bottle."

"On it!" Stella reached for the second expensive bottle of Bordeaux and the corkscrew.

"Mine didn't sprout," said Karen. "I didn't think I wanted it to, but now that it didn't, I'm a little disappointed."

There were two quick knocks on the door.

"Just a sec!" Mercury called. Then she whispered, "Where's the trash can?"

"Here!" Imani reached down to the side of her bed and lifted a small wooden bin that was obviously more decorative than functional. She handed it to Jenny, who passed it to Mercury—who scooped the potatoes into it and then put it quickly on the floor between the beds.

"Come in!" Mercury called.

Gemma's head poked around the door and into the room. "Do you guys mind if I hang with you for a while?"

"No! Not at all," Karen made an expansive gesture. "Got plenty of room here." She patted the mattress beside her.

"Thanks." The teenager came in and then stopped as her lips curled up. "The five of you look like you're slumber partying."

"There's a bathrobe in the closet over there if you want to get out of those clothes," said Imani.

"Sounds good to me." The teenager peeled off her blood- and gore-spattered clothes as she ducked into the bathroom. The sink went on, and they heard her splashing water.

"Hey, where's your mom? Does she want to join us?" Mercury called to the girl.

Gemma emerged from the bathroom, wrapped in a big, white robe and drying her face and arms with a washcloth. She kicked her discarded clothes into the bathroom before sitting beside Karen on the trundle. "She wants me to think that she's sleeping, but she's really curled up in a corner, crying." She sighed and picked at the tie to her robe, not meeting anyone's gaze while she spoke. "Mom and Dad are close—like super ridiculously, embarrassingly close. I don't mean that's a bad thing, but it kinda makes me feel like a third wheel, especially now that I'm older. Since I've been a teenager, it's like they don't even try to hide how wrapped up in each other they are." She shrugged. "My friends tell me they're jelly—that they wish their parents trusted them more and didn't watch their every move. But there's a big difference between being trusted and being forgotten. Not that my friends get that, though." Gemma wiped her face with the washcloth again before she looked up at Mercury. "But to answer you, Mom acted like she was okay earlier when you met her, but it was just because she didn't really believe Dad was, um, dead." Gemma wiped her face with the washcloth again before she said, "So, she's really not okay. And no, she wouldn't want to join us."

"How are *you* doing?" Imani asked her.

Gemma met her gaze. "I dunno. How are *you* doing?"

"Not for shit," said Imani.

"Yep," Gemma nodded. "Me too." She looked at Stella, who was holding the newly opened bottle of Bordeaux. "Can I have a glass?"

"Aren't you sixteen?" asked Karen.

"Yeah. I'm also the sixteen-year-old who held three people as they bled out today and worked beside a doctor to take care of a bunch more."

"We don't have an extra wineglass," said Stella, "but there are water glasses in the bathroom."

"I'm not picky." With the litheness of the young, Gemma jumped up, hurried into the bathroom, and came back with a small water glass, which Stella filled. The teenager sat back beside Karen and took a drink. She looked up at Stella. "It kinda tastes like red chalk."

"It'll grow on you," said Stella.

"That's good, 'cause it's pretty gross."

Mercury snorted a laugh. "Your second glass won't be. So, how is it out there? Anyone, um . . ." Her words trailed off as she realized she wasn't sure how to ask if more people had bled out like Bob.

"Die?" Gemma volunteered the word.

Mercury nodded. "Yeah, that."

Gemma took another gulp of wine, grimaced, and said, "Nope. I don't think any more of the wounded people out there will either."

Karen patted her knee. "I hope you're right."

"Me too, but why do you think that?" asked Stella.

Gemma moved her shoulders up and down. "Just a feeling I have."

Stella and Mercury shared a look.

"The green fog hit you and your mom, right?" Mercury asked.

The teenager nodded. "Yep. It was weird. Afterward was when people started, like, dissolving."

"What did you feel when the fog hit you?" asked Imani.

Gemma took another sip of wine as she considered. "It hurt. Like bees inside me. And then I woke up and was a little achy, but pretty much okay. I actually forgot about that until now."

"Jenny, Karen, did the two of you feel anything when the fog hit us?" Stella asked, her voice bright with excitement.

Karen shrugged. "I don't really know. I dropped down to the ground and covered my head. I don't really remember feeling anything except that I was terrified."

Jenny chimed in. "I hit the ground, too. I just remember being freaked out about Amelia, who was crying really hard beside me."

"Gemma, I want you to do something for me, and it's going to sound really crazy," said Mercury as she reached for the little trash bin that rested on the floor between the beds.

"'Alright. I guess. Wait. What do you want me to do?"

Stella felt around the foot of the bed until she found one of the knives. "She wants you to cut your finger and bleed on a potato."

Mercury lifted one of the two unsprouted potatoes from the bin.

Gemma's gaze went from the knife to the potato and back to the knife. "You didn't get me drunk to perform weird experiments on me, did you?"

"Are you drunk?" Mercury asked.

"Not yet."

"Well, then. If we were being nefarious, we would've waited until you actually were," said Stella.

"Tell her," said Imani.

Mercury sighed and reached back into the bin for a sprouted potato. "See this?"

Gemma nodded slowly. "You mean that old potato?"

"Yeah, only it's not old," Mercury said. "It was just like the other one until Imani's blood got on it. Right here." She put her finger on the base of the sprout where the skin of the potato was stained dark red.

"So, you're telling me Imani's blood made the potato grow?"

"Yeah. Her blood can do that. So can mine and Stella's," said Mercury.

"Mine doesn't make anything grow." Karen held up her bandaged finger. "But I tried."

"Neither does mine," said Jenny. "Which is actually kinda annoying—especially 'cause I have a master's in botany."

Gemma turned to the woman beside her. "Here, Karen, hold my glass."

"No problemo," said Karen.

Then Gemma reached out her hand. "Gimme the knife and the spud."

Karen patted her knee again. "Good luck."

Stella leaned into Mercury and whispered. "Who would've believed that Karen's a happy drunk?"

"Right?" Mercury whispered back. "And she's way more messed up than I thought."

Stella snorted softly. "I think I might actually like her."

"I've been thinking the same. Must be hell freezing over."

"Or it's an apocalypse," said Stella.

"So, now what?" asked Gemma as she put down the knife and reclaimed her glass from Karen.

Stella lifted her goblet as if toasting the teenager. "Now we drink and wait."

Gemma took another sip of wine and nodded. "Yep. I like this waiting to see if I'm a superhero party." She held her bloody spud up to eye level.

Karen said, "Honey, don't forget your Band-Aid."

Gemma glanced down at her thumb. "Don't need it. It's already stopped bleeding." She put the potato next to her on the trundle but continued to watch it, so when she spoke, it seemed she was talking to the spud more than the women who surrounded her. "Do you think we're the last people left alive in the world?"

Stella answered without any hesitation. "No, but it's not ever going to be like it was just this morning."

Karen sighed. "Just this morning. It feels like it was only minutes ago."

"No," Imani's voice was flat. "It feels like a lifetime ago."

Gemma looked up from the potato. "You seem like a really good mom; the kind of mom any kid would be lucky to have. I just wanted you to know that."

Imani nodded but couldn't speak.

"I wish I'd been a better mom," said Karen. "I could've made my boys better men."

"I don't think anyone can *make* another person be better," said Mercury. "So, don't beat yourself up about something you can't change."

Karen met Mercury's gaze. "That was kind of you to say."

"It's just the truth," said Mercury as she swirled her wine and watched it refract the flickering light from the fireplace.

Gemma spoke up. "I wonder what it's gonna be like now."

"There'll be a lot fewer men," said Stella.

"Well, if that's true, I hope women do a better job of running things," said Karen.

Stella snorted. "It'd be damn difficult to do worse."

"We're going to do a better job," said Gemma firmly.

Imani lifted her glass to the teenager. "I like your conviction."

Gemma shrugged. "Yeah, well, anyone who's been in school knows girls are more mature than guys, and now some of us have superpowers." She lifted the potato that rested beside her and turned it so that the women could see the green sprouting proudly from its bloodstained skin. "I think we should tell Dr. Hilary about this."

Mercury and Stella exchanged a long look, and then Stella nodded slightly.

"Sounds like a plan," said Mercury. "But not tonight. Tonight we drink and sleep. Tomorrow we start our new world."

"Okay." Gemma nodded and then held her glass out for a refill. "You're right about the red chalk. It's more like weird vinegar now."

"Child, you blaspheme, but I won't hold it against you." Stella poured a little more wine into Gemma's cup. "Instead, I'll make it my mission to educate you. So, let's talk about tannins . . ."

Mercury leaned back on the mound of pillows she'd propped against the head of the bed and listened to Stella explain red wine to Gemma—with occasionally semi-helpful comments from Jenny and Imani while Karen put her empty glass down, curled up, and fell instantly to sleep.

Mercury sipped her wine and stared at the crackling hearth fire. The flames reminded her of the firepit in her parents' yard, and longing washed over her so thick, so dense that she almost couldn't breathe. She missed her family. She missed Oklahoma—the smell of her mom's butterfly bushes and the fireflies that lit up the yard on warm nights. She ached for the heat of a clear summer day and the thunderclouds that would roll in from the west to bring rain to wash the thirsty prairie and put the green in Oklahoma's nickname, Green Country.

How am I going to live without my home? I'm never going to see Dad and Mom or my brothers again. Are they all dead? Even my little nieces and nephews? What about my tribe of friends? Teresa, Kim, Robin, Shawn, Lola, Sher, Sharon, Kristin, Bridget, Gena, Jill, and Kresley. I can't say it out loud yet, but inside I know it. I know they're as gone as my home—my Tulsa.

Without missing a beat in her wine lecture, Stella reached out and took her hand. She didn't look at Mercury. She was just there—warm and alive and solid. Mercury clung to her hand and promised herself solemnly. *We'll make a better world. For everything—everyone we've lost. And make sure this never fucking happens again.*

CHAPTER

13

PISSED OFF VOICES woke Mercury. For a moment she didn't know where she was, and then Karen snored softly and Gemma murmured something in her sleep. *Oh shit! The apocalypse.* Mercury sat straight up. Imani was gone. Stella was gone. Raised voices drifted through the cracked door to the suite, which made Gemma stir in her sleep. Mercury quietly got out from under the covers she'd burrowed beneath and tiptoed to the door and opened it.

"Shh! Y'all are gonna wake up Gemma and Karen—" Mercury swallowed the rest of her admonishment when she realized the two people who were arguing in the hall were Imani and Sadie—Gemma's mom. "Oh, hi, Sadie. Gemma's inside, but she's sleeping. She got up several times last night to check the wounded, so we should probably let her sleep, but if you—"

Imani stopped Mercury's words with a lifted hand. Then she turned to Sadie. "Tell Mercury what you just told me."

Sadie sighed heavily. Her shoulders were bowed. Her hair was lank and greasy, and dark circles made her eyes look bruised. Sadie looked a decade older than she had the day before when they'd met her on the side of the road. She reluctantly lifted her gaze from the floor and spoke in a hushed voice. "I know Gemma was up most of the night, so I figured she'd still be asleep. I came by to ask you ladies to give her this for me." The hand Sadie lifted held an envelope that had *Gemma* written in bold letters across it.

"Wait—why? She'll be up in a little while," said Mercury.

Sadie's gaze shifted back to the floor. "I won't be here."

"I don't understand," said Mercury.

"She's fucking leaving with Ken to go to Government Camp—which no longer fucking exists—and then they think they're just going to take a day trip or whatever to Gresham, a suburb of Portland, which also *does not fucking exist anymore,* to try and find her husband."

Mercury closed the door softly behind them. "Sadie, you will most likely die if you head into Portland, though I don't know how you're even going to get there. The highway west of the turnout where our group was when the bombs hit is destroyed."

"Yes, I understand that," said Sadie.

"Do you really?" Mercury asked. "Portland was on fire. Leveled. Gone. For miles and miles. Not to mention that there was some kind of biological agent released in that green fog. You've seen what it can do—how it makes people dissolve. So heading into a huge area that's on fire, with a biological agent drifting around, is not a rescue mission. It's a suicide mission."

Sadie's grief-shadowed eyes lifted to Mercury. "I have to go to him. He's my *husband.*"

Imani shook her head and let loose a verbal attack on the woman. "Gemma is your *child*! Do you know what I'd give to see my babies again? *Anything.* Literally I would give *anything.* And you're just going to walk away from yours on a fool's chase."

Sadie slowly took one of Imani's fisted hands in both of hers. "Then if I don't come back, I know you'll be there for my Gemma."

Imani yanked her hand from Sadie's grasp. "This is the stupidest white woman shit I've ever in my life experienced—and that's saying something because white women do some stupid shit."

"She's not lying," said Mercury.

Sadie turned to Mercury. "Will you give Gemma this?" She held up the envelope with her daughter's name on it.

Mercury nodded and took the envelope.

"You don't understand, but Gemma will. And thank you. I know you'll look after her." Then Sadie turned and walked away without looking back.

"Jesus Christ," said Imani.

Mercury shook her head. "This is horrible for Gemma. Should we wake her up? Maybe she can catch her stupid mom and stop her."

"And what if her stupid mom doesn't stop? Or stops only until the next time Gemma's asleep?" Imani blew out a long, disgusted breath. "No. Let the child sleep. Maybe Sadie will get a clue and come back—before someone worse than that douchebag who tried to take your truck gets a chance at her."

Mercury stared down at the envelope in her hands. "God, I hate that I have to give the kid the letter that will basically tell her she's an orphan."

Imani gently took the envelope from her. "I'll do it. Sadie was right about one thing. I'll be here for her child."

Mercury met Imani's eyes and felt a rush of compassion for her friend. "Gemma said it best last night. You're a really good mom."

"Being there for your babies isn't being a really good mom. It's just *being a mom*."

"Still. You're a really good mom."

"Thanks." Imani folded the envelope and put it in the pocket of her jeans, which Mercury realized were clean—along with the thick "BLM" sweatshirt that actually fit her, unlike the giant lumberjack PJs Mercury was still wearing.

"Wait, where'd you get real clothes?"

"Oh, my luggage was being stored at the bellhop station while I was hiking. I got it when Stella woke up. I didn't really sleep much last night. But you have clothes in the room. Stella's been up forever. She went out to the truck when it was barely dawn and brought back a big bag she'd filled with stuff for you guys. She even found something not too hideous for Gemma to wear. Everything is on the couch in the sitting room of the suite." Imani gave her an appraising look. "You, Gemma, and Karen could probably sleep through the next apocalypse. You didn't so much as twitch when Stella dragged all that stuff in."

"Oh yeah. My ability to sleep deeply is a gift. I'll bet Gemma and Karen's is a gift given to them by Bordeaux."

"Ha! Gemma wasn't drunk. The child quit drinking because she said she had to check on 'her patients.'" Imani made air quotes. "But you're totally right about Karen. Girlfriend cannot handle her booze."

"That's the truth." Mercury peered down the gloomy hallway. "What time is it? It looks like it's still dark."

"Actually, it's midmorning, but dark as hell. And it stinks like a nasty burn pile outside."

"Shit. That can't be good, but it's not exactly a surprise. The number of bombs we saw was terrifying, and that many—and the fires they cause—have got to affect the atmosphere."

"I just hope there's nothing worse up there in those clouds than ash and crap like that," said Imani.

"What about the green stuff?"

Imani shrugged. "I haven't been outside. I'm not a damn fool."

"Where's Stella now?"

Imani jerked her chin in the direction of the foyer. "She's made breakfast, set up lunch, and finished the stew, which she says will last for dinner today and at least tomorrow. I think she's taking inventory of all the food now. I tried to help, but she said that I'm not a very good sous chef and shooed me away."

"She's pretty picky about her kitchen help," said Mercury. "Took me years to get a passing grade from her."

Imani shrugged. "I'm not complaining. I can make my auntie's biscuits. That's about the extent of my kitchen expertise. Curtis is the cook in the family." Her face went soft with the memory, and Imani smiled as she spoke. "He loves the kitchen. Curtis can cook anything. His favorite is to make an elaborate breakfast spread on Sundays while I sleep in—with fresh-squeezed OJ for my mimosas. He calls it our family brunch and . . ." Imani's words fizzled out. Tears spilled down her warm beige cheeks. "*Called*, not *calls*. I have to start thinking of him in the past tense."

There were no words that would end Imani's grief, so Mercury pulled her friend into her arms and let her sob.

"Um, you guys okay out there?"

They jumped at Gemma's voice. She'd cracked the door and was watching them with concerned moss-green eyes.

Imani stepped out of Mercury's arms and hastily wiped her face with the sleeves of her sweatshirt. "Sorry—we didn't mean to wake you."

Gemma yawned. "That's okay. I'm starved. Hey, uh, there're clothes and stuff piled on the couch. Would anyone care if I borrowed something? What I wore yesterday is super gross."

"Stella found some clothes for you. I'll show you," said Imani. "But first we need to talk."

"Who died?" Gemma switched from teenager to healer in a breath. "Come on. Show me what clothes are for me. I need to give Doc Hilary some backup. She'll be real upset if another—"

"No one died!" interrupted Mercury. "Or at least I don't think anyone did. Did they?" she asked Imani.

"No. I don't think so. Everyone looked alright to me."

"Well, then why do you *look* like someone died?"

"Let's go back inside," said Mercury.

She and Imani went inside the suite, with Gemma on their heels. Karen was rubbing her eyes. She squinted up at them from her trundle.

"What time is it?"

"Midmorning," Mercury said quickly as she and Imani led the teenager to the sitting area of the suite. Over her shoulder she told Karen, "I hear Stella made breakfast. She also brought clothes in for all of us."

"Do you think there might be coffee somewhere?" Karen asked as she gingerly stood and massaged her temples.

"There's coffee in the foyer," said Imani. "I recommend lots of water and an analgesic for that hangover."

"I am not hungover." Karen winced as she spoke too forcefully. "Never mind. Perhaps I did imbibe too much last night." She paused and a smile lifted the corners of her lips. "Though I do not regret it." Then she disappeared into the bathroom.

"Apocalypse Karen is nicer than regular Karen," said Mercury.

"I was just going to say something like that," agreed Imani.

They went to two overstuffed chairs that sat in front of a coffee table and a newly obsolete flat screen TV. The chairs were loaded with clothes and toiletries. Mercury easily picked out a pair of her favorite jeans and her "Rogers Ropers" sweatshirt. The khaki slacks, beige blouse, and flowered cardigan were obviously Karen's, which left a pair of boyfriend jeans, a cream-colored tank top, and a red cable-knit sweater for the teenager.

"Here ya go," Mercury said, handing the clothes to Gemma. "Stella foraged these for you."

"Thanks." Gemma took them and then sat on the end of the coffee table. "Tell me what's up."

"I'm gonna always be straight with you," said Imani as she sat on the chair closest to Gemma. "So you know I'm being honest when I say I'm pissed as hell, but your mom asked that we give you this." She took the envelope from her pocket and offered it to Gemma, who reluctantly took it.

Gemma's finger traced her name on the outside of the wrinkled envelope before she looked up at Imani. "She's gone, isn't she?"

"Yes," Imani said. "She left with Ken. She's going to try to get to your dad."

Gemma's gaze went from Imani to Mercury. "But you guys think he's dead."

It wasn't phrased as a question, but Mercury answered. "From what we saw when the bombs went off in Portland and the surrounding area—as well as Salem and the area around it—no one could've survived that. If we thought for an instant something different, we would tell you.

Gemma nodded somberly. "And then there's the green fog that's probably still around. It did something good to us. Or at least it seems good so far. But it kills other people—other male people."

"Do you remember whether your mom said anything about feeling funny when the fog went over you?" ask Imani.

Gemma shook her head. "No, we didn't talk about it at all. We were too busy trying to take care of the people who were still alive." She looked down at the envelope again and slowly opened it.

"Would you like us to give you some privacy?" asked Imani.

"No. I'm a fast reader." Gemma's gaze flicked back and forth across the handwritten page. When she was done, she smoothed it carefully before refolding it and putting it back in the envelope, which she gripped in both of her hands as she stared at it and spoke softly. "They left me years ago. This pretty much just makes it official."

"That doesn't make it any easier," said Imani. "I'm here for you."

"So am I." Mercury spoke up. "So are Stella and Jenny and Karen. "

Gemma's eyes lifted from the envelope. They were dry. They were also decades older than sixteen. "Aren't you going to leave too?"

Imani leaned forward and looked into the teenager's old eyes. "If we do, I give you my word that it won't be to head to a bombed city, and if you want to come with us, you absolutely can."

"We promise," said Mercury.

"I'll try not to be a pain," said Gemma softly.

"You're not a pain. You can make things grow, remember?" Imani said.

"Well, potatoes for sure," added Mercury.

"We should go tell Doc Hilary," said Gemma.

"Agreed, and we need breakfast," said Mercury.

"I could use some coffee," said Gemma as she stood, took off her bathrobe, and began pulling on the clean clothes. She left behind the neatly smoothed envelope with the goodbye letter from her mother, lying on the coffee table like a lost dream.

"Coffee? Really? Are you sure you're sixteen and not sixty?" Mercury said.

Gemma's head poked out of the sweater as she answered Mercury. "Does how old I feel count?"

"In every way," said Imani.

"Then I am definitely not sixteen today."

CHAPTER

14

When Mercury, Imani, and Gemma stepped into the foyer-infirmary, the aroma from the trays of breakfast casseroles Stella had made, mixed with the distinctively cloying scent of burning marijuana, almost cloaked the sharp smell of ash that rested like a shroud over everything.

Mercury sniffed the air. "Is that weed?"

"Yep!" Gemma nodded enthusiastically. "Doc Hilary is prescribing it for pain and anxiety."

"I'm gonna have to get on her prescription list," muttered Mercury. Stella waved them over from her place at the low table they'd commandeered the night before.

"Coffee is over there by the cups and such," Stella said as the three of them joined her. "There's another breakfast casserole on warm in the kitchen. Is Karen seriously still asleep?"

"No, she was just getting out of the shower when we left the room," said Imani.

"Hey, thanks for bringing us clothes," said Mercury.

"Yeah, you did good," Gemma said.

Stella shrugged. "No biggie."

"Imani, if you and Gemma pour the coffee, Stella and I will get the casserole," said Mercury as she sent Stella a "come-with-me" look. Friends for too long to ignore the look, Stella stood, and together the two women made their way through the room of wounded people to the kitchen. "So, they're smoking weed."

"Yeah," said Stella. "It's great for pain relief and anxiety. Apparently, some of the full-time staff—all dead now, by the by—had a reefer grow station set up in the basement, with lights, dirt, fertilizer, giant plants, and lots of mason jars of dried bud—the whole deal."

Mercury stopped and looked at her. "For real?"

"Absolutely. There's enough stuff down there for an entire greenhouse. Doc Hilary was thrilled. She's a naturopath who knows a lot about plants, and a *whole lot* about medical marijuana in particular. She's writing down recipes for me to make salve and tinctures, and butter for edibles."

"Huh. That's a bright spot in a dark day—literally and figuratively."

"You can say that again." She gestured toward the wall of boarded-up windows. "It's a dark mess out there. I plan on joining the weed smokers after I get the stuff the doc needs made and dinner simmering."

"I'll help."

"I'm counting on it. Imani's useless in the kitchen." Stella glanced at her friend as they entered the kitchen, and she switched on one of the floor lamps. "I assume you want to talk about how we're going to tell Doc Hilary about the blood stuff," said Stella as she grabbed plates from the wire rack.

"Well, yeah, but first you should know that Sadie, Gemma's mom, left."

Stella's hands stilled as she reached for oven mitts. "What?"

"Yeah, she dropped off a letter to Gemma while she was still sleeping. Gave it to Imani, who is mad as fuck all."

"Of course she is! Imani just lost her kids, and now Sadie abandoned her daughter? I'm mad as fuck all and I'm not even a mom." She shook her head in disgust and took the casserole from the oven. "How's the kid taking it?"

"Like someone a lot older than sixteen. She hasn't cried. At all. Imani and I promised her we wouldn't abandon her." Mercury grabbed enough forks for everyone.

"Of course we won't abandon her. When we leave, she comes with us."

"Wait. *When we leave?*"

Stella spooned the steaming egg casserole as she spoke. "We're not going to stay here. Not forever."

Mercury touched her arm, and Stella put the spoon down and met her gaze. "You've always had great intuition. You've always listened to it."

Stella snorted. "Not always. Just in the decade or so you've known me. I had to live awhile first and screw up several times—hence my two marriages—before I learned to trust my gut."

"'Kay, yeah, but since I've known you, it's been a thing. Wait . . . I want you to think about your intuition. Has it gotten clearer, or however you'd describe it, since the bombs?" Mercury held up a hand to stop Stella as she began to answer. "No, really think about it."

"I don't need to. I know the answer. It's hell yes. My intuition has been pretty clear for the past decade or so, but since yesterday it's *loud*. I don't mean literally. I don't hear voices or anything like that. But the feeling is crazy strong. I knew from the moment Karen said something last night that we are going to leave." She picked up three of the five plates, balanced them expertly and then jerked her chin at the other two. "Can you handle those and the forks?"

"Got 'em." Mercury picked up the plates with the forks and as they retraced their steps to the main room, she asked, "Hey, where's Jenny? I thought she was out here with you."

"She was, but she and Tyler are going around with the housekeepers, boarding up broken windows, collecting supplies from the rooms, etcetera—basically making this place into as much of a fortress against whatever is out there as possible."

"Sounds smart," said Mercury.

"Definitely."

"But we're not staying?" Mercury asked with a sideways glance at Stella.

"Absolutely not. We won't be here very much longer. That came to me this morning when I went out to the truck. By the by, there's a camper shell from a wrecked Chevy in the parking lot that just might fit on the bed of our truck. We should check it out as soon as possible."

Mercury stopped in the hallway just outside the foyer. "And you're not scared about going out there?"

"I'm fucking terrified, but we gotta go. Don't know when yet, but soon. Don't know why yet, but I do know it's the right thing for us to do."

"Us?" Mercury said. "As in you, me, Imani, Gemma, Jenny, and Karen?"

"Us as in any one of those you just mentioned who want to leave with us. Mercury, you should be ready for some *not* to want to leave—and if that happens, we don't argue. We go and let them stay."

"You know that for sure?"

"My gut does."

"That's good enough for me. Let's eat and then fill the doc in on the blood stuff," said Mercury, and they headed for their table, where Imani and Gemma, joined by Karen, waited with steaming mugs of coffee.

They ate mostly in silence, appreciating Stella's delicious casserole and enjoying the sound of giggles that came from the wounded, who were happily filling the space with their own harmless version of green fog.

As they finished breakfast, Dr. Hilary joined them with several sheets of the lodge's stationery, on which she'd written recipes.

"Stella, I have to tell you again how much I appreciate your skill in the kitchen," said the doc. She was wearing another floor-length boho skirt that billowed around her long legs. She'd pulled her hair back, but little tendrils had escaped to halo her head. "These recipes are pretty simple. I'll have Tyler bring you some of the mason jars of bud. If you have any questions, though, please do not hesitate to come to me."

Stella took the pages, glanced through them, and then nodded to the doctor. "This is doable. I'm pretty sure we have all of these supplies in the kitchen."

Hilary smiled. "You should. *I'm* pretty sure the staff has been making edibles for years. Amanda, the young woman who was hostess for the Cascade, had a real gift for cannabis truffles. I wish she'd been in the restaurant and not out by the pool when the earthquake hit." The doctor shook her head sadly. "I'll miss her sweet smile."

"Dr. Hilary," Mercury began, "could you spare a few minutes to speak with us? In private, in the kitchen."

"Well, I was going to change the dressing on Marge's leg. That break is pretty nasty."

"I'll do that, Doc," said Gemma. "You're gonna want to hear what they have to say."

"You're certainly capable of changing Marge's dressing," Hilary told Gemma. Her gaze went back to Mercury. "And I'm becoming intrigued."

"Well then, let's go to my office," said Stella.

Stella led the way. Hilary, Mercury, and Imani followed. Karen stayed to assist Gemma, and Jenny was still working with Tyler. They made their way to the rear part of the kitchen. Stella turned on the two floor lamps to illuminate the rear counter on which sat the potatoes Mercury's blood had spattered the night before. The sprouts had continued to grow and were now easily showing six inches of vibrant green. Beside them were a spotless potato, a carrot missing its green top, a golden beet also minus any greenery, a big red tomato, and a pile of dried lima beans. A chef's knife rested beside the line of vegetables. The group stopped in front of the table.

Hilary looked from the vegetables to the three women. "Now I am entirely intrigued."

"Tell her," Stella said to Mercury.

"Oh, okay. Well, Dr. Hilary, this is going to sound crazy, but we've discovered that our blood can make things grow. Some of our blood, that is. We can't all do it. I can. And so can Stella, Imani, and Gemma—but not Jenny or Karen."

She paused and Stella continued to explain. "Last night Mercury accidentally cut her finger. Some of her blood got on a bag of potatoes. The potatoes she bled on started to sprout—right away. She tried it again. Same thing happened. Then last night all of us tried it, which is how we know whose blood has the ability and whose doesn't."

Mercury lifted the finger she'd sliced into to show the doctor. "See this tiny pink line?"

Speechless, Hilary nodded.

"Last night it was a cut that bled. A lot. It might've even needed stitches. I can't tell you for sure because it healed too fast for me to worry about it."

"May I?" Hilary held out her hand.

"Sure." Mercury let the doc examine her finger.

"This is healed. Almost completely," said Dr. Hilary.

"Ours too." Imani said. She and Stella showed the doctor their fingers, which looked like Mercury's.

"Where were you when the bombs went off?" asked Stella.

"I was just through there," Hilary pointed back at the dining room. "Outside on the patio, enjoying a cup of tea and some scones."

"Did you see the green fog?" Mercury asked.

Hilary nodded. "Yes, it swept over everything out there not long before the first earthquake. I remember vividly that I thought I was on fire because my skin burned. Then I believe I lost consciousness, but not for long. I woke in time to run inside. I was in the foyer."

"All of us whose blood made the potatoes sprout felt something when the fog hit us," explained Imani. "And we also lost consciousness."

"Jenny and Karen didn't, or at least they didn't remember it happening to them, and their blood also didn't do anything to the spuds," said Stella.

Hilary turned to Mercury and held out her hand. "Cut me."

Without hesitation, Mercury took the knife and pressed it to Hilary's thumb. The doctor squeezed until blood welled. "Should I start with the potato?"

"Might as well. I brought out the other vegetables so we could see if it's *just* potatoes," said Stella.

Hilary nodded and wiped scarlet on the potato. Then she shrugged and said, "While I'm bleeding, I might as well spread it around." She squeezed her thumb several more times so that it bled freely, then dripped blood on each of the other vegetables. When she was done, Stella handed her a piece of gauze.

"I'd give you a Band-Aid, but I have a feeling you're not going to need it," said Stella.

"How long does it take?" asked Hilary as she stared at the vegetables.

"It was pretty fast last night," said Mercury. "It should only take a few—"

"Hey, Doc? Ladies? You in here?" Tyler's voice drifted from the front of the kitchen.

All six women jumped.

"Here! Cover them." Mercury grabbed a dishtowel and tossed it to Stella, who draped it over the row of veggies.

"Yeah, we're back here!" Imani called.

Tyler jogged to them. "Oh good. Um, some guy just drove up."

"Is he injured?" asked the doc.

"Nah, I don't think so. Jenny and I were outside getting more boards for the windows and we saw him. We yelled for him to park on the side of the road 'cause the parking lot is pretty dicey, and he's driving the front part of one of those big eighteen-wheelers. He waved and yelled okay, and then backed out. He didn't seem hurt, but I thought I should get you guys."

"Yes, absolutely. We're coming," said Dr. Hilary.

"Awesome!"

When he just stood there, Stella said, "Tyler, could you bring the breakfast dishes back here to the sinks so we can get them cleaned up?"

"Oh, sure! I'll do anything for someone who can cook like you." He flashed a besotted grin at Stella before he scampered away.

"Ah, youth," said Stella. "He's lucky I'm not a decade younger. My line is drawn at thirty years young, though."

"Well, it is the apocalypse . . ." Mercury waggled her brows suggestively.

"Interesting thought," murmured Stella as she turned back to the counter with the shrouded vegetables. With a flourish she pulled off the dishcloth.

Every vegetable had sprouted.

Hilary gasped. With a hand that trembled, she reached out and stroked the green that spiked the top of the carrot.

"'Kay, don't be freaked," said Mercury. "We can all do it—and we feel just fine."

Hilary turned, eyes washed in tears, to Mercury. "Freaked? I am astounded! Delighted! Amazed!" The doctor laughed joyously. "This is miraculous!"

"It is," said Stella solemnly. "It is also how we are going to survive."

CHAPTER

15

"You do not know how glad I am to see living people!" A bulldog of a man jogged up the broken parking lot to where Mercury, Stella, and Hilary waited to greet him. His hand was out before he even reached the women. "Ladies, it is so damn good to see you. Name's Jebediah Simpson, but most folks just call me Sim."

Dr. Hilary stepped forward and took his hand firmly in hers. "I'm Dr. Hilary. The ladies behind me are Mercury and Stella. I believe I recognize you. Aren't you a regular at the Sunday brunch buffet?"

Sim's cheeks became two cherry dots as he grinned. "Yes, indeedy! Whenever I'm not on the road, that is. I do like a good Sunday brunch." He nodded to Mercury and Stella. "Nice to meet you." Then he looked behind them and whistled. "The mountain sure made a mess of Timberline."

"Part of it's still habitable," said Hilary.

"Yeah, and you're welcome to come in," said Mercury. "We can feed you, and we'd like to hear anything you can tell us about what it's like out there." She made a vague gesture meant to take in the rest of the country.

"I do 'preciate that. Can't stop long, though. I need to get to my family's cabin. It's about twenty miles north of here off Route 35. My husband and our five kids went there for spring break. I was supposed to join them yesterday, but . . ." He shrugged.

"The apocalypse got in the way?" Mercury said.

"Seems like it. Here's hoping the fam is fine. Can't reach 'em on the radio in my rig, but that could just be because there's no electricity. Hope that's all it is." He wiped a hand across his face. "Hey, is Bob around?"

The women turned and began walking back to the lodge with Sim falling in beside them. Hilary shook her head sadly. "Bob died yesterday. We'll miss him."

"Well, shit. What about Ken? He's been here 'bout as long as Bob."

"Ken left to try to find his family, with a couple other people from here," said Mercury.

"Isn't he from Government Camp?" Sim asked.

"Yep," said Mercury.

"The mountain covered it in an avalanche. There's nothing left of it," said Sim.

"Yeah, we know." Mercury nodded. "We were on the highway on the way to Portland when the bombs hit. We managed to get back here, which means we passed Government Camp on the way. We told Ken it was gone, but he left anyway."

"That's a damn shame." Sim gave her a considering look. "Don't sound like you're from around here. Do I hear Texas in your voice?"

"Oh, hell no!" said Stella. "You hear a much more refined accent. We're Okies."

"Okies! Tulsa is one of my favorite spots to stop when I'm on the job. I usually just sleep in my rig, but I make an exception there and stay at a little VRBO called the Hotel California in Reservoir Hill. The place is owned by one hell of a cook. I always look forward to a big, delicious breakfast there." He sighed and shook his head. "Hard to believe it's not there anymore."

Stella and Mercury froze. Hilary and Sim took a step or two past them, and then they stopped too.

Mercury fisted her hands at her side because they were suddenly trembling. "Wait. What do you know about Tulsa?"

Sim ran his sausage-like fingers through his short, graying hair and sighed again. "They bombed it. A buddy of mine was on the Turner Turnpike halfway between OK City and Tulsa when the bombs started falling. He managed to broadcast that both cities took direct hits, and then there was nothin' more from him."

Stella reached out and pried one of Mercury's hands open so she could hold it. "You're one hundred percent sure?"

Sim nodded. "I am. From what I can make out from those of us who can still communicate." He jerked his chin back toward his rig. "We have a com line going with our radios. The capitals of every damn state were hit, as well as anywhere that had a military base or decent-sized airport."

"The 138th Fighter Wing," Stella said softly. "I used to date a fighter pilot who flew F-16s from the Air National Guard Base by the airport. Shit, just shit." She shook her head.

Mercury didn't realize she was crying until her nose got snotty. She wiped at it angrily. "Who the fuck did this to us?"

"No one I've talked to knows for sure," said Sim. "Though we did get off our ICBMs. Truckers saw 'em launch. So, whoever did it is fucked and won't be follow-up attacking us. Pardon my language, ladies."

"Your language doesn't need a pardon," said Stella.

"So every state was attacked?" Hilary asked.

"Yep, some lots worse than others, of course. Haven't heard one word from anyone east of the Mississippi. And California—most of it's gone. Whole damn coast changed. When the earthquakes started, the San Andres Fault broke. All of it. A shitload of the West Coast slid into the ocean."

Mercury felt lightheaded, like she'd stood up too fast, and she clung to Stella's hand to steady herself. She met his eyes. "You know this for sure. It's not just hearsay?"

"Truckers reported it. For most of them, it was the last thing they did."

Mercury fired another question at him. "What about the green fog? Did everywhere get bombed with that too?"

"Hell yes! It's still floating around. I sped through patches of it between here and Madras."

"But when the bombs went off, did the green fog hit you?" Stella watched him closely as she waited for his answer.

He shook his head. "Nah. I was taking my morning shower in a truck stop not far from Madras—basically in the middle of nowhere, Oregon. The men's showers there are like a cement bunker—no windows—shit, no air circulation at all. The guys and I call it the dungeon. Everything started shaking and going to hell, and there I was, stuck in the showers, naked as the day I was born. When I managed to get dressed and outta there dead people were everywhere, but the green stuff was gone. Like I said, though, I've seen it. Between there and Madras, and between Madras and here."

"Madras? That's where you came from?" Hilary asked. Then she quickly added for Stella and Mercury, "Madras is a modest-sized town about seventy miles south of here."

"Yeah, but that seventy miles took me more than half a day to travel. I left this morning at dawn. Good thing my rig drives like a tank, though I had to leave my load in Madras. Never woulda made it a mile, let alone all the way here still hauling. The road's almost impassable. Lots of vehicles stranded. Lots of dead folks. It's terrible. But Madras is still there. Parts tore apart in the quakes—and of course there's the dead. Doesn't seem to matter that no bomb fell on the city. They just died anyway. But their mayor, Eva Cruz, is on it. She's got a hospital set up as her headquarters and is rounding up folks and helping 'em. She's got a radio set up and is tryin' to contact other drivers. This mornin' she told me herself to spread the word to survivors that Madras will welcome them."

"Sim, we'll have more questions, and we'd really like it if you talked to the people in the lodge, but first how about some coffee and some lunch?" Hilary said.

"That sounds great. I do appreciate your hospitality. Can't say I'm good at public speaking, though. Don't much like crowds."

"Then you have nothing to worry about. There aren't enough people left here to be a crowd. It's more like you'll just be chatting with us," clarified Hilary. "There are about thirty wounded inside and besides us, only a handful more non-injured."

Sim shook his head slowly. "I really hoped there were a hundred plus folks up here who survived the bombs and such. Damn, just damn." He and Hilary led the way with Mercury and Stella, still holding hands, following slowly.

"I knew it was probably gone," Mercury said softly as she wiped at her nose again. "But I had some hope."

Stella squeezed her hand. "I know. We gotta tell Jenny and Karen—and Imani. Shit, shit, shit, I'm tired of giving good people bad news."

"We can grow things," said Mercury. "I'm going to hold onto that."

"Right there with you, girlfriend," said Stella.

Mercury paused long enough to turn and face her best friend. "I don't care where we go, but wherever we end up from today on, we have to make the world we live in better, kinder, more fucking reasonable than the one that exploded yesterday. If we don't, none of this—none of these deaths—will have meant anything."

"Agreed. One hundred percent agreed."

Sim got comfortable at the coffee table Mercury and her friends had been using as a dining table. Imani and Jenny were helping Tyler board up the last of the foyer windows while the three housekeepers, Mary, Rachel, and Veronica, collected all the fans they could find and positioned them so that they blew air away from the foyer—just in case the green fog descended on the lodge. Karen was assisting Gemma as she changed Marge's bandages. While Stella disappeared into the kitchen to make a plate for Sim, Mercury gathered her three friends, who threw the trucker curious glances but followed her to their bedroom suite.

Mercury closed the door softly behind them and turned on the little bedside lamp. Then she faced the women.

"That man's a trucker," she said without preamble. "He's been in contact with other truckers. I'm just gonna say this fast and get it over with. Tulsa is gone. San Diego and the entire West Coast of California is gone too."

"Oh!" Karen sat heavily on the bed and clasped her hands together, closed her eyes, and as tears leaked down her cheeks, she prayed softly.

Jenny's face had blanched a sick, curdled milk color. "He's sure?" she asked.

Mercury nodded. "Yes, one hundred percent sure."

Jenny sat heavily beside Karen. She stared up at Mercury with eyes that were glossy with tears that stubbornly refused to fall. "My mom. My dad. My sister. They all live in Jenks. They're dead, aren't they."

Jenny didn't phrase it as a question, but Mercury answered her. "They are. Jenks is basically Tulsa—like Bixby, Broken Arrow, and all those other suburbs. Remember how much damage the bomb did in Portland? Nothing surrounding it could've survived. It has to be the same in Tulsa. And even if some people survived, like around my parents' place east of Broken Arrow, we have to be realistic. There's really no way we can get from here to there—not somewhere that's several days drive away."

"I know . . . I know . . ." Jenny's gaze slid from Mercury to the embers in the fireplace. She stared as tears leaked from her eyes, down her pale cheeks.

"I hope it was fast." Imani's voice was whisper soft. "It was early. My babies are good sleepers. They were probably in bed with their daddy 'cause they always climb in bed with Curtis when I'm gone." Her gaze met Mercury's. "Please let it have been fast. Let them all have been curled up together asleep."

"They were," Mercury said. "I'm going to believe they were."

"I—I have to get some air." Imani turned and quickly left the room.

Mercury stared at the closed door. "I don't know whether I should go after her or let her have some time alone."

"Do both." Karen looked up as she wiped her eyes with the sleeve of her cardigan. "Give her a little time, and then go after her. And I'll pray for her. I'll pray for all of us."

Mercury nodded. "We definitely need all the help we can get. I wanted to tell y'all the news in private, but Sim—that's the trucker's name—is going to talk to everyone after he gets done eating. Thought you'd like to know if there're any questions you want to ask him."

"I wonder how the rest of the world's doing." Karen spoke to her clasped hands.

"Bad. He said he hasn't heard anything from anyone east of the Mississippi. I think we need to focus on here and now if we're going to survive this and build a new life for ourselves," said Mercury.

"Why? What for?" Jenny asked as she looked up at her friend and mentor. "Who's left alive to care?"

Mercury squatted in front of Jenny. "We are. We're alive. We're healthy. We can build a world where this never happens again."

"I'm not sure I have the energy," said Jenny.

"That's okay. You're not gonna have to do it alone." Mercury pulled the younger woman into a hug.

Sim put away a huge portion of reheated breakfast casserole and three big mugs of coffee. As he ate, Tyler gathered anyone who had been strong enough to leave the foyer infirmary, and by the time the trucker belched and wiped his beard free of egg debris, everyone in the cannabis-perfumed room was watching him expectantly.

"Damn good food," Sim said as he stretched.

Hilary seemed to materialize before them. "Sim, our people would appreciate it if you'd update them on what you know."

Sim nodded. "Yep. I can do that." He lowered his voice and added, "Do you want me to sugarcoat it or tell it like it is?"

"Tell it like it is," said Stella. "There's no point in anything else."

"I agree," said Hilary.

"Well, then, here we go." Sim stood and followed Hilary to stand before the constantly burning hearth.

"He seems like a good guy," said Mercury to Stella. "I hope his family is alive."

Stella spoke immediately. "He is a good man, and they are not alive."

Mercury stared at her as Sim introduced himself and began repeating to the group of raptly listening people much of what he'd already told them.

"Is that your gut talking?" Mercury asked her best friend.

Stella moved her shoulders. "Must be. I didn't even think, but the words just came—and when I spoke them, I knew they were true."

"That's happening more and more, isn't it?" Mercury said.

Stella nodded. "Seems so. I'm trying not to let it freak me out, but *hello*! It's freaky."

"Your gut is gonna keep us alive," said Mercury. "Don't be freaked. Be as grateful as I am."

"Doin' my best," murmured Stella as the two women turned their attention to Sim.

"So, that's about it. Not much east of the Mississippi 'pears to have survived—or at least not enough to get word out yet. Oh, one more thing: there's a major storm brewing. Shouldn't be news to any of you who are regulars. Storm was predicted last week, which is why I was on my way to my cabin north of here to hunker down before it hits. But FYI, I got word from a park ranger in the Cascades that conditions are right for a blizzard. Should start tomorrow afternoon or so up here. God only knows how long it'll last."

A hand went up and Sim nodded at a young man whose face, arm, and leg were swathed in bandages.

"You said you came from Madras?"

Sim nodded. "Yep."

"Any word from Bend?" he asked.

Sim blew out a long breath. "It wasn't bombed, but it's a mess. The quakes caused massive destruction and loss of life. Also, from what I've heard, the green fog was especially bad there. And Redmond—for those of you from out of state, that's a town between Bend and Madras—is gone. Not because of bombs, but my friends reported that the entire town was on fire."

As several people began to ask Sim questions, Stella turned to Mercury. "That's it. Our cue to leave."

Mercury tilted her head to Stella's and whispered. "What? You mean the storm?"

Stella nodded. "Exactly what I mean. We cannot get stuck up here. Time to make our move, like, ASAP."

"'Kay. Crap. Do we need to figure out how to bring all these people with us?" Mercury's stomach heaved at the thought. How the hell were they supposed to move all these hurt people?

"No. Or at least I don't think so. Here's what I know for sure—you and I and Imani need to go. Now. Before the damn snow hits. If Jenny and Karen want to come—fine." She paused as Gemma walked past with a handful of bandages. "Well, shit. Gemma needs to come with us too."

Mercury blew out a long breath. "All right. Is first thing in the morning fine?"

"Not really, but it'll do. I feel a great sense of urgency to get out of here before the snow starts."

Mercury turned to meet her best friend's gaze. "Are we leaving all these people to die?"

Stella brushed her mane of silver-blonde hair back from her face and shook her head. "I don't know! I hope not. I don't get a terrible feeling when I think about them staying here. At least not for now I don't. But I don't really understand how this shit works. All I can do is tell you what my gut is saying—and it's screaming loud and clear—*get out!*"

"Is your gut also telling you where we should go?" Mercury asked.

Stella jerked her chin in the direction of the trucker, who was patiently answering questions. "Madras. But I don't feel like it's our final destination. It's more of a stopover. That's all I know for sure right now."

"All right, then. We'll talk to the rest of our group and see who wants to come with us, and then let Hilary know," said Mercury.

"I sure as hell hope I'm right," muttered Stella.

"How often was your gut wrong before the bombs?"

"Almost never," said Stella.

"I'm gonna believe that's still true," said Mercury.

CHAPTER

16

"DAMN NICE OF you ladies to fix me up with this bag of goodies." Sim smiled at Stella and Mercury, and shifted the laden bag to his hip so he could offer his hand to shake. "My husband will especially 'preciate the wine. Travis likes to think of himself as an amateur sommelier."

Hilary took his hand warmly in both of hers. "Sim, I want you and your family to stay away from that green fog. It's deadly, especially for men."

Sim sobered and nodded. "Yes, ma'am. I already kinda figured that from what I've seen."

Hilary smiled. "Good. Stay safe. And after the storm passes, you and your husband and kids should come down to the lodge. Travis can check out the lodge's wine collection."

"We'll do that," Sim grinned, which made him look like Santa out of uniform. He turned to Stella. "That casserole fixed me right up." He rubbed his belly. "When I come back, I'll get the recipe, if you don't mind." He offered his hand to her.

Sidestepping his hand, Stella gave him a hug and kissed him noisily on the cheek. "I don't mind. You're a good man, Jebediah Simpson. Thank you for bringing us the information you did."

"Hey, no problem. Glad I could help."

Less of a hugger than her friend, Mercury took Sim's offered hand in both of hers. "Yeah, thanks. We needed to hear what you had to say."

He shook his head sadly. "Sorry about your home. Wish I'd had better news."

"So do we," said Mercury.

"Well, I better head back to my rig. Gotta get to my family," said Sim.

"Mercury and I will walk you out," said Stella.

Mercury sent Stella a surprised look but shrugged and headed to the door with them. As Mercury, Stella, and Sim picked their way carefully to the parking lot, she shivered. The air was already colder than it'd been since her group had arrived six days before. *Six days?* The thought flitted through her mind. *How could the world change so completely in just six days?*

The parking lot came into view, with its piles of dirty snow, jumbles of vehicles, and stains of red that marked where so many people had taken their last breaths. Imani stood at the edge of the lot, facing out away from the lodge. She was utterly still, her face turned from them.

"Is she okay?" asked Sim.

"Her husband and kids were in San Diego," answered Mercury.

He shook his head. "That's tough."

"I'll go to her," said Mercury.

"Both you ladies go to her. I can make my way back to my rig just fine. I'll give you a honk and a wave as I pull away."

"Okay then, take care, Sim." Stella bumped Mercury's shoulder and jerked her chin toward Imani.

"Yeah, be safe," said Mercury as she and Stella headed to Imani.

"See you ladies after the storm." Sim pretended to tip a nonexistent hat to them before he turned and hurried across the broken lot to the exit and the highway beyond.

Mercury and Stella trudged through dirty snow, up an incline, to Imani. Mercury glanced up at where Imani stood so still—almost as if she'd been formed from the land beneath her. She could only see the side of her friend's face, and for a moment Mercury thought she caught a flash of light—green light—in Imani's chestnut eyes. Mercury paused, blinked, and it was gone.

She tugged on Stella's arm. "Hey, do you feel anything weird coming from Imani?"

Stella shrugged. "She's sad, but I don't need my gut to tell me that. Why?"

Mercury shook her head. "Nothing. Just wondered."

They climbed the rest of the way to Imani silently. From her vantage point, they could see the two-lane Timberline Highway and the front part of Sim's rig, which was parked half off the road in a little dip right before the turn into the lodge parking lot.

"How you doing?" Mercury asked as they joined their friend.

Imani didn't answer. She just kept staring out, away from the lodge.

Mercury cleared her throat and tried again. "Sim's leaving. He says there's a big winter storm coming. Should get here tomorrow afternoon."

Imani didn't so much as glance their way.

Mercury opened her mouth to say something else—anything else—that might get Imani to speak to them, but Stella's lifted hand stopped her words.

"What are you looking at?" Stella asked Imani.

Imani drew in a deep breath, which made Mercury realize she hadn't been breathing before then.

"San Diego was there—out there—southwest of here. I'm looking toward my babies." Her voice was brittle, like the words she spoke should fall to the ground and shatter around their feet.

"We'll look with you if you don't mind." Stella's voice was hushed.

"I don't mind," said Imani. "I just . . . I had to come out here and look toward them. This is as close as I'm going to get to them for the rest of this lifetime."

Stella stepped up to stand on one side of Imani, and Mercury moved to her other side. The women stood together in the cold, gray day, looking to the southwest.

"No! Shit!" Stella suddenly broke their silence. "Sim! Hey! Stop!"

"What is it?" Mercury blinked and then squinted through the ashen day down at the road beneath them. She could see Sim's back as he trudged toward his rig. The front grill of the big truck was all they could see from where they stood, but Mercury instantly understood the urgency in Stella's voice. Across the road behind Sim a fat finger of green fog wafted lazily from the ditch. It swirled and curled and drifted with the chilly wind, closer and closer to the trucker.

Mercury cupped her hands around her mouth and shouted. "Sim! Sim!"

He kept walking, completely oblivious to their calls and to the emerald fog that appeared to follow him.

"Together! All of us call his name on three," Mercury said. "One, two, three!"

"Sim!"

The trucker paused and turned. He was smiling. The bag of supplies rested on his hip and his hand was raised as he waved at them.

"RUN!" yelled Mercury.

But Sim had already seen the green fog. He began to scramble backward, like he was unable to take his eyes from the encroaching mist.

"Just turn around and run!" shouted Imani.

"It's too late," Stella said softly. "Too fucking late." Unable to watch, she turned her head away, and as she did, Sim spun around, finally realizing he needed to sprint to his rig.

Panicked, he dropped the bag of supplies. The two bottles of red wine broke against the asphalt with the sound of muffled gunshots. They bled scarlet across the highway as Sim stepped on a rolling apple. His ankle twisted, and with a cry of anguish he fell.

The green fog swept over him. For a few moments it obscured the man enough that Mercury couldn't see what was happening with him. Then Sim stood. He lurched forward with a terrible limp. For a moment it seemed he might make it to his rig—he might be okay. He reached the grill and fell heavily against it. He turned, lifted a hand to the women as if to say he was okay. Mercury could even see the flash of his teeth as he smiled.

Then Sim coughed.

Once. Twice. With the third cough blood spewed from his mouth. His hands went up to clutch his throat and he fell to his knees as he vomited blood and bile and chunks of Stella's breakfast casserole. Then he toppled forward onto his face. He writhed and screamed wetly.

"We need to help him!" Imani said. She started to move forward, like she was going to rush to him, but Stella snagged her wrist.

"He's a dead man," Stella said. "You can't help him. And I don't know whether or not that green stuff will kill us too."

Imani shook her head. "We can't just let him die alone."

Sim's screams had stopped. His body twitched several times. It was over fast. He went still within seconds, surrounded by an expanding pool of scarlet.

"He's gone," Stella said. "And he wasn't alone. We were here. Up until the last moments, he was happy and sure he was going to join his family." She paused and sighed heavily. "And now he is."

"They're dead?" Imani's voice was soft.

"They are," Stella said.

Imani faced Stella. "You know things now, don't you?"

"Yes," Stella said. "But I can't control it. I can't make whatever *it* is tell me stuff. Things just come to me, and so far when I *know* things, they come true. Like I know we have to leave here. No later than tomorrow at dawn. You, Mercury, Gemma, and me. If Jenny and Karen want to come, that's fine. If anyone else wants to come that's fine too. But *we have to leave.*"

"Why?" Imani asked. "Why the hell should we go on?"

Mercury spoke the words etched on her heart. "So we make a world where this kind of shit never happens again."

Imani's dark eyes searched hers. "Can that even be done?"

"I don't know, but I want to try. I want to fight for something better than the mess that got us here," said Mercury.

"It can be done." Stella's voice took on a soft, rhythmic cadence. "We can't change the entire world. We can make a new one for us—for people like us. A world that sings with our voices. A world that is better, brighter, more beautiful than what was before."

"What does that even mean?" Imani asked.

Stella shook herself like she'd just come in from the rain and said, "Hell if I know, but I want to give it a try."

"I do too," said Mercury. She looked at her friend. "Imani, will you choose to live? Will you come with us?"

"Yes. But I can't promise I'll be much help building this dream world of yours. I'll always be looking toward San Diego."

"That's okay," said Stella. "We need someone who can see beyond us."

CHAPTER

17

"AND YOU'RE COMPLETELY sure you must leave?" Dr. Hilary stood to the side of the massive kitchen as Stella, general-like, collected supplies to take with them, put the finishing touches on the enormous pot of stew that had been simmering for a day, and made notes about the inventory she'd taken that morning.

Stella glanced up from the sheets of paper she'd been filling with lists and amounts and simple recipes. "Yes. No later than dawn. But you and whoever stays with you aren't in any immediate danger—especially since you'll be snowed in here for a couple weeks. Just be sure you have plenty of wood. You should be able to make the food last for almost three months—and that's without you growing any new veggies. I've written down ways to stretch the inventory, but you need to make use of that reefer grow setup in the basement and your magic blood. Plant the potatoes already sprouting, as well as carrots, onions, tomatoes, and such. Keep the meat frozen and use it sparingly. You'll be fine."

Hilary's gaze went from Stella to Mercury, who was putting marijuana buds in mason jars—and checking to be sure there were seeds with the buds. Mercury paused and nodded. "Just FYI, Stella knows stuff now. It's part of whatever changed our blood to grow things. She's always had great intuition, but now it's like superhero level."

"Though not quite as predictable as X-ray vision or leaping tall buildings in a single bound," muttered Stella as she went back to her lists.

"Well, I'd rather you stay, but you must do what you believe is best," said the doc. "What do you think we should do about our blood?"

"Do about it?" Mercury asked. "I don't think there's anything we can do about it except to try to figure out the extent that green fog changed us."

"No, she means should we tell people about our changed blood." Stella didn't look up from her lists. "And not only should we tell the people here, but they should all be given a spud and a knife." She did look up then. "We can grow things. This is an apocalypse. We will never again be able to run down to Whole Foods and grab a bag of salad and some bread, and then go by the deli for salmon steaks. To survive, we'll need to grow our food."

Hilary nodded. "So, you think we just take potatoes and knives into the foyer and start cutting?"

"Yep. Mercury will talk to the group and let them know what's up," said Stella.

"I will?"

Stella nodded. "Use your teacher classroom-management skills. You'll do great. We can handle hundreds of teenagers a day. Thirty wounded people are the size of a normal classroom. Keep that in mind."

"Good point." Mercury nodded, feeling relieved. Stella was absolutely right. Compared to a classroom of thirty-plus hormone-filled teenagers, the adults in the foyer were easy.

"While you're doing that, I'll be sure the back of our truck is loaded with supplies. It's a major relief that that camper shell fit." Stella made a shooing motion. "Go on. I need to concentrate. It's almost dinnertime. I have to be sure all this is set for y'all after we leave, which is going to take me a good part of the evening. Then we need to sleep so we can get out of here at first light."

"'Kay, let's get this done, Doc," said Mercury.

Together Mercury and the doctor selected a variety of veggies that could easily be planted under the basement grow lights if they did sprout, and a few razor-sharp chef's knives. They put everything in a big stainless steel mixing bowl. On the way to the foyer, they stopped in the lodge's boutique, which had become a makeshift medical supply area, and grabbed a bottle of alcohol and some baby wipes. Then, together they wound their way through the mattresses, where the wounded napped, quietly read books, or played cards. Mercury thought how interesting it was that this little group had settled in so well. A few of the thirty had retreated into themselves and either slept constantly or just stared and cried, but the majority of the survivors seemed to be in halfway decent spirits.

Mercury couldn't figure out if it was good or bad that no one appeared scared shitless.

She and Dr. Hilary reached the enormous fireplace that crackled and popped and lent warmth and comfort to the large room. Hilary lifted her hand and cleared her throat. Every head turned in their direction as the room went expectantly silent.

"Some of you have already met her," Hilary began, "but for those of you who don't know, this is Mercury Rhodes. She has something very important to speak with you about. Please know that she has my full support." Then the doctor stepped aside.

"Hi," Mercury said. She'd already decided that it was stupid to equivocate. So, she launched directly into the truth. "When the bombs exploded yesterday, they released some kind of green fog." She paused as people nodded. "We only know a few things about that fog. One is that it kills people—terribly. Another is that it doesn't kill everyone, though it seems men are way more susceptible to it than women. Recently, we've discovered that it changed some of us—or rather it changed our blood."

Marge propped herself up on her elbows. "What do you mean by *changed*?"

"My blood makes things grow," Mercury said. "So does my friend Stella's and Imani's and Gemma's."

"And mine as well," added the doctor.

"That's sounds like sci-fi stuff," said Marge's partner, Nathan.

"Yep, but that doesn't change that it's the truth. Watch." Mercury took one of the knives from the bowl. Hilary handed her an alcohol-soaked wipe. She disinfected the blade and her thumb, then she quickly cut herself, picked up the top half of a carrot, and smeared the drops of blood that welled onto it. Then she faced the room again. "Along with being able to make veggies grow, we believe that other things have changed about us too, though we really don't know much more than the fact that some of us have heightened intuition, and we heal faster than before."

"This is really hard to believe," said a middle-aged woman whose head was bandaged and her ankle splinted and elevated.

Gemma stood from where she'd been crouched beside a mattress, finishing a bandage change on a man whose arm had a nasty gash from shoulder to elbow. "Yeah, Janet, it is, but it's also true." The teenager looked around the room at the people she had been treating—the people who had already come to respect her. They watched her intently as she continued. "My blood makes things grow, but I also *know* things about you guys. I can feel when you hurt. And I knew Bob was going to die before he started to bleed out."

Mercury blinked in surprise at the girl, but before she could say anything Janet scoffed. "Oh, come on! That's not even possible."

Gemma met her gaze unblinkingly. Her voice was firm and much older than a sixteen-year-old's. "Why would I lie? Why would *we* lie?"

"We wouldn't," Mercury spoke up before Janet could continue. "Plus, what's the point? It's not like you couldn't disprove what we're saying—but we *can* prove it." She lifted the carrot that had already begun to sprout green tufts from its top. "Clearly, we're not lying."

The group murmured excitedly, but Mercury shushed them.

"Stella, Imani, Gemma, and I are leaving at dawn before the snowstorm that Sim told us about hits. You're set up here with shelter and a nice amount of supplies, but you're going to run out. Hilary's blood grows things. Who else wants to test their blood?"

"Why are you leaving?" Marge asked. "And hell yes, I want to test my blood."

"Good choice," Gemma said as she retrieved the knife, alcohol wipes, and the bowl of veggies from Hilary and headed to Marge.

Mercury met Marge's gaze and continued to tell the truth. "We're leaving because Stella says we need to, and we trust her gut instinct."

"Are you coming back?" asked another woman.

"I don't know, but Tyler is removing the CB radio from Sim's truck so we can take it with us. This morning he found the lodge's radio that Bob told him about, which means we can stay in touch. You can't leave. We already talked with Hilary about it."

"No, it wouldn't be wise to move any of you, not even those of you who aren't badly wounded," said Dr. Hilary. "Besides the coming storm, we really don't know what *out there* is like. You may have to walk—or run—for your lives."

"Or fight," Mercury added. "But we're heading to Madras. As Sim said, the mayor there has made it a sanctuary city. We're hoping that we'll be able to send help back after the storm." She held up one of the knives. "Anyone else want to get tested?"

Hesitantly at first, and then more eagerly, every hand in the room went up. The testing went fast. If a veggie didn't sprout within just a few minutes, it didn't sprout at all.

"Only five grew anything?" Nathan asked and then grimaced and rubbed his taped ribs.

"Only five," Mercury nodded. "But at least we know some things that are similar in everyone whose blood changed. All of us were outside and breathed in the green fog."

"Yeah, and it hurt—like stinging bees," said Gemma.

"Also each of us lost consciousness, if only for a minute or so," added Hilary.

Nathan frowned and shook his head. "And it didn't change the blood of even one man. That doesn't seem fair."

Marge looked at her partner. "I think you should be grateful our car didn't come to a stop in the middle of that green stuff, because it seems every man who comes in contact with it dies."

Nathan grinned at his partner. "Oh, honey, I *am* grateful. I also wish my blood could grow things."

"So, do you think whoever engineered this particular biological agent made it to wipe out men?" Janet sounded equal parts pissed and skeptical.

"We can't know for sure if it was created to be that specific or if it's just a fortuitous byproduct." Heads turned as Stella joined them in the foyer.

"Fortuitous?" said one of the other three men as he carefully sat up. His arm was in a sling, and his thigh and head were heavily bandaged. His age was hard to determine as the gauze wrapped around his forehead also covered the side of his face, but Mercury guessed he was somewhere between forty and fifty.

"Well, let's see." Stella tapped her chin with exaggerated contemplation. "Who's been in charge of the world until now?"

"Men," said Gemma.

"Exactly." Stella put her fists on her waist and faced the wounded man. "Women saved you. Women bandaged you. Women will continue to be sure you heal. Remember that."

"Is that a threat?" asked the man.

"What's your name?" Stella countered with.

"Keith Carter."

"Well, Keith, we're not like that," said Stella. "We're simply speaking to you honestly. This new world is going to be different. We're not going to tolerate misogyny. That's not a threat. It's the truth."

"Exactly. We're being truthful and making it clear more things have changed than our blood," Mercury said.

"Guess it's good you're leaving," muttered Keith.

"No, Keith." Hilary spoke firmly. "We'll have none of that. Mercury and Stella are correct. Our blood has changed and so has our world. We're not going to bicker with you. And we're not going to be bullied by you either. We will be compassionate. We will be truthful. We will be *fair*. And we will work together to survive this. If that is not how you want to live, you are free to go."

"I—I can't leave. I can barely walk," said Keith as the part of his face not bandaged flushed scarlet.

Another man—the younger guy who had multiple cheek, shoulder, and leg lacerations—spoke up. "Well, dude, then I guess you'll have to learn how to get along with people, and by people I mean women."

"Good advice," said Nathan as he reclined back with a sigh. "We do need to work together, and to tell you the truth, I'm glad I'm not in charge."

"Oh, my love," said Marge with a fond grin. "I'm glad you're not in charge too."

CHAPTER

18

"OH, GOOD! YOU guys are all here." Gemma walked into the suite and plopped down on the trundle beside Karen, who was already sipping a glass of another excellent red Stella had chosen. "Thanks to marijuana, Stella's amazing stew, and Imani's ridiculously delicious biscuits, everyone is tucked in and half asleep already."

"Here, kid. Tonight I brought you a real wineglass." Stella poured a little red into the stemware and handed it to Gemma. "Don't forget to swirl it like I taught you last night."

"Did you already let it breathe?" Gemma asked as she swirled the wine semi-professionally.

"Of course," said Stella.

"I'm impressed," Imani bowed from where she sat beside Jenny on the second queen bed.

"Me too," chimed in Mercury. "I think we should lower the drinking age in our new world."

"I vote yes for that." Gemma grimaced after she took a sip. "Though red wine does take some major getting used to."

"Keep working on it. You're a fast learner," laughed Stella.

"Will do." Gemma took another small sip, this time without grimacing. "So, who all's leaving in the morning?"

"We were just getting to that," said Mercury. "The three housekeepers, Mary, Rachel, and Veronica caught me right after dinner. They've decided to stay."

"So has Tyler," said Jenny.

"Okay, so, right now it's Mercury, Imani, and me leaving." Stella swirled her wine. "What about you three? Coming or staying?"

"I've been thinking about it a lot," Gemma said. "I know I could stay here and learn a lot from Doc Hilary. Plus, there is a small chance my mom might actually come back here." She sighed and then shook her head. "But I don't really believe that. I don't think she'll want to live without my dad; she'll just give up." Gemma blinked rapidly and continued. "I want to go with you. You make me feel like I have a family."

Imani reached over and squeezed the teenager's hand. "You do. We're your family. I'm glad you're coming with us."

"We all are, kid," said Stella.

Jenny cleared her throat before she spoke. "Mercury, you know I love you, right?"

"Well, yeah. Love you too."

"Which makes this really hard for me to say, but I don't want to leave," Jenny finished in a rush.

Mercury's insides constricted. She'd assumed Jenny would go with them. Jenny had been her intern, and then her colleague and friend. She automatically opened her mouth to talk her out of it—or at the very least to ask her to reconsider—but Stella's hand touched her leg. Without looking at Mercury, Stella shook her head quickly and subtly. Mercury bit her lip and rearranged her thoughts.

"Please don't be mad." Jenny sounded so damn young.

"Oh, honey!" Mercury leaned forward and touched Jenny's cheek gently, like a mother would. "I'm not mad at you. I'll miss you, though."

Jenny squeezed her hand and sniffled, wiping away an escaping tear. "Me too."

"Why do you want to stay?" Gemma asked.

"Well, I don't have magic blood, but I do have a master's in botany. They're going to need someone who knows plants to tend to and harvest what they grow. But, um, the biggest reason is something I'm not proud of." She sighed before she continued. "I'm scared of what's out there. I know it's probably delusional to think that we're actually safe up here, but it *feels* safe, and right now I need that feeling." Her gaze lifted to meet Mercury's. "I hope you're not too disappointed in me."

"I'm not disappointed in you at all, and I understand completely," said Mercury quickly.

"Plus, you're right," said Stella as she saluted her with her wineglass. "Just because our blood makes veggies sprout doesn't mean they can stick them in dirt and expect them to grow. The people here need you."

"I'm scared of what's out there too," said Karen softly as she stared into her wineglass. "But I would like to come with you."

Mercury was as shocked at Karen's desire to leave as she had been surprised that Jenny wanted to stay. "It's going to be dangerous."

Karen nodded. "I know. That's why I'm afraid. And I'll understand if you don't want me to come with you."

"Why do you want to leave?" asked Stella.

"I want to be part of the new world, and I believe that means I need to go with you." She lifted her shoulders and let them drop. "It's as simple as that."

Stella turned to Mercury. "It's your decision."

Mercury sputtered mid-sip of the excellent red and almost snorted it out of her nose. She swallowed quickly and stared at her best friend, "Mine? Why mine?"

"Don't know why. Just know it is."

"'Kay, well, I only have one question." Mercury turned her gaze to Karen. "Will you be proselytizing?"

"Do you mean praying for and with people?" Karen shot the question back.

"No I don't mean that. As you know very well the definition of *proselytize* isn't about praying for or with someone. It's about converting others' beliefs to your own. Will you be doing that?"

"I assume you won't allow me to come with you if I say yes."

"More than that," Stella said. "If you lie, we will leave you wherever the hell we are—even if it's on the side of the road. We have no space or patience for liars. Just be honest, Karen. Tell the truth. It'll come out eventually anyway."

"Fine. I will only share my faith with people who ask about it. That is a truth I can live with. Can you, Mercury Rhodes?"

"Yep. Easily. That's how I live my life. How many years have you known me?" She leaned forward and spoke earnestly to Karen, willing her to understand.

"I'm not sure. Eight or so years, I guess," said Karen.

"It's been over a decade," Mercury said. "In that decade have I even tried to convert you to Paganism?"

Karen jerked back like Mercury had slapped her. "No! That would be inappropriate."

"And yet you have—over and over—made references to your religion and to the fact that I'm going to go to hell unless I believe as you do. *That*, Karen Gay, is actually inappropriate."

"And rude," said Stella, nodding.

"And disrespectful," said Jenny.

"I agree. And I'm Christian, from a family of faith-filled, church-going, strong, blessed black women," said Imani.

"Adults are so ridiculous about religion." Gemma took a long drink of her wine and shuddered slightly.

"What do you mean, Gemma?" Karen asked.

"Well, your lives are usually screwed up. Um, no offense, 'cause I don't know you guys super well yet, so I'm just talking about the adults I've known, but that's what I've seen over and over. But instead of, like, working on themselves, adults are real quick to tell other people what they're doing wrong instead." She rolled her eyes. "It's stupid."

Mercury barked a laugh. "You know, you're absolutely right, Gemma." She met Stella's gaze. "Let's change that in our new world."

Stella lifted her glass and clinked it against Mercury's. "Agreed."

"Karen," Mercury said, "you may come with us."

"Thank you." Then Karen added slowly, carefully—as if she had to search to find the correct words. "And I will try to be respectful of everyone, no matter their faith."

"That's all we ask," said Mercury. "And once you practice respecting other people—no matter their faith—I think you'll realize that it's easier and a lot less stressful than trying to make everyone fit into your mold."

"She means what works for you doesn't have to work for everyone. And that's not a bad thing," said Gemma.

"You're a smart kid," said Stella.

"Yep. I know. And I'll take more wine, please."

"Is there anything else we need to do before we leave?" Imani asked as Stella refreshed her wine.

"We need to tell Tyler, or whoever will be running Timberline's CB—"

"That'd be mostly me," interrupted Jenny. "Tyler doesn't know much about them. Thankfully, Imani and I chose to take that workshop on radio waves, which included some archaic but now surprisingly useful info on CB radios."

Imani nodded. "Which is why I know how to work one too."

"That's excellent," Stella said. "So, Jenny, keep a listen to the CB, but don't broadcast much. Don't tell people your position or give them other details. Don't even talk to anyone except us."

"What's going on?" Mercury asked her.

"I don't know yet. All I know is that Timberline will be safe as long as it's secluded." She turned to Jenny. "We're not going to be completely forthcoming with info when we first get to Madras. We won't tell them about the CB, or about Timberline, until we know we can trust them."

"Sounds smart," said Jenny. "I'll get the CB set up in the boutique we're using as a supply room. That's pretty central. We should be able to hear if you call."

"Other than an emergency, don't call us," said Stella. "And if you do, make up a location away from here."

"Got it." Jenny nodded.

"Do we have backpacks?" Gemma asked.

"Backpacks?" Mercury echoed.

"Yeah, I'm assuming we're gonna be super cautious about everything, which means we won't be driving into Madras with our truck and all our supplies—including that CB radio—but we're gonna need some of our stuff, clothes and toothbrushes and such. So, we'll need backpacks."

"Excellent idea, kid," said Stella. "And something I hadn't even thought about."

"There were new backpacks in the boutique. We moved them, along with clothes and that other stuff to the little store at the end of the hall today," said Jenny. "I can go grab five of them for y'all."

"That would be great, Jenny," said Mercury.

"Hey, I'm not going with you, but I still wanna help." She got up and gave Mercury a quick hug before heading for the door.

"I'll miss her," Mercury said softly.

"You'll see her again." Stella paused, then grinned. "I like good news like that way better than knowing stuff like poor Sim dying."

"That sucked," said Mercury.

"He's happier now," Imani murmured as she stared into the crackling fire. "He's with his family."

"Hey," Mercury took Jenny's place beside Imani and put her arm around her friend. "Stay with us, 'kay?"

Imani nodded slowly. "I'm doing my best."

CHAPTER

19

STELLA WOKE THEM a little before dawn. The five women dressed quietly and made their way to the kitchen, where Stella had prepared a big breakfast—which they ate in the rubble of the Cascade Dining Room so they wouldn't wake the wounded, sleeping comfortably in the hearth-warmed foyer/infirmary. As they were cleaning up the dishes, Dr. Hilary joined them in the kitchen.

"I still wish you were staying," she said after she hugged each of them.

"You're a good leader," Stella told her. "The people here will be safe as long as they listen to you."

"And if they don't?"

"You shouldn't force anyone to stay," Stella said. "Let anyone who wants to—or who causes problems—leave. Do it with goodwill and send them off with supplies, but in return make it clear that Timberline must remain a secret."

The sharp-eyed doctor nodded somberly. "I understand. If anyone leaves, I'll willingly help them but also get their word that they'll keep us a secret. And you have the route written down? It's not difficult at all. Take a left onto highway 26 out of Timberline Highway."

Stella nodded. "And follow it down to Madras. I didn't need to write it down because Jenny found an actual *paper map* of Oregon in the boutique. It's already tucked away in the glove box of the truck with Sim's CB that Jenny and Tyler installed."

"Jenny is brilliant." Mercury hooked her arm through Jenny's and grinned, though her eyes were suspiciously bright.

"If you cry I will lose it. I mean it," said Jenny.

"Right. No tears. Promise." Mercury wiped quickly at her cheek.

"Changing the subject!" Jenny said firmly after she wiped at her own cheeks. "So, what are you going to tell people about where y'all have been since the bombs?"

"Mercury has that covered," said Stella. "She's a good storyteller who should've taken those manuscripts out from under her bed and sent them to a publisher."

"Huh? You write stuff?" Gemma asked.

"I did. Just for fun. And those manuscripts aren't hidden under my bed. They're hidden in my computer. Well, they were. But I actually have been thinking about a story we can tell," said Mercury.

"Told ya so." Stella grinned cheekily as the group turned expectantly to Mercury.

She drew a deep breath, released it, and then launched into her fiction. "'Kay, well, a foundation in fact helps fiction to be believable."

Gemma nodded like she was an aged professor. "That actually makes sense."

"Thanks, but I can't take credit for it. My creative writing teacher at OSU–Tulsa, Tess Miller, said it—and I've never forgotten. So, we were camping at—" She paused and then quickly added, "Uh, I have to check that map and find the name of a campground somewhere around here."

"Frog Lake," said Gemma. "Say that. My parents and I have camped there a bunch of times, and we're tent campers, not glampers."

"Girl, you can pitch a tent?" Imani looked impressed.

"Totally," said Gemma.

"Good to know," said Stella. "So, we were tent camping at Frog Lake."

"Yep," continued Mercury. "We're teachers who take off every spring break and do something together. This break we came here. When the bombs hit, we didn't know what to do, so we didn't do anything until it started to snow. Then we knew we had to try to find help—and we ran into Sim on the highway. He sent us to Madras."

"Good story," Imani said. "But it doesn't explain Gemma. She could pass for eighteen, but that's not old enough to be a teacher."

"My story is that I live nearby and my family was camping at Frog Lake for spring break. My parents died in the first blast."

The women were silent as they gazed at Gemma. Mercury was trying to figure out something adult and wise to say when Imani spoke as she put her arm around Gemma. "And then our group found you."

Gemma looked up at Imani—her eyes bright with unshed tears. "No, *I* found *you.*"

Together the group followed Stella, who led them from the dining room. They paused in the hallway to retrieve the filled backpacks they'd left there. As they picked their way through the foyer, several of the wounded stirred enough to wave goodbye—mostly to Gemma. Marge sat, stopping the teenager so she could hug her, and then thanked Stella again for not leaving her and Nathan to die on the side of the road. Then the teenager approached the doctor and handed her an envelope that had "Mom" written on it. "In case she comes back."

Gemma was crying silently when they finally stepped outside. Imani took her hand. "It's okay. Stella says we'll see them again."

"She didn't say *I* would," Gemma muttered, but she held onto Imani's hand tightly.

"You will, kid," Stella said.

"What about my mom?" Gemma asked.

"I'll only tell you what I know to be the truth, and right now my gut tells me you will see at least some of those people again—Doc Hilary for sure. I'm sorry. I don't get anything when I think about your mom, which isn't good or bad."

"If you do get something about her, will you tell me?"

"Absolutely," said Stella.

Mercury finally released Jenny's arm. "Let's say goodbye here. It's too damn cold for you to go out to the parking lot."

Jenny bit her bottom lip and nodded. She turned to Stella first and hugged her quickly. "Keep them safe, okay?"

"I'll do my best."

Then she hugged Gemma, Imani, and Karen before returning to Mercury. "I always wished I had an older sister. Someone who would clue me in about important life stuff. Someone I could hang out with—tell my secrets to—and know she's always there for me." Jenny drew a deep breath and cleared her throat before she continued. "You answered my wish. You'll always be my big sister."

"Oh, Jenny! Come here." Mercury pulled the young teacher into her arms and held her tightly. "You be careful. Listen to your gut. And don't take shit from anyone."

"Okay." Jenny stepped out of her arms. "Please don't get dead."

"I'll do my best." Mercury repeated Stella's words. "I love you, Jenny Kimpton."

"I love you too, Mercury Rhodes. And I'm going to go inside and not stand here and blubber while you drive away." Without another word, Jenny turned and jogged back to the lodge.

Stella walked beside her as Mercury wiped at her cheeks and dug a tissue from her jean's pocket to blow her nose. "I fucking hate goodbyes."

"I know you do," said Stella. "But it's really just 'see ya later.'"

"Yeah, well, that's the only reason I'm not a snotty mess right now," Mercury said.

Stella snorted. "You are a snotty mess, but I still love you."

"Like Sam would say—ditto." Mercury shivered as they picked their way down to the parking lot and their truck, which Stella had moved from its hiding spot up as close to the lodge as possible. "Goddess, it's freezing!"

Karen looked up at the lightening sky. "Snow. Those clouds look heavy with it."

Stella nodded. "Yeah, and I hope the snow keeps the green crap from floating around."

Mercury gave the sky a suspicious glance. "I hope the snow doesn't have the green crap in it."

"I don't think it does," said Imani. "I've watched it and it's heavy. Remember how it acted with Sim? It didn't lift to him. It wafted around him sluggishly with the breeze. It was in the ditch and then around his knees and only covered him when he fell. It's denser than the air, so it's not going to float easily, and instead it'll settle into low spots."

"Are you saying that because your intuition is telling you to?" asked Mercury. "Like Stella?"

"No. I'm saying that because—science."

"I wish we knew whether it was dangerous to touch or whether that green crap has to be breathed in to kill," said Mercury.

"Zero clue," said Imani.

Everyone looked at Stella, who shrugged her shoulders. "I got nothin'."

"Well, either way the lodge really should be safe. It sits up pretty high," said Mercury. "The initial blasts forced it up here, but like Imani said, it's heavier than air, so it's probably less of a threat the higher the elevation."

"I *told you* they'd be safe," repeated Stella. "Though I do agree with science-checking things. I may be an art teacher, and now some kind of weird seer or whatever, but only the willfully ignorant ignore science."

"Preaching to the choir, sis," said Imani.

Karen cleared her throat as they reached the truck. "Ladies, how are five of us fitting in that cab? It was already crowded on the way here, and there were only four of us."

"Well, I thought y'all could take turns riding back here. I made a fairly comfy nest-like area in the middle of the truck bed." Stella put down the tailgate and lifted the hatchback of the camper shell they'd managed to attach to the old pickup. The inside was carefully packed with supplies—everything from food to clothes, to camping equipment the housekeepers had found in one of the suites—and, of course, a more than decent supply of wine. In the center of the strapped-in piles of supplies was a mound of blankets and pillows.

"Ooh, I'll go first!" said Gemma. "This is seriously too early for me. I'll be out like a light as soon as you start driving."

"Sounds good," Stella said.

"Gemma, would you mind if I took a turn with you?" Imani asked. "Long car rides makes me sleepy. Always have. And you're right about it being too early."

"Don't mind at all!" Gemma grinned over her shoulder at Imani as she crawled into the bed of the truck.

"If you need anything—like you have to stop to pee," Mercury said, "just rap on the window."

"Okay," Imani said as she followed Gemma into the truck bed.

Stella closed the hatch behind Imani and headed to the driver side of the cab. As she carefully steered the truck around the obstacles that still littered the broken parking lot, Mercury swiveled and peered out the back window, through the camper shell, and out its cloudy rear window at the sleepy lodge.

"It's harder to leave than I thought it would be." She kept the lodge in view as long as possible before turning around.

"It made me feel safe." Karen spoke softly. She'd taken her place on the bench seat near the door.

"I think that's it," agreed Mercury. "Reasonable or not—the lodge seemed a sanctuary."

"It is for the people who remain there," said Stella. "Just not permanently, and not for us."

Carefully, slowly, Stella followed the one-way exit from the lodge that wound around and eventually joined the two-lane Timberline Highway that they'd driven up just two days before. The truck's headlights pierced through the dawn gloom, but it was still slow going.

"At least I don't recognize any new cars—or see any more dead people than I did driving up," Stella said.

"The road's still crappy," said Mercury. "I hope there are no more earthquakes." She gave Stella a side glance. "Will there be?"

Keeping both hands on the wheel, Stella shrugged. "No clue, but I wouldn't be surprised if there were."

It seemed that it took less time to make their way down Timberline Highway than it had to go up it, which Mercury realized was because Stella could drive a little faster without having to worry about jostling wounded people in the bed. The headlights illuminated the stop sign that signaled where the road to Timberline emptied into highway 26—east and west. Stella had begun to slow when she suddenly stomped on the brakes, narrowly missing a heavily pregnant doe who dashed across the broken two-lane. She put the truck into neutral and let it idle while she wiped the sweat from her palms on her jeans.

"Shit!" Stella sounded shaky. "That was close. I have to remember that with hardly any traffic, wildlife will be more likely to cross the highway."

"Is there a rush to get to Madras?" asked Mercury.

Stella opened her mouth to answer, paused, and then blew out a long breath before she answered. "Actually, no. I can calm down. The rush was to get off the mountain before the snowstorm hit, and we're on our way, so we should be good."

"So, just relax and take it slow." Mercury bumped her friend's shoulder with hers. "Plus, our truck bed passengers aren't injured, but I grew up riding in the bed of my dad's ranch trucks, and I promise you that going fast is going to jostle them like crazy."

Karen pressed her thin lips into a thinner line. "Children riding in the beds of trucks is so dangerous. It's one of the few things I ever spoke against Michael about."

Mercury and Stella turned to Karen, brows raised.

"Do tell," said Stella.

"Yeah, spill the tea, girl," added Mercury.

"The tea?" Karen's brow wrinkled.

"It means to give us all the gory details about—" Mercury jumped and yipped at three sharp knocks on the glass behind her. She turned to see Imani looking at her.

"Gotta pee!" she shouted through the muffling glass.

Stella nodded and made the "okay" sign with her right hand. She pulled beside the broken "Timberline Lodge" sign that used to point up the highway and put the truck in neutral.

"Sorry, guys," said Imani as she and Gemma crawled out of the bed of the truck with a roll of toilet paper.

"Too much coffee," Gemma said around a yawn.

"Hey, no problem," Mercury told them, remembering the big deal Mr. Hale had made about Amelia needing to stop for a pee—which had probably saved their lives.

Mercury stretched and walked a little way into the middle of what was left of the highway. From there she had a decent view of the bottom slope of the mountain. The sky had become light enough that it allowed her to see the broken trees and torn land that was dotted by the orange glow of uncountable fires. She wanted to look away. It made her sad and angry and frightened to see evidence of how much her world—the entire world—had shifted in just a couple days, but it also pulled her attention, like passing a bad wreck. She had to look.

"It's crazy, isn't it?" Stella said from beside her.

Mercury jumped. "Goddess! Make some noise, would ya? You move like a cat."

"Thanks. That reminds me of how much I miss my house panther." She hooked her arm through Mercury's.

"Cash Money was an awesome house panther," agreed Mercury.

"I'm glad I'm as between cats as you are between dogs. I'd hate to think about what woulda happened to them." She lowered her voice. “It sounds strange, and unintentionally callous, but you know my parents and my older sister have been gone for years, so my fur babies *are* my family. Glad I got to say goodbye to Cash Money and didn’t lose him in this mess.” When Mercury didn’t say anything, Stella added. “Hey, I didn’t mean to make it seem like I’m comparing my cat to your mom and dad and brothers.”

“Oh no. I get it. I know you’re not making light of anyone’s loss. And I’m glad Kong went to frolic with the Goddess last year. I’d hate to think about him scared and dying without me.” She paused and then continued in a soft voice. “It’s not real yet. I–I still feel like as soon as we’re in cell range, I could call my parents, my brothers, or their wives, and they’d answer and want to know when the hell I was coming home.”

“Glenn would grumble at you and tell you that you should be a better sister and keep in touch with your brother,” Stella said with a smile.

“Oh, for sure. He’s been overly sensitive since he was a kid, and Lionas and I lured him into drinking pee by saying it was lemonade.” Mercury laughed.

“Right? He’s still weirdly touchy about that.” Stella echoed her laughter.

“Probably because Glenn’s the baby of the family,” said Mercury.

Stella nodded. “Oh, for sure. And Lionas is the more reasonable one.”

“Yep. He’d say, ‘No problem, little sis—you’re busy.’” Mercury shook her head. “I don’t know when it’s going to feel real, but I’m pretty sure I don’t want it to. Right now it’s like going away to summer camp when I was a kid. I used to miss my parents so, so much. I mean, I ended up having fun, but I missed them the entire time and was so damn glad to see Dad drive up in his truck to take me home.” Her breath caught on a sob.

Stella squeezed her arm. “Be kind to yourself. Everyone grieves differently.”

“Like Imani said yesterday—I hope it was fast. It was Sunday morning. Dad and Mom were probably having breakfast out front.”

“Using that big rock as a table,” said Stella.

“Yeah. Dad was probably spiking his coffee.”

Stella grinned. “Right? I’d forgotten he’s where you got your love of Kahlúa coffee.”

"And my love of mimosas—the tree and the drink." She laughed a little and her gaze lifted, as if she might see her father reflected in the dove-colored clouds above them, and through the grayness she caught the silver outline of an almost full moon low in the sky. "Wait! What's today's date?"

Karen joined them, rubbing her arms vigorously. "Well, let's see—Sunday was the last day of spring break, which means it was March nineteenth. It's dawn on Tuesday, so it's the twenty-first."

"Tomorrow's the spring equinox, which means Ostara." Still staring up at the sky Mercury spoke wistfully. "This year it also falls on a full moon."

"That's right," said Stella. "You have a big Gathering planned for Ritual."

"Had," Mercury corrected with a sad sigh.

"Hey, we're done peeing!" Imani and Gemma joined them.

Gemma held out the roll of toilet paper like a prize. "Anyone need this?"

"Nah, I think we're good for now," said Stella.

At that moment fat snowflakes began falling from the sky.

"Shit! It's starting. We need to get to a lower elevation before we get stranded up here," said Stella, and the women scrambled for the truck.

CHAPTER

20

THE SNOW QUICKLY increased from fat, lazy flakes to sheets of never-ending white. The old truck's windshield wipers weren't fabulous, and even with the defrost turned all the way up, Stella was soon forced to peer through a soggy, streaky circle of melting snow and ice.

"If you want me to take a turn at driving, I will," said Mercury.

"How long's it been since you've driven a manual?" asked Stella.

"Last summer. I drove Dad's old truck while he and his temp worker guy tossed hay bales onto the trailer."

"Okay, I'll keep that in mind if I need a break." Stella slowed and flexed one hand, wiped it on her jeans, and then flexed the other. Her knuckles cracked, and she never took her gaze from the snow-covered road. "Well, the one good thing about all this snow is that it's easy to see the half of the highway that's gone." She jerked her chin to the right. That side of highway 26 was impassable—whether from it having slid down the side of the mountain, or whether the asphalt was just too broken to drive over—and the settling snow accentuated the broken and missing areas like a highlighter on a page of dark print.

Stella downshifted and slowly steered the truck around the blackened shells of wrecked vehicles.

"That's another good thing about the snow," said Karen as she stared at the skeletal vehicles. "It's covering the bodies." She shuddered and rubbed her cross between her forefinger and thumb, but didn't look away from the wreckage. "Don't worry, though. I'm still looking for any sign that anyone's alive out there."

"Good job, Karen," Mercury said. "The snow makes that easier too. You'll be able to tell if anyone has been walking around."

"So far—nothing." Karen continued to stare out the window. "I'm not sure if I should be relieved or not about that."

"Both." Stella accelerated again and the rear of the truck fishtailed. She steered into the spin and righted it with no problem, but muttered, "I'm gonna stop soon. I was hoping we'd get far enough down in elevation to be out of this snow, but that doesn't look like it's going to happen anytime soon—which means we need to put the chains you found behind the seat on the tires."

"'Kay, yeah, I helped Dad put chains on his truck tires more times than I can count," said Mercury. "It's not hard. Hey, how's our gas gauge?"

Stella glanced down and frowned. "I'd forgotten what a gas hog these old trucks were. I'll stop next time we see a vehicle that isn't burned to a cinder. I can use that section of hose Tyler cut us to siphon gas while you put the chains on the wheels."

Karen sighed. "We've been driving through this mess for hours, right? Or does it just feel like it?"

"No, it's definitely been four hours. And we've officially gone"—Stella paused and glanced at the odometer—"almost nineteen miles from Timberline."

Mercury swiveled around to peer through the window into the camper shell and the back of the truck. She smiled. "Imani and Gemma are still curled up together like puppies and sound asleep."

"It's good for them," Stella said.

"Sleeping?" asked Karen.

"Well, that and being together. None of us will make it through this alone, but those two in particular need each other."

"I'm glad they're together," said Mercury. "Hey," she said, pointing as she squinted through the streaky windshield and the unending snow, "up ahead that looks like a bunch of stalled vehicles."

"Sure does." Stella began to slow. "Also looks like it's an exit from the highway."

"I saw a sign a little way back that said Oregon highway 216 east was ahead," said Karen. "And I really would like to use the facilities." She stared out the window and shrugged. "Which seems to mean making the side of the road a lady's room, as I didn't also see a sign for a rest stop."

"Trust me, Karen." Stella downshifted. "You wouldn't want to go inside a rest stop right now."

Karen shivered delicately. "I believe you. I shall brave the snow."

"Atta girl, Karen," Mercury said. "You're practically a pioneer woman."

Karen sat up straighter. Her narrow lips tilted up. "Well, I can churn butter."

"That's an excellent skill to have," Stella said. "We'll have to catch us some cows and get you a churn."

As they drew closer to the widening in the two-lane several cars, SUVs and trucks materialized from the snow. Three had been involved in a T-bone accident—a really bad one. But none of the others appeared wrecked, although one SUV clung precariously to the broken side of the highway, looking like it could tumble over the side of the mountain if the wind shifted.

Stella drove slowly past the SUV and the wrecked pile of vehicles—all covered with snow—and finally came to a stop beside the gas tank of a Ford Exhibition. She put the truck in neutral and pulled up the emergency brake.

"I don't like how this feels," Stella spoke as she studied the area around the outside of the truck and the Exhibition.

"Then maybe we shouldn't stop here." Karen gave their surroundings a suspicious look.

"Honestly, I can't tell if it's my intuition saying don't stop or the fact that it's blizzarding out there, and any sane human wouldn't want to leave this warm truck." Stella shrugged. "What I do know for sure is that I'd rather fill up now versus running out or even getting near empty in this storm." She frowned up at the seemingly endless supply of snow falling from the slate sky.

"And you've been slipping around a lot the past couple miles. I need to put those chains on," Mercury said.

"Do it fast," said Stella. "I'll siphon quickly. Karen—"

"I'll use the pretend facilities quickly. I don't want to be out in the cold either," Karen said.

Mercury looked behind them to see Imani stretching and Gemma covering her head with a blanket. She mouthed, "Break time," at Imani who grinned and crawled to the tailgate.

"Let's do this. Fast," said Mercury. The three of them exited the cab of the truck, and Mercury sucked in a breath. "Goddess! It's freezing out here!"

"Yeah, but nice and warm back there in the bed." Imani yawned magnificently as she joined Mercury. "What's up?"

"Karen has to pee, Stella's siphoning gas, and I'm getting the chains on those tires." Mercury tilted the bench seat forward and opened the dark duffle that was filled with random tools, duct tape, zip ties, and—thankfully—a new set of tire chains.

"I'll help." Imani squinted against the unending snow. "It'll wake me up." She held out her arms. "Just load me up and tell me what to do."

"'Kay, these are the kind of chains that are really easy to install. Here, check it out." Mercury moved to the front driver-side tire and held up one chain. "All you have to do is unhook the clasps here—and here." Mercury demonstrated. "Then you just position them on the tire and reclasp the chains together." She did so, grunting as she kneeled in the snow. "Ugh, the knees of my jeans are gonna be wet."

"Better than sliding off the road, though," said Imani as she peered over her shoulder. "What're the weird-looking red plastic things for?"

"They're how you finish. They kinda rest over the hubcaps. You use the straps to attach them to the chains to hold them into place. Like that." Mercury stood and wiped off her jeans. "Got it?"

"Sure. Looks easy." Imani held up a jumble of thick metal-wrapped wires. "But these don't look anything like chains."

"Be grateful for that. These are, as my dad would say, newfangled, fancy tire chains. Putting actual old chains on tires was a pain in the ass and really hard on tires." Mercury headed around the truck. "I'll get the front if you get the rear."

"Will do!" Imani disappeared around the rear of the truck as Mercury knelt by the next tire.

"Fuck! That's vile!" Stella spat into the snow twice after she stuck the end of the hose that went from the gas tank of the Exhibition into their truck's half-empty gas tank. "I shoulda known better and grabbed a bottle of water to rinse with." She spat again and shuddered.

Karen appeared from around the far side of the Exhibition. "I'll get you a bottle of water. I put several in my backpack, and it's just inside the tailgate." She tromped past them to the back of the truck.

"How're your spidey senses?" Mercury asked Stella as she snapped the front tire chain into place.

"Telling me we need to be quick," said Stella.

"Yeah, well, the front tires are done. I'll help Imani with the rear ones, and we can—"

"Hey there, missus!" a deep voice boomed from the rear of the truck.

"Shit!" Stella hissed the word. She ducked behind the side of their truck as she pulled the hose from the gas tank and quickly screwed the cap on. She met Mercury's gaze and whispered, "Get the gun."

Mercury nodded and slowly, quietly, opened the passenger door, popped the glove box, and took the .38 out of its holster. She released the safety and pulled the sleeve of her sweatshirt down so that it covered her hand and the pistol.

"Ladies, we have a visitor." Karen came back into view through the snow. Her face was chalk pale. She walked slowly along the driver side of the pickup. Following her was a barrel-chested man who could've been anywhere between forty and sixty. His beard was unkempt salt and pepper. He wore a red cap, a thick down coat, and jeans tucked into wading boots. Resting in the crook of his arm was a long hunting rifle with a scope Mercury recognized as a Winchester 70—the same weapon her dad used to hunt deer the few times he didn't use a bow.

"Well! This is a nice surprise. I didn't expect to find anyone out here in this storm, let alone a *working* truck full of women." The man smiled, showing tobacco-yellowed teeth below a bulbous red nose. "Name's Mack Stanley. I imagine you girls will be glad to hear that several of us have a settlement just up 216." He pointed through the snow at the turnoff behind him. "I have a snowmobile parked by the exit. You can follow me to what we're turning into a pretty nice shelter."

Mercury spoke up. "Nice to meet you, Mack. That's a lovely offer, but my friends and I are just passing through. We only stopped here for a quick sec. We'll be on our way now."

Imani's head popped up from the rear passenger side of the truck. She walked toward Stella and Mercury, her dark eyes trained on the man, who caught sight of her and frowned. "I see you have a colored woman with you." He shrugged. "Guess that's okay. Anyone else? No menfolk?" He tried to squint into the camper shell, but the fogged-up window obscured his view—though while he was looking away, Karen had continued walking so that she was now just on the other side of the open passenger door from Mercury

Imani halted like she'd walked into a wall. Stella moved to stand between Mercury and the open door to the truck. "Like my friend said—we're just passing through." Stella slid quickly into the cab and scooted behind the wheel.

"Well, now, why would you want to keep driving in this mess?"

Imani skewered Mack with her narrowed gaze. "Because this isn't where we planned to stop."

Mack barely glanced at her. "I didn't ask you, missy." He took a step closer to the driver door as Stella released the parking break with a creaky snap. "Hey there," he called to Stella. "What's your rush? Come on up to our place and get yourselves warm."

Mercury faced Mack as she motioned for Karen to get into the cab of the truck. "We're in a rush because of the weather. Like you already mentioned—it's a mess," Mercury said. "We plan on getting out of this snow before dark so we don't have time to stop and get warm, but we do appreciate the offer."

Karen got into the cab, which left only Imani and Mercury outside the safety of the truck. Mercury was trying to decide whether she should shout at Imani to get back into the bed, or squish her into the cab with them when Mack raised his rifle and pointed it at Mercury.

"Well, now, ladies. I'm gonna have to *insist* you come with me. The boss man who's in charge of our camp is pretty clear about being sure we take care of any females we find out here. It's for your own good, really. It's too dangerous now for women to be on your own. You, there"—the rifle bobbled as he gestured at Mercury—"go with the colored girl and get into the bed." He took another step closer to the cab. "Your friend is going to need to slide over so's I can drive."

Mercury put her thumb on the hammer of the .38 so she could cock, lift, and fire the revolver, when a figure materialized out of the snow behind Mack. Gemma lifted a tire iron and swung it at Mack's kneecap as she shouted, "Fuck you!"

Mack screamed in pain, clutched his knee and dropped to the snow. His rifle skidded across the snow-slick asphalt and came to rest against the front tire of the truck. Stella opened the door, reached down to retrieve the rifle, and yelled, "Let's go!"

Gemma and Imani bolted for the rear of the truck and climbed back into the bed as Mercury jumped into the cab and slammed the door. Imani hit the glass of the camper shell behind them. "We're in! Go! Go!"

Stella put the truck in gear and floored the gas. The newly chained tires caught and spewed snow and dirt over Mack as they sped away.

CHAPTER

21

Stella didn't stop until she found a turn off a road lined with broken trees. She pulled the pickup behind a clump of toppled pines, effectively hiding it from anyone zipping past on a snowmobile. The three of them piled out of the cab and hurried to the rear of the truck, opening the tailgate so they could help Imani and Gemma out.

Gemma's face was pale, and her hands were still shaking, but she smiled at the women. "I did good, right? Imani said I did."

"You did fucking fantastic, kid," said Stella as she hugged her.

"I couldn't hit him on the head," Gemma said as she detangled herself from Stella and shivered. "I just couldn't."

"What you did was perfect," Imani assured her.

"Yeah." Mercury smiled at the teenager. "Plus, hitting him on the head might not have hurt him at all. He didn't seem very smart."

"Racist asshat," muttered Imani.

"Seriously," said Gemma.

"I believe I may have to rethink my stand on violence," said Karen.

"We're all going to have to rethink a bunch of what we considered normal before this. Though I've always believed racists need to be kneecapped," said Stella. She wiped her hand across her face. "But we did get some gas."

"And four chained tires," added Imani.

"We need to get on the CB and let Jenny know to pass the word—if someone wants to leave Timberline, they need to know there're armed men at the Oregon 216 turnoff," said Stella.

"Men? As in plural?" Mercury asked.

Stella nodded. "Yeah, you heard that douchebag. There's some boss man calling the shots—and it sounds like they're collecting women. Even through the snow, I could see vehicles that at first appeared to be stalled or wrecked had actually been pulled into place to block the turnoff. No way potbelly Mack did that by himself."

"Jesus, it's like something out of *Mad Max*," said Imani.

"I'm afraid as more time passes and groups of survivors band together, that analogy is going to be too accurate for comfort," said Stella.

"Why the hell can't good people band together?" Mercury brushed her hair from her face and retied her ponytail. "Why is it always the assholes?"

"It's not always," said Gemma. "We've banded together and we're definitely not assholes."

"The kid makes an excellent point." Stella nodded.

"And wherever we end up settling we're not going to be *those* kind of people." Karen jerked her chin back the direction from which they'd come.

Imani opened the glove box, took out and unfolded the extra-long antenna she and Jenny had rigged, and placed it on top of the hood of the truck. She handed Mercury the mic and flipped on the radio, which had already been dialed into channel five. Then she nodded. "Okay, go ahead and shout out to Jenny."

Mercury squeezed the button on the mic and spoke slowly and clearly into it. "Jenny, this is Mercury. Are you there?" She paused as her group gathered around to peer over her shoulder. "Jenny, Mercury here. You listening?"

There was a crackle, and then from far away came Jenny's tinny voice. "Mercury! I'm here! Y'all okay?"

"Yeah, just fine. But pass along to Hilary and any idiot who wants to leave there that there's an armed blockade 216 exit from 26 east, and probably a whole camp of asshats somewhere up 216 not far from there."

"Shit! Okay, got it! And you're all okay for real?"

Mercury smiled. "For real."

"Still snowing where you are?" Jenny asked.

"Blizzarding is a better description," said Mercury.

Jenny's laughter echoed through the speaker. "Can't even see outside here. We're all hunkered down, getting lunch ready. You at Madras yet?"

"Not even close."

There was a weird crackling sound, and through a tide of static, they could just make out a man's voice saying, "What's your twenty, ladies?"

"Uh-oh," said Mercury. "Jenny, shutting this off. More later."

"Got it. Be safe."

As Imani reached for the power switch, the same man's voice, stronger this time, blared. "Ten–nine! Repeat that last transmission! I didn't get your loca—"

Imani turned off the radio. "And you won't get our location either."

"Asshats everywhere," grumbled Stella.

Mercury took the antenna from the roof of the truck, wiped off the snow, and secured it beside the radio—and the revolver, which she'd returned to its holster—Stella's newly acquired rifle was tucked in the truck bed. "Hey, I wonder where this side road leads?" She put her hand over her eyes and squinted against the snow as she tried to look through the sheet of whiteness. "Maybe we should follow it a little way and see if we can find another vehicle. Unless you had time to fill the tank up before Mack interrupted us."

"Got the tank about three-fourths the way full." Stella shrugged. "We may as well drive a little way along this road. All I need is one vehicle, and I could easily top off the tank. I like having it full, that's for sure."

"Imani, do you mind taking a turn with me?" Karen asked. Her eyes were bloodshot and she frowned at the snow she kept wiping from her cardigan.

"I'd be happy to. I'm wide awake," said Imani.

"Hey, do you guys care if I squish into the cab?" Gemma asked. "After smacking that guy, I'm pretty sure I may never sleep again."

Imani put her arm around Gemma. "You'll sleep again—just get ready for nightmares."

"That's not very comforting." Gemma rested her head on Imani's shoulder.

"But true," said Stella. "And we can squish. You're not very big."

The five of them shook off snow like cats, got in the truck, and Stella began to slowly follow the winding one-lane. But they hadn't gone far when they had to stop because several huge pines had snapped in half and completely blocked the road.

Stella braked and put the truck into neutral. "I'm gonna get out and see if I there's a way around those trees."

"Hey, we shouldn't take any chance on getting stuck," Mercury called out the open door to her friend. "We can stop and top off the tank at the next truck we come to on the highway, and—"

Stella held up a hand, silencing Mercury. Imani, who was sitting closest to the passenger door rolled down the window as everyone listened. The wind had died and the snow fell vertically, covering the broken trees and torn earth like a shroud. So, the sound of weeping carried eerily to them, as if the cries had found their way between flakes.

"Someone's crying," whispered Imani.

Stella hurried back to the truck. "Did y'all hear that?"

"Sounds like a child crying," said Imani.

Stella nodded somberly as Karen came around the side of the truck. "I think I hear a baby crying."

"Yeah, we all hear it." Stella met Mercury's gaze. "There's no way to safely drive the truck around those trees. Get the gun and come with me."

Mercury didn't hesitate. She popped the glove box and pulled out the revolver.

"Who else besides Mercury can drive a stick?" Stella asked.

"I can," Gemma said.

"Okay, kid, I'm going to turn this truck around. Then you get behind the wheel and get ready to drive like a bat outta hell away from here if we need a quick getaway."

Gemma grinned and rubbed her hands together. "I've always wanted to be a getaway driver."

"Uh, no offense, Gemma, but can't you drive a stick, Imani?" Karen asked.

"Nope. Zero clue," said Imani. "But don't stress. If Gemma says she can do it—she can do it."

"Hey, I was my parent's designated driver," Gemma said. "I've driven Dad's truck home from a family dinner that included way too many beers for him and way too many white zinfandels for Mom—about a zillion times. I can do it with no problem."

"She drank white zinfandel in front of you?" Stella shuddered. "Child abuse."

While Gemma grinned and Karen sighed and shook her head, Stella quickly turned the truck around, put it into neutral, and motioned for Gemma to get behind the wheel.

"Okay, keep a lookout for us," said Stella.

"I'll do that," said Imani. "I'll stand outside the passenger door and watch and listen. First sign of anything iffy, and we'll be ready to get outta here."

"I'll be in the bed of the truck," said Karen.

"That's fine," Mercury told Karen, "but before you pull the covers over your head, give Imani the rifle." Then she and Stella began to tromp through the calf-deep snow up the little country road.

The crying—high and thin and heartbreaking—got closer and clearer. The two women came to a dirt road completely covered with untouched snow. Facing the paved one-lane was a mailbox shaped like a log cabin. On the side of the green tin roof there were five stick people painted with huge smiles: a mommy, daddy, and three little kids. "The Smythe Family" was written in bold white letters beneath the stick figures.

"Shit," Stella said.

"Fuck," said Mercury.

Side by side, they started up the dirt road. Even broken and battered, the trees in the forest surrounding them were thick. They caught the snow in mounds on splintered trunks and fallen branches. Sound was further muffled up the little lane, so that it seemed the sobbing echoed from everywhere around them.

From out of the snowy landscape, a Subaru SUV materialized. It had smashed against one of the toppled pines and burned so that there was not much left of it but a snow-covered shell. Small tracks led from it back to a raised clearing, in the middle of which was a large, two-story log cabin. Mercury could just make out that a heavily blanketed someone sat on the porch swing—and that someone was crying.

"Shit," Stella repeated as they paused at the SUV. "We gotta look."

"I hate this," Mercury said. "I really, *really* hate this. Did I tell you why I changed my major from a pre-veterinary focus to secondary education?"

"Yep, many times, Acorn. You realized you hated dead things and parasites," said Stella as they stared at the snow-covered wreck together.

"Yet here I am, in the fucking apocalypse, surrounded by dead things."

"Yeah, well, at least there're no parasites," quipped Stella.

"So far." Mercury sighed and stepped forward to peer into the burned vehicle. She quickly turned her gaze away. "I saw two bodies in the front."

"Me too." Stella took a step back. "I'll look in the rear seats." Stella bent and peered through the shattered back window. "Nothing."

"That means the kids are probably at the house," Mercury said.

"Yeah, let's get it over with." Stella started to walk the rest of the way to the cabin, following the small footprints in the snow, but Mercury lagged behind. Stella turned to her. "What?"

"Get what over with?"

"Finding out what we're faced with. You know, how many kids—alive or dead," Stella said. "One's obviously alive. She's crying."

"And we do what with her?"

Stella's brows lifted. "We take her—and any other living kid—with us. Actually, we hope that there's family close by who are alive, so we can take the kid or kids there, but we can't leave them here. Alone."

Mercury nodded and resumed walking beside Stella. "So, we shouldn't stay here?"

Stella glanced at her. "Oh, *that's* why you're giving me that look. Hell, no. Mack and what I suspect is a whole cluster of likeminded douchebags are way too close. Plus, this isn't where we settle. I'm sure of it. When we do settle, it won't be a few yards off a main highway—and that's not just my gut talking. That's common sense."

"Whew. I didn't think we'd be staying, but . . ." Mercury shrugged.

Stella met her gaze. "No. It's absolutely not safe here. Actually, we need to bundle up whoever we find and get the hell outta here ASAP."

"Agreed," Mercury said. "I have a crawly feeling in the back of my neck."

"Yep, intensify that by one hundred, and that's how I feel." She gestured at the snow-covered forest. "Don't let all of this silence fool you. Mack's buddies are close."

Mercury shivered and nodded.

They followed the small tracks to the wide porch that framed the front of the spacious cabin. As Mercury and Stella reached the porch, the sobbing stopped like someone had pressed "Mute." On the swing, held aloft from the ceiling of the porch by spotless, well-oiled chains, was a mound of blankets. In the center of the blankets three little faces peered at them. Each face was blotchy and tear-stained, and the children stared at the two women with wide-eyed fear.

"Hi." Mercury stopped at the bottom of the porch stairs. "I'm Mercury and this is my best friend, Stella." Beside her Stella lifted her hand and waved hello. "We were driving by on that road out there, but our truck couldn't go any farther because trees blocked us. When we got out to see if we could get past the trees, we heard someone—and thought we'd follow the sound and see if we could help."

"Yeah, we're teachers, so we're used to helping kids," added Stella. "What's your name?" she asked the center face, a girl who sat up higher and looked older than the other two children.

The girl cleared her throat and used the blanket to wipe her eyes and nose. "My name is Georgiana, but everyone calls me Georgie. These are my brothers, Jayden and Cayden. They're twins."

"How old are y'all?" asked Mercury.

"I'm eleven. Jaden and Cayden are six." The twins looked up at her, and Georgie sighed before she added. "Okay, yeah. I'm *almost* eleven. Are you really teachers?"

"Yep," said Mercury. "All the way from Tulsa, Oklahoma."

Georgie lifted her chin. "That's like, in the Wild, Wild West, right?"

A smile tugged at Stella's lips. "Right," she said.

"What grade do you teach?" asked Georgie. The boys remained completely silent, but their bright little eyes had returned to looking back and forth from Mercury to Stella.

"High school," said Stella. "I'm an art teacher and Mercury is a science teacher."

"Shouldn't I call you by your last names, like Mrs. Someone or Miss Someone, if you're teachers?" said Georgie.

"Normally, yes," said Mercury. "But we're not at school right now, so it's okay to call us by our first names. Georgie, are your mom and dad home?"

The two little boys, one on either side of Georgie, jolted like Mercury had hit them. Silently, tears started to leak down their cheeks. Georgie lifted the blanket so that she could tuck it more securely around her brothers. She kept her arms draped over their narrow shoulders, like her touch was all that held them together. She met Mercury's gaze without flinching.

"Yes. They're in our car over there." She moved the fingers of one hand off her brother's shoulder long enough to point at the wrecked Subaru. "They've been there since Sunday morning when the bad things started happening." She paused and chewed her lip before she continued. "The twins found them. We—we couldn't get them out of the car 'cause it was burning real, real hot."

"Georgie," Mercury said, "you couldn't have saved them even if you could've gotten them out of there."

"Yeah, I know. Mommy and Daddy went out to get our Sunday morning donuts. They—they didn't really come back."

"Sure they did," Mercury said softly. "They couldn't help what happened, but they absolutely came back to you three." She paused and then added, "There are just three of you?"

Georgie nodded and sniffed.

"Where were you and your brothers when all the bad stuff happened?" Stella asked.

"Upstairs in our bedrooms." Georgie caught Stella's gaze.

"Did you see any green fog-like stuff?" Mercury asked.

Georgie nodded. "Yeah, at first. It was outside, but it didn't get to the upstairs into the house. Then it earthquaked. That was really scary. When everything stopped shaking, the green stuff was gone. That's when we saw our car on fire and ran out to try to help Mommy and Daddy." She paused and had to wipe at her face again. "There were bombs, right? You can tell me the truth. Jayden, Cayden, and I can take it."

"Of course you can. I can already tell how strong the three of you are. And yes, there were bombs. I'm not going to lie to you. Neither is Mercury. Is there anything else you want to ask us?" Stella said.

The little girl nodded slowly. "Is almost everyone out there dead?"

Stella breathed out a long sigh. "Well, a lot of people have died, that's for sure. We can't tell exactly how many because most communication is down."

"Are we having a war?"

"From what we've heard there's no one left to fight us, but that doesn't mean that it's safe out there. Hey, do you have any family that live close? Like grandparents or maybe an aunt or uncle?" Stella asked.

Georgie shook her head. "No. It takes a long time to get to our Meemaw and Peepaw's house in Portland. And Gramps and Gran are even farther away—over by the ocean, with Aunt Gertie and Uncle Sam. They live right next door. It's pretty there. We were there until a little while ago when Daddy finished building our cabin. Daddy builds houses—log houses—he's real good at it, and—" Her words broke off and her brown eyes filled with tears. Her voice dropped to a shaky whisper. "He *was* good at it."

The boys cried harder.

"Hey, Georgie, have you and your brothers eaten recently?" Mercury said.

"I, um, opened all the cans of ravioli Sunday, but it was pretty gross because the electricity is off and the microwave and stove don't work." Georgie sniffled and wiped her face with the blanket. "Yesterday I opened cans of soup and we had crackers. We ate it, but it was gross too. This morning we had cereal, but the milk smelled really bad—like everything else in the fridge. The boys ate all the cheese, but it gave them tummy aches and the poo-poos."

"Well, we have sandwiches already made and ready to eat at our truck—and a camper shell on the back of it, so it's kinda like camping," said Mercury. "How about we go inside and pack bags for each of you, and then you can come with us?"

Georgie narrowed her eyes. "Where?"

"We're going to Madras. Have you ever been there?" Stella asked.

Georgie nodded. "We went to the movies there with Mommy and Daddy."

"Well, that's where we're going," Mercury said. "We think you and your brothers should go with us."

Georgie stared at her so long Mercury thought she wasn't going to answer, but finally the little girl said, "We can't stay here by ourselves."

The little girl didn't frame it as a question, but Stella answered. "No, you can't."

"We could if I was older. I'd stay here and take care of Jayden and Cayden myself."

"You'd do a good job of it too. You've taken care of them by yourself for three days." said Stella. "But now it's time for us to help you."

"Us? Are there more teachers?" Georgie's gaze swept behind them.

"Yeah, there's another science teacher and a history teacher back at the road with our truck. And there's also a teenager with us who just lost her parents too," said Mercury.

Georgie's gaze found her. "We didn't lose our parents. They died."

CHAPTER

22

IMANI WAS PACING back and forth in the snow beside the old Chevy when Mercury and Stella returned. As they emerged from the wall of white, Imani whirled to face them, hands on hips, mouth open to chastise them for taking so long—when her gaze found the silent little boys walking between them, and the stone-faced girl who held their hands.

"Well, hi there!" Imani crouched so that she was at eye level with the kids. "This is a nice surprise. I'm Imani."

"Which kind of teacher are you?" Georgie asked.

"I'm a science teacher," answered Imani.

"Oh my! Hello, children." Karen came from around the rear of the truck.

Gemma stuck her head out of the open driver window. "Hey, can I get out of the cab now?"

"Yeah, but leave the truck running. We're out of here as soon as we settle the kids in the back with something to eat and I fill up the gas tank with this." Stella lifted a full red plastic container that said "Gas" on the side of it, which she'd found in Mr. Smythe's well-organized garage—along with a bow and an arrow-filled quiver she'd slung over her shoulder, three fishing poles and a tackle box Mercury carried, plus a nice selection of hunting and fileting knives.

"So," Mercury said as Gemma joined them, "this is Georgie and her brothers, Jayden and Cayden. Kids, this is Imani, who you've already met. And Karen—she's the history teacher. And Gemma, who is a really excellent doctor."

Georgie studied Gemma. "You're too young to be a doctor."

"Yeah, up until three days ago I woulda said the same thing." Gemma shrugged. "But now I get that age isn't that important."

Georgie nodded slowly. "Like before Sunday I didn't think I'd have to take care of my brothers all by myself."

"Exactly," said Gemma. "But you did, even though people might say you're too young."

"Exactly," Georgie echoed.

"Okay, I'm gonna top off the gas tank, and then let's get back on the road," Stella said.

"While you do that, we'll get Georgie and her brothers settled in the back with sandwiches," Mercury said.

"I'll help," said Gemma. "I totally know all about the sammi-ches." She grinned at Georgie and her brothers.

"Thanks, Gemma," Mercury said. "They brought their favorite things in their backpacks, so be sure to find a special place for them."

"Oh, for sure," Gemma said as she led the kids through the snow to the rear of the truck.

"I'll be there in just a sec," Imani called.

"No problem. Take your time," said Gemma.

Imani and Karen closed in on Stella and Mercury. Stella held up her hand before either woman could say anything "I'll make this fast because, unlike what Gemma just said, we shouldn't take our time. Georgie is ten. The twins, Jayden and Cayden, are six. Mercury, tell them the rest while I dump this gas into our tank so we can get the hell outta here."

Mercury explained, "Their parents are dead inside their wrecked SUV right in front of their house. The kids watched them burn, and the boys haven't spoken since. Georgie said they spoke just fine before that, though."

Imani nodded. "It's called selective mutism. I remember from one of my child development classes. It happens after a major shock, especially to children. They'll probably speak again—when they're ready and they feel safe. We shouldn't force them, though."

"Is there some reason why we're *not* returning to their home to fix them a hot meal and take our time to figure out what to do with them?" Karen asked.

"Yes. Stella says it isn't safe. Plus, we already know what to do with them. According to Georgie, their family was in Portland and on the Oregon Coast. Neither is an option. So now they're our responsibility," said Mercury.

"Poor babies," Imani said. "They've been all alone for three days?"

"Yeah, with their dead parents in a burned-up SUV right outside their front door. No electricity. No communication with the outside world, and running out of food. It's a damn good thing we heard them. Oh, and the reason we did is because all three of them were on the front porch, crying."

"It's so awful," said Imani.

"Yes, of course it is," Karen said. "But how are we supposed to take care of three small children and—"

In the distance from the direction of the highway came the whine of motors—not like the sound of a car or a truck—but something more high pitched and moving fast. The engine sounds carried easily through the silence of the ravaged, snow-covered forest.

"Now!" Stella jogged around the truck with the empty gas container in one hand and Mack's rifle in the other. "We gotta leave *now*!"

"I'll get in the back with the kids and Gemma," Imani said.

"Karen, get in the cab," Stella snapped orders. She handed Mercury the rifle. "I'm assuming you can shoot this?"

"Yep," Mercury said.

"And you're a decent shot with it?" Stella asked.

"More than decent."

"Good. Do you know how many shells it has in it?"

Mercury examined the rifle, silently thanking her dad for teaching her to respect firearms, which included learning to clean and care for a Winchester almost identical to the one in her arms. "It's fully loaded. One in the chamber and five in the cartridge."

"Get in the back. Keep the window to the camper shell raised and the safety off," Stella said. "Now!"

Mercury's stomach roiled as the engine drone got louder. "Fucking snowmobiles."

Karen hurried to the cab as Stella met her best friend's gaze. "Don't question whether you should shoot or not. No second thoughts. If they catch us we'll be Stepford-ed or Handmaid's Taled—or worse."

"Got it," Mercury said. "Just drive and don't worry about me."

"Can't we just stay here? Hide until they've passed?" Karen spoke through the open door.

"When they don't find us on the highway, what do you think their next move will be?" Stella asked while she jogged around the truck to the driver side. "They're from here. They know this area. They know the side roads. They'll start searching them. There is no one to stop them from doing whatever they want to us *except us*. We need to get out of here. Not later today. Not tomorrow. Fucking now!" She caught Mercury's eye before she closed the door to the cab. "Get the kids down. Tell Gemma and Imani to hang on. Mercury, *do not let them catch us*."

Mercury didn't waste time responding. She knew what she had to do. She raced to the rear of the truck, climbed in and pulled the tailgate closed behind her—though she left the rear camper shell window propped open. As the truck retraced the way to the highway, Mercury arranged their backpacks and containers of supplies so that she could sit comfortably just inside the raised tailgate and aim the rifle out the back window. Without looking at the two women behind her or the cowering children, she said, "Imani and Gemma—get the kids down! And then hold on. Stella is going drive as fast as she can."

"What's wrong?" Georgie sounded young and terrified.

Mercury couldn't take time to look at her, but she kept talking as she readied herself to protect them—to not let anyone get to them. "A bad man tried to hurt us not far from here. We got away from him."

"I broke his knee," Gemma said with more than a little satisfaction.

"Yeah, she did. But it seems his friends, who are probably also bad men, have come after us."

"That noise. It's snowmobiles," Imani said.

"More than likely," Mercury agreed as she rested the gun on the tailgate and sighted. She'd been worried earlier that Mack's Winchester had a scope. She understood how accurate that would make his aim. Now she sighted the rifle with an immense sense of relief. Mercury was a good shot—a better than good shot—but she was also in the bed of a truck that bounced and shook and was the opposite of good for her aim. The scope would, hopefully, make up for that.

"Are you going to shoot the bad man?" Georgie asked from behind her.

"I hope not. I don't *want* to shoot anyone," Mercury said. "But I can promise you I won't let any bad men get to us, so if I say cover your ears—do it."

"Okay," Georgie said. "Jayden and Cayden, you heard Mercury. Cover your ears when she tells us to."

The truck reached the highway and Stella didn't hesitate. She turned onto what was left of 26 east and accelerated. The powerful engine of the old Chevy growled, and the newly installed chains clawed the snow. The truck shot forward. Mercury pulled the rifle inside and rested it across her lap as she sat cross-legged and tried to see through the wall of white.

It hadn't stopped snowing since dawn, but in the time that they'd tromped to the cabin, the flakes had changed from lots of big Christmas lace to smaller, more serious frozen drops that pelted everything and effectively whited out the road. Mercury was impressed that Stella could maneuver around the vehicles, fallen rocks, splintered trees, and broken asphalt at their current speed. They drove like that for several minutes without Mercury seeing anything or anyone behind them except abandoned vehicles and forest debris. Her shoulders were beginning to relax as she considered the fact that maybe the snowmobiles they heard were actually picking up wounded Mack, when the pointed front end of a snowmobile materialized through the curtain of snow. A heartbeat later a second one came into view beside the first.

Mercury gripped the rifle, though she didn't lift it yet. Keeping her eyes fixed on the snowmobiles—and the men driving them—she said, "Knock on the window and be sure Stella knows they're right behind us."

Gemma pounded on the window and shouted, "Snowmobiles!" A moment later she shouted to Mercury. "Stella nodded. She knows."

"'Kay, stay down and hold tight," Mercury said.

The snowmobiles drew closer. Mercury didn't know much about them. There really wasn't any use for one in Tulsa—not even on her dad's property—but at last year's teachers' conference at Timberline, she and Stella had gone on a snowmobile excursion, and she was only too aware that they were faster and more easily maneuvered than their truck. As they drew close enough to make out the men's faces,

Mercury could see that the two of them were wearing goggles to protect their eyes—and then she felt like she'd been hit by a jolt of electricity as she recognized the closer of the two.

"Fucking Alvin Rutland!" Mercury ground through her teeth.

He was only yards off their tailgate when Rutland bared his teeth in a feral version of a smile. The stubble on his upper lip was stained red by his perpetual nosebleed. He lifted his hand and pointed a Glock at Mercury. He shouted something and motioned with his weapon for the truck to pull over as he began to edge even closer. The driver of the other snowmobile didn't appear to have a weapon, but he split off to Mercury's left. It was obvious what they were going to do—crowd the truck and threaten them with the gun until they pulled over.

Mercury didn't question her instinct. She didn't hesitate. Stella had been right. There was no damn way she could let Al Rutland catch them. "Cover your ears!" She yelled over the engines, and then, with one smooth movement she lifted the rifle, sighted, and squeezed the trigger.

Rutland was close enough that she saw the shock on his face. His Glock fired immediately, but he'd flinched at her shot and he didn't even hit the truck. Mercury didn't flinch. She took aim again and fired—and even over the ringing in her ears, she heard the whine of the healthy snowmobile engine change to a clanking that sounded like the engine was eating itself. The snowmobile sputtered and slowed. But before it dropped out of sight, Mercury shifted her position and took aim at the second vehicle's engine. Its driver was still staying even with the rear of the truck, but kept glancing over his shoulder at Rutland.

Mercury squeezed the rifle's trigger. The driver jerked the wheel hard to the side, and the snowmobile's outside runner hit debris from a wreck that Stella had narrowly avoided. The front of the little vehicle crumbled and the driver was expelled from his seat and thrown into the car on which the splintered top half of a fallen pine had landed.

Still Mercury didn't relax. She kept the rifle up and ready, reminding herself she now had only three shots left. But no high-pitched engine whine echoed from behind them—and nothing malevolent materialized from the snow.

"Sh-should I tell Stella everything is okay?" Gemma's voice was shaky.

Mercury kept staring behind them. "Not yet. Let's get some distance between us and them first." She continued to keep watch, the rifle resting in her lap, and the end of a blanket Imani draped around her shoulders, as the truck increased the distance between them and the deadly 216 turnoff.

CHAPTER

23

STELLA DIDN'T SLOW until the forest gave way to land that was a lot browner and flatter than the slopes of Mt. Hood. The snow changed with the topography, and the relentless white shifted to beads of stinging ice. The highway widened to a consistent four lanes, though the number of stalled vehicles and clusters of accidents drastically decreased.

The children had devoured several sandwiches from the mountain of them Stella had premade, and were curled together between Imani and Gemma, sleeping so soundly that they didn't so much as twitch when Stella slowed and stopped.

"I'm gonna go to the cab and talk to Stella." Mercury spoke softly so she didn't wake the children.

"I'm coming with you," Imani said.

"I'll stay here in case the kids wake up," whispered Gemma as she opened the lid of the prepacked cooler that was strapped to the side of the truck bed. She pulled out three sandwiches and handed them to Mercury. "You and Stella and Karen didn't get to eat. We still have sandwiches left. Stella made a ton of them."

"Thanks." Mercury took the sandwiches, but before she followed Imani out of the camper shell, she hesitated and turned back to Gemma. "Have you ever shot a rifle?"

"Nope. That's something I need to learn."

Mercury nodded. "Yeah, unfortunately it is. I'm going to leave the rifle here. The safety is on, but don't mess with it."

"Okay, no problem."

"If you hear or see anything weird, knock on the window. I'll leave the camper shell open back here so you have a good view of anything coming up behind us."

"Okay, cool," Gemma said. "But you know Stella wouldn't have stopped if the coast wasn't clear."

"Things change," Mercury said.

"Got it," Gemma said. "I'll knock."

Mercury climbed out of the bed of the truck, closed the tailgate but left the camper shell propped open, and jogged through the sleet to the cab. Karen was scrunched against Stella, with Imani smashed against her to make room for Mercury, who closed the door quickly. She shivered while she handed sandwiches to Karen and Stella.

Stella took hers and lifted it in salute to Mercury. "Girlfriend, you did great!"

"It was Alvin fucking Rutland." Mercury almost spit the words.

"Oh lord!" Karen gasped and clutched her imaginary pearls.

"Holy shit! That had to be who Mack was talking about when he said 'boss man.'" Stella shook her head. "It's what one of his men called him, remember?"

"I do," said Karen. "I'll never forget that whole encounter."

"Who the hell is Alvin Rutland?" Imani asked.

"The misogynist douchebag who tried to take our truck from us before we made it back to Timberline," said Mercury.

"Is he the guy who flew off the snowmobile or the other one?" asked Stella.

"The other one. He wasn't hurt at all," said Mercury.

"That's too bad, but at least Jenny and the rest of them have been warned," said Stella. "And, Acorn, that was some damn fine shooting."

"Actually, it was freakishly fine shooting," Mercury said around a mouthful of sandwich. She swallowed and explained. "I'm a good shot, and I've had a lot of practice hunting with my dad and entering marksmen competitions with him, but the truck was *not* a stable place to shoot from. I shouldn't have made those shots."

"What exactly are you saying?" Imani asked.

"That there could be more about me that's changed than just the fact that my blood can grow things." She gestured at Stella. "Her blood can grow things, but she also *knows* stuff."

"Didn't you say that before the green fog Stella was in touch with her intuition?" Karen asked.

Mercury nodded as Stella answered. "Yeah, I was."

Karen continued. "Well, before the green fog you were already a good shot. You've told us that."

"Yes, that's true," said Mercury.

"So, you think the green fog may enhance abilities we already have," said Imani.

"Yes, I do," answered Karen. "Imani, what were you particularly good at before the fog?"

Imani looked down at her hands. "I was a good mother. I took care of my family. I watched over them and all of the neighborhood kids. My home—" She had to pause, take a deep breath, and clear the tears from her throat before she finished. "My home was the hangout for everyone. Didn't matter about color. Didn't care which church, if any, they attended. Didn't matter whose mom or dad had money or didn't. Everyone was welcome. My family—my neighborhood—were my life."

Mercury covered Imani's hand with hers, and on her left, Karen lifted her hand and placed it over Imani's other one.

"To be such a wonderful mother—such a good nurturer—is a true gift," said Karen softly. "It's one I wish I had."

"I'm so glad you're with us," said Stella. "We need you."

Imani shook off their hands so she could wipe the tears from her cheeks. "Maybe someday, with your help, I'll stop wishing I'd died with them."

"And when you do, that will be another gift," said Karen.

"That's very wise of you," said Imani as she met Karen's gaze. "I was wrong about you before all of this."

Karen's smile was sad. "No, honey. You weren't." She turned her gaze to Mercury. "You didn't aim at the men. Even though one of them was that horrid Rutland person," Karen said. "I commend you for that."

Mercury lifted a shoulder. "No reason to commend me. I don't ever *want* to shoot anyone, but I can tell you, had those shots not worked—not disabled or crashed those snowmobiles—my next two bullets would definitely have been aimed at those men, Rutland first and foremost." She shivered again, this time not from the cold. "I'm pretty sure that second guy is dead. Makes me sick."

"Your sickness is one of the things that separates you—and us—from those monsters," said Imani. She turned to Stella. "Do you know what would've happened if they'd caught us?"

Stella swallowed a bite of her turkey sandwich before she answered. "All I know is what my gut told me, which was that we needed to do anything we could to keep them from catching us." She looked through the streaky, still-swiping windshield wipers at the land that surrounded them. "Out there changed pretty quick. Mercury, pop the glove box and get out the map. Karen's old-timey wristwatch says it's one thirty. I can make better time since we're off that mountain and the highway is a lot less messed up—though I don't know how long that'll last. But we need to see how much farther it is to Madras. After that run-in with Rutland, I want us off this road and tucked into some civilization as quickly as possible."

Karen took out the neatly folded map and spread it across their laps. Before they'd left Timberline, Jenny had highlighted the route from the lodge to Madras, which Mercury gently traced with her finger.

"Thank you, Jenny," she murmured.

"We're right about here." Karen pointed to a spot midway on the section of highway 26 that ran through an area outlined by a brown boundary labeled "Confederated Tribes of the Warm Springs."

"That blue broken line must be the partially dried up river I've seen off that side of the road." She gestured to their left. "And see this little gray line that intersects with 26?"

The three women nodded.

"I believe that's the one-lane road we passed just a short way back."

"You're really good at map reading," said Imani. "All those lines and symbols make zero sense to me. I'm a 'Google-my-route-to-my-favorite-restaurant' kind of a girl."

"It's part of my fascination with history," said Karen. "I've studied lots of maps, especially old ones—like of Lewis and Clark's expedition, which actually wasn't too far from here. I used to dream about being an explorer."

"Is that before or after you wanted to be a dancer?" Mercury asked.

Karen's lips twitched, like she almost wanted to smile. "During. But neither career was appropriate, so I went to school to be a history teacher—though my father would've much preferred if I'd taught something more sensible, like math."

"I think a ballerina explorer is an excellent job choice," said Mercury.

Karen did smile then. "Well, my childhood obsession is certainly coming in handy now—though I'm pretty sure my map-reading skills are more useful than my ability to relevé."

"You might need to dust off your ballet moves," Stella said. "I'm pretty sure you're our prima ballerina."

Karen's eyes sparkled. "Well then, I may consider it. But for now I shall just hone my map skills." She refocused on the map and put her finger on a dot labeled Warm Springs. "According to the map's legend, I can estimate that we're about twenty-ish miles north of this little town, which means . . ." She paused and shifted the map around. "Ah, here it is: Madras is about another fifteen miles from there."

"So, thirty-five miles to go until we're there," said Stella.

"Do you think we can make it before dark?" asked Mercury.

Stella shrugged and swallowed another bite of sandwich. "I'm going to try like hell, but it really depends on whether we run into more creepy men. Also, we haven't gone through a town yet, so we have no clue what we're going to find when we reach Warm Springs." She paused contemplatively before adding, "Karen, can you tell if we can take that little side road around Warm Springs to Madras?"

Karen squinted at the map. "It loops around and crosses the Warm Springs River, but then it looks like it feeds directly into the town."

"And wasn't that just a kinda crappy side road?" Imani said. "This weather and crappy roads do not seem to mix."

Karen nodded. "From the glimpse I got as we drove past, I believe it looked pretty rough—like it was an old state highway in disrepair. We are on reservation land, which means poorly maintained roads and schools. The only thing well maintained would be poverty." She shook her head in disgust. "As if pushing Indigenous people off their ancestral lands isn't bad enough."

"Karen, you sound awfully liberal," quipped Mercury.

Karen didn't even look up from the map. "That's not being liberal. That's just being a decent human being. And I agree with Imani. Taking a side road we don't know in this weather isn't a good idea."

"Okay, then we stay on 26 to Warm Springs and hope for the best. We'll revisit the side road thing if the highway gets dicey," said Stella. "Y'all agree?"

The three women nodded, then Imani sighed. "I hope we're done with the crazies. Those poor kids have been through enough."

As if on cue, Gemma rapped hard against the rear window. The four women jumped and then turned quickly to see the teenager gesturing wildly at the open camper shell as she mouthed, *"FOG!"*

"Oh shit!" Imani said. "Fucking green fog!"

The breeze had picked up as they'd come off the mountain, until it'd become a pretty decent tailwind. And now in that wind they could clearly see emerald green. It hugged the ground, but was definitely being pushed forward toward them.

"Time to go!" said Stella.

"I'm going to stay up front." Mercury opened the passenger door and braced herself against the stinging rain.

"I'll get in the back with the kids," said Karen. "Imani, you coming with me?"

"Yeah, coming!"

As Imani got out of the cab, Mercury snagged her arm. "I left the rifle back there. It's loaded, but the safety is on."

Imani nodded. "Want me to bring it to you?"

"Can you shoot it?"

Imani shook her head. "I could shoot the pistol, but I have no idea what to do with that long gun."

"Rifle," Mercury said. "Yeah, bring it up here."

"Fast!" said Stella.

"Will do!" Imani sprinted to the back of the truck.

"Is that green crap going to chase us the whole way to Madras?" Mercury asked.

"No clue," said Stella as she drummed her fingers impatiently against the wheel. "But the wind definitely isn't blowing forty miles per hour, which is the pace I'm going to try to keep between here and there."

Gemma appeared, carefully carrying the rifle. "Imani said to bring this to you. Is it okay if I take a turn up here?"

"Yeah, yeah, get in kid!" Stella grumped.

Mercury double-checked the safety on the rifle, put it carefully behind the seat, and then slid to the center of the bench so that

Gemma got in beside her and closed the door. Stella immediately put the truck into gear and accelerated.

"Hey, you know this rain isn't just rain, right?" Gemma looked around Mercury to Stella. "It's ice rain. That means it's slick."

Stella snorted a laugh as Mercury chuckled softly.

Gemma frowned at them "Why are you two laughing at that? I'm, like, *super* nervous about it."

"We're from Oklahoma," said Stella, as if that explained it.

Mercury added, "Winter in Oklahoma gives us a break from ticks, fleas, snakes, and tornadoes. In exchange, we are blessed with freezing rain and all-out ice storms. You learn to drive on roads that are, as my dad would say, *"slick as snot,"* or you stay home most of the winter."

"Oh, good. That makes me feel better. You two don't seem like the stay-at-home types," said Gemma.

"Like I said before—you're a smart kid," said Stella. "Now, keep watch for any more green fog."

"Or people. Living people," Mercury said.

"I can see the fog in the side mirror," Gemma said as she peered outside the truck. "It's way back there now."

"I'm not worried about *that* green fog," said Stella.

"What? There's going to be more?" Mercury stared at her best friend.

"Yep, Acorn. I think so. And I don't think next time it's going to be so easy to get rid of."

Mercury blew out a long sigh. "Shit."

CHAPTER

24

STELLA WAS ABLE to maintain her forty miles per hour goal over the next several miles. The freezing rain had changed almost completely to regular rain, which pattered against the hood of the old truck with the comforting familiarity of rain on a tin roof. But with the smoke-darkened sky and dusk getting closer and closer, visibility was poor—though good enough to see that the land around them was sparsely populated. There were some homes near the highway, but the only movement around them was farm animals—mostly goats. Fires were visible, close to the highway and distant, though the rain had reduced the majority of them to smoking skeletons.

Throughout the entire area, they glimpsed pockets of green. It tended to rest close to the ground, but once it got rolling and the wind caught it, the fog lifted and curled and drifted—almost as if it was sentient. Twice it covered the road. Stella sped through it, and the fog scattered and billowed in their wake like they were a boat cutting through a river of green.

Gradually, from the rain-soaked, smoke-ravaged landscape, canyons and huge gulches began to appear, like oasis dreams in a desert. There was a stark, raw beauty to the land that intrigued Mercury. The brownness with scrub, sagebrush, and twisted juniper trees reminded her of parts of Oklahoma, which alternatively made her feel at home and made her heart ache.

They only saw one other living person. A woman sat on the porch of a rundown ranch-style home that had been built close to the road. A tin roof protected her from the rain. She was wrapped in a coat several sizes too big. Goats climbed the porch around her. She stood and held a rifle in her arms as she eyed their passing truck.

"I'm not stopping," said Stella.

"You won't get an argument from me," said Mercury.

"Me either," added Gemma. "Gotta figure if someone greets you with a gun—it's not gonna be a friendly meeting."

"Good point," said Stella.

Gemma sighed as she stared out the window. "I hope we don't have to camp out here tonight."

"Us too, kid," Stella said.

"I've been thinking about that Rutland guy," said Gemma. "I wonder why he isn't dead."

"Huh?" Mercury turned to face the teenager.

"Yeah, uh, he had a nose bleed three days ago. It killed Bob in a day. I just wonder why it didn't kill Rutland."

"I hadn't thought about that, but I did see blood below his nose, so he still has the nosebleed. Your spidey senses tell you anything about that?" Mercury asked her friend.

Stella paused before she sighed and shook her head. "Nope. Other than common sense—that we have no idea what the green fog actually is, so it's tough to even hypothesize about what it does to us, or how fast."

"I have a guess," said Gemma.

"Let's hear it, kid," said Stella.

"I'll bet it has something to do with how much green stuff they were exposed to—and might also be affected by other conditions they had. Like, Bob was a super sweet guy, but he also had diabetes."

"Really?" Mercury said.

"Yep. He told me that while I was doctoring him. And, not to be mean because, like I said, Bob was a nice guy, but he was also pretty chubby. I remember Rutland. He looked like he was in super good shape, which doesn't always mean anything, but . . ." She shrugged. "In AP chemistry, just before spring break we learned about viral loads. That's, um, well, how much of the particles of a virus a person has to breathe in, or come in contact with if it's not airborne, to make that person sick. Remember that big Winnebago that was crashed next to where you found mom and me?"

"Yeah, your mom said Rutland and his people hunkered down against it when the second blast hit," said Mercury.

"So maybe Rutland and his men were shielded from enough of the green stuff that it's kept him—and them—from dying," said Gemma. "Todd and Jason—the guys in the Winnebago—weren't so lucky. They were inside and passed out when the green stuff hit, but the green fog was inside with them. They definitely breathed in more of it than Rutland, which is why they died sooner."

"That does make sense," said Stella.

Mercury nodded. "Yeah, it does. Here's hoping Rutland breathed in enough of it to eventually kill him. Our new world doesn't need men like him. Our old one had enough of them."

"Agreed" said Stella.

"Not possible now, of course, but I'd love to see a scientific study on it," said Mercury.

Gemma nodded and then folded her hands in her lap. "Um, can I ask something?"

"Sure. Anything," said Mercury.

"When we get to Madras, can I stay with you guys?"

Stella glanced away from the road for a moment. "Well, yeah. Of course."

Mercury nodded and echoed her friend. "Yeah. You can stay with us as long as you want."

"Even though you think you're probably gonna leave Madras?" Gemma studied both of the women. "I mean, I know I'm a kid, which can be a pain in the ass for you, but I want you to know right now that, no matter what, I want to be with you guys. Even if it looks like it'd be a better choice to leave me at Madras."

"We've already told you that you're not a pain in the ass. And better choice for whom?" said Stella, her eyes back on the road as she slowed and steered around two stalled trucks and an SUV on its side.

"Me. Well, *or* you guys."

"It's not better for us to leave you somewhere, and if you want to stay with us, then that's the best choice for you," said Mercury firmly. "You're one of us now. Plus, Imani would be really pissed."

Gemma grinned. "She's a mama bear." Then her smile slid from her face. "But, um, what if whoever is in charge of Madras says I should stay?"

"No one in Madras is the boss of us," said Mercury.

"And no one will take you away from us." Stella sighed. "We won't let anyone take those kids in the back away from us either. Not if they want to stay with us."

"Shit," said Mercury.

"Right?" said Gemma, her grin returning. "I told you kids are a pain in the ass."

"*Little* kids are a pain in the ass," countered Mercury. "You're a teenager. We're used to your particular brand of ass pain."

The rapping on the rear window made them jump.

"Shit! I wish we had a better system for that," said Mercury as she turned to look behind them. "Every damn time I almost pee myself."

Imani shouted through the panes of glass. "The kids have to go potty!"

Mercury nodded and gave her the thumbs-up sign. She turned around. "Did you hear that?"

"Yep," Stella said. "I'll find a place. I'm pretty sure we're close to Warm Springs, so it's a good idea to stop before we have to deal with whatever as I do my best to speed through that town."

"I gotta pee too. Like, bad," said Gemma.

Mercury raised her brow. "For how long?"

Gemma shrugged a shoulder. "Awhile."

"Next time only hold it if we're fleeing for our lives," said Mercury. "The last thing any of us needs is to deal with a UTI."

Stella shuddered. "The scourge of womanhood."

"Seriously," muttered Mercury.

"Oh, hey! That looks like a river ahead!" Gemma pointed to the left side of the road.

"Good eyes, kid," said Stella. "And the rain has finally let up. We can stop by the river so everyone can wash their hands and whatnot before we head out."

Stella pulled to the side of the road in an area clear of stalled cars. There were no homes anywhere around them, and as they sat in the cab studying the land, they could see no movement except scrub and junipers swaying in the breeze. The highway was above what, upon closer inspection, looked more like a deep gulch that was swollen with rain than a true river, though they could see a rickety wooden bridge several yards away, perched over the rapidly moving water.

"Does anyone see any green fog?" Stella asked as she rolled down her window and peered through the gloom.

"I don't," said Gemma.

"Neither do I. What does your gut tell you?" Mercury asked.

"That we should stop here. That's it. Right now I can't tell if it's *me* worried about the green stuff and bands of marauding assholes, or my intuition."

Mercury scanned the area around them as she spoke. "I say let's all get out, have a bathroom break, confer with Karen about where we are, let the kids stretch their legs, and then head into the last stretch without stopping."

"My gut says that's a decent plan," said Stella.

They climbed out of the cab and went to the rear of the truck to let down the tailgate and lift the camper shell window. Karen crawled stiffly out of the bed of the truck, with Imani and the three kids following closely.

"'Kay, huddle up for a sec," Mercury said, and the small group clustered around her. The twins held their sister's hand and remained silent, though they didn't look as wan as they had when she and Stella had plucked them from their porch. All three kids, as well as Gemma, gravitated to Imani, which didn't surprise Mercury at all. "So, we'll stop here to go to the bathroom and whatever else you need to do." She pointed down at the river. It flowed well below the level of the road, and the current moved so quickly that white caps lifted around boulders and hunks of dead trees. The steep bank that framed it gave way to a wide, rocky shoreline. Just a few yards to their left was a small cluster of junipers and shorter, gnarly-looking vegetation Mercury thought might be sagebrush. "You can have some privacy over there by the junipers, but y'all need to listen up: *Be vigilant.*" She paused when Georgie raised her hand. Mercury called on the girl. "Georgie?"

"Jayden and Cayden don't know what that means."

"Oh, sorry." She smiled at the silent boys. "It just means not to get distracted. Keep an eye on what's going on around you."

"Like, in case there are more bad men?" asked Georgie.

"There are no bad men close to us right now," said Stella.

Mercury nodded. "If Stella says that, you can be sure it's true. What we're mostly worried about is the green fog. You know it's dangerous, right?"

Georgie nodded somberly.

Mercury drew a deep breath before she continued. "So, you and Jayden and Cayden understand how important it is to stay on the lookout for it, right?"

Georgie nodded again and the boys mimicked her.

"Do not let it touch you," said Stella. "If you see any, get away from it as fast as you can, and holler for help."

The kids stared from Stella to Mercury with wide, frightened eyes.

"Hey, I have to pee. How about I go with you three down to the river?" Gemma made a show of squinting her eyes and peering at the bank. "I see some crazy big boulders down there. We could each potty behind one—no problem."

"That sounds like a great idea," said Imani. "I'm going to talk to Mercury and Stella for a sec, then I'll join you down by the river. It'll feel good to walk around a little. Jayden and Cayden, I'd love for you to help me with one of my favorite hobbies. Can you two guess what that could be?"

The boys didn't say anything, but their eyes brightened as their gazes lifted from scanning the riverbank to Imani. Slowly, both shook their heads.

"I collect heart rocks!" Imani said with a grin. "And you two are the perfect height to make sure I don't miss any. Plus, I'm a science teacher, and I can tell you what the rocks are made of and maybe even how old they might be."

"Oh, they'd like that," said Georgie.

"Then it's a date! Gemma, I'll be down there soon. Oh, and here." Imani reached inside the open tailgate, grabbed a roll of toilet paper, and tossed it to Gemma. "Don't forget this."

"Got it!" Gemma tucked the roll under her arm and led the three kids to the incline. She helped them down, and then they made their way to the bank. Gemma slid down it first, then turned and lifted each of the three kids down.

"She's a really good girl," said Imani as they watched the four young ones walk over big, round rocks as they headed to the river.

"Yeah, she's a keeper," said Stella. "Ladies, I have a prickly feeling about Warm Springs *and* Madras."

Mercury's brows went up. "Should we not go to Madras?"

"I still believe we have to, especially knowing Rutland and his goons are somewhere behind us, but I don't think we'll be staying long. No, my prickly feeling says that we need to gas up, drive fast through Warm Springs, and then—somewhere close but still outside Madras city center—hide the truck and walk the rest of the way."

"Stella, we have three children with us." Karen picked at the hem of her cardigan. "They cannot walk miles."

"I don't mean *miles*. We can hide the truck inside the city limits somewhere. But I know *for sure* we should not drive it very far into Madras."

"Then we won't. We'll hide it. And we'll carry the boys if we have to. They're small and skinny. They can't weigh much," said Mercury.

"I still wish we didn't have to walk." Karen's lips pressed into a line.

"We all wish that," said Stella. "But we can't chance losing this truck."

Karen sighed. "Do you know *why* you don't think we're staying in Madras? Didn't that truck driver—"

"Sim," Mercury said.

"Yes, Sim. Didn't he say that Madras is governed by a woman? Surely we'd be safe there with her," said Karen.

"Then stay there," said Imani, though not unkindly. "I'm doing what Stella says. Period."

"I'm not saying I won't do what she says." Karen put her hands on her round hips. "I was just asking why."

Stella shrugged. "Karen, I've told you everything I know. I've only had this superhero intuition thing for three days. I don't know how it works. It's telling me that Madras is questionable, though exactly what that means I don't know. It might be as simple as it's just not the right fit for us, which doesn't have to mean it's a den of inequity. Imani is right. If you want to stay in Madras we won't stop you. Just because it's not right for all of us, doesn't mean it's not a good fit for you."

"I don't want to be separated from the rest of you," Karen said softly.

"Then don't be," said Mercury. "But you need to understand it's your choice to make—just like it's our choice to leave."

"I have to pee," said Stella. "But first I'd like Karen to check out the map and try to figure out exactly how far from Warm Springs we are. We should leave the truck with a full tank, and I need to know if I should fill up at the next car we see or if it can wait until we're through the town."

"Yes, okay, I can definitely help with that," said Karen. "I would imagine we're very close to Warm Springs, but I'll check the map and see if I can figure out our exact location." She headed to the cab to retrieve the map as Mercury stretched mightily with a quick yoga sun salutation.

"Hey, I'm gonna go down to the river with the kids," said Imani. "Unless you need me up here?"

"No, go ahead," said Stella. "Actually, Mercury, you can go too. I'll do the map stuff with Karen and then pee over there behind a bush or whatever." She nodded at some scrub bushes roadside.

"Okay then, heading down. You coming Acorn?" Imani slid down the incline from the highway and grinned cheekily up at her.

Mercury frowned at Stella. "Look what you've done. The Acorn thing is spreading."

"I hold your dad responsible," said Stella. "He started it."

Mercury had just turned to follow Imani down the incline when a terrified scream echoed up from the riverside. Her gaze shot to the bank. One of the twins was standing close to Georgie and Gemma, at the edge of the water. He'd turned toward the clump of junipers several yards to their left and was pointing as he screamed again.

Mercury followed his finger to see that the other boy had climbed up on a boulder and appeared to be frozen as he stared down at the base of the rock where green fog lapped against it like emerald water.

CHAPTER 25

TIME BLURRED FOR Mercury. The twin who had screamed sprinted toward his brother—and the green fog that was lazily rolling with the wind along the riverbank toward him.

"Gemma! Stop him!" Mercury shouted.

As Gemma raced after the boy, Georgie slipped on a wet rock. Her arms windmilled as she tried to get her balance. Then, with a cry of terror, she fell backward into the raging water. Her head went under the whitecaps.

"Georgie!" Imani shrieked.

Mercury hurled herself down the incline and sprinted past Imani. As she did, she shouted to her friend. "Stay on top of the bank! Gemma and I will get the kids and hand them up to you."

Mercury moved faster than she ever had in her life. She leaped down the bank, assessing the situation as she ran. Gemma was struggling with one twin, who was kicking and screaming and trying to get away to go to his brother. Georgie's head surfaced. The current had already pulled her into the middle of the river and was carrying her past them. She sputtered, coughed, and then cried for help. The second twin was still frozen on the boulder.

The wind continued to push the green fog toward them.

"I'll get the girl! Save the boy!" The shout came from across the river where a man had thrown off a huge backpack and was sprinting into the water. He dived in and surfaced fast. "Hold onto that rock!

I'm coming!" With powerful strokes he closed the distance between himself and Georgie.

The rapid current had carried Georgie to a cluster of rock and tree debris, and she managed to pull herself up a little way out of the churning water, where she clung precariously to a craggy boulder as the man swam toward her.

As much as she wanted to, Mercury couldn't save all of them by herself. She had to trust the man if she was going to get to the twin perched on the boulder, now an island in the middle of the expanding sea of green fog.

She reached Gemma, who was still struggling with the kicking, screaming boy. Mercury paused only long enough to grab the kid's shoulder and turn him to face her. "Enough! You're not helping! Go with Gemma. I'll get your brother. Now!"

The kid's face was covered with tears and snot and dirt, but he nodded shakily and went limp in Gemma's arms. Mercury met Gemma's frightened gaze. "I don't know whether we have to breathe in the green crap to be affected by it or not, but here's hoping it can't hurt us unless we do. Carry him to the bank! Keep him above the fog! Imani will grab him! Run Gemma!"

She didn't wait for Gemma's response, but turned to see the twin who was still frozen on the boulder. His face was bloodlessly white. Even from a distance his big brown eyes looked glassy with shock.

Mercury had zero clue which twin it was, but with a fifty–fifty shot at getting it right, she called, "Cayden!"

The boy looked up from staring at the green fog. He blinked several times but finally focused on her.

"Do *not* move! When I get there, I'm going to turn my back to you. Climb on my shoulders. You'll be fine up there. The fog can't get you." Mercury desperately hoped she was right about that. "Do you understand?"

The little boy nodded shakily.

Fear roiled in Mercury's stomach. The fog was only inches from her. It hugged the rocky riverbank in swirling eddies that lifted about to her thighs, maybe her waist. She looked at the boy again. His eyes were trapped on her. Tears leaked from them, and he had wrapped his arms around his narrow chest like he was trying to hold himself together.

Mercury closed her mind to the memory of Amelia, Mr. Hale, and Coach Davis; Todd and Jason; Bob and Sim bleeding out because that green crap had taken them.

I believe I'm going to be okay. I'm not going to breathe it in. I'll grab the kid and get out us out of there.

Mercury sprinted forward, slipping and sliding on rain-slick rocks. The swirling fog parted, as if welcoming her, and then it lapped around her legs and waist. Mercury ignored it. She kept her gaze locked on the boy. She reached the boulder, turned her back to Cayden, and crouched just low enough for him to climb awkwardly onto her shoulders.

"Hang on!" Mercury couldn't sprint back. The fog now blanketed the entire riverside, completely obscuring the rocky ground. She was too afraid she'd slip and the boy would fall from her shoulders. She had to walk slowly, carefully instead. Her gaze darted to the river, where the man had reached Georgie and was talking to her. Georgie had stopped sobbing and nodded as she clung, monkey-like, to his back.

Mercury looked from the river to the steep bank where Imani, Stella, and Karen urged them on, waiting to lift up the other twin and Gemma. She hadn't been able to get the boy up to her shoulders, so Gemma carried him half in her arms, half over one shoulder to keep him above the fog that billowed around her waist. Like Mercury, she couldn't move quickly, but had to pick her way blindly over the slick, wet rocks.

Mercury increased her strides. Her long legs brought her closer and closer to Gemma until she reached the bank just behind the teen.

"Here! Take Cayden!" Mercury leaned forward as Stella and Karen grabbed Cayden and pulled him up off her shoulders. Mercury turned quickly to help Gemma, whose arms were shaking with the effort it took to hold the boy above the green tide.

"I'm—I'm gonna drop him!" Gemma panted.

"Got him!" Mercury hooked her hands under his arms and lifted Jayden, who felt like he weighed nothing, from Gemma up to Imani. "Now you!" Mercury turned back to Gemma and took a firm hold under the teen's elbow.

"Reach for my hand! I'll pull you up!" Stella stretched her arm down as far as she could—hand open to grab Gemma's.

Gemma nodded.

"On three, start scrambling up there," Mercury said. "One, two, *three*!"

Gemma's hands clawed at the vertical wall of dirt and rock and exposed roots while Mercury tried to boost her up without bending down for leverage because the pernicious green had risen with their movements and wisps of it were twisting up their chests. Gemma lifted one hand from its clawlike hold on the bank to reach for Stella, and the root where she'd wedged the toe of her shoe snapped. Stella tried to snag her hand, but Gemma couldn't reach her, and the teen toppled backward, taking Mercury with her to the ground.

Mercury was too shocked to hold her breath. As the fog closed over their heads and they fell to the rocky shore, she breathed in the green. Even as Mercury reached out for Gemma and tried to struggle to her feet and lift the girl with her, the scent of pine and earth, grass and wildflowers filled her nose. The fog sizzled through her body and with a strange detachment Mercury thought, *Gemma was right—it feels like bee stings under my skin.* Then her vision tunneled as someone's hands touched her shoulders and then grabbed onto her arm before her emerald world went black.

"Mercury Elizabeth Rhodes, don't you dare fucking die on me!"

Stella's voice penetrated the blackness. Mercury drew in a deep breath and sat up as she coughed and coughed. Her eyes began to frantically scan her surroundings even before her vision had cleared.

"Gemma!" she croaked. "The kids!"

Stella was on her knees beside her. "The kids are safe. Gemma is right there next to you. She's breathing."

"Bleeding?!" Mercury's insides heaved.

"No! *Breathing.* Jesus Christ, relax. Just breathe in and out. I will kill you if you die."

Mercury didn't lie back down. Instead, she slowed her breathing and blinked her vision clear. Just as everything stopped looking like she was peering at it through a blurry fishbowl, beside her Gemma moaned and her eyelids fluttered. Karen put her hand on Gemma's shoulder. "You're okay. Just take it easy."

Gemma rubbed at her eyes, and then her gaze found Mercury sitting beside her. "We aren't dead?"

"I don't think so," said Mercury.

Gemma started to struggle up. "Georgie? The boys?"

"They're fine. Everyone is fine," Stella said. "Look." She pointed up behind them. Mercury, Gemma, Karen, and Stella were just below the incline, above which was the road and their truck.

Mercury's gaze followed her finger to see the two boys sitting on the open tailgate of the truck with their sister, wrapped in a blanket, between them. Imani was cleaning a bleeding wound on the forehead of the guy who had jumped in the river after Georgie.

"He's hurt," said Gemma. "I need to look at his head. He may need stitches." She started to get to her feet, but Stella jumped up from between them and pressed her shoulders down so that she had to sit.

"How about we be sure you're okay before you go doctor someone else?"

Gemma smoothed her long, tangled hair back from her face and looked at Stella. "I'm fine. Let me stand up and I'll show you."

Stella took her hands off the girl's shoulders, and Gemma stood without even a wobble. She looked down at Mercury and said, "Do you feel like anything is broken inside?"

Mercury did a quick internal check before she answered. "Nope. I feel pretty good actually."

"Well then, come on. If I'm fine, you're fine." Gemma paused at the incline. "Who got us out of that green stuff?"

"All three of us," Stella said. "Imani, Karen, and me. I got on my belly and reached down into that mess to grab each of you, and Imani and Karen anchored me, then pulled me up."

"Did you breathe any of it in?" asked Gemma.

"Nope. It stopped drifting up, and I could reach y'all without sticking my face into it." She jerked her chin down at the riverbank. "Then it spread out and kinda floated around down there."

Mercury looked at the riverbank that was blanketed with green. It had spread out all along the water, but it looked like it was only a few inches deep.

"Well, thanks for grabbing us," said Gemma before she scrambled up the incline and headed to the truck.

"I'm going to stand up now." Mercury eyeballed Stella. "You going to let me?"

Stella held her hands up, palms out. "Absolutely. You're alive, so I'm fine with you falling on your ass."

"Well, at least now we know that crap has to be breathed in to affect us."

"You didn't feel anything when it was lapping around you?"

"Nope. Nothing." Mercury stood and was surprised at how great she felt. The bee sting sensation was gone. The disorientation was gone. And her vision was completely clear. She glanced up at the truck, where Gemma was already inspecting the man's wounds.

"What happened to him?" Mercury asked.

"While Georgie was being a monkey on his back, he swam with the current downstream until they were past the green crap. Then he cut to the shore, and as he did, a log broke free from a pile of tree debris and a bunch of other nasty-looking stuff. It should've knocked Georgie off his back, but somehow he managed to spin around and instead of it hitting the kid, the edge of a log smacked his head. For a moment I thought they were both going to drown, but he got them to shore before he collapsed."

"How bad is he hurt?" Mercury asked.

"He probably needs stitches and for sure should be watched. I wouldn't be surprised if he has a concussion. He puked his guts up after he crawled to shore, and he's been pretty dizzy."

"The boys are really okay, right?" Mercury's gaze met Stella's. "No coughing? No bloody noses?"

Stella shook her head. "Nope. They're freaked out but physically seem fine. Georgie is waterlogged and exhausted, but she's fine too. What about you? What'd you feel before you passed out?"

"It was like the first time. The green stuff smelled like trees and dirt and stuff, and it burned like crazy—and then everything went black."

Stella wiped a shaky hand across her face. "I thought you were gone. I thought I'd lost you."

Mercury pulled Stella into a tight hug. "Not a chance." When she finally released her best friend she continued. "Guess I should meet our new guy."

"Our?" Stella's brows lifted.

"Just a figure of speech. But if he has a concussion because he saved Georgie, it's not like we can just leave him on the side of the road. Or can we? What's your superpower tell you about him?"

Stella cocked her head to the side as she looked up at the man. "He's one of the good guys."

Mercury rolled her eyes. "From what we've seen he could be one of the *only* good guys out here."

"Yup," said Stella. "Want me to boost you up that incline?"

"Nah, I've got it." With ease Mercury reached up, grabbed the lip of the incline, and almost without touching the steep side of it, she was up over the edge, standing on the side of the road, brushing her hands on her jeans. Then she looked down, saw Stella struggling, and grabbed her wrist and pulled her up so that she stood beside her.

Stella stared at Mercury.

"What?"

"You're strong," Stella said.

"Well, yeah, you know I work out." Mercury shrugged. "I like free weights."

"You were fast down there," Stella added.

"Adrenaline," said Mercury.

"We'll see," said Stella.

Mercury looped her arm through her best friend's. "Don't be a crazy person. I'm just me."

Stella snorted but didn't say anything else.

CHAPTER

26

TOGETHER THE TWO women walked to the mini-clinic Gemma was setting up at the rear of the truck. The kids had scooted over so that the wounded man could sit on the end of the tailgate with them. Gemma had the first aid kit she and Dr. Hilary had put together by loading a fancy tackle box from Timberline's boutique with whatever the lodge could spare and Hilary thought they might need—which included needles and suture thread as well as alcohol, painkillers, bandages, and a very few precious antibiotics.

Mercury rounded the truck, where she finally got a good look at the man who had saved Georgie. He was holding a square of bloody gauze against a gash in the side of his forehead.

"Ah, found it!" Gemma pulled out a tube of something with a victorious grin.

"What is it?" the man asked.

"You'll be happy to hear it's lidocaine," Gemma said.

"So, you have to stitch this up?" he asked her.

"Only if you want it to heal right," said Gemma.

He paused and then flashed straight white teeth at the girl. "You're right. I'm happy it's lidocaine."

Mercury had to cough to cover a laugh, which had the man turning his attention to her. *He has a nice face . . .* His hair was dark sable, with just a hint of silver around his temples. It was long—past his shoulders. It'd been tied back, but most of it had escaped the leather-wrapped band so that it hung in damp clumps he'd pushed behind his ears. His eyes were rich, golden amber, much like his melanin-kissed skin. His full lips, framed by a closely shorn salt and pepper goatee and beard, lifted at the edges as one of the twins jumped off the tailgate and hurled himself at Mercury. The boy wrapped his arms around her waist and stared up at her adoringly.

"Hi there, uh, Cayden?" Mercury glanced at Georgie, who grinned at her and nodded. "Glad to see you're okay."

The boy's grip on her tightened. Mercury ran her fingers through his corn silk hair. "And I'm okay too."

His eyes filled with tears, which he blinked rapidly to try to keep them from overflowing. Mercury untangled his arms from around her waist and crouched in front of him. "I'm really okay. Look at me." She stood and turned in a slow circle before crouching back before him. "See? Totally fine."

His chin quivered and a tear escaped his eyes. He didn't need to talk; she read the guilt in his gaze and pulled him into her arms so that his little head rested against her shoulder as his back shook with his sobs. Mercury thought her heart would melt inside her chest. She held him tightly and murmured over and over, "I'm okay. The fog isn't your fault. None of this is your fault. I'm okay."

When Cayden finally stopped crying, Imani handed her a few squares of toilet paper, and Mercury cleaned off his face and told him, "Blow." Then she smiled at the boy. "You were very brave. You did exactly what I asked you to do. I'm really proud of you."

Cayden's soft little post-crying hiccups and the way his eyes never left her made Mercury feel like she was queen of the world.

"Come on—I need to meet the man who saved your sister." Mercury took his hand and led him to the tailgate. She lifted him and set him back beside Georgie before she turned to the man. "Hi, I'm Mercury Rhodes," she said, holding out her hand.

He enfolded her hand in his, which was strong and warm and calloused. A smile hovered in his eyes. "Nice to meet you. I'm Oxford Diaz, but most people call me Ford." Then he winced as Gemma took the gauze from him, blotted the gash in his forehead, and began applying lidocaine as close to the laceration as possible.

"Hold still," Gemma said. "I'm technically not supposed to use this on an open wound, but Doc Hilary told me in a pinch I can spread it as close to the suture site as possible, and it'll help with at least some of the pain."

"Some relief is better than none." He didn't take his resin gaze from Mercury. "So, the green stuff doesn't kill people every time it touches them."

"What we've discovered is yes and no," Mercury said. "It doesn't kill women. So far, though, we're pretty sure it does kill every male who breathes it in—though not always right away."

"Well, then, I'm glad you saved the boys," he said.

"And I'm glad you saved Georgie," said Mercury.

Imani turned Georgie so she could towel dry and comb out her long hair. "We're all glad you saved her."

"I was lucky that I was there," he said and flashed a wide grin at the girl. "Right, *pequeña dama*?"

"Sí!" said Georgie. She sat up a little straighter and announced, "I went to a Spanish immersion school when we lived with Gramps and Gran." The girl looked at Ford. "But your accent is different from my teacher's."

"Where was your teacher from, *niñita*?"

"Mexico City," said Georgie proudly.

"Ah. I'm from here, but my grandparents were born in Puerto Rico, and when I speak Spanish, I speak it with their accent."

"Okay, just sit there for a few minutes and let the lidocaine do its thing, and then I'll sew you up," said Gemma. She studied Ford for a moment and then added, "And thanks for not freaking and saying I'm too young to doctor you."

"Oh, there is no doubt you're a healer," Ford told her.

"Why do you say that?" asked Stella.

Ford lifted his broad shoulders. "My mother is a nurse. Gemma's touch reminds me of hers."

"Nurses are awesome," said Gemma. "That's a massive compliment."

"Do you mind me asking where your family is?" Mercury said.

"Not at all. They're at our annual family reunion in Puerto Rico. I was supposed to join them yesterday." His gaze slid to the horizon. "I must hope that whoever did this to us forgot about Puerto Rico."

"Hey, Ford," Georgie waved a hand at him to get his attention. "Did you know some people don't even understand that Puerto Ricans are US citizens?"

Ford's lips lifted again. "Yes, *niñita*, I do know that."

"Well, maybe the bad guys *don't* know and your family is okay." Georgie crossed her arms over her chest and nodded as if she'd just solved all the problems of the world.

"That is exactly what I pray for," said Ford.

"Are you Christian?" Karen's head popped out of the back of the truck like someone had called her name.

"I was raised a Catholic who genuflects on autopilot," said Ford. "But I'm more of an agnostic—or maybe just a worshipper of nature."

Mercury grinned internally as Karen disappeared back inside the truck.

Ford sucked in a sharp breath when Gemma stuck the needle through one edge of the laceration. Without looking away from the wound she was stitching Gemma said, "Keep talking, Ford. It'll help take your mind off what I'm doing. Just don't move, or I may stab you in the wrong place."

Ford's gaze returned to Mercury. "Mercury . . ." Ford said. "That's an unusual name."

"So's Oxford. Is that where you were born?" Mercury asked.

"Nope. My parents went to England on their honeymoon. And by naming me Oxford, forevermore all of my friends and acquaintances know that's where I was made. Not a big deal now, but very much not cool when I was a kid. What about you?"

Stella spoke before she could. "Her name is Mercury Elizabeth Rhodes. Her nice but nutty parents loved queens."

Mercury grinned at Stella. "'Nice but nutty' is a great way to describe them." She turned her attention back to Oxford. "So, what are you doing out here by yourself?"

"Backpack camping. I always take a solo trip during spring break."

"Holy shit, don't tell me you're another teacher," said Stella.

"No, I'm an electrician, but I block out at least a week every spring, summer, and fall to backpack and camp. I've been exploring Oregon for decades like that. It keeps me grounded. Are all of you teachers? Well, except the doc here and the kids."

"Yes, we are," Karen answered as she reemerged from the camper shell and began handing sandwiches and slices of apples to everyone. "Mr. Diaz, I have one saved for you."

Ford turned his endearing smile on Karen. "Please, call me Ford."

Mercury was surprised to watch Karen blush as she replied. "Oh well, then I shall. And you may call me Karen."

"It would be my pleasure—ooo!" Ford jerked a little and sucked air. "That one stung. Sorry, I didn't mean to move."

"It's okay. I wasn't stabbing you at that second, so you're fine. Keep talking. I'm about a third the way done."

"Ford, do you live in Oregon?" asked Mercury.

"Yeah. I do—or I guess after the bombs it'd be more accurate to say I *did*—a few acres that was a Christmas tree farm in North Plains, which is just on the other side of Portland."

"How did you avoid the green fog when the bombs hit?" Stella asked as the group clustered around the tailgate, ate sandwiches and apples, and watched Gemma sew up Ford's forehead.

"Just got lucky," he said. "This spring my campsite was at the very top of one of the canyons. When those bombs hit, and then the green spread after them, I was having my morning coffee above everything." His open, friendly expression became somber. "From where I was, I watched the fog engulf a group of men working on a fence repair at the base of the canyon. It killed all of them. I knew then that I had to avoid it."

"You don't have a vehicle?" Imani asked.

"I did. It was parked at the end of the service access road I took to the canyon. I'd left it there and then hiked to the top. When the green stuff cleared, I hiked back to find that the earthquake had shaken it off the canyon service road. It rolled into a gully. No way could I get it out, so I made my way to the highway and followed it until yesterday when I met a truck driver. Nice guy named Sim, who was on his way north."

"Oh my Goddess!" Mercury said. "We met Sim too!"

"That's wild," said Ford—his grin back. "He gave me an update on the destruction, so I knew it wasn't safe to head toward Portland, and he told me that Madras is the place to go. That's where I've been headed. I hope he made it to his family."

The ladies avoided his gaze while Mercury thought about how much she hated having to tell him about Sim.

"Oh," said Ford. "He didn't make it."

"No," Mercury said. "But it was quick and he didn't suffer long. Sim is why we're headed to Madras too."

"Dios descanse su alma en paz," Ford said softly. Then he genuflected with a motion that was so natural, so easy, it was clear he hadn't been exaggerating about it being second nature to him.

"If you're heading to Madras, why were you on that side of the river and not by the road?" Stella asked.

"I was cutting around Warm Springs."

"Why?" Mercury asked.

"Since yesterday I've been avoiding the highway. Instead, I headed cross-country and followed service roads. I don't know where you ladies came from, but there are some bad types roaming up and down 26."

"Preaching to the choir," said Imani. She was leaning against the tailgate, nibbling her sandwich. She'd put her arm around Cayden, whose head kept bobbing against her shoulder as he struggled not to fall asleep. "We've almost lost the truck twice because of assholes."

"I'm not surprised. That's why I cut cross-country. See that canyon top over there?" Gemma had just snipped the end of a stitch, so Ford took the opportunity to jerk his thumb behind them at a tall, rocky canyon. "I camped up there last night 'cause I realized pretty quickly that green stuff likes to stay low. Anyway, this morning I could see Warm Springs from the canyon. It's just around that bend in the road ahead of us. Have you ladies ever been to Warm Springs?"

"Not any of us teachers. We're from Tulsa and San Diego," said Mercury.

"Well, Warm Springs is a little town built around a big casino," Ford explained. "The town's in a valley surrounded by these canyons—it's pretty—especially as the Deschutes River is just on the other side of it. Anyway, that's not the point. The point is I could see the town, or at least the part of it the highway goes through. It's covered in green. All of it."

"Like, so much you wouldn't even drive through it?" Karen asked.

"Not me, no. Maybe you ladies would be okay." His gaze cut to the sleepy twins. "But . . ."

"Not all of us would be," Mercury finished for him.

"Yeah. Exactly," said Ford.

"Do you know a way our truck can cut around Warm Springs so we can still head to Madras?" Karen asked. "We have a map, and I searched for a side road, but the only one I found fed straight back into the highway in the middle of the town."

"You won't find the way on a map. They don't print cell access roads or farm roads. But yeah, I've been camping in this area for years. I can show you how to get the truck around the town."

"Done!" said Gemma. "Let me put a bandage over it. Sorry I didn't really have anything to numb it with, but you were excellent at holding still."

Ford touched his wound gingerly and shrugged. "It didn't hurt much. Your touch is very gentle."

"Thanks!" Gemma taped gauze over the stitches. "You're good to go."

Stella walked over and stood before him. "Oxford, we would like to offer you a ride to Madras with us, but there are conditions."

"That's fair. I promise I'm not a serial killer."

"I already know that," said Stella, waving away his comment. "I need you to give me your word that you will keep anything we tell you in confidence."

"Will any of your secrets hurt others?" he asked.

"Absolutely not," said Stella.

"Then I have no problem with that condition."

"Good, second condition—and I'm going to be blunt because we need to get out of here ASAP."

"I prefer blunt," Ford said as he watched her closely. "I also prefer the truth."

"As do we," agreed Stella. "So the truth is we're in charge. Mercury and I make the decisions for the group, though we listen to what everyone has to say. If that's not okay with you, then we should part ways now. We'll be sure you're safe, though, and we'll leave you with enough food to get to Madras."

"I joined the Air Force out of high school—before I went to Journeyman school. I'm comfortable with the chain of command," said Ford.

"Which means?" Mercury asked.

"It means you outrank me, so I'll do what I'm told to do." He flashed his charming smile. "My truth is that it'd be my personal nightmare to be in charge and responsible for all of your lives. I'm perfectly happy to turn over command to you."

"Deal." Stella offered him her hand.

"Deal." He shook it. "Hey, I should cross that little bridge downstream and get my backpack. All of my supplies are in it." He stood and immediately his swarthy complexion blanched to the color of curdled milk. His hand went to his forehead as he swayed.

"Nope, nope, nope!" Gemma turned from where she was disinfecting her needle, grabbed his arm and guided him back to the tailgate, where he sat heavily and gulped air as sweat suddenly beaded his forehead. "You aren't walking anywhere. I also don't want you sleeping for at least a few hours. I'm pretty sure you have a concussion."

"I'll get your backpack," Mercury said.

"Are you one hundred percent sure you don't feel broken at all?" Gemma asked her.

"Do you?" Mercury said.

"Nope."

"Me either." Mercury looked at Stella. "Do I need to hurry?"

"Definitely," said Stella. "While you're getting the backpack, the rest of us will load up. Ford needs to be in the cab so he can tell me which way to go."

"Stella?" Ford called after her. Stella turned to look at him, and he added, "I don't suppose you have any wire cutters? It'd definitely make getting this truck cross-country easier."

Mercury answered. "Oh yeah, we do! They're in that black bag behind the bench seat."

"I'll get them out," said Stella.

"We're sleepy," said Georgie around a giant yawn. "Imani, would you stay in the back with us?"

"Of course, baby," said Imani, brushing back the girl's hair before she smiled at Stella. "I'll get the kids loaded."

"And I'll be back in a sec," said Mercury as she started jogging along the road heading downstream to the wooden bridge about half a football field away. She glanced down at the rocky river side, relieved the green fog hadn't spread that far. *Well, here's hoping that backpack isn't as heavy as it looks.*

OXFORD DIAZ

CHAPTER

27

THE WOODEN BRIDGE was one of those old plank things—and several of the planks were either missing or rotted and splintered. Hoof prints in the dirt and droppings on the bridge showed that goats had been using it. There was no railing—nothing except some crappy-looking horizontal pieces of wood nailed to what looked like not much more than salvaged two-by-fours. She hugged the left side of the little footbridge, tiptoed quickly across it, and refused to look down at the murky, angry water swirling not far below.

Once over the bridge, Mercury jogged upstream several yards until she found Oxford's hastily discarded backpack. It was a *real* backpack, not like the schoolgirl ones she and Stella and the rest of their group had crammed into the bed of the truck. This one was a long rectangle that was obviously filled with serious camping supplies. It was in good condition but was also well used—and completely full.

Mercury sighed and picked it up by one of its wide straps—and then wanted to laugh. It wasn't even close to as heavy as it looked! She slipped her arms through the straps, looked across the river, downstream to where Stella was standing by the rear of the truck, staring at her. She grinned and waved at her friend, who made more of a shooing gesture than a wave in return.

"Coming!" Mercury shouted between cupped hands before she jogged back to the bridge.

At the footbridge Mercury remembered to stick to the side, now on her right, that had been semi-stable on her way over. Not anticipating any problems because her newly acquired weight just didn't add that much, she walked out onto the bridge and began to retrace her path.

Mercury's stomach growled, and she was wondering what besides sandwiches Stella had packed for them, when a board gave way under her left foot, falling into the raging water just inches beneath. Struggling to regain her balance, Mercury staggered into the center of the bridge.

With a deafening *crack*, the planks beneath both of her feet broke and dropped into the river, with Mercury following close behind. The backpack caught on a plank behind her, halting her fall, but that plank was thoroughly rotten and it gave way quickly so that she continued to plummet downward. As her legs went under the water, Mercury frantically grasped at the bridge planks in front of her. She managed to grip a splintered piece of wood and held on while the current sucked at her body like it was the throat of a ravenous giant.

She could hear Stella shouting and knew her friends must be running to save her, but the board she clutched moaned beneath her weight.

It wouldn't hold her long.

The board's splinters sliced into her fingers and the palms of her hands, but Mercury didn't let go. The backpack pulled her down, but she gritted her teeth, and instead of allowing the current to take her and pull her to the bottom, Mercury grunted and concentrated. Then she attempted something she'd been trying to accomplish in the gym for years. Using an overhand grip on the rough plank, she pulled herself up until her chin was above the board, and then methodically Mercury straightened her arms, heaving up until her chest had cleared the board and her waist was even with it. She swung her legs to the side, up and over, and with abs of steel she had zero clue she owned, Mercury powered up the rest of the way onto the bridge, landing in a crouching position.

There was a sharp *crack*, almost like gunfire, and the footbridge disintegrated beneath her. Without conscious thought, Mercury shouted, "Shit!" and leaped at the bank that was still at least ten feet in front of her. As what remained of the bridge crumbled into the river, Mercury catapulted to land with an *oof* as the backpack's weight made her roll onto her back, turtle-like, in the dirt.

"Mercury! Jesus fucking Christ! Are you okay?" Like a major league pro heading into home, Stella slid to her. She grabbed her arms and pulled her to a sitting position. "Are you broken? Gemma! Get your butt here!"

"I'm here! I'm here!" Gemma sprinted up and went to her knees beside them. "Let me look at you. What hurts?"

"I'm okay," Mercury said. She lifted her hands. Her fingers and palms were a mass of blood and splinters. "These hurt, but other than that I'm okay."

"Fuck!" Imani ran to them. "Get that giant pack off her."

"Guys, really. I'm okay except for my hands. The pack's fine. It's definitely not as heavy as it looks. Help me up."

Stella and Imani took her elbows and guided Mercury to her feet. She moved her shoulders and shifted the backpack before smiling at her friend. "See, good as new. Goddess! That bridge really sucked."

"G-give me that pack." Ford was staggering to them. His pale face made him look as dead as Mercury almost had been.

"No!" Mercury told him. "I've got it. It's not even heavy. Dude, you look like you're gonna pass out."

Gemma whirled around and made a little squeaking sound as Oxford swayed like a willow in a gale.

"Help him! I'm good." Mercury frowned at Ford.

Gemma put her arm around Ford's waist. Imani went to his other side and did the same to stabilize him.

"You better follow us back to the truck. Like, *right now, Acorn!*" commanded Gemma as she and Imani turned Ford and began trudging to the truck.

"Damn, she's getting bossy," said Mercury. "Right?" She glanced at her friend. Stella's glacier-blue eyes were trapped on her. Her face was unreadably somber.

"What? I'm okay. Really."

Stella kept staring at her.

"Stella! Why are you looking at me like that?"

"Give me that backpack." Stella held out her arms.

"Fine, but I really can carry it. It's just my hands that are cut, not my back." She glanced down at them as she wriggled out of the pack. "Ugh, splinters are the worst, aren't they?" Mercury let the pack drop to the ground. "Sorry, if I hand it to you that really will hurt me."

Saying nothing, Stella bent to pick up the backpack. She lifted it about a foot from the ground before letting it drop back. "You said it was light."

"It is."

"No, Mercury Elizabeth Rhodes. That thing weighs at least fifty pounds."

"Oh my Goddess, Stella. That's insane."

"No, what's insane is that you're carrying it around like it's nothing, and you just did a straight arm pull-up with that fucking thing on your back right before you jumped, flat-footed, from the middle of that bridge onto the bank a good ten feet away like *goddamn Wonder Woman!"* With a trembling hand Stella brushed strands of her wild hair from her face. "You have super strength."

"I do not." Mercury hooked one of the backpack straps through her arm and with a single movement, slung it up to her shoulders.

Stella's brows lifted into her hair. "I could barely pick that thing up."

Mercury stared at her friend as her heartbeat calmed. She looked behind Stella to the skeletal remains of the footbridge that clung to the opposite bank. Then she met Stella's gaze again. "I did a dead-arm pull-up. I seriously pulled my body weight up like it was nothing."

Stella nodded. "With a fifty-pound backpack. Then you jumped. *Jumped!* And went flying a bunch of feet—don't know how many because I was flat out running to try to save you while you did it—to the other fucking side of the river."

Mercury felt nauseous and dizzy. "What's happening to me?"

Stella touched her friend's shoulder. "You're still *you*. Remember that. We all have to remember that. But you have changed."

"The green fog," Mercury whispered. "I got a second dose."

Stella nodded. "Yeah, but you were already strong before that. I watched you leap down the bank to save the kids. You were *fast*. And I noticed it again when you lifted Gemma onto the bank. She's gotta be a hundred and twenty-ish pounds. You grabbed her under her elbow and hefted her up like she weighed nothing. The only reason she fell back was because she slipped."

Mercury stopped and turned to face Stella. "Tell me the truth and don't fucking sugarcoat it. These new abilities—are they a good or a bad thing?"

Stella paused and tilted her head to the side in what was becoming her familiar listening pose. "Good and bad. That's all I get right now."

"That's not very comforting."

"If it helps, I don't feel any danger warnings about you—or Gemma," Stella added.

Mercury wiped her sweaty forehead with a shaky hand. "Gemma! Does she have super strength too?"

Stella snorted. "Not hardly. Imani had to help her get Ford back to the truck. Speaking of, come on. We really do have to get out of here."

The two women walked in silence for a little way before Mercury cleared her throat. "Um, did everyone see what happened?"

"Yep. When that first board broke, it sounded like a gunshot," said Stella.

"Even the guy?"

"Absolutely." Stella glanced at her. "Unless you're prepared to leave him by the side of the road with a concussion, we're going to have to take him with us, which means we're going to have to trust him."

"And is he trustworthy?"

"Acorn, if he wasn't, I wouldn't have stopped here. Nor would I have given him the conditions for traveling with us. Like I told the kids. *There are no bad men in the area.*" She paused and added. "I think I was compelled to stop because we were destined to meet him. And the green fog redo was important too."

"Okay, so I'll trust him. Feels kinda weird, though. Men have been awful since this thing happened."

"Oh, Mercury, don't blame it on the apocalypse. You haven't trusted men for many years." Stella wrapped her arm through Mercury's. "Not that I disagree with you. I just like to play with them more often than you do."

Mercury arched one brow up. "Stella Carver, are you going to *play with him*?"

Stella bumped her shoulder and waggled her eyebrows at her best friend. "No, *I'm* not."

A small boyish tornado sprinted the distance left between the two women and the truck, and Cayden ran to Mercury. He skidded to a stop in front of her and stared up at her with big fawn eyes as his chin quivered.

"Cayden! Thank you for coming out to meet me." Mercury smiled at the little boy.

Stella released her friend's arm. "Now that you're in Cayden's capable hands, I'm going to be sure everyone's situated so that as soon as Gemma's done taking care of your cuts, we can get out of here. We have about an hour until dusk. Ford says if nothing crazy happens, we'll make it to Madras by then, but crazy is *all* that's been happening these days. We need to get going." Stella gave her a quick hug. "Stop almost getting dead," she whispered before she let go of

Mercury, ruffled Cayden's hair, and then hurried the rest of the way to the truck.

Cayden was staring at Mercury's hands. The stinging in her palms and fingers had faded to an ache. So had the bleeding, but scarlet had pooled in her palms and as she turned them so that the boy couldn't see the lacerations, little drops of blood spattered onto the cracked asphalt.

"Hey," Mercury said, and Cayden's gaze lifted to her eyes. "I'm okay. Really."

Cayden closed the last few feet to her, and with a sigh too ancient for his six years, he wrapped his arms around her waist and hugged her while he cried softly.

"Oh, sweetie. I know this is all really scary and hard, but we're going to be okay. I mean it. I'm not just saying it because that's what people say to kids. I promise you Stella and Imani and Karen and I are going to find a place—find a way—for all of us to be safe again." With the back of her hand she caressed his soft hair. "Hey, you want to know something?"

Cayden pulled back, wiped his cheeks with the back of his sleeve and nodded.

"I'm really, *really* glad we found you and Jayden and Georgie."

Then, for the first time since she and Stella had found the kids on the porch of the cabin with their dead parents in the driveway, Cayden smiled. The grin lit his face and his eyes, and the puzzle piece that had been missing in Mercury's life slid firmly, irrevocably into place in her heart.

"I'll *always* be glad you're with us—with me," she told the little boy. "I'm going to keep you safe. I promise."

"Of course you will." Georgie was standing just a little way from them. "You're our protector."

Still grinning, Cayden nodded like a little bobblehead doll and hugged her again. Mercury looked down at him to see that all around them, everywhere her blood had spattered against the broken road, wildflowers pushed up as if they, too, were looking to her for safety and love.

CHAPTER

28

"THERE IT IS! Take a left onto that gravel road." Oxford sat in the center of the cab, his long legs stretched in front of Mercury, who sat nearest to the passenger window. He pointed at a narrow, rocky area off the side of 26 that looked more like a mistake than an actual road. As Stella braked and turned, he added. "You'll need those wire cutters pretty soon."

"Yep," said Stella as she eased the old truck onto the gravelly path and then pointed to the floorboard. "I got 'em out while Mercury's hands were being doctored. They're right down there."

"Oh crap. That's more rain." Mercury craned her head back and looked up at the slate sky that had started to spit drizzle again. "Are we going to get stuck?"

"Shouldn't," said Ford. "The land is dry out here and soaks up rain pretty fast. The access roads I've been following didn't look too waterlogged, and you do have those chains. They'll help." He sat up a little straighter. "Okay, here's the first gate. Mercury, I wish I was steadier on my feet, but I have one hellacious headache. I'm afraid if I go out there, I'll cause more problems than be helpful, but if you do need more muscle, I'll try."

"Gemma wouldn't stand for it," said Mercury. "And no big deal. I'm used to being what my dad liked to call 'Gate Girl.' I'll jump out and see if I can open the gate. If not, I'll just cut it open." She peered through the rain. "It doesn't look too sturdy."

"She's not going to have any problem with the gates. Any of them," Stella said as she braked.

"That's right." Ford nodded. "For a sec I forgot about the bridge."

Mercury wasn't sure what she should say. Her feelings were at odds about her newly discovered strength. It seemed like a good thing, but it also made her stomach a little sick. Mercury held out her hand like a surgeon asking for a scalpel. "Wire cutters!"

"Here ya go." Stella handed her the tool. "Don't think I don't recognize your Meredith Grey voice. You go out there and perform fence surgery, Acorn."

"Acorn?"

Ford's voice followed her out of the open door to the truck as she hurried through the rain to the gate. It was a simple barrier of aluminum attached to a wooden post with a chain and a padlock. Mercury sighed. The damn chain was thick and rust-free. It was going to take some major strength to cut it. She opened the mouth of the wire cutters as wide as possible and managed to slide a link of the chain inside the sharpened edges. Then she gritted her teeth, gripped the two arms of the tool, and pressed them together—hard—and cut through the link like it was a wet spaghetti noodle.

"Super strength definitely comes in handy," she murmured as she shook out the chain, opened the gate, and then jogged back to the truck.

"Do you think I should get out and close it?" she asked as Stella drove through.

Ford shook his head. "I hate to say it, but from what I've seen traveling by these little roads for the past day or so, I don't think there're enough people left alive out here to worry about it. There are a bunch of goats, some cattle, a few horses and—believe it or not—a herd of alpacas that would probably appreciate being able to roam free for food and water."

"Alpacas? That's weird," said Mercury as she wiped her face dry with the sleeve of her sweatshirt.

"Yeah, kinda," Ford said.

"How're your hands holding up?" Stella asked as she navigated around a big hole in the dirt road.

Mercury studied her hands. Gemma had removed the splinters and cleaned the cuts before wrapping them in gauze. "I think they're fine. They don't hurt at all." She unwound the gaze and grinned. "They're perfect, actually."

Ford's gaze went from her healed hands to meet her eyes. "That's weirder than the alpacas."

Mercury shrugged and said, "Yeah. I heal fast."

"Did you heal this fast before the green stuff got you?" Ford asked.

Mercury only hesitated a second. "Nope."

He cleared he throat. "Well, speaking of weird—you're strong."

Mercury nodded.

Ford looked from Mercury to Stella. "I gave you my word I wouldn't tell anyone your secrets. You don't know me yet, but I always keep my word."

"The green fog changes some women," said Stella. She was driving two-handed again and kept her gaze on the dirt and gravel road, steering carefully around potholes and newly formed cracks in the land.

"But you're not all strong like Mercury," said Ford.

"So far that's just me," said Mercury reluctantly.

"Tell him," said Stella.

Mercury sighed. "A few of us—Stella, Imani, Gemma, and I—can make plants grow with our blood. We also heal faster than normal."

Ford blinked several times before he said, "Are you messing with me?"

"Nope," said Stella. "Tell him the rest."

"Stella knows things now. She's always had great intuition, but since the green fog, it's been supersized. She's saved us a bunch of times already."

"I didn't save y'all. *We* have saved ourselves. I just gave us a heads-up," explained Stella.

"Huh. That's good to know. Also will come in handy in the future." Ford nodded. "What about Gemma and Imani?"

"They can make plants grow, and small cuts heal fast with them, but we're not sure about what else they can do," said Mercury.

"Gemma's a healer," said Ford. "That's obvious. Not only is she good at it, but now that I know more, I realize it wasn't my imagination. As long as she was touching my forehead, it didn't hurt at all for her to stitch me up—my cut didn't ache or anything. It's only when she wasn't touching me that it hurt." He reached up and pressed his fingers to the bandage and grimaced. "Like now."

"I believe Oxford is correct about Gemma," said Stella.

"Do you know what's up with Imani?" asked Mercury.

Stella moved her shoulder. "I can't tell yet, but I promise you there's more than just the 'my-blood-grows-plants' thing."

"What about Karen? Did the green fog not touch her?"

"It did," said Mercury. "She was with us when it covered us, but her blood hasn't changed—or at least not in a way we can tell yet. There was another woman with us who survived the first blast but whose blood also doesn't grow plants."

"Did she die?" Ford asked quietly.

"No, she stayed at Timberline with a doctor and the survivors," said Stella.

Ford turned his head quickly to look at Stella. "Timberline's still there? I've skied Mt. Hood many times from that lodge."

"It's there—partially," said Mercury. "Half of it's gone, but what's left makes a pretty good shelter. And they have plenty of supplies."

"I'm surprised you didn't stay there," said Ford.

"Blame Stella. Her new spidey senses said we needed to leave," said Mercury.

"If we hadn't left, those kids and Ford would've died." Stella pressed her lips together.

"Wait, what?" said Ford.

Mercury patted his knee. "It's probably better if you don't ask."

"She's not wrong," Stella muttered. "Gate girl!"

"Got it!" It only took a few minutes for Mercury to cut through and discard the chain and open the gate. Then she was back inside the cab, wiping rain from her face again. She turned to look at the man beside her. "So, Oxford, you said you know the area?"

"Yep, well."

"And also Madras?"

He nodded. "I've been there many times. They have—well, I suppose it's *had* now—a few excellent local restaurants in the heart of the town. I like to treat myself to a nice meal before I leave on a backpack trip, and again right after."

"We need to hide the truck," said Stella. "Do you know where we can do that and still not be so far from town that it'll be tough for the kids to walk it?"

"Hmm, from what Sim told me, the mayor has set up shelters in the center of town. So, yeah, I think know where we can stash the truck."

"We're gonna need to access it quick," said Stella. She glanced at Ford. "I don't think we're going to stay in Madras long."

"Why not?"

Stella shrugged. "Don't know that. All I know is that I have a feeling it's not the place for us."

Ford smoothed his neat beard. "I know a spot that will work if the earthquakes haven't destroyed it. So, you think you'll leave Madras because something's wrong with staying there, or because you'll be scouting survivors and bringing them back to safety?"

"Could be either." Stella sighed. "I just don't know, which is frustrating as hell. Ford, the road 'T's' again. Which way?"

"Right," said Ford. "And we're only about a couple miles from where this will feed into highway 97. We'll be on the outskirts of Madras. From there I can show you how to cut along the edge of town to the place we can hide the truck."

Stella turned right and bumped along a rough patch of the road that had gone from gravel and dirt to dirt and mud. The path curved around the base of a tall basalt-wrinkled canyon that loomed above. The rain, clouds, and encroaching dusk had already limited visibility. Stella reluctantly flipped on the headlights.

"I haven't wanted to turn these on. Didn't want to call needless attention to ourselves, but the shadow of the canyon has blocked what's left of the light and—shit!" Stella jerked the wheel hard to the left to avoid the rear end of a worn, late model GMC truck that had been abandoned in the middle of the road.

"They okay back there?" Stella asked.

Mercury peered through the gloom into the bed of the truck. Gemma gave her a thumbs-up and then pointed at the three sleeping children and shrugged.

"Yeah, they're okay. I think those kids could sleep through a bomb," said Mercury.

"I think they already slept through one bomb," said Stella. "That's probably what saved them—being asleep in the top story of their cabin." She gestured to the stalled truck. "Here's hoping that thing has a full tank of gas."

"I'll do it this time," said Mercury. "I've already been rained on."

"Do what?" asked Ford.

"Syphon gas," said Mercury. "While I'm out there, want me to put up the antenna, and you can let Jenny know we're almost at Madras?"

"Sounds good," said Stella.

"Huh?" Ford said.

As an answer Mercury popped open the glove box to expose the revolver and the CB radio. She pulled out the extendable antenna and opened the door as Ford whistled softly in appreciation.

"Damn, you ladies have all the best stuff."

Mercury grinned over her shoulder at him. "You better believe it!"

She unfolded the antenna and stuck it to the top of the truck before she rapped on the window twice and gave Stella and Ford the okay sign. Then she jogged to the back of the truck. Imani had already opened the camper shell and had the piece of hose ready for her. "I'm assuming we're stopping for gas."

"Yeah, thanks. Ford says we're only a mile or so from where we join highway 97, which will take us to Madras. He knows a place just outside town where we can hide the truck."

Imani glanced at the sleeping children. "How far are they going to have to walk in this rain?"

"He says not far."

Imani frowned. Her gaze kept returning to the sleeping children.

"Here," Gemma reached around Imani and handed Mercury a puffy down jacket. "Take my coat. It's waterproof. You can hold it over your head while you're syphoning gas."

"Thanks." Mercury took the coat and returned to the side of the truck. It didn't take long for her to open the gas caps, insert the hose, and then sputter and cuss as she spit out a mouthful of gas before she shoved the end of the hose into the truck's gas tank.

The door to the truck opened and Ford stuck his head out as he handed her a bottle of water. "Stella said you'd want this."

"Yeah, that gas is disgusting. Thanks." She took the water, rinsed her mouth, and then drained the rest of it. "Which reminds me that I have to pee. Ford, would you keep an eye on the hose while I duck back behind there for a sec?" She gestured to the rear of the GMC truck.

"No problem. Be careful."

Mercury nodded and went to the back of the trucks. They'd left the camper shell window propped open, so she paused. "I need some of that toilet paper," she whispered into the dark bed.

Gemma's head popped up. "Some or the whole roll?"

"Some. I don't want the whole roll rained on."

Gemma handed Mercury a wad of toilet paper. Then she ducked behind the truck to squat awkwardly while she held the jacket over her head. When she was done, she stood and was zipping her jeans when something a couple yards from her caught her eye. The wind lifted part of what she'd thought was just a pile of rock and dirt and made rain-darkened fur flutter.

Mercury shivered and clutched the coat tighter around herself as she walked slowly down the road to the thing. She got closer and was able to see that it was a baby goat. It looked newborn. It was curled up, almost like it was asleep, but when Mercury crouched to touch it, the little creature was cold and stiff. She looked around to see if the mother was nearby, but nothing in the bleak landscape moved.

Gently, Mercury stroked the soft fur on the baby's head. It was so sweet—so young and innocent and alone; tears mixed with rain to wet her cheeks. Mercury's heart hurt for this little one and so, so many others.

"I'm sorry," she murmured to the small body. "I wish you'd been born in a better time—a safer time." Mercury stood and held her hand out over the still body. She raised the index and pinky fingers on her right hand and the rest she folded into a clenched position, making the Pagan symbol for the Horned God, or Green Man, the masculine personification of nature. "Little friend, in the name of the Earth goddess, Gaia, I encourage you to forget this broken shell. In the name of the Green Man, the Horned God, patron of things wild and free, I bid you go beyond and enjoy the Summerland."

Mercury closed her eyes, and as she made the sign of the pentagram by touching first the center of her forehead, then her right breast, left shoulder, right shoulder, left breast and forehead in turn, she imagined that a glowing door opened before them, and the spirit of the tiny goat bucked and kicked and frolicked joyfully through it to a verdant valley beyond. "Blessed be, small friend, and farewell."

She finished the impromptu ritual and turned back toward the truck—and from the bed she caught the flash of a muted light.

Mercury squinted into the still open rear of the camper shell, expecting to see that Imani had turned on the flashlight they'd brought from Timberline, but there was nothing but darkness within, from which Karen stared at her with an oddly intense expression.

Mercury tossed Gemma's coat inside the camper. Before she closed the window, she spoke softly to the adults. "Okay, we're out of here. Hold tight. We'll be in Madras soon."

"Sounds good." Gemma whispered back to her, and Imani gave her a thumbs-up.

Karen refused to meet her eyes.

CHAPTER 29

As Ford had said, the dirt road emptied into highway 97 about a mile later. Stella turned left and immediately they saw a sign that read "Madras—1 mile." She'd turned off the headlights as soon as they'd left the shadow of the canyon, and had to slow the truck so that she could steer around the mess of wrecks and stalled cars they'd avoided by cutting cross-country.

"Okay, Ford, what's the plan?" Stella gripped the steering wheel tightly and kept her eyes on the dark, rainy highway.

"Mercury, look to the right side of the road for a little convenience store gas station combo called 97 Mart. We need to take a left there."

"Is that it? Looks like a burnt-out gas station." Mercury nodded to the right of the highway.

"Yeah, I'm pretty sure it is. Stella, go left at that intersection."

Stella turned left and had to leave the road and drive in the ditch to get around a truck that had smashed head-on into the front of an SUV.

"When did these people have time to run into each other?" Stella shook her head. "I just don't get it."

"The EMP pulse stopped their engines, but that doesn't mean the vehicles stopped," said Mercury. "And panic does crazy things to people."

"Careful, there's a tree down ahead," Ford said.

"I see it. I'll just stay in the ditch until we get past this mess," said Stella.

"Okay, up that little incline on your right. See that cemetery?" Ford pointed.

"Yep," said Stella.

"You can turn right directly after it."

Mercury looked in the side mirror. "Oxford, it looks like we're getting farther away from the center of town."

"Yeah, we are, but not too far for us to walk—even if I'm not very steady on my feet. There—take this right," said Ford, "and pretty soon we should come to a small, overpass-like bridge. Here's hoping it's still standing."

"I see it! It's just after that big clump of pines," said Mercury. "Careful, looks like several of them have splintered."

"Yeah, I see 'em," said Stella. "I can take the ditch to get around them."

"The bridge is still standing! That's a relief," said Ford. "My idea is to have you pull off the road and park under the bridge. It goes over Willow Creek, which winds through Madras. The creek is pretty intermittent and dries out a lot, especially in the summer. It hasn't been raining long, so I figured it wouldn't be too swollen."

"I think I can pull off on the right side. Doesn't look too steep. Mercury, maybe you should get out and scout down there, though, and see if there's anywhere for me to park under the bridge."

"No problem." Mercury left the truck and made her way down a gentle incline that led to a shallow creek. She felt a wave of relief as she studied the area under the bridge, and then returned quickly to the truck. "It's perfect—just like underneath a highway overpass. There's a cement section down there where you can park the truck. The creek has water in it, but it's shallow—nothing like that river back on 26. And I didn't see any sign of green fog, but if you back the truck in, you could park it so that it'd be positioned to get the hell out fast."

"Good idea," said Stella, who expertly guided the truck down the incline and then backed it under the bridge and parked it where it was securely out of the rain and poised to be driven away.

The kids were awake, but sleepy-eyed. They yawned and stretched as everyone climbed out of the truck, but unlike normal six-year-olds under normal circumstances, the boys didn't need to be told to stay close. They remained in their sister's shadow—and their sister stuck to Imani like a refrigerator magnet. But Mercury had no doubt which twin was Cayden. Wherever she was, she felt his intense gaze following her.

"Okay, let's get our backpacks on and head to the heart of town," said Mercury.

Stella spoke to the three kids. "It's going to seem like a long way, but once we get there, we'll be able to rest. And if we don't like it in Madras, don't worry. We'll leave. That's why we're not taking the truck with us—so that no one can take our wheels and stop us from leaving."

The twins huddled closer to their big sister, who draped her arms protectively around their shoulders. "But what if the people there won't let us leave? What if they try to take us away from you?"

Cayden nodded his head emphatically and stared at Mercury as his eyes filled with tears.

"You know I'm superhero strong, right?" Mercury asked all three kids, but her gaze remained on the twin she thought of as her special boy.

The three children nodded.

"Well, I give you my word: I won't let anyone take you away from us," said Mercury.

Georgie blinked fast as she attempted to keep frightened tears from spilling down her round cheeks. "Okay, we'll try really hard to keep up with you and to be really good."

"I need to speak with the adults—all of you. Over here. Gemma, would you stay with the kids?" Imani asked. Gemma nodded, and then Imani turned and marched several yards, with the adults following her.

"What is it?" Mercury asked.

"The kids need to stay here. They're terrified—again—and this is one terror too many in a long list of what they've already been through to survive. Stella, you don't think this is our permanent place?" Imani said.

Stella nodded. "I still have the feeling that we're not staying here, but I can't tell why."

"Then what's the point of dragging three exhausted, traumatized children into town? I'm one hundred percent against it," Imani said firmly.

Mercury let out a long breath. "I can't say I disagree with you. Would you want to stay here with the kids?" she asked Imani.

"Absolutely."

"Stella?" Mercury turned to her friend.

"It would definitely be easier to get in and out of town without kids. Anyone who wants to stay with the truck and wait for us to come back should stay," said Stella.

"I should go to Madras with you," said Ford.

"Yeah, thanks. We seriously won't know our way around without you guiding us," said Mercury.

"No problem. I'm more than willing." He smiled at Mercury.

"I refuse to remain here." Karen's thin lips disappeared as she pressed them into a colorless line.

"Karen, no one is excluding you," said Mercury.

"Well, good." Karen's face looked pinched as she refused to meet Mercury's gaze.

"Okay, so, that's settled," said Mercury. "Let's tell the kids and Gemma."

They rejoined the four young people, and Stella smiled at the children. "Change of plans. We decided it would be best for the kids to stay with the truck while just a few of us check out Madras."

"You're leaving us?" Georgie clutched her brothers' narrow shoulders.

"No!" Mercury quickly explained. "Or at least not for more than—" she glanced at Stella.

"Two nights," Stella said. "No matter what, we'll be back to check in no later than the next morning."

Mercury nodded. "Yeah, and if we decide to leave, we'll leave then. Together."

Imani put her arm around Georgie's shoulders. "I'm going to stay here with you."

"So will I," said Gemma.

"When are we leaving?" Karen asked as she picked at the hem of her cardigan.

"Now." Stella spoke firmly. "Or as soon as we put on coats and get our backpacks together."

The group worked silently and quickly. Even the children helped, though as they struggled to pull Ford's heavy backpack from the bed of the truck, Gemma stepped in.

"Hey, Ford can't carry this." The teenager fisted her hands on her hips as she faced Stella and Mercury, who were slipping on their own backpacks. "I don't even like the fact that he's up and walking around. Are you sure he needs to go with you?"

Ford opened his mouth to respond, but Stella beat him to it. "Yes. Ford must come with us."

"I'll carry his pack," said Mercury. "And he can carry mine."

"Are you sure?" Ford eyed her. "It's fifty pounds."

Mercury raised a brow. "Remember the bridge? I'm pretty sure I can manage."

Ford dipped his head to her. "Then I bow to the lady's superior strength—with gratitude."

Mercury sloughed off her backpack and handed it to Ford and then reached past the kids into the bed and, like it weighed five pounds instead of fifty, she pulled it out and slid her arms through the straps. Then she went to the cab and returned to the group with the Winchester and the .38.

"You look like something out of *Mad Max: Fury Road*," said Ford. "And I mean that as a compliment."

"Thanks. Charlize Theron is a badass." Mercury turned to Stella. "I think I should take the revolver with us and leave the rifle, but I want to know how you feel about that."

Stella tilted her head to the side. "Yep. Take the pistol. Leave the rifle."

"Would you show me how to shoot it?" Imani asked. "I hope I don't have to use it, but I'm not going to let anyone hurt these kids."

Mercury nodded and gave Imani a quick lesson in how to fire the Winchester. "Basically, don't aim for the head or legs. Just point it at the biggest target you have—the center of the body. Squeeze, don't jerk the trigger, and hold it snug against your shoulder, like this." She demonstrated. "It'll kick, but if it's firmly against you, it won't be bad."

"Got it." Imani handled the rifle carefully, respectfully, and slid it back behind the bucket seat of the truck. When she returned to the group, she asked, "What should we do if the green fog rolls in under the bridge?"

"Drive that truck out of there," said Stella.

"Sis, I can't drive a damn stick," said Imani.

"I'll drive it," said Gemma. "I can do it."

"Okay, Gemma can do it," said Imani. "Where do we go? You'll need to find us on your way out."

"Go back to the cemetery up the street," said Ford. "It's on higher ground than this part of the road, and you should be able to find a place to hide in the middle of the graves."

"Good idea," said Mercury. "Gemma, if you have to do that, look for a mausoleum. That'll help you hide."

"Okay, got it," said Imani. "Do you think it's safe for us to build a little campfire and heat up some of the stew we brought? I know we have lots of sandwiches and granola and fruit, but it'd be good for the kids to have something warm in their bellies."

"Stella should weigh in on this, of course," said Ford, "but we're far enough from the town center, which is where Sim said the mayor was housing survivors, that you should be fine if you keep the fire small and under the bridge. I'd build it down by the water and have someone keep a lookout while you're cooking. If anything stirs, you can kick it into the creek."

"Sounds like a solid idea," said Stella.

"It's going to be really dark." Georgie's voice was small and scared.

"Yeah, it is," agreed Mercury. "Imani, I know we're saving the batteries of the flashlight we brought, but this is probably a good time to use it."

Stella nodded. "Turn it on when you're in the camper shell. Don't feel bad about using the batteries. If it makes you and the kids feel better—use it."

"I have a flashlight with me," Ford said. "So, we'll have a spare if the batteries in the one you have give out."

"Okay," said Imani. "Don't worry about us. You just get in there—figure out what's going on—and get out."

"That's the plan," said Mercury. "We'll see you no later than the day after tomorrow."

"If we're gone both nights, be sure you have the truck loaded and ready to go early the next morning. Just in case," added Stella.

"Be safe." Imani hugged each of them—even Ford.

"Hurry up and come back." Gemma hugged Stella and Mercury before she went to Ford. "Bend down. Let me see your dressing."

Ford did as she asked and sighed in relief when she touched his forehead.

"How bad does it hurt?" Gemma asked.

"When you touch it—not at all. Otherwise, it aches and I have one hell of a magnificent headache."

"I'll get you some ibuprofen." She started to turn to the truck, but Stella touched her shoulder to stop her.

"Instead, just press your hand to his wound and think about the pain going away."

"That's cra—" Karen began, but Stella shushed her.

"Let the kid work through it," Stella told the history teacher.

Karen's lips disappeared into a tight, disapproving line.

"Try it," Mercury said to Gemma. "The worst that can happen is nothing, but it could be like this backpack—light and easy to handle."

"Okay," Gemma said. She wiped her hands on her jeans, drew a deep breath, and then, as Ford bent down, Gemma pressed the palm of her hand over the gauze bandage.

"Concentrate," Stella told her.

Gemma closed her eyes. Her brow furrowed.

Ford closed his eyes too, and within just a few heartbeats his face relaxed into a smile. "Such a relief," he murmured.

Gemma bit her lip as she continued to concentrate. Sweat beaded her face, and she began to shiver. Gooseflesh prickled the small hairs on her forearms.

Stella touched the teen's shoulder. "That's enough."

Gemma's hand dropped heavily from Ford's head. She opened her eyes and blinked several times, and then rubbed at her forehead—in the exact spot of Ford's wound.

"D-did anything happen?" asked the teenager.

Ford straightened. His smile widened. "Absolutely. My headache is completely gone, and I don't feel dizzy anymore."

"Really? That's awesome!" Gemma spoke enthusiastically and then grimaced in pain and staggered so that Stella had to steady her.

"How are *you* feeling now?"

"My head hurts and I'm kinda dizzy," said Gemma. "And, uh, I may puke."

Stella nodded slowly. "Imani, I think you should warm that soup. Be sure Gemma eats—slowly—and also drinks a full bottle of water and then rests."

"I—I don't want to take water from the kids," said Gemma as she rubbed her forehead.

"I have a water purifier in my pack." Ford gestured for Mercury to turn around. He unzipped an outside pocket and pulled out a neatly packed water purifying kit. "You can get all the fresh water you need. The instructions are still in the case."

"Y'all, it's dusk. We need to go," said Mercury.

"Where are we going to say we've been?" asked Karen.

"I have our fiction ready. I'll give you the details on the way," said Mercury. "See y'all soon." She turned to head up the gentle slope when Cayden detached himself from his sister and ran to her, wrapped his arms around her waist and hugged her tightly. She smoothed his hair and rubbed his back. "Thank you for the hug."

He looked up at her, tears poised in his worried gaze.

"Hey, I'm coming back. Promise."

Cayden released her, but instead of returning to his sister, he stared up at Stella.

"Oh, I get it," Stella said. "Yes, we're coming back—and that includes Mercury."

Cayden nodded somberly and turned back to hug Mercury again, and as he did, she glanced at Stella—and Mercury's breath caught in her throat. Her best friend wasn't looking at her, but instead stared into the distance as pain flashed across her face—and Mercury Elizabeth Rhodes shivered as if someone had just walked over her grave.

CHAPTER 30

"I DO NOT LIKE a town with no electricity. Right now in particular." Karen spoke softly, rubbing her crucifix between her forefinger and thumb. They were walking down the center of the residential street Ford said would lead them back to highway 97 and the best way to enter Madras. "It may seem childish, but I have never been comfortable with the dark. I don't mean to be ghoulish, but it makes the houses seem like tombs, especially as we know there are probably dead people within."

Stella wiped at the rain slipping past the hood of the jacket she'd taken from Timberline's boutique. She, too, spoke in hushed tones, as if not wanting to disturb the dead. "It reminds me of the Tulsa icepocalypse of 2007. Remember, Acorn?"

"I'll never forget it. And I'll always be glad we were having wine at my condo the night it hit. We were totally iced in for a week."

"Your fireplace saved us," said Stella.

Mercury laughed softly. "I still thank the Goddess that I'd just made a run to Columbia Liquor and was stocked up." She glanced at Karen. "How long were you without electricity?"

"Ten days. It was miserable," said Karen.

"I remember reading about that," said Ford. "The pictures looked like a hurricane had hit Tulsa."

"It was bad," Mercury said. Then she grinned at Stella. "But those snow days were so, so good."

"Fuckin' A they were." Stella returned her grin.

"All those snow days really messed up my lesson plans," said Karen.

Even in the dark Mercury and Stella shared an eye roll.

"There's the highway," Ford said. "Good. My head's starting to ache again." He glanced at Stella as the four of them climbed the on ramp and walked down the middle of the deserted highway into Madras. "So, Gemma's extra powers definitely have to do with healing."

"About that," Stella said. "We need to not say anything about our, uh, *extra* abilities. And I mean none of them. Agreed?"

"Yes, ma'am," said Ford.

Karen nodded slowly. "I do not usually hold with lies, but these are desperate times, and strangers do not need to know our business."

"Karen, it's not just strangers who don't need to know details about us," said Stella. "Let me make this perfectly clear. Even if sometime tomorrow you get all comfortable and decide someone here is your friend—even if you realize you want to stay—don't tell anyone shit about us. Not about Timberline. And most definitely not about our fucking blood."

"Stella Carver, you do not have to be so vulgar, *and* you do not need to take that tone with me." Karen glared at her through the spitting rain.

"Karen Gay, do you not understand that this is life and death, and your prudish, naive ideas of right and wrong take a backseat to what's actually best for us?" responded Stella.

Mercury stepped between the two women. "Karen, we've been through this already. If you don't like cuss words, then don't use them, but it is not your business to tell anyone else what words or what tone they should or shouldn't use. And it's ridiculous that *shit* and *fuck* are what you're focused on instead of what Stella is saying—that it isn't safe to tell people secrets about us because divulging too much can get us dead. Do you understand that?"

Karen frowned. "Well, yes. Of course."

"Good. End of discussion," Mercury said.

They walked on in silence as the stalled vehicles increased. Mercury kept her gaze averted from the cars and trucks and SUVs—as well as the gelatinous looking mounds of clothing that used to be men, which littered the highway. Though the rain was cold and miserable, she was glad it and the darkness obscured her view of the nightmare around them, especially as they entered the town proper. Buildings had crumbled in the earthquake. Power lines were down across the road, which was one of the few good things about not having any electricity. Some businesses and homes smoldered. Everything was dark and eerily silent.

Ford's voice sounded muffled by the rain, and Mercury strained to hear him. "Soon we should be passing a street named after a tree—can't remember if it's Maple or Oak . . . I remember because that's where a hiking trail feeds into town. We might want to—"

Lights blazed so that the four of them stopped abruptly and lifted their hands to shield their eyes.

"Hello, folks!"

A woman's voice called from behind the blinding light, which Mercury realized was coming from several side-by-side vehicles that blocked the road.

"Hello!" Mercury called back. "We heard there's shelter in Madras."

"Is that all there is? Just the four of you?" asked the woman.

"Yeah," Ford said and then repeated the story Mercury had concocted. "I'm Ford Diaz, a backpack guide. These three ladies are teachers from out of state. They were on a spring break camping trip with me when all hell broke loose. Walking down the highway yesterday, we met a trucker named Sim who told us this was a safe place."

There was a pause and then the wall of lights extinguished. Mercury blinked hard, trying to clear the spots from her eyes as the warm glow of an oil lantern replaced the glare of headlights. The lantern bobbed toward them, and soon Mercury could make out the figure of a woman, flanked by two men, walking toward their little group.

"Sim! He's sent us several groups of good people." The woman's smile flashed white in the darkness behind the lantern. "I'm Amber Watson, executive assistant to the mayor of Madras, Eva Cruz. Welcome to our town."

As the woman was smiling at Ford, he extended his hand first. "Nice to meet you, Ms. Watson."

Her smile was warm. "Oh, just Amber is fine. And who are your ladies?"

Mercury forced a smile as she extended her hand. "Mercury Rhodes."

"And I'm Stella Carver."

"I'm Karen Gay. It is s-so l-lovely to finally get here!" gushed Karen through teeth that chattered with cold.

Mercury stepped forward, smile still in place, and offered her hand to one of the two men flanking Amber. "Hi, I'm Mercury. Nice to meet you."

The man hesitated, glanced at Amber, and then took Mercury's hand. "Ron Shaddox."

Mercury noticed Ron kept sniffing and wiping at his nose. Even in the dim light of the lantern the dark stain on the wad of tissue in his hand looked like blood.

Mercury turned to the second man, and Amber stepped forward, gesturing behind her at the line of cars that blocked the road and spoke quickly. "Oh, Karen, your teeth are chattering! What's wrong with me? I shouldn't keep you out here in the cold and rain. If you come with us, we'll get you settled in one of the facilities Mayor Cruz has designated for housing newcomers." She motioned for them to follow her as she briskly led them to the vehicles that had been blinding them. "I'm assuming you ladies would like to room near one another?"

"Yes," Stella said. "We can share one room for the three of us. No need to take up more space."

"And I'd like to be close to the ladies," Ford said.

Amber tossed her long, strawberry-blonde hair back and grinned over her shoulder at Ford. "Well, of course you would. You've been taking care of them all through this nightmare. We'll be sure to put you in the same building with your ladies."

"Thanks," Stella said. "We'd appreciate that. We have come to depend on Ford."

"I'm not surprised at all. Such a tall, capable man." Amber gave Ford an appreciative look. "Follow me and let's get you out of this cold."

Beside Stella, Mercury whispered, "The misogyny is strong with that one."

Ford covered his laugh with a cough.

Amber took them to a big Suburban that didn't just look new, but as she opened the back door, new car smell wafted through the rain to them.

"If you hand Ron and Wes—" Amber laughed softly—"oops, sorry I cut the introductions short—this is Wes Marshall." She gestured to the second man, who dipped his head but said nothing. "If you give the men your backpacks, they'll put them in the rear so you have plenty of room in the seats. We're not going far, but you might as well be comfortable."

Mercury glanced at Stella, who surreptitiously nodded and then slid her backpack from her shoulders and gave it to Wes.

"Thanks," Mercury said when she slipped out of Ford's backpack and handed it to him. She watched his eyes widen as he felt its weight. She shrugged. "I log a lot of gym time."

They climbed into the Suburban. Amber got behind the wheel, leaving Ron and Wes at the roadblock.

Mercury leaned forward as Amber put the big SUV in gear. "We've hardly seen any vehicles still running—and this one looks brand new—like those other SUVs blocking the highway."

Amber smiled and nodded. "Oh, it is! We're fortunate that our Chevy dealership was hardly damaged in the quakes. Any vehicle not running when the bombs went off is in perfect working order."

Mercury sat back as Karen said, "That does seem very fortunate."

"And please understand"—Amber caught Mercury's gaze in the rearview mirror—"the only reason we've blocked off the city center is so that we can better help survivors find shelter."

"That's kind of you," Karen said.

"We count our blessing here in Madras. We also have a farm supply store that was almost untouched by the quake. It has a great selection of generators, which is why you'll see"—she paused as she took a left, and suddenly lights glowed from the windows of a few buildings—"that we do have some electricity!"

Mercury stared out the window. The shimmer of lights through the rain should've been comforting, but instead she shivered—chilled by more than the cold.

"The lights on your left are coming from our city library. It, the Fellowship Church, and our elementary school are the shelters Mayor Cruz has designated for newly arrived survivors."

"It doesn't look like this part of town was damaged very badly," said Ford.

"Oh, here in the heart of downtown we did pretty well, but what you can't see at night is that many of the building are cracked and unstable. That's another reason we've isolated this section of the town. We're housing survivors here, but we can't allow people to just go into any building they choose. It's not safe."

"Did you lose many of your citizens?" Stella asked.

Amber's perkiness dimmed. "Yes. It has been tragic. Before the disaster our population was at about seven thousand souls. Right now we have a little under four hundred healthy citizens, with several dozen wounded. And we're learning that sometimes those who don't seem badly hurt suddenly die for no discernable reason."

"Do you have a working hospital?" Mercury asked.

"Our hospital was severely damaged in the quake, but we managed to save quite a lot of medical supplies, and we have two doctors who survived. Mayor Cruz has set up a temporary hospital in the courthouse."

"Your mayor has been a busy woman," Stella said.

Amber's smile returned. "She's a dynamo! And here we are—the elementary school. It was already a designated disaster shelter for the community and had several working generators, so it was easy to turn classrooms into temporary housing. The water lines are intact to the school, which really helps as there are plenty of bathrooms and two locker rooms with working showers—*and* hot water."

"A hot shower sounds heavenly," said Karen.

"As I said, Madras is truly blessed." Amber parked in front of a large brick building with a row of blue doors and lights glowing from within. "Okay, let's get you settled."

They filed out of the Suburban, paused to reclaim their backpacks, and then followed Amber through the blue doors into the foyer of the school. Mercury couldn't help it—the instant they were inside the school, she felt the tension in her shoulders start to relax. All schools had things in common: the shiny linoleum floors, the trophy cases, the walls of lockers, the florescent ceiling lights. And to Mercury, that meant home and safety and familiarity.

"Down this hallway are the classrooms we've turned into shelters." Amber guided them past the administrative offices situated inside the front doors of the school, and turned left. The hall was wide, with classrooms on one side and lockers topped by narrow rectangular windows high above them on the other. Only a very few of the overhead lights were on, but every classroom they passed had the glow of lights that were softer than florescent seeping under the doors. From some of the classrooms, muffled sobs spilled into the hallway with the light.

"It's so very sad." Amber shook her head and hurried them along. "So many losses. Mayor Cruz has vowed to put together a team of therapists to counsel people. Are any of you therapists or have mental health training?"

"No," Stella said. "We're just teachers."

"I'm definitely not a therapist," said Ford.

Mercury noticed he did not offer up the valuable information that he was an electrician.

"Oh, there's nothing *just* about teachers!" Amber gushed. "The surviving children will certainly need you."

"We're always happy to help children," said Karen.

Mercury and Stella said nothing.

As they continued down the hall, Mercury studied the doors to the classrooms. The glass pane in each door had been painted black. They passed two sets of double doors on their right that also had the glass blacked out and were chained and padlocked closed.

Mercury paused. "Amber, why are all the windows painted black?"

Amber halted and looked around as if she was confused. Then she smiled. "Oh, I see what you mean. Not *all* of our windows are painted—just the doors to the classrooms. It was a school ordinance passed by the Board of Education some time ago because of the tragedy of school shootings. Not that we've ever had anything like that happen here. We're a godly town, but it's best to be safe."

"Amen!" Karen said.

Mercury pointed at the padlocked double doors to her right. "Are there classrooms on the other side of those doors? And why are they chained and locked?"

"No, those lead to the courtyard, which is where we have extensive gardens the children tend, though it's early in the year and they're a mess. Someone must have accidentally painted over the glass, and I hadn't even noticed they were chained. But you ladies are teachers. You know the importance of controlling the entrances and exits to our schools."

"I smell fresh paint," said Stella.

"Yes, well, it was just spring break. No doubt many little touch-ups happened during that week. Now, shall we continue to your—"

The door to the classroom they were standing near opened, and a middle-aged woman stepped into the hall. She had long, thick dark hair that was streaked with silver. Her eyes were ebony and glinted with anger. The tawny brown skin that stretched smoothly over her high cheekbones was flushed with two dots of angry mauve.

"Amber! I thought I heard your voice. As I said this morning, I am more than ready to return to my ranch. I have goats to milk."

Amber took the woman's elbow and attempted to return her to the classroom, but the woman shook off Amber's hand and planted her feet.

"You've avoided me all day. I won't be dismissed any longer."

Amber's cheerful smile was gone like she'd flipped a switch. Her green eyes narrowed and her voice hardened. "Moira, now is not a good time. Our new arrivals are exhausted, hungry, and wet. I need to show them to their rooms."

Moira crossed her arms over her chest. "Then I will wait right here for you. You cannot put me off, and I will not stay away from my ranch for one more day. Had I known it was this difficult to get out of Madras, I would've remained on my property."

"All right then, just let me get these good people settled. I'll be back to speak with you in a moment."

"I'll be here—though here is absolutely *not* where I want to be." Moira leaned against the door to the classroom and stared unblinkingly at Amber.

Amber's cheery smile was strained as she turned her back to Moira and continued to usher them down the hall.

None of the four of them spoke, but Stella and Mercury shared a looked that telegraphed "What the fuckery?"

Just before they reached the end of the hall, marked by signs on the concrete walls that said "Girls Restroom" and "Boys Restroom," Amber stopped, opened a classroom door, and walked into the dark room. "Hang on just a sec so I can find the lamp. We want to save as much energy as we can, so we're only using a very few of the florescent lights in the hallways, cafeteria and gym. It's a blessing that our light fixture store is always closed Sundays, so all of the lamps were turned off, and those that didn't fall over and break in the quake still work."

There was a click and yellow light glowed from a floor lamp to illuminate a modest classroom where the desks had been replaced by four cots, each neatly arranged against one of the four walls. Tacked to the ceiling in front of each cot were long, floor-to-ceiling drapes. They'd been tied back, but could be easily closed to provide some privacy. She turned to the four of them, motioned for them to join her in the classroom, and closed the door softly behind them.

"Before we continue, I really must apologize for that little scene with Moira."

Stella spoke immediately. "Why can't she go home?"

"It's sad, really, and under normal circumstances I wouldn't share this with strangers—though I mean no offense in calling you that."

"No offense taken," Mercury said. "We are strangers to you—just like you are a stranger to us."

"Well, yes, I suppose that's true. Anyway, poor Moira is mentally ill. She thinks she has a goat ranch about ten miles outside town. She does live on the remains of what used to be a ranch, but several years ago she went bankrupt. She hasn't had a goat in years and has been selling eggs and homegrown vegetables at our farmers market to get by. This disaster has unhinged her mind. We're trying to get her to stay in town because we're worried about her."

When Mercury and Stella said nothing, Karen spoke up. "That is sad. I commend you for working to keep her safe."

"Well, we're a Christian town. We take care of one another here in Madras." Amber's smile blazed at Karen. She included Mercury, Stella, and Ford in her show of exuberance, but when none of them spoke, she cleared her throat and continued. "Ford, the only other classroom here that has men in it is already fully occupied. I would take you to one of our other shelters where there are a few other men you could room with, but you did say you wanted to be close to your ladies."

"That I did," Ford said.

"Well, the classroom right next to this one is the last empty one in this wing of the school, and I thought I'd put your ladies there." She looked through long lashes at Ford and added. "You might not know it yet, but this thing has been pretty hard on men. There aren't many who have survived, and we want to be sure those of you still with us are happy."

Beside Mercury, Stella snorted softly.

"This will work perfectly," said Ford.

"Good! Now, ladies, like I said, your room is just next door. You might have noticed the restrooms are down the hall. Take a right at the restrooms, and about halfway down the hall you'll find the gym on your left. We have the doors open so that it's easy for you to find the locker rooms. The girls' is marked clearly on the left of the gym—the boys' on the right. The locker rooms have been fully stocked with towels, soap, shampoo, and such." She grinned and lowered her voice conspiratorially. "As I already said, we do have hot water, though please keep your shower time to a minimum. You wouldn't want to make the generator work too hard. When you're all showered and refreshed, keep going down the hall from the gym, and you'll come to the cafeteria. I believe there's still some dinner if you're hungry."

"We're definitely hungry," said Ford.

Amber laughed and gave his shoulder a little push. "Of course you are! Would you like me to show you to the cafeteria?"

"No, I believe I'll take a shower first and change into some dry clothes," Ford said. "Then the ladies and I will see about dinner."

"Well, I'll show your ladies next door. Oh, one more small thing. Tomorrow we'd like all of you to stop by our makeshift hospital in the courthouse—don't worry, we'll shuttle you there after breakfast," Amber said.

"We're feeling fine," said Stella.

"But I see Ford has been wounded. I'm sure he'll need that dressing changed. And Mayor Cruz asks that all survivors take a blood test. Just a little stick to fill up a small vial—there's nothing to it." Amber waved her hand as if brushing away even the thought that the blood test would be uncomfortable.

"Why does the Mayor want us to take a blood test?" Mercury asked.

"Just to be sure you're healthy. You know that green stuff is pretty nasty." Amber paused. "Or do you not know how destructive it is? Did it touch you at all after the blast?"

Ford spoke up quickly. "No. We were camping on the top of a canyon not far from Warm Springs, which gave us a great view and also kept us above the green fog."

"Though we did see how dangerous it is as it engulfed and killed the people below us," added Mercury.

"Yes, that is why we avoided it on our trek here," said Karen.

"And also why it took us so long to hike here," said Ford. "We had to keep going around the green stuff."

"That was wise," said Amber. "Tomorrow you'll see that Mayor Cruz has directed that industrial fans, the kind used in hemp farming, be placed in key locations in the heart of the town so that if the fog rolls in we can turn them on and keep our citizens safe by blowing away that nasty stuff." She shuddered delicately.

"That's a good idea. That fog is definitely dangerous, but like Ford said, we've avoided it completely," Stella said. "So there should be no reason for us to have our blood tested."

"Oh, it's not *just* to check your health. Mayor Cruz has also set up a blood bank. We'll be typing your blood and in the event survivors need transfusions, that will help us know who to go to for a lifesaving donation."

"I know my blood type," said Mercury. "O negative."

"Mine is O positive," said Stella.

"Well, it's convenient that you know that, now isn't it?" Amber patted Stella's arm as she moved past her to guide them to their classroom. "But we all want to be sure, and of course there's the problem of the green fog. Even breathing in a tiny bit of it can be harmful. You might not have known you were exposed."

Ford propped the door to his room open with a backpack and went with the silent women, who followed Amber to the next classroom. All four of them peered down the hallway to see Moira standing exactly where Amber had left her. She stared at them expressionlessly as they waited in the hall while Amber turned on another floor lamp, which shined on a room set up very much like Ford's.

"There you go! Come on in! So, do you have any questions?" Amber folded her hands before her and waited expectantly.

"No," Stella said. "You've been very helpful."

"And what about you, Ford? Is there anything else I might do for you?" Amber blazed her smile at him.

"Nope—what Stella said: you've been great. We've been walking for three days, and we're pretty beat. I'm sure we'll be asleep very soon."

"Well then, I will see you tomorrow. Oh my goodness! I almost forgot. Tomorrow evening we're going to have a gathering at Sahalee Park, right down the street from here. There will be food and music. The mayor calls it our first Post-Apocalypse Madras Festival." Amber laughed softly at their surprised expressions. "Yes, I know. It seems odd to have a festival in the middle of a disaster that has changed our world and cost so many their lives, but Mayor Cruz believes it will be good for morale to remind everyone that some normalcy remains, as well as joy."

"I think that sounds lovely," said Karen.

Amber squeezed Karen's arm warmly. "As do I. Welcome to Madras." She breezed past them, and the door closed silently behind her.

"Jesus Christ. She's a Stepford wife," said Stella.

"Shh!" Mercury said as she hurried to the door. She paused, and then very carefully cracked it, pressing her ear to the small opening. She heard Amber and Moira's voices—Amber's cool and reserved—Moira's louder and obviously angry. Though she strained, she couldn't make out words. Then the voices stopped, and the door to the classroom down the hall slammed shut. Silently, Mercury closed the door. "I couldn't make out what they were saying, but Moira is definitely pissed."

"And mentally ill," said Karen.

"Oh please, Karen. We don't know that's the truth," said Mercury.

"We also don't know that it *isn't* the truth," insisted Karen.

"Fine. We'll leave the topic of Moira's mental health for later, but blood tests?" Mercury said. "Blood fucking tests?"

"Perhaps Amber is being honest," said Karen as she walked to one of the cots and put her backpack down beside it. "Why does everything have to be nefarious?"

"Seriously, Karen?" Stella shook her head.

"Well, one can hope!" Karen said.

"They know!" Stella rounded on Karen. "Stop being so fucking naive and desperate to like that woman and this place because Amber kept saying they're *blessed* and the town is *godly*—which is a stupid fucking reason to think a school can't have a shooter."

Truth!" said Mercury.

"I refuse to judge her prematurely." Karen set her chin stubbornly.

"Wake up, Karen. They know the green fog changes blood, and they clearly want to know whose blood has been changed. If it wasn't for 'nefarious'"—Stella air-quoted the word—"reasons, Amber would be honest with us, like we were with the doc and the rest of the survivors back at the lodge after we figured it out. Shit, Karen, I don't even need my ramped-up intuition to understand that— just half a damn brain and a dose of common sense."

Ford nodded. "I gotta agree with Stella. Amber sounded fishy as hell, especially about that woman down the hall. Also, am I the only one who noticed those two men, Ron and Wes, were concealing handguns under their jackets?"

"Oh shit! I didn't notice that," said Mercury.

"Neither did I," said Stella.

Karen sighed dramatically. "*We're* carrying a concealed weapon in our backpack. For protection! Why can't it be as simple as that with those two men?"

"The short answer is because Stella's gut says something could be off here," said Mercury. "The longer answer is we've been here less than an hour, and I don't need Stella's gut to tell me Amber isn't being honest with us."

"Not to mention the chained-up doors and windows, which are *not* to classrooms, painted black," Stella said. "You know that's not normal."

Ford ran a hand through his dark hair. "I don't know about school stuff like the three of you, but I do know they won't be taking my blood."

"Ditto," said Mercury.

"Right there with the two of you," said Stella.

Karen began going through her backpack and pulling out semi-dry clothes. She said nothing.

CHAPTER

31

MERCURY AND FORD exchanged backpacks, and then the four of them each pulled out a change of clothes from their packs and made their way through the silent halls to the gymnasium. From there it was easy to find the locker rooms. Mercury wanted to stand in the stream of hot water forever, but whether Amber was nefarious or not, it wasn't right to selfishly use up generator power.

Newly showered and wearing clean clothes, the women joined Ford—who looked well scrubbed and relaxed—to explore the cafeteria. The two women working there nodded politely and offered them delicious spaghetti and a succulent salad bar loaded with fresh greens and veggies. The four of them ate ravenously, talking of nothing in particular as they were all too aware how often the two women stopped by their table to "just check in" on them.

At the open door to their classroom, Ford stopped. "Ladies, I'll say goodnight here. I don't think I've ever been this tired."

Mercury studied the dark circles under his amber eyes. "How's your head?"

"It wishes Gemma was here, but it's definitely better. Hey, I'd really like to be sure we stay together—the four of us. I suspect I'm going to sleep longer than usual. If I'm up, I'll prop the door to my classroom open. If you wake before me, please knock on my door and get me up. I don't know how else to put this, but it isn't a comfort to think about sleeping late," Ford said.

"No worries. We'll be sure you're up," Stella said. "And we do need to stay together. Plus, we have a festival to go to."

"We're actually going to that?" Mercury said.

"Oh, absolutely," said Stella.

"I for one am looking forward to it," said Karen. "Goodnight, Ford." She went to the cot she'd already claimed as hers and began untying her shoes.

"Night." He grinned at Mercury and Stella before exiting their classroom and closing the door behind him.

Mercury picked up her backpack and went to the cot adjacent to the one by which Stella had tossed her pack. She unzipped her backpack and held her carefully folded dirty clothes with one hand as she reached inside the main part of the pack for the holstered .38. Mercury frowned. She put the clothes on her bed and crouched beside the bag, opening its mouth wider so she could look inside.

"Fuck! The gun's gone."

"What?" Stella hurried to her.

"Yeah, I put it in the main part here, inside a plastic bag I found in the truck, and then I packed my clean clothes over it. It's gone."

"Oh no!" Karen rubbed her crucifix. "What could've happened?"

Mercury frantically felt around her pack. "I don't know! I—" Her words broke off and she unzipped the small pouch in the front of the pack and pulled out the crumpled plastic bag. She opened it to find the pistol inside its holster. Mercury took it out and checked the magazine and the safety.

"Is it okay? Loaded and everything?" Stella asked.

"Yeah," Mercury put it back in the plastic bag, tucked it inside the main part of the pack, placed her dirty clothes over it, and zipped it shut.

"Well, that's a relief," Karen said. "You must have forgotten you put it in the outside pouch."

"I didn't," said Mercury.

"But that's where you found it," Karen insisted.

"I know. *But I did not put it there.*"

Karen pressed her lips together and returned to her cot.

Mercury met Stella's gaze. "I seriously didn't put it there."

"I seriously believe you. We'll ask Ford tomorrow if he moved it. He was carrying your backpack," Stella said.

Mercury blew out a relieved sigh. "You're right. Ford could've moved it."

"Well, that's the only thing that makes sense," said Karen from across the room.

"It would also make sense that someone went through our things while we were gone," said Mercury.

"Let's see what Ford has to say tomorrow," Karen said.

"Oh, for sure." Mercury said. "You brought wine, didn't you?" she asked Stella.

Stella snorted. "Fuckin' A right I did." She went to the backpack she'd put on the floor beside the cot adjacent to the one Mercury had placed her backpack on, unzipped it, and brought out a bottle of Domaine Serene Monogram Pinot Noir 2012 from the Willamette Valley in Oregon. Stella sighed happily as she reached back into the pack for a corkscrew. Then she turned the label toward Mercury and Karen, who was sitting on her cot watching them. "I checked the wine list before we left Timberline. This lovely bottle of pinot noir sells for just over one hundred dollars. It has a nose of bright red cherries with a lavender finish."

"Brava!" Mercury clapped her hands. "Open it!"

"I shall, though I must apologize that my presentation does not include stemware—or any kind of ware. We'll have to be barbarians and drink out of the bottle."

"Totally cool with me. I don't mind cooties from y'all," said Mercury.

"Are you two really going to get drunk?" Karen asked.

Mercury sighed. "Karen, there are four glasses in a bottle of wine. It is *literally* impossible for Stella or me to get drunk on two glasses of wine. Not to mention we were intending to share with you."

"No thank you. I'm exhausted. I shall just bid you goodnight." Karen pulled the curtain across her section of the room and disappeared behind it.

Mercury kicked off her shoes and joined Stella on her cot. They passed the bottle back and forth silently for several minutes as they savored the excellent pinot noir. Soon Karen's soft snores echoed through the flimsy privacy curtain.

Eventually Mercury whispered, "What the fuck's wrong with Karen? I was just starting to like her, but she's reverted to the stick-up-the-butt Mrs. Gay we all knew and did *not* love."

Stella drank contemplatively before passing her the bottle and answering in an equally low voice. "Karen wants to return to what's familiar to her."

Mercury swallowed. "Being a judgmental bitch?"

Stella shrugged and whispered. "Yeah, pretty much, but that's a simplification. It feels normal to Karen to trust people who appear to be like her, who believe like her, who dislike the same people she does, and exalt the same things she does. It means home and safety, and she wants that desperately."

"So do we!" Mercury struggled to keep her voice low. "I'm sorry, I hear what you're saying, but I just don't get it. Karen has witnessed, more than once, that your intuition is right. You made it clear before we stepped foot inside this town that things might not be on the up-and-up here. And yet from the second we got to town, she has a big ol' hard-on for Amber and all things Madras."

"We may lose Karen here. I can't tell for sure yet, probably because she's not certain about what she's going to do." Stella took another long drink of pinot noir. "But, Acorn, the truth is this place may be a great fit for her. Her blood isn't special, so she's in no danger of being discovered and used or whatever they want to do with those of us who did change. It seems like conservative Christians are firmly in charge. We know what that's like. We're from the damn Bible Belt. But what's uncomfortable and narrow-minded to us is homey to her. Here she could fall back into old, familiar habits. It might be an easier place for her to live out the rest of her life."

"Easier?"

"Acorn, you know our path is absolutely *not* going to be easy, right?"

Mercury exhaled a long breath and held her hand out for the bottle. "Yeah. I know."

"And if you could find a spot in this new, terrifying world where you felt safe, wouldn't you take it?" Stella whispered the question to her.

"Depends," said Mercury.

"On?"

"On what kind of person that makes me. Stella, Amber is lying. I don't need your intuition to tell me that."

Stella nodded. "Yeah, I think she is too."

Mercury bumped her shoulder. “Do you know what all she’s lying about?”

“Not for sure. It feels like everything she said had truth and lies woven together into one cloth,” said Stella.

“That’s poetic.”

“Thanks, but to complete the metaphor—the cloth would be a shroud for us,” she added.

“Absolutely right.” They drank in silence for a while before Mercury continued. “Amber was all flirty and eye-batty at Ford.”

“Can’t blame her. There aren’t many men left, and he’s not just handsome—he’s a good guy.” Stella turned her head to meet her best friend’s gaze. “You and he make a cute couple.”

“Oh please, woman. An apocalypse is a stupid time to take a lover.”

Stella snorted softly. “Acorn, listen to me carefully ’cause I should only have to say this to you once. An apocalypse is a *perfect* time to take a lover.”

“Huh. We’ll see.”

Stella smiled knowingly. “Yeah, we sure will.”

CHAPTER

32

SUN BLAZING IN through the classroom windows and the smell of coffee woke Mercury. She yawned and stretched and wished she'd had even a moment where she'd forgotten the apocalypse and thought she was back in her antique cherrywood bed in the silver and gray bedroom of her midtown condo, and the coffee she smelled was Café du Monde's dark chicory blend coming from the preprogrammed machine in her immaculate kitchen.

"Here, Acorn. It's about time you woke up. It's almost noon." Stella handed her a mug of black coffee.

Mercury rubbed her eyes and then sipped the hot coffee. She sighed appreciatively. "Thanks. This isn't bad for school coffee."

Stella snorted. "Oh please. You're just desperate. And you should be. I doubt if we'll have coffee wherever we end up."

"Do not blaspheme like that!" Mercury lowered her voice and added, "Where is Karen?"

"She told me she was going to church," Stella said. "Though she must be doing one hell of a lot of praying. She's been gone for hours."

"Hours? How long have you been up?" Mercury raised her hand to stop Stella's words. "Never mind. I shoulda figured not even a damn apocalypse could change the fact that you wake up with the chickens."

"We should get some of them too. Chickens, I mean, not more apocalypse or church," said Stella. "Come on, get yourself together. Ford's in the cafeteria. I told him I was going to wake you, and then we'd join him for something to eat."

Mercury put her coffee mug on the floor and pulled on her "Notorious RBG" sweatshirt and jeans before she sat to shove her feet into her Ariats. "Then what are we going to do?"

"Explore the town a little—see what supplies we might be able to subtly confiscate—and while we do that, eyeball what's going on with those roadblocks in case Moira's not crazy and the *godly people of Madras* aren't as willing to say goodbye as they are hello."

Boots on and coffee mug in hand, Mercury stood and they headed to the door. Then she stopped and returned to her cot to pick up her backpack and sling it over one shoulder. "I'm not leaving this again."

"Sounds smart."

"Did you say supplies? Anything in particular we should look for? I mean, I'm not going to want to schlep bags of groceries back to the truck."

"I was thinking more like pharmaceuticals and tampons," said Stella.

"Ooh, Xanax?"

"Well, sure, though you know I'm a bigger fan of CBD than Xanax. It works better to manage anxiety and is a lot healthier for us—not to mention sustainable. When I said pharmaceuticals, I meant birth control and antibiotics." Stella paused before she opened their door. "I probably don't need to say this, but just in case—we shouldn't talk about anything more than the weather and such where we can be overheard."

Mercury nodded. "Yeah, I get that. Hey, have you seen Moira this morning?"

"Nope, and I've been looking for her. Moira—is it bad that every time I hear that name I think of *Schitt's Creek* and am overwhelmingly sad that I'll never see an episode of Moira Rose's brilliance again?"

"Hell no, it's not bad, and don't remind me. It was horrible enough that we only got six seasons of it, but at least I could binge them over and over." Mercury sighed heavily. "I need to stress eat. Let's go."

The two friends made their way to the cafeteria. When they passed the second set of blacked-out, chained doors, Mercury whispered to Stella, "Have you gotten a glimpse of that courtyard?"

"No," Stella whispered back. "I tried, though. I thought I'd open one of the doors as far as the chain would allow so I could peek out there, but it was a no go. The doors are locked *and* chained *and* padlocked. There's no way to see out, and the windows are painted from both sides because I used my fingernail to scrape away some of the paint. I also got *lost*"—she air-quoted—"and wandered to the other wing of the school. It's the same over there, except the halls are full of the desks they moved from these classrooms. Doors are blacked out, chained, and locked over there too."

"They *really* don't want people looking out to that courtyard."

"They sure don't." They paused in the open doorway to the cafeteria to see Ford sitting at a table with four women clustered around him. "Yep, he's definitely popular."

"They're like a swarm of mosquitos," said Mercury.

"Jelly much?"

Mercury bumped her shoulder. "No. Just making an observation."

Stella laughed softly. "A catty one, that's for sure. I don't think you need to worry, though. I'm pretty sure he's only interested in—"

"Mercury! Stella! Over here." Ford waved his arms at them like he was sitting in the middle of a packed cafeteria instead of one that had less than a dozen people scattered at several tables.

"Come on—let's go rescue him," said Stella.

"He is kinda cute when he looks desperate," she whispered to Stella, and then, as they approached Ford's table, Mercury smiled at the women surrounding him. "Hi, I'm Mercury and this is Stella."

The tallest of the four young women, who had straight blonde hair that reminded Mercury of Marcia Brady, gave her a tight-lipped smile. "Hiya, I'm Lenore, and these are my sorority sisters, Michelle, Katie and Bec." She pointed to each in turn. "We were just asking Ford if he is going to the festival tonight." The smile she aimed at Ford lost its tightness and became authentic.

"And I just told these young ladies that I will definitely be there with my friends," said Ford. "These are two of my friends. There's one more, but I don't know where our Karen is."

"Oh, I'm sure she'll materialize before the festivities start," said Stella. "Lenore, are you and your friends from Madras?"

"Yeah, we sure are. Born and raised here. We're seniors at OSU in Bend." Lenore's smile faded. "Bend is, um, gone now. The only reason we weren't at the sorority house and, um, dead is 'cause it's spring break."

"It's very sad," said Bec as the other girls nodded somberly. "Are you from around here?"

"No, we're from Tulsa," said Stella. "We came here for some backpacking over spring break. Ford is our guide."

"Lucky you!" Lenore said. "Well, byeee. See ya at the festival tonight Ford. And, uh, you two also."

Mercury and Stella sat across from Ford, who grinned at them. "Good morning! I'm really glad to see you two. When I was young, I used to think it would be great to be the only man on Themyscira, but I take it back. Maybe my teenage or twenty-something self would've liked it. My grown self feels a little like a piece of beef being led to slaughter, and those girls are way too young."

"You're a fan of Wonder Woman?" Mercury asked.

"Who's not?" Ford said with a grin.

"Only soulless people and misogynist asshats," said Stella.

"Oh, hey, quick question." Mercury leaned forward and lowered her voice. "Did you move the gun from the main part of my backpack to the outside zip pocket?"

Ford's eyes widened. "No. Absolutely not. Why?"

"Someone moved it. Last night. While we were showering and then eating."

"So they know we're armed," said Stella.

"That's why you're carrying your backpack," said Ford.

"Can I get you some coffee or something to eat?" asked a woman who approached their table with a smile. She was round and apple-cheeked, like she'd be a perfect Mrs. Claus.

The three of them instantly stopped their conversation. Mercury pointed at Ford's tray, which was filled with half-eaten scrambled eggs and hash browns. "Actually, I'll follow you to the kitchen if you have any more left of what he's eating."

"I believe we do. Come on back and I'll load you up," said the woman.

"That sounds great." Mercury stood. "Stella, you want anything?"

"You can refill my coffee, but that's it. I ate a couple hours ago. I'll just sit here and protect Ford while you're gone."

"Muchas gracias," he said with a wink to Stella.

Mercury was back in a few minutes with her plate filled with eggs, hash browns, and thick, bright red slices of fresh beefsteak tomatoes. "They said it's lunchtime, but I lucked out 'cause they had hash browns and eggs left over from breakfast." She salted a slice of brilliant red tomato and shoved it in her mouth, moaning in pleasure. After she swallowed, she said, "Y'all, these tomatoes are amazing." Then she lowered her voice. "Before we leave I'm going to stick a few in my backpack. We gotta have some of these wherever we end up."

Stella picked up one of the slices from Mercury's plate and nibbled delicately. "I'm in total agreement with that."

Mercury and Ford made fast work of breakfast, bussed their table, thanked the kitchen workers, and headed out the blue front doors of the school.

"Hey there!" A man who had been leaning against a black Tahoe SUV straightened and waved at them. "I'm here to shuttle newcomers to the courthouse. Hop in and I'll give you a ride."

"That's okay," Mercury said. "It's such a beautiful day that we'll walk."

The man frowned. "Do you know your way around Madras?"

"Sure do," said Ford. "Been here many times. I'll make sure the ladies get where they need to go."

"Well, okay then." The man continued to frown, but went back to leaning on the SUV.

The three of them walked briskly away. Mercury shielded her eyes as she looked up into a bright sky made all the more brilliant by the distant clouds of smoke and snow that surrounded them.

"Why is it not all smoky here?" Mercury asked as they walked down the sidewalk in front of the school and then took a right toward the heart of downtown Madras, which was only a few blocks away.

"I think we're just having a temporary reprieve because of wind patterns mixed with rain. We're also very lucky those bombs didn't go off a few months from now, when we'd been in the middle of Oregon's fire season. We had a wet winter and early spring. If not, most of the state would be an inferno right now."

Stella shivered. "That sounds awful."

"Yeah, for sure. Wildfires are scary," agreed Ford. "Hey, what's going on over there?"

They'd come to the intersection of what the lopsided street signs proclaimed were Fifth and E Streets. In the middle of Fifth Street, white tents had been pitched. People walked up and down the street, stopping at the tents. There weren't a lot of people—Mercury quickly counted fifty or so—but if it hadn't been for the caution tape strung across the doorways of most of the downtown shops and the fact that several of the buildings that housed those shops had cracked facades, broken windows, and caved-in roofs, it could've been an afternoon farmers market on a pretty spring day

"This, lady and gentleman, feels like smoke and mirrors," whispered Stella. "But let's pretend we don't know that and see what we can scavenge."

They headed to the first tent in the line of several, and Ford cleared his throat, catching the women's attention. He cut his eyes to the end of the block, where a row of SUVs formed a barricade.

The three of them turned their gaze to look at the other end of the street. There, too, was another SUV barricade.

"I think," Ford said quietly, "that if we walked up and down the streets that frame downtown we would find that each of them are blocked."

"I think you're right," said Stella.

"Good thing we don't need to drive out of downtown," said Mercury. Stella and Ford silently nodded.

The first tent they came to was filled with toiletries—toothbrushes, toothpaste, shampoo, conditioner, razors, etcetera. The gray-haired couple in charge of the tent grinned at them.

"Hi there! I'm Elizabeth, but you can call me Beth, and this is my hubby, Fred."

"Howdy." Fred raised his hand and gave them a friendly wave.

"It's nice to see new faces, though you really should get that bandage changed, sir. Do you know where we've set up the clinic?" Beth asked Ford.

"Yes, ma'am," Ford said. "Amber told us last night when we arrived that it's in the courthouse, and if I remember correctly, that's not far from here."

"You're right about that," Fred said. "We're on Fifth and the courthouse is on Second."

"But before you head that way, is there anything you need from here?" Beth gestured like Vanna White turning letters.

"Well, Beth, some toothpaste would be nice," said Mercury. "But I'm out of cash, and I'm pretty sure you don't take credit cards."

Beth laughed softly. "Oh no, you don't need money here. Mayor Cruz asked us to set up tents for new arrivals and survivors. Madras takes care of her own. Please, take what you need."

"Wow, that's really nice," said Mercury. "But what if we don't plan to stay?"

The woman's smile faded. "Why would you want to leave?" She lowered her voice. "I've heard horrible things about what's happening out there. That green fog kills people, and the people it doesn't kill have turned into marauders."

"Marauders?" Stella asked. "Really?"

Fred nodded. "Yup. That's what the mayor says. Best to just stay here. Madras is a great place to live."

"We'll definitely consider it," said Ford.

Beth's smile returned. "How lovely! Fred, dear, don't we still have some beard conditioner left back there in the right-hand corner by the razors?"

"I believe so, Bethy. Follow me, young man. I'll be happy to show you," said Fred.

"Oh. That'd be great. Thank you, sir." Ford headed with Fred to the rear of the tent.

"Um, I was wondering," Mercury said. "Would you point us to the tampons?"

"We're out of tampons," said Beth.

"Well, pads will do," said Mercury.

"Sadly, we're out of them too. Fortunately, the mayor found us plenty of these." She reached behind her and handed Stella and Mercury each a box that was labeled "Intimina Lily Menstrual Cups."

"As a woman Mayor Cruz understands the importance of feminine hygiene products, and in these troubling days, having something for *that time of the month* that's reusable only make sense. I'm beyond the need for these, but I certainly wish I'd known about menstrual cups when I was younger. It boggles my mind to think of how much money they would've saved me."

Stella looked up from reading the box. "So, these save your flow instead of absorbing it like a tampon."

"That's right, dear. Then you just pour it out, wash the cup, and reinsert it. They can be used for years and years, and each box comes with three cups."

"I've wanted to try these things. I just never got around to it. Guess this is the perfect time to give them a go," said Mercury. "Ma'am, could Stella and I trouble you for a couple more boxes? We have other women in our party."

"Of course, dear. Here you go."

Mercury put the boxes in her backpack, as well as Ford's beard conditioner, wished Beth and Fred a great day, and headed out of the tent.

"What was all of that about?" Ford asked under his breath.

"Blood," said Stella. "And how to save every drop a women has."

"I cannot tell you how creeped out I am," whispered Mercury.

"Keep it together, Acorn. We're gonna get our asses out of here soon. Real soon," said Stella. "Meanwhile, let's hunt and gather."

"Holy crap. There're clothes. Like, new dresses and such," said Mercury as she stared into the next tent, which was filled with colorful spring dresses hanging on metal rods and blowing slightly in the soft breeze like butterflies.

"Come on in! I'm sure we have something that'll fit you!" The plump thirty-something woman who sat on a stool near the front of the tent grinned at them and gestured for them to enter her makeshift store. "I'm Abby. I'd love to help you ladies find something pretty to wear tonight to the festival. And in case no one's told you yet—everything out here is free."

"So we've heard," said Mercury.

"Yes, that's very nice," said Stella.

"Well, that's Madras." Abby grinned. "A very nice place. The festival will be at Sahalee Park not far from here, on Seventh and C Streets." Then her gaze shifted to Ford. "And two tents down you'll find menswear."

Ford shrugged. "I'm fine with what I have on."

Stella looked him up and down. "Well, that's great if you're ready to be completely out-dressed. I mean, how many opportunities are we going to have to attend a festival?"

"Well," Abby said conspiratorially, "she hasn't announced it officially, but rumor has it Mayor Cruz is going to hold a festival every month. She says it's good for morale."

"I guess it wouldn't hurt to get dressed up," Ford said. "I don't want to embarrass you ladies."

"Good choice, Ford," Mercury said. "Let's shop!"

CHAPTER

33

"KAREN! THERE YOU are! We've been worried about you." Mercury had the absurd notion to hug Karen, who was sitting cross-legged on her cot, reading the Bible, when she and Stella came into their room.

Karen closed the Bible and gave Mercury a tight-lipped smile. "There was nothing to worry about. My day has been quite nice."

"We want to hear all about it, but first we have a surprise for you," said Mercury as she opened her backpack.

"A surprise?" Karen leaned forward. "What do you mean?"

"Have you heard there's some kind of gathering or festival or whatever happening at the park?" asked Stella. "It starts in just a little while."

"Yes, Amber mentioned it last night, and the good people at the Fellowship Church told me more," said Karen.

"Yeah, well, Stella and I thought it would be a treat to have new outfits for the gathering," said Mercury. "Oh, here it is." She turned and held up a cornflower-blue broom skirt, a buttery-colored cotton blouse, and a matching blue cardigan. "Ta-da! We found this downtown at that farmers market thing. I just guessed about the sizes, so I hope they fit."

Karen stood and went to Mercury. Reverently, she took the outfit, fingering the soft cotton and smoothing the cardigan. When she looked up at Mercury, her eyes swam with unshed tears and her voice shook. "Th-they're beautiful. I especially like the cardigan. I don't know how to thank you."

"You just did," said Mercury. "Karen, I don't know what's been wrong between us for the past day or so, but whatever it is, I hope we can get past it."

"Yeah," Stella added. "Even if you've decided to stay in Madras, we need to part as friends."

Karen clutched the clothes to her breast. "I agree. I've been conflicted and have let some things bother me. I haven't liked our recent estrangement either."

"Well, let's get all prettied up and have Ford escort us to the party!" Mercury said as she handed Stella a white cotton eyelet dress that looked like a something a 1950s housewife would wear if she had a 1960s hippy vibe. "Here's your dress. Hang on." She searched around in her backpack and then brought out a silver pashmina decorated with tiny garnet-colored sugar skulls. "I think you're kinda macabre, but you already know that."

"What?" Stella wrapped the scarf around her shoulders. "I think it's extremely appropriate for apocalypse wear. Plus, it matches my boots. Hello!" She lifted her jeans to expose the cutout leather sugar skulls on her Justin cowboy boots.

Karen sighed. "Oh, Stella." Then she turned to Mercury. "What are you wearing?"

"Ooh, I'll show you!" Mercury shook out her dress. "Isn't it perfect?"

Karen touched the material of the flowy dress that had a turquoise and ruby floral design printed on a creamy background. "It's a pretty pattern. It's very Western—like home."

"Right? And check this out." She held the dress up. "It looks like it's a maxi dress, but the front is asymmetrical and cut to mid-thigh."

Karen's smile had relaxed. "I wish I could still wear something so revealing."

Mercury returned her smile. "Karen, it's a brave new world. You can wear whatever the hell you want."

"Sometimes you two make me feel so young," said Karen.

"That's a really nice thing to say." Mercury pulled off her sweatshirt and kicked off her boots as the other two women began changing. "Hey, what did you do today?"

Karen turned her back to Stella and Mercury and began to take her clothes off and fold them carefully. "Well, first I shuttled to the courthouse and gave them a sample of my blood."

Mercury froze halfway out of her jeans. "You did what!"

Karen held her new cardigan up to cover her plain white cotton bra when she turned to face the two women. "I let them take my blood."

"Why would you do that?" Mercury asked.

"Two reasons," Karen explained. "First, because we already know my blood hasn't changed, so it can't hurt for them to have a sample of it, especially as it reinforces the story we gave them that we weren't exposed to the green fog. Second, because I may stay in Madras."

Stella finished unbuttoning the plaid shirt she'd layered over a tank top and dropped it onto her cot. "That was smart, Karen."

"Thank you, Stella," Karen said.

"So, you haven't decided if you'll stay or go?" Mercury said as she finished getting undressed.

Karen's shoulders drooped. "No. Not yet."

"We'll support your decision," said Stella. "No matter what it is."

Karen said nothing but turned her back again and continued to change her clothes.

"That didn't take all day. What else did you do?" Mercury asked.

"I spent most of the day in prayer at the Fellowship Church just down the street from here. I found it very peaceful."

"That's good." Mercury slipped on her dress and buttoned the bodice to the deep V-neck. "Didn't Amber say that the Fellowship Church was another building set up for survivors?"

"It is. They've moved the pews and placed beds there instead, but the sanctuary is still intact," said Karen.

"Were there many people there?" asked Stella as she stepped into her dress.

Karen pulled on the broom skirt and tucked the blouse into it before she turned to face them. "Oh, probably only about twenty or so. The church is more cozy than spacious."

"Did you happen to see Moira today?" Mercury asked.

"No, I didn't, though I did look for her." Karen draped the new cardigan over her shoulders and smoothed her skirt. "Oh, I think everything fits!"

"You look great!" said Mercury. "What do y'all think? Wait—gotta finish my ensemble." She bent to pull on her cowboy boots. "How's that?" Mercury twirled so that the skirt billowed around her.

"Very pretty," said Karen.

"Totally fuckable." Stella wrapped the pashmina artfully around her neck. "What about me?"

"Not a day over forty," said Mercury.

"Perfection. Let's get Ford and go. I'm getting hangry," said Stella. They headed for the door, but Stella stopped them with a lifted hand. "Wait. I cannot believe I almost forgot." She went to her backpack, opened the small outside pocket, and brought out a black and gold lipstick case. She popped the top off to expose a creamy, brilliant red lip color. "This, my friends, is Guerlain KissKiss Lip Color's Red Insolence, which is the closest thing to the shade Marilyn Monroe used to wear as we can get. It's all the makeup we have right now, but it's absolutely enough." She applied it expertly and then handed the tube to Mercury.

"Ooh, thanks!" Mercury spread it on her lips and made kiss noises at Stella. "Want me to put it in my backpack? I'm definitely not leaving that gun here." She paused and turned to Karen. "FYI, Ford didn't move the gun. Someone else did." Karen started to respond, but Mercury kept talking. "You don't have to say anything. I just want you to know so you figure that into your decision about whether you should stay or not." Then Mercury said to Stella, "Hell, yeah, I'll put that gorgeous lipstick in my backpack, but let Karen put some on first."

Karen shook her head. "Oh no. Red is too bright for me."

"Red will illuminate your face," Stella said. "Trust me. You'll look beautiful."

"Well, I suppose it couldn't hurt." Karen hesitantly applied the lipstick and then blotted it on her finger. "Are you sure?"

"Absolutely!" Mercury and Stella said together.

There were two knocks on the door to their classroom, and Ford's voice spoke through it. "I swear I can smell the barbeque cooking. You ladies ready yet?"

"Coming!" Mercury slid her backpack, purse-like, over one shoulder, and the three of them filed out of the room.

"This feels bizarre." Mercury said under her breath to Stella. She, Stella, and Karen stood not far from the four big grills that were fired up and aromatic with burgers and hotdogs. Long, trestle picnic-style tables had been set up under the park's pavilion, where there were big tubs of icy wine, beer, and sodas, as well as a condiment table and an impressive salad bar bursting with luscious fresh veggies. A couple hundred adults stood and sat in little groups, eating and talking—though several of the adults were bandaged and/or in wheelchairs—but everyone looked relaxed and happy.

A dozen children, mostly preteens, were either eating or hanging out on the playground equipment. They were quieter than what would be considered normal for kids that age, and their play had an intense "I'm-determined-to-have-fun" vibe to it.

And, of course, women outnumbered men at least ten to one.

The park was pretty, tucked into a residential neighborhood that was dark and silent, though Sahalee Park was neither. A generator hummed behind the pavilion, lending power to strands of globe-shaped lights that had been hung all around its roof. They also dangled in long, starry ropes from the pavilion to a basketball court that had been turned into a dance floor. In a circle around the makeshift dance floor and throughout the park, big iron firepits blazed with crackling wood fires. On a little table beside the square of cement that was the dance floor, an ancient boom box with a stack of CDs beside it blasted eighties and nineties tunes.

"Yeah, it feels very Shirley Jackson's 'The Lottery,'" said Stella. "And if they bring out a box and ask us to draw slips of paper, I'm running for the hills. Literally."

"I'm with ya, girlfriend," said Mercury.

"If that happens, I'll race you out of here," whispered Karen.

"Red for you," Ford said as he rejoined them and handed Mercury a plastic cup of wine. He looked handsome and well groomed in his new outfit of dark jeans, a deep burgundy button-down shirt, and a black leather jacket.

"You just became my hero," Mercury said.

"Wish I'd known wine was all it took for that to happen." Ford grinned at Mercury before turning to Karen. "And also red for you, though only half a glass." He gave Karen a cup.

"That's very kind of you, Ford. Thank you," said Karen.

"You're welcome. White for you," he handed Stella a third cup and kept the last one for himself.

"Thanks," said Stella. "I'm usually a red wine girl, but this white dress is a stain magnet, and it may be the last new dress I get for a *very* long time. I'd like it to last."

The four of them sipped their wine and people-watched until Ford cleared his throat and said, "Does anyone else feel like they're stuck in an episode of *The Twilight Zone*?"

"Yeah, we were just talking about that," said Mercury. "Not that having a festival is a terrible idea. I can see what the mayor is trying to do—lift morale and all—but it just feels off."

"It's too soon," said Stella. "It's only been four days. People are still in shock."

"I do agree that this is rather forced levity," said Karen. "But the sentiment is sound."

"Well, I'm looking forward to slapping one of those thick beef-steak tomatoes you ladies raved about earlier on my burger—or rather, *burgers*," said Ford. "And did you see over there next to the condiments and salad stuff that there's an enormous vat of potato salad?" He lifted his cup. "Here's to it *not* having raisins in it."

Mercury clinked her cup against his. "I wish, but there are *a lot* of very white people here, so don't get your hopes up."

There was a stirring in the people in the park as a black SUV pulled up. Ron Shaddox, who still carried a tissue to blot his perpetually bleeding nose, got hastily from the driver seat and opened the back door. A tall, lean woman wearing a cream-colored pantsuit with a sparkly USA flag lapel pin and bright red stilettos got gracefully from the backseat and made her way through the park, followed closely by Amber. The woman's long blonde hair was straight and precisely cut at her shoulder blades. She was pretty— beautiful even—with big, dark eyes and glossy pink lips that formed a perfect Cupid's bow. She could've been anywhere from thirty-five to fifty-five. Like Stella, a woman who aged gently and somehow defied gravity and time.

People greeted her and she smiled radiantly as she shook hands and waved. On the basketball court turned dance floor, a man Mercury recognized as silent Wes from the night before turned over a wooden box and then offered the woman his hand as she carefully stepped to the top of it. He handed her a microphone, which was attached to the dated boom box.

"Ron and Wes are carrying again," Ford whispered to Mercury just before the woman began to speak.

"Good evening, Madras!" Her voice was strong and steady, and it reflected her smile. "For those of you who don't already know me, I'm Eva Cruz, the mayor of this wonderful town."

There was a spattering of applause, which her raised hand quieted.

"Some may say it is too soon to have a gathering, a Madras festival, but I am a great believer in hope, and I mean for our monthly festivals—starting with this one tonight—to be an outward sign of our hope for the future. I want to share some news the good people manning our radios have relayed to me. As we already knew from a truck driver who passed through here yesterday, the West Coast is gone—and east of the Mississippi has been hit so hard that there is little to no communication coming from there, though we will continue to try to reach out to survivors."

"Hit by what, Mayor Cruz?" a man's voice called from the crowd.

"Franklin, I was just getting to that. Because our great nation's communication has been severed, we will probably never truly know who bombed us. The information we do have has come from truckers and amateur radio enthusiasts—may God bless them. We know that firebombs exploded and then detonated a sonic element that released a toxin into our atmosphere."

"The green fog?" A woman called.

"Yes, exactly," said the mayor. "The capitol of every state was hit, as well as our major military installations. We believe our allies were targeted too, but with everything except the most basic forms of communication destroyed, it's difficult to know exactly which countries might have survived the attacks. We have heard nothing from Canada, and that saddens me terribly.

"What we do know is that our brave military retaliated before their bases were destroyed. According to our own retired Colonel Dees." She paused there and looked around the crowd. "Is the Colonel here tonight?"

Franklin's disembodied voice responded. "No, Mayor. Haven't seen her yet."

"Well, then I'll go ahead and pass along what our military expert shared with me earlier today. The Colonel assured me that we do not have to worry about being invaded—thank the good Lord. Our ICBMs, that's intercontinental ballistic missiles, for you civilians"—Cruz smiled to take the sting from her words—"would have decimated our enemy, but even though there is no longer a threat of invasion, we will have to deal with fallout, as our retaliation was nuclear."

"The bombs that hit us—the green fog—do we know whether it's nuclear or not?" Franklin shouted over the murmuring crowd.

"We have not seen any evidence that the bombs that hit us were nuclear. Our guess—and that's really all it can probably ever be—is that our enemies counted on the biological agent to wipe us out." Her voice hardened. "My additional hypothesis is that they meant to invade us, which is why they chose not to use nuclear devices—so that our beautiful, God-fearing country would remain fertile and be able to support our enemies." The mayor waited for the angry shouts of the crowd to die, and then she continued. "I'm sure we'll be debating for generations what happened, how, and why. But for now we must focus on surviving and rebuilding in a world that has been permanently changed, but that is something we can do, *will do*—together with the help of our blessed Savior, who has answered our prayers and made Madras a true sanctuary!"

The mayor paused as people applauded.

"I know this news is a lot to take in, but I must remind you that if you have not gone by our courthouse, which has been repurposed as a clinic, and let our nurses draw your blood, please do so sooner rather than later. We've all seen evidence of the horrifically destructive nature of the green fog. Now we know it is a weaponized biological agent. In order to study it and be ready for whatever it might do to us as time passes, we need to understand it. So, especially those women who were exposed, please—for the good of the community—I ask that you get your blood drawn." She paused again to smile at the crowd. "Well, I can smell the delicious food cooking, so I won't keep you from—"

"From going home? From leaving this hellhole?"

Everyone turned to look at the woman who had interrupted the mayor.

"Oh, shit! It's Moira," said Stella.

Moira strode onto the basketball court. Ron and Wes had stepped away from Cruz but now, like members of the Secret Service, they moved closer to the mayor while Amber met the woman and stood in front of her, blocking her from reaching Cruz.

"Moira, we've talked about this and—" Amber began, but Moira sidestepped her and kept walking toward the Mayor.

"No! I will not be patronized and lied to anymore. I came to town to get supplies. You know—the stuff the *good people* of this town are giving away free to anyone who wants or needs it. *Unless* you don't intend on remaining in Madras. Then what? Then we're shoved in a classroom, forced to give blood, and kept from leaving."

"Moira," said the mayor, "no one is forcing you to remain in town. No one is forcing *anyone* to remain in town or do anything they do not wish to do."

"Oh bullshit!" Moira shouted. "I got here the afternoon of the nineteenth, and I've been asking for my truck to be returned to me so that I can leave since then. It's the twenty-second. I gave my damn blood like you said I had to do. And now I want to go home."

"Moira, you know that we've been talking with you about your home." The condescension in Amber's voice was so clear Mercury wanted to cringe. "It's not the way it was before."

"Oh, Amber, shut the hell up. I'm not stupid or crazy. Of course it's not the way it was before. *None* of our homes are as they were! My home is *my* business, not yours." She turned to face the mayor. "Are you going to let me leave or lock me back in that damn classroom again."

Mayor Cruz pressed her hand to her chest. "Moira! No one would lock you in anywhere!"

Moira laughed humorously. "Really? Then I guess my door was *stuck* last night after I had words with your lackey, as well as today until dusk. Whatever. I want to leave. Now. I do not give two shits that it's dark. I could find my way home blindfolded."

"Then, by all means, you may definitely leave," said the mayor. "Ron, please give Moira a ride back to the school. Have her truck loaded with whatever supplies she needs, and let her be on her way. Moira, I sincerely apologize if it seemed as if we were keeping you here against your will. We only want what's best for you."

"Eva, I'm a grown woman who is a good decade older than you. Hell, I babysat you when you were a kid! I know what's best for me. And I don't need a ride back to the school. Just get my truck and meet me there." Moira whirled around and marched from the park.

Mayor Cruz's smile was forced and tight. "I apologize for that disturbance, but I'm glad it's given me the chance to right a wrong. Amber, could you please go to the school and be sure Moira is well cared for?"

"Of course, Mayor Cruz!" Amber hurried off, with Ron trailing after her.

"Now, let's return to our festival," said the mayor. "Abby, please put on my favorite song, and let's all remember that hope is alive while we eat, drink, and make merry! May God bless Madras and

America!" Eva clapped her hands and the crowd joined her—at first quietly, and then more enthusiastically as the woman who had been so helpful at the clothing tent cranked up the volume of the boom box. The opening lyrics to Whitney Houston's 1980s hit "I Wanna Dance With Somebody" blasted from its archaic speakers.

Mayor Cruz lithely stepped down from the box and motioned for everyone to join her on the dance floor. Like that had released a dam, people began dancing, and within minutes it was as if Moira had never existed.

"That was some shit," said Mercury.

"Well, we know that poor woman is mentally ill," said Karen.

Stella shook her head. "No, we don't. We only know what Amber told us last night, and like I already said, she lies."

"So, your intuition is telling you Amber was lying about Moira?" Karen asked.

Stella let out a long, frustrated breath. "You know it doesn't work like that. I don't get a list I can check off. All I'm sure of is that Amber has lied. A lot. And, Karen, I want you to think about this. Why are you so willing to believe these strangers over me?"

Karen opened her mouth to respond but was interrupted when Mayor Eva Cruz appeared suddenly in front of their little group. Her smile was radiant. "You good people must be the group Amber told me arrived late last night. Teachers from out of state and their backpack guide, correct?"

"That's right." Mercury held out her hand. "I'm Mercury Rhodes, and these are my friends and fellow teachers, Stella Carver and Karen Gay." The mayor shook their hands. "And, of course, our guide—Oxford Diaz."

"Nice to meet you, ma'am," Ford said as he shook the mayor's hand.

"When I found out we had a group of teachers join us, I had to welcome you personally. Now more than ever the education of our young people is so important."

"We certainly agree with you on that," said Karen.

"I hope you're settling in nicely. I believe Amber has you at our elementary school."

"She does," said Stella.

"The hot showers were quite a lovely surprise," said Karen.

"Well, please know that those rough accommodations are only temporary. As soon as we're sure which homes are sound enough for occupants, we'll be moving people to more permanent shelters. As teachers, I assume you'd like to live close to the school." Cruz's smile included the three women. She turned to Ford before they could respond and continued. "And our engineers could certainly use your muscle, Mr. Diaz."

"I'm always happy to help," said Ford.

"Well, then, I look forward to getting to know the four of you. Madras is now your home. Oh, just a small thing—as I said earlier, please go by the clinic to get your blood drawn." The mayor patted Karen warmly on her shoulder. "Though I believe I heard that you already did so."

"Yes, I did. The nurse was quite pleasant," said Karen.

"See!" Cruz's smile beamed. "There's nothing to be worried about."

Wes materialized behind the mayor and cleared his throat before saying, "Excuse me, Madame Mayor, one of the doctors would like a word with you."

"Thank you, Wes. Well, duty calls. It was so nice to meet all of you. Please, enjoy our little festival, and again, welcome to your new home." She nodded congenially at each of them before she followed Wes back through the crowd.

"She seems lovely," said Karen.

"*Seems* being the key word," said Mercury. "What do you think, Stella?"

"I think she was telling the truth—just not all of it," said Stella.

"Must you see evil in everything?" Karen whispered angrily.

"Look, I didn't say she was evil. All I said is that she's not telling us everything," said Stella. "And as I was saying before the mayor graced us with her presence—I want you to think about why you're so willing to believe everything these people tell you and question everything I tell you. Do that and get back with me later. Now, I'm going to chug the rest of this mediocre wine and then get out on that dance floor before we have to leave."

"We're leaving tonight?" Ford asked.

"Well, not yet. But we won't be here tomorrow at this time," said Stella. She grabbed Mercury's hand. "Come on, Acorn. Let's cut a rug."

CHAPTER

34

MERCURY WIPED THE sweat from her forehead as Prince's "Little Red Corvette" came to an end.

"Holy shit, I'd forgotten how much I love those old songs," said Stella, who used her pashmina to fan herself. "I haven't danced this much and sung this badly at the top of my lungs for years."

"Me neither, and I need something to drink."

"Wait! Is that . . ." Stella paused and then, as a new song began, she grinned. "It is! Springsteen! "Dancing in the Dark"! OMG, slow dance with me!"

But before Stella could start twirling her around the basketball court, Mercury felt a tap on her shoulder.

"Do you mind if I cut in?" Ford asked her.

Mercury shrugged. "Sure, you can dance with Stella, but be warned. She has the endurance of a marathon professional."

"He's not asking to dance with *me*, Acorn." Stella winked at Ford. "I'll see if I can pry Karen off that picnic bench. Here's hoping she's finally liquored up enough to dance."

"Gracias!" Ford returned Stella's wink before he turned to Mercury and offered her his hand.

She took it and he began leading her around the court in a smooth two-step with the easy confidence that marks all good dancers.

"So, how many of those burgers did you eat?" Mercury asked playfully as she fell into rhythm with Ford.

He laughed. "Only two. I just pretended to eat more as an excuse not to dance."

"But you're a good dancer."

Ford twirled her around and dipped her before he replied. "Yes, I am. But the woman I wanted to dance with was having a really good time with her best friend, so I waited."

"Oh. That was, uh, very patient of you." Mercury was glad she was already flushed from dancing with Stella because she knew Ford had just caused her to blush magnificently.

"I can be a very patient man. I know when to take my time, and prefer slow and thorough to fast and finished too quickly." He held her gaze as a smile lifted the corners of his sexy lips.

"You definitely lead well," said Mercury.

"That's not all I do well."

"Really?"

"Absolutely." Ford led her through a series of intricate spins and turns that caused her dress to swirl alluringly around her and had her laughing like a girl.

The Springsteen song ended, and Toby Keith began singing about how he "Should've Been a Cowboy." Ford easily changed tempo and continued to guide her around the dance floor.

"So, before the apocalypse what did you like to do besides hike and dance?" Mercury asked as she followed Ford's lead.

"I'm a big bike rider, an amateur foodie, and I also like going to the movies."

"Bike as in motorcycle or bike as in pedal?" she asked.

"Pedal, for sure," he said. "And I love books. Powell's—that's a big independent bookstore in Portland—used to be my favorite place to spend a rainy Sunday afternoon."

"You read? For pleasure?"

He laughed. "Absolutely. Why do you look so shocked?"

Mercury opened her mouth—thought better of what she was about to say—closed it, and reconsidered her response. As Ford held her close, she finally said, "I've been trying to figure out how to answer that without sounding like a man-hater and I'm not being very successful."

Ford grinned. "It's not man-hating to tell me you haven't met a lot of grown-up men who read for pleasure. I don't know many besides the men in my family either."

"Well, good. Then that's my answer. What kind of books do you like?"

"I read across genres. The truth is that I hate genre labels. I think they keep people from reading."

"Oh my Goddess! I've been saying that for years! Like, even though there are some awesome romance books that I know my male students would love—because they're labeled *romance*, it's almost impossible to get guys to give them a try."

Ford nodded. "Exactly. I really enjoy science-fiction and fantasy—especially sci-fi/fantasy written by women." He grinned at her shocked expression. "Women tend to add more complex character development and—get this—*sex* to the genre. I enjoy both."

"Seriously?"

"Seriously."

Mercury studied him with new eyes as they moved together around the dance floor. "What's one of your fav sci-fi or fantasy books?"

"That's easy. I love the queen of sci-fi/fantasy, Anne McCaffery."

Mercury thumped him on his broad chest. "Get out! Pern is my go-to comfort world!"

Ford's grin was boyish with enthusiasm. "Hey, I've always wanted to be Jaxom and Impress my own white dragon."

Mercury laughed. "I named my first dog Ramoth, after Lessa's golden queen dragon."

"No way! When I was a boy I called my bike Mnementh and used to pretend that I was riding on the back of a dragon."

"F'lar's big bronze dragon!" Mercury's cheeks hurt from grinning at him—not that she minded.

"Small world," Ford said as his amber gaze met and held hers.

"Small world," she said, still smiling up at him.

The Toby Keith song ended and the next began, with Tina Turner singing "What's Love Got to Do with It?"

Mercury stepped out of Ford's arms and blotted her face. "This is an excellent song, but not great to dance to, and I'm really thirsty."

"Want to get something to drink?"

"Absolutely."

Together, they walked to one of the big troughs full of wine bottles floating in ice water. Ford poured them two plastic cups full and then sipped silently as they watched people dance.

"In this moment it's easy to forget we're living in an awful apocalypse," said Mercury. "Actually, I'm suddenly getting big *Romancing the Stone* vibes." She glanced at him. "But you probably didn't see that movie."

"Joan Wilder? *The* Joan Wilder?" Ford said in a very thick Colombian accent, which caused Mercury to crack up.

"Oh my Goddess, I love that part."

"I'm actually pretty fond of the festival scene. You know, where Joan Wilder and whatever Michael Douglas's character's name was—"

"Jack T. Colton," Mercury said.

Ford grinned. "Yeah, that was it. Where Jack T. Colton and Joan Wilder have their first *moment*. That's my favorite part."

"Oxford Diaz, are you a romantic?"

"Oh, completely." He held Mercury's gaze and added, "I wish it could last. This night—this festival . . . But I agree with what Stella's been saying. We cannot stay. I also feel—"

The women closest to them sent Ford shocked looks, and Mercury took his arm and lowered her voice. "Let's check out one of these firepits—away from listening ears."

"Good idea."

They walked slowly to a firepit far enough out of earshot that they could speak easily. Beside it on the park's verdant grass was a pile of wood, which Ford fed to what was already burning so that the fire leaped and made the bears cut out of the iron sides of the pit appear to sway in time with the licking flames.

Mercury sipped her wine and gazed up at the sky—and then sighed wistfully. "That full moon is gorgeous tonight."

"It is, but why do you sound sad about it?"

"Oh, I'm not sad. It makes me homesick, that's all. Today is Ostara, and a full moon on a Sabbat is particularly fortuitous. I had a huge Ritual planned."

"Ostara—isn't that the original Easter?"

"Sorta. It's the Pagan celebration of the Spring Equinox, named after the Anglo-Saxon goddess of dawn, Eostre. Christians adopted it for their Easter like they did several other Sabbats—Samhain, or Halloween, and Yule, or Christmas, in particular." Mercury sipped her wine and then continued. "Have you ever wondered what bunnies and eggs have to do with zombie Jesus rising from the grave?"

"I've never really thought about it. My grandparents were strict Catholics, but my parents not so much—and me, not at all. Like I said before, I'm more of a nature worshipper than a sit-in-a-church-and-pray-to-a-distant-but-judgmental-God guy."

Mercury smiled at him. "That's very Pagan of you."

"Thank you. So, my guess is that the baby animals have a lot more to do with the Goddess than Jesus."

"Right you are! The Easter bunny and colored eggs come from an Eostre story. It's said the Goddess heard the pleas of a little girl beseeching her to save a bird that was frozen and almost dead. Eostre interceded and saved the little creature by turning it into her sacred animal, a white hare. But, because the hare was really a bird, it laid eggs in the colors of the Goddess's rainbow."

"I had no idea," said Ford.

"Yeah, Pagans would draw symbols of the goddesses and gods on the eggs and then use them to decorate their altars and bring prosperity and fertility to their crops and families."

"Well, that makes more sense than Jesus coming out of the tomb with bunnies and eggs," Ford said with a laugh. "What would you have done at your Ostara Ritual?"

"I'd planned to have my friends Gather at Woodward Park, which is in the heart of midtown Tulsa. It's filled with azaleas that would've been in full bloom. I'd have an altar set up. We'd circle around it and call in the elements. Then everyone in the circle would write on their piece of prayer paper what blessing they'd like to beseech the Goddess for, in the form of the Lady of the Earth, and the God, in his form of Lord of the Wood, in the coming season." She paused and then added. "Just to be clear, I choose to worship a female deity, but I do include men in my Rituals. Then we light the prayer papers and toss them into the air, ask the Goddess and the God for their blessings, close the circle, and feast. There's lots of dancing and merrymaking and harmless drunken revelry that follows."

"That sounds like something I'd be a lot more interested in than sitting in church," said Ford. "Hey, why don't you and I do a mini-version of your Ritual right here—right now?"

"Really?"

"Sure, why not? Just tell me what I need to do or say."

A rush of unexpected happiness made Mercury feel incredibly light. "Ford, that would mean a lot to me."

His gaze held hers. "Then let's do it."

"How are you at adlibbing?" Mercury asked.

"Not bad, but I don't want to mess up your Ritual."

"You won't! There is no right or wrong way to do it," Mercury explained. "The acceptance and the freedom to each having our own beliefs is one of the first things that drew me to Paganism. So, we're not going to cast a true circle, but it's respectful to acknowledge each of the five elements before we wake and greet the Lady and Lord."

"Five elements? I know earth, air, water and fire. What am I missing?"

"Spirit is the fifth element," she said.

"Okay, got it. So, we acknowledge the five elements, then what?"

"Then we'll wake the Goddess and God. I'll greet the Lady. After that a priest greets the Lord—which means you just kinda mimic what I say with a masculine edge. Like, if I greet the Lady and ask her to grant us her power to enchant and create, what would be the male equivalent of that?"

Ford rubbed his beard and then said, "To grant us his power to desire and appreciate the beauty around us?"

"Yes! That's great! We do that and then we speak aloud what we'd like the Lord and Lady to bless us with in the coming season. Then we can toast to the goddesses and gods—and pour the wine on the ground as an offering." Mercury grinned up at Ford. "That would be a very nice little Ostara Ritual."

"Let's do it. I'm ready."

"Okay, we'll face each other. I'll start by calling the elements and waking the old gods from their winter sleep." Mercury turned so that she and Ford faced each other. She tossed back her hair, drew in a deep breath, and then began—hesitantly at first, but soon Mercury relaxed into the abbreviated version of the familiar, beloved Ritual. "Air, fire, water, earth and spirit—I ask that you bear witness to our Ostara Sabbat this Spring Equinox night. From the far lands and secret, wild places I ask the old goddesses and gods to awaken from their sleep to bring forth the warmth and light of springtime, and the bountiful harvest that, with your blessings, will follow." Mercury raised her cup and pretended that it was the chalice that rested on her altar filled with rich, red wine. "We greet you, oh loving and gracious Lady of the Earth! Goddess of the fields and meadows, Queen of forest and stream, mountains and lakes. With the spring you bring beauty and fertility and prosperity, and we ask, Great Lady, that you lend us your power to enchant and create." Mercury lowered her cup and nodded encouragement to Ford.

Ford cleared his throat, lifted his own cup, and in a strong, deep voice invoked, "We greet you, oh friend and protector, Lord of the Wood! God of the wilderness and guardian of all things wild and free. With the spring you bring the heat of the sun that makes everything green and grow, and we ask, Powerful Lord, you to lend us your power to desire and appreciate the beauty that surrounds us." Ford lowered his wine cup and watched Mercury expectantly.

Mercury lifted her hand that wasn't holding the cup. She pinched her fingers together as if they held a thin slip of prayer paper. "Lady of the Earth, I beseech you to bring prosperity and safety to us in the season to come." Then she pretended to toss the paper up and even looked above them as if expecting it to blaze into light and then burn before it touched the ground. "Now you," she said to Ford.

Ford also pretended to hold a paper in his hand. "Lord of the Wood, I beseech you to bring us home and to fill that home with love and protection in the season to come." Then he tossed the invisible paper in the air with a little laugh.

Mercury raised her cup again, and this time, when Ford did the same, he held it close to hers. "Blessed be field and forests—lakes and streams!"

Without being prompted Ford said, "Blessed be the great powers of life, symbolized by the beautiful Lady of the Earth and the protective God of the Woods!"

Mercury nodded and then closed the Ritual with, "The Goddess and the God—the earth herself has been awakened and honored. This rite of spring is done. Merry meet, merry part, and merry meet again! May we blessed be!"

As their cups touched in a toast, Ford said, "Blessed be!"

Then, laughing together, Mercury and Ford poured their wine onto the verdant earth.

"You did so great!" Mercury told him. "Don't tell Karen, but you're an excellent Pagan."

"Oh, I won't." He grinned. "I'm not one of those kiss-and-tell guys, Bellota."

The word *kiss* hung around them like smoke from their firepit. Mercury felt flushed again, and not just in her cheeks. "What does *Bellota* mean?"

His smile was slow and intimate. "Acorn, of course."

Their gazes met and held. In the anticipatory silence, the opening lyrics to "Strawberry Wine," a slow, sensuous country hit from the nineties drifted to them.

"I love this song." Mercury spoke softly, trapped in Ford's intense amber gaze. "Such a beautiful waltz. "

"Then let me waltz you around to a song that's almost as beautiful as you." Ford offered his hand.

With no hesitation, Mercury took it and let him pull her into his arms. She leaned into his warmth as he guided her in a circle around their firepit.

"This is my favorite Ostara dance ever," she murmured as she rested her head against his chest.

"May the Goddess and the God grant that it's just the first of many," said Ford as he held her close and danced her into the night.

KAREN
GAY

CHAPTER

35

THE FIRST MADRAS post-apocalypse festival ended not long after Ford danced Mercury intimately around the firepit. Slightly tipsy, the four of them walked slowly back to the school. Ford fell into step easily beside Mercury, and every so often his hand brushed hers in the dark, which made her feel as if they shared a delicious secret.

At the door to Ford's classroom, they paused. Other festival attendees were filing into their rooms down the hall, so Stella kept her voice low. "Y'all, pack your things tonight. You can go to bed, but be sure you're dressed. My spidey sense says when it's time for us to go—we need to *go*."

"It's still tonight?" Ford asked in an equally quiet voice.

Stella nodded. "Yepper. Pretty sure before dawn."

"Then why don't we just leave in a few hours when everything gets quiet?" Mercury whispered.

"It's not time yet, Acorn, but you'll know it when it is." Stella grinned and swayed a little, then she reached out with her pointer finger and bopped Mercury on the nose. "Boop! As Alexis Rose would say."

"Oh my Goddess. You're drunk," Mercury said.

"Nope, just toasty. Someone over-served me tonight."

"That would be you who was the over-server," Karen said and then snorted a laugh.

Ford looked from Stella to Karen. "Are you going to come with us?"

Karen's tipsy humor slid away. She picked at the hem of her new cardigan. "I'm not sure yet. I wish I knew why Stella is so set on leaving."

"I wish I knew for sure why too," Stella said. "All I know is that we are leaving, and whatever you decide we'll be cool with. Until that time we should sleep."

"Good night, ladies," Ford said. He caught Mercury's gaze. "Rest well, Bellota. I hope your dreams are filled with dragons." He smiled, winked at Stella, and disappeared into his room.

"Dragons?" Karen asked.

"Yep, dragons. He's a fan," said Mercury.

"Come on, Acorn. I'll help you wipe that drool off your chin." Stella hooked her arm through Mercury's as Karen laughed softly and they walked the few yards to their room.

"You *like* him," Stella said while they changed back into their jeans.

"I think Ford is a lovely man." Karen said. "So polite and so handsome."

"I'm not going to talk about it. Seriously. Nothing happened."

"*Something* was happening over there by the firepit. I could practically see the sparks between you two." Stella lay back on her cot and wagged her brows at Mercury.

"We just invoked a little Ostara blessing and danced," said Mercury with a nonchalant shrug. She noticed that Karen watched her sharply, which made her cheeks flush with heat. "But for the record, I think he's a lovely man too."

"I knew it!" Stella said with a fist pump.

Mercury giggled a little woozily and then told her best friend, "Go to bed. All three of us need to sleep off this wine if we're going to leave without staggering and laughing."

"I am not dru—" Karen began, but hiccupped loudly instead of completing her sentence.

"Karen, whether you stay or go, you're going to have to work on your wine tolerance level," said Mercury.

"Fuckin' A right!" said Stella.

Karen said nothing, but Mercury noticed she'd changed into travel clothes with the rest of them. *Maybe Karen will leave with us,* was her last thought before red wine and the memory of a perfect dance waltzed Mercury to sleep.

Mercury's eyes opened and she ran her tongue across her teeth and shuddered, suppressing the *ick* she wanted to say, so she wouldn't wake her roommates. Her hand searched blindly along the floor beside her cot, where she usually kept a full bottle of water—and then she had to suppress a groan of frustration. Because of her state of semi-drunkenness when she'd fallen asleep, Mercury hadn't thought to fill up her water bottle in anticipation of her current cottonmouth and headache.

Mercury sat and peered through the dark room to see that Stella was curled on her side, sound asleep. Her gaze went to Karen's bed, but the older woman had pulled the privacy curtain.

Quietly, Mercury crouched beside her backpack, unzipped it and pulled out the empty water bottle. Then she tiptoed to the door and opened it carefully, closing it softly behind her as she headed to the end of the hall and the water fountain located outside the girls' restroom.

The building had that eerie silence that permeated all public schools when they weren't filled with teachers and students. Mercury had long thought that empty schools felt haunted by the dreams of generations of young people. As she padded in sock feet silently down the hall to the water fountain, she found herself listening for the voices of those long-gone students, which reminded her of how much she missed her own classroom and her own students.

They're dead. They're probably all dead.

Mercury shut down that thought fast. Later. She'd think about her students later and leave an offering to the Goddess in their memory. But now she'd fill up her water bottle and try to get a little more sleep before whatever was going to happen that would tell their little group it was time to leave.

She held her bottle under the arched stream of water, and as it filled, her gaze wandered over the lockers. She smiled nostalgically at the posters, which clung stubbornly to the walls. Some called for students to audition for the spring musical, *Camelot*, and others announced that Mrs. Rowland and Mrs. Wente were planning a summer trip to Italy and gave a time and date for the informative meeting about it.

Her gaze continued down the hallway, and she felt a little jolt of happy surprise as a sign over an inside door at the dead end of the hall proclaimed in red letters on a white metal sign: "Roof Access/Do Not Enter."

Fuck it! I'm going up on the roof!

Mercury willed the water to run faster, drank several long chugs from the fountain, capped it, and turned to tiptoe to the closed door to the roof—then she heard the sobs. Mercury froze and held her breath while she listened. Yes, the sound of a woman weeping was coming from the open door to the girls' bathroom beside her. Her first thought was that it must be Moira. *Those assholes! They didn't let her leave!* As Mercury entered the bathroom, she decided that Moira must be the reason they hadn't left yet. *I'm supposed to find Moira crying and sneak her out with us!*

So it was a shock when Mercury's eyes acclimated to the little nightlight-like lamp that was the only illumination in the windowless bathroom and she realized the woman sobbing on the closed toilet lid in the last stall wasn't Moira, but Karen.

Mercury must have made a small sound of surprise, because Karen's tear-streaked face lifted from her hands. Hastily, she unrolled a wad of toilet paper and wiped at her nose.

"Oh my Goddess, Karen, what is it? What's happened?"

Karen shook her head back and forth, back and forth. "Nothing. I'm fine."

"Don't do that. You're obviously anything but. Talk to me."

Karen looked up and met Mercury's gaze, and her eyes welled and overflowed again as she spoke. "W-why is it so easy for you and Stella to let me go?"

"What?" Mercury moved closer to Karen and leaned against the open stall door.

"I know I'm not best friends with you two, but I—I thought we were becoming close—all of us." She dabbed her face with the toilet paper again.

Some of the toilet paper stuck to her damp face, and Mercury leaned forward to brush it off. "I thought we were too, and then you returned to being cold and shut off right before we got here. Stella and I realized that you were really unhappy, and if this place makes you happy—which it seems to do—then you *should* stay."

Tears washed down Karen's round cheeks. "I wasn't unhappy. I was frightened."

"Frightened? You mean of the green fog and the men out there?"

Karen shook her head and slowly said, "No. Of you."

"Me! Why?"

Karen drew a long, quivering breath. "I—I saw you. Out there in the shadow of the canyon. After you peed you made Satan's horns with your fingers and then traced the sign of the devil's pentagram. And then I saw it—the glowing thing, door, entrance to Hell, whatever it was, and that little sparkly goat trotting through it."

Mercury just stared at Karen.

"Then tonight, when you were over by the firepit with Ford, I saw you throw sparks into the air like it was nothing. I don't know why Ford didn't see it, but *I did*," Karen insisted.

"Karen, holy crap, you're blowing my mind. I hardly know where to start. Um, okay, first—this," Mercury held up her right hand, pointing finger and little finger extended and the other fingers held down by her thumb, "isn't the sign of Satan's horns. It represents the Lord of the Woods, the Green Man, the incarnation of the masculine aspect of nature. It's a ward *against* evil—a protective sign. Karen, most Pagans, especially those of us who follow Wicca or any of the many forms of witchcraft that blur the line between Pagan traditions, *do not believe in Satan*. He is a Christian creation, not a Pagan one."

"But I saw you make the sign of the pentagram."

Mercury nodded. "Yes. In the Pagan tradition, the five points of the pentagram represent the five elements: air, fire, water, earth, and spirit. A pentagram can help call the elements. It can also be used for general invocations or banishments. When I used it yesterday, I invoked the protection of the elements as I bid the spirit of the newborn goat I'd found dead on the road to cross over to the Summerlands to be with the Goddess."

Karen sniffled and blew her nose. "It—it wasn't Satanic?"

"Absolutely not. Karen, please listen to me—I do not believe in Satan. I do not believe in hell. I try my best to live by the main tenant in the Pagan Rede of Chivalry: *"Always contemplate the consequences of thine acts upon others. Strive not to harm."*

"Then what did I see? What was that glowing thing? And those sparks you tossed into the air tonight?"

"Yeah, I want to hear more about what you saw. But not here. Not crouched in a girls' bathroom, like freshmen cutting class."

"Stella's asleep. I don't think we should wake her," said Karen as she stood, tossed the wad of teary and snotty toilet paper into the toilet, and flushed.

"Hey, come with me to the roof! I was just going up there when I heard you crying," Mercury said.

"The roof? How?"

"Come on! I just saw the access door while I was filling up my water bottle. But, *shh.* I'm pretty sure we're not supposed to be up there."

Karen's lips flattened as she pressed them together.

"Be a rule breaker with me—just this once," Mercury grinned.

"Well, okay, but I have a feeling this won't be *just once.*"

Mercury hooked her arm through Karen's, much like she did with Stella. "There's nothing wrong with being a rebel—as long as you're rebelling against the right things."

"And going on the roof is one of those things?"

"Tonight it definitely is," Mercury said.

They padded to the door, which was chained closed with a padlock.

"Well, I guess that's that," said Karen.

"Nah, hang on." Quietly, Mercury pressed the metal handle of the door and breathed a sigh of relief as it gave way and opened the few inches the chain allowed to show a stairwell that led up. "All I need to do is get this chain off, and we can go up there."

"But how—"

"I've got this." Mercury took the simple padlock in the palm of her right hand. She closed her hand over it and squeezed as hard as she could—and the metal lock shattered.

Karen squeaked. "Oh my Lord!"

"I forget how strong I am now." Carefully, Mercury drew the chain from around the doors and then opened one of them all the way. She motioned Karen through before she bent and propped the door open by catching the chain in it. "That's in case it locks behind us. I could probably pull it off the hinges, but that would definitely wake everyone."

The school was only one story tall, so it was an easy climb to the rooftop access door, which was also chained and padlocked shut. Mercury broke that lock too, and used the chain to prop that door open. Then they were out on a wide widow's walk with high, brick railings on either side that led to the tall dome of the gym, and the air conditioner and heating units lined up there like metallic soldiers.

Karen gazed up. "The stars!" she said in a hushed voice. "They're magnificent."

Mercury tipped her head back and stared up at a fat full moon the color of heavy cream. Without light pollution, the stars were so brilliant they left spots in her vision when she looked away from them. "One fall, Stella and I went to Cody, Wyoming, to the Buffalo Bill festival they have up there. The stars were my favorite part of the entire trip. It was like I could reach out and touch them. These are even more spectacular." Mercury sat with her back against the lip of the roof and patted the space beside her. "Karen, I'd like to ask you a question that might seem a little too personal."

"All right. I'll answer it if I can."

"Why didn't you dance tonight?"

Karen moved her shoulders. "Because a father's voice is difficult to drown out, even by wine and eighties and nineties hits."

"I'm sorry," Mercury said.

"As am I. Maybe someday he'll be silenced, but that day wasn't today."

"Well, I hope that day comes for you soon. So, let's talk about the rest of it." Mercury turned to face Karen.

Karen sat primly beside her, buttoning her cardigan to keep out the chill night wind. "You mean the glowing and the sparks?"

"I do. I've never seen either of those things."

Karen stared at her. "You didn't see the shining door-like thing that opened or the baby goat?"

"Nope. What I did over the body of the goat was tell it how sorry I was that it had died, and then I urged its spirit to go free—to enter the Goddess's realm, which Pagans often refer to as the Summerlands. Karen, I *imagined* a glowing entrance and the spirit of the goat trotting happily through it."

"Mercury, that is exactly what I saw. I–I'm not making it up!"

"I believe you. I'm shocked, but I believe you."

"And what about the sparks you threw with Ford?"

"Today is Ostara, the Spring Equinox. It's a Sabbat—a sacred Pagan holiday—like Easter is for you. I usually have friends over for Ritual. To simplify it greatly, that means that we call on the elements, as well as the goddesses and gods; honor nature; and then, as part of my Practice, we write blessings on pieces of prayer paper, light the papers, and toss them into the air, where they flame and then extinguish in a second or two. Ford and I performed a mini version of my Ostara Ritual and I *imagined* that I was tossing prayer paper into the air after lighting it."

Karen looked stunned. "I saw it . . . just like the glowing door and the spirit of the goat. What does it mean?"

"Well, I think we should talk with Stella about it, but I have a feeling it means that your blood might actually have been changed too. It seems you're able to see the—"

"Get in there! Now!"

"Ron, there's no reason to be rough with her. You know I abhor violence and do not condone torture."

From the far side of the roof, voices lifted with the wind. Mercury pressed her finger against her lips as Karen's mouth dropped open. Then, she gestured for the older woman to follow her as she crawled across the roof and slowly, silently, got to her knees so that she could look down on the courtyard that was so carefully concealed from everyone. Beside her, Karen did the same.

Amber had certainly been telling the truth about one thing: the large, square courtyard was covered with garden beds, but they weren't any kind of a mess. They were *bursting* with vegetables. In the center of the courtyard, surrounded by dozens of tomato plants, were two familiar male shapes—Ron and Wes. Wes carried a lantern exactly like the one Amber had led them to the Suburban with the night before. He placed it on the earth in a round space between the tomato beds. Even in its wan light, Mercury could clearly see the beefsteak tomatoes that swelled on the vine, ripe and ready to pick.

Then Ron stepped aside and Mercury realized that Amber and Mayor Eva Cruz stood near the third woman. She had been knocked to her knees before them. Her hands and ankles were duct-taped—as was her mouth. The full moon glinted off the silver in her long hair as she glared up at the people who held her captive.

"It's Moira!" Karen whispered.

CHAPTER

36

MERCURY FELT ODDLY detached as she watched the scene unfolding below them. She didn't notice the roughness of the roof against her knees. She didn't feel the cold bite of the wind. Her whole being was focused on Moira.

Mayor Cruz moved so that she stood in front of Moira. Mercury couldn't see the mayor's face, but she had a clear view of Moira. The woman didn't cringe. She wasn't crying and didn't even look frightened. She simply stared defiantly at Eva Cruz.

"I hate that you've forced me to do this." The mayor spoke softly, but the courtyard amplified her voice, lifting it to the rooftop. "Had you simply cooperated, everything would have been fine. I would've brought your goats into town. I've even set up a pen for them in Cowden Park. You could've chosen from any of the houses near the park and lived there happily, comfortably. But no. You couldn't be a team player."

Even through the duct tape covering Moira's mouth, Mercury could see that woman sneered at the mayor.

Cruz shook her head. "I couldn't let you go out there, back to your dingy ranch in the middle of nowhere. You'd get snatched by marauders in an instant." The mayor crouched before Moira so she could look into her eyes. "You green bloods are too valuable for that. We're in an apocalypse, you know. Food is going to get tough to come by pretty soon."

Moira's brow furrowed as she stared at Cruz.

The mayor laughed humorlessly. "You don't even know, do you? Your blood—it causes plants to grow."

Ron coughed, a wet sound that made Mercury cringe. Beside her, Karen gripped her hand as tightly as a lifeline.

Amber rounded on Ron. "Did I not tell you to see a doctor about that cough and that godawful bloody nose?"

"I did. Said there wasn't a reason for either and they'd probably just go away," Ron muttered.

"Ugh. It can't be soon enough," said Amber. "Madam Mayor, would you let Ron and Wes and me take care of the rest of this?"

Eva Cruz stood and brushed dirt off her hands. "Yes, I believe I will. I'll be out in the Suburban. Please be quick. I have a decent bottle of wine waiting for me to wash away that festival swill." She looked down her pert, perfect nose at Moira. "I really wish you'd been a team player." As she strode to the exit, the mayor told Wes, "Put her over there by the potatoes afterward. We've discovered from the last two that even their meat makes things grow."

As soon as the mayor was gone, Amber went to Ron, who stood closest to Moira. He coughed again, sniffed, and spat.

"Ron, that's disgusting. Get out of my way. I'll do it." Amber grabbed something out of Ron's hand and moved behind Moira. Moonlight glinted off the blade of a hunting knife. As Mercury clutched Karen's hand, Amber fisted Moira's hair. In one swift motion she pulled back her head and slit Moira's throat.

Blood spurted in a wide arc, washing the eager beefsteak tomatoes while Moira's body gurgled, spasmed, and fell to the side between two huge, fruit-filled plants.

Mercury felt Karen's body tremble through their joined hands. She had to quickly swallow the liquid that filled her mouth as she forced herself not to puke.

"You heard what the mayor said. Bury her over there by the potatoes. And hurry up. It'll be dawn in an hour, and some of the new people at the school are ridiculously early risers." Amber turned to hand Ron the knife, but the man's body was wracked with coughs. "Jesus Christ, stop it!" She hissed the words at him. "You're going to wake someone. Wes, maybe you should finish this on your own while Ron reports to the clinic."

Ron nodded jerkily and tried to speak, but his cough turned into scarlet vomit. His blood mixed with Moira's as he fell forward on his face. His legs kicked spasmodically, and then he was still.

"Well, shit. Now I'm going to have to help you bury Ron's dumb ass, and I'll probably break a nail. Go get another shovel and tell the mayor what happened. She'll need to drive herself home while we clean up all of this."

"Yes, ma'am," Wes said before he jogged to the exit.

Mercury and Karen ducked back under the lip of the roof.

"We need to get out of here. Now!" whispered Mercury through lips that felt numb with fear.

"I'm coming with you," Karen's face was drained of color, but her voice was firm. *"Now."*

Mercury led the way back down the stairwell from the roof. She looped the chain around the handles of the doors on the ground floor so that they appeared to still be locked. Then the two women sprinted in their sock feet to their classroom and burst through the door to see Ford stop, mid-pace.

"There you are!" He pulled Mercury into a fast hug. "Stella woke me. Said we were going to go soon, but we had no idea where you two were."

"Th-they killed her. Slit h-her throat!" Karen spoke through teeth that chattered with fear.

"Her?" Stella asked.

"Moira," Mercury said as she went to her cot and pulled on her boots. "Karen and I were up on the roof talking when Ron and Wes, Amber and the fucking mayor dragged her into the courtyard. She was duct taped. Couldn't talk. Couldn't run. Couldn't do anything except wait on her knees."

Ford shook his head and genuflected.

"You were right, Stella. I am so, so sorry I doubted you." Karen passed a trembling hand across her brow. "They know. She called Moira a green blood. Said they couldn't let her go because of it, and then—" Her words broke off as she sat heavily on her cot and sobbed.

Mercury went to her and rested a hand on her shoulder as she told Ford and Stella. "And then fucking Amber wrenched Moira's head back and slit her throat. You know those delicious tomatoes we've been gorging on? *Moira bled all over them.* And she couldn't have been the first person—the courtyard was filled with bed after bed of supersized vegetables."

"Did you see the mounds?" Karen looked up at Mercury as she wiped at her cheeks.

"No, I was too busy staring at Moira," said Mercury.

Karen shuddered and rubbed her golden crucifix between her thumb and forefinger. "There were mounds all over the courtyard—body-sized mounds. It's where they've been burying people." She looked at Stella. "The mayor said even the green bloods' *meat* is valuable. She was talking about women—about the bodies of women."

"We go. Now," said Stella. "Ford, I know you're feeling a lot better, but trade packs with Mercury again. We can't afford you getting dizzy and weak. We need to move fast. Mercury, get that pistol out of your backpack. Is it safe to put it in your jean's pocket?"

Mercury nodded as she opened her backpack and fished out the revolver. "Yeah, it's holstered and the safety is on, but it's better in my jacket pocket."

"As long as you can access it easily. Ford," Stella said, "how do we get out of here and back to the truck?"

"We return to the park and keep going past it, heading east. Eventually we'll come to Willow Creek. It winds through Madras. Three years ago there was a drought, and I used the dry bed of the creek as a hiking trail through town. The creek isn't dry now, of course, but it'll take us to where we parked the truck—and on the off chance someone notices we're gone and comes looking for us, they definitely won't think we're walking along the bank."

"Are we ready?" Mercury asked as she exchanged backpacks with Ford and put the holstered pistol in the deep pocket of her jacket.

Everyone nodded. Stella turned to Ford. "We'll follow you."

"Amber said it's an hour before sunrise," said Mercury.

"That's enough time for us to get to the truck and be well outside Madras before it's light," said Ford. "They won't even know we're gone for hours, but just in case, I think we should stay off the main roads."

"Agreed," said Stella. "Show us how to cut cross-country on the access roads, like we did to get to Madras."

"Where are we going to go? Back to Timberline?" Karen asked hopefully.

"No. We need to head east," said Stella.

"Okay, east it is," said Ford. "Stay close and try to be as silent as possible. The lack of electricity is on our side. Surprise is on our side. But don't forget that Ron and Wes are armed."

"Ron bled out in the courtyard," Mercury said. "Fucking Amber discarded him like he was trash."

"I thought she was a nightmare from the first moment I glimpsed her, but Ron's no loss. One less goon," said Stella. "Let's go."

Together, they moved quickly and quietly down the hallway to the front doors of the school. There they paused.

Ford slid Mercury's backpack from his shoulders, handed it to her, and spoke softly. "I'll go first. If anyone's around, I'll say I needed some air. If you see me go left instead of right, that's because someone's out there. Don't worry about me. Just give me a few minutes to distract whoever it is, and then get to the park. I'll circle around and meet you there."

Mercury touched his arm. "Be careful."

"Always, Bellota."

The women waited in the shadows just inside the front doors and watched Ford expectantly. He walked to the middle of the sidewalk and made a show of stretching and yawning as he turned in a slow circle. There was no Suburban parked in front of the school. Nothing appeared to stir. In moments Ford was back. He took the pack from Mercury. "All clear!"

The women followed Ford outside. They took a right and walked briskly toward the park. Dawn was just beginning to turn the sky from coal to deep sapphire. The town was silent and dark. No lights glowed from any building. Nothing moved except the limbs of the trees in the chilly breeze.

Mercury felt as if she walked through a crypt.

The park was deserted. The strands of lights had been turned off, and the firepits gave off a feeble orange glow as wood embers slowly died.

In the shadow of the pavilion, Ford huddled them up and whispered. "The street that runs along the north side of the park there"—he pointed—"is B Street. If we turn right onto it, we'll eventually come to the edge of town, where Willow Creek runs parallel to Madras. All we have to do is follow the creek north to where we left the truck."

"I don't think we should walk on B Street," whispered Mercury. "That's one of the main roads in town, and from what we saw today, they have roadblocks on the main roads."

Ford nodded. "Right. We'll cut through the neighborhoods that frame the street. Stay close."

The neighborhoods that flanked B Street were deserted, dark, and utterly silent. Ford, with Mercury beside him, led them through yards and across alleys as they wound around privacy fences and avoided anything that appeared to be a major street.

They found dead bodies. A lot of dead bodies, deflated and with their fluids drained away to leave limp sacks of fetid skin and clothes. Ford grabbed Mercury's arm and pulled her back just before her boot sank into the flattened gut of what used to be a man. She had to press her hand against her mouth to keep from screaming.

The wind picked up as they got closer to the edge of town. It was cold, but not freezing, though the scent of rain was on the breeze. Finally, the houses gave way to scrub and a few ramshackle trailers. On their right was what looked like a roomy home with a neat yard and a broken sign that proclaimed that not long ago "Beeson's House" had been a bed and breakfast. On the left side of the road was a scraggly park—and at the intersection that marked the edge of town, were two SUVs parked side by side, blocking the road.

Ford stopped and then silently backtracked before he whispered, "Let's cross the street and cut through that park to get past the roadblock. I could just make out the outlines of playground equipment. That should give us some cover. On this side of the street, there's nothing but scrub and sagebrush—nowhere to hide. Sound good?"

The three women nodded.

The little group sprinted across the street in twos—Mercury and Ford first, followed by Stella and Karen. Then they entered the park. They had to move slowly to keep from making noise or running into slides or teeter-totters, and it seemed to Mercury that it took them forever just to get halfway through the park.

"I can't believe Ron's dead." A male voice Mercury recognized as the mostly silent Wes drifted to them from the road, and they froze. "As if we haven't lost enough men."

Another male voice answered, one Mercury didn't recognize. "Hey, look at it this way: fewer men mean more women sniffing around after us. I mean, there are so many of them now compared to us that they're in charge. Shit, we deserve some kinda compensation."

"Totally agree with ya, bro," said Wes.

Ford motioned for them to keep walking, which they did—even more slowly—until Amber's voice broke the silence from only a few feet in front of them.

"You two are disgusting. As my mother often said, it takes a very good man to be better than no man at all, and neither you, Wes, nor you, Mitch, are good men. One of the many wondrous things this apocalypse has done is to finally put the entitled white man on the endangered-and-soon-to-be-extinct species list."

Ford had put his hand up to stop them. He motioned for them to retrace their steps, but what Mercury had assumed was a short, squatty bush suddenly stood. As she pulled up her pants, Amber lifted her head and looked directly at Ford.

CHAPTER

37

"WELL, HELLO THERE." Amber wiped her hands on her jeans. "Good thing I had to take a pee break, or you would've passed right by without us seeing you. That would've been a shame, wouldn't it?" Then her gaze found Mercury, Stella, and Karen, and her pretty eyes widened. "What are you four doing out here?"

Ford stepped a little forward so that he stood between Amber and the women. "No big secret. We decided to leave Madras. I have friends who live south of here, outside Odessa on a potato farm. I heard from a lady in town today that she thinks Odessa made it through the bombs, so we thought we'd check it out."

"Don't you really mean you thought you'd sneak out of Madras before dawn?" Amber's voice held a sarcastic edge as she mimicked Ford.

"No sneaking involved," said Mercury as she stepped up beside Ford. "We just wanted to get an early start."

"Interesting," said Amber. "But I'm going to have to insist you return to the school. It's not safe for you to leave town on foot, especially with only the few supplies in your backpacks."

"How would you know what we have in our backpacks?" Mercury asked.

Amber's eyes glinted with irritation. "Common sense. Which is the same thing that should tell you it's smarter to return to town and let us fill up an SUV with gas and supplies for you. Then you'll be free to drive to Odessa in relative safety—though the stories Mayor

Cruz has heard of atrocities on the road should make you think twice about leaving at all."

"You mean like you did for Moira?" Mercury said.

Amber narrowed her eyes. "Yes, exactly."

Stella and Karen moved to Ford's other side. "We're fine as is," Stella said. "We like to backpack. So, thank you for your hospitality, but we'll be on our way now."

Stella strode past Amber with the rest of their group close behind her.

"I'm afraid I'm going to have to insist—for your own good—that you return to town," said Amber.

Without slowing, Mercury said, "No, thank you. We'll take our chances in Odessa."

"Wes! Mitch! Escort our guests to an SUV, please, and give them a ride back to the school."

"Get ready to run," whispered Ford.

"They'll chase us with the SUVs," Stella cupped her hand over her mouth and spoke softly.

"I can take care of one of the SUVs. Mercury can shoot the other if she needs to. Just be ready to run when I tell you to."

Mercury nodded as two men materialized from the slate-colored predawn.

"Yes, ma'am," said Wes. "Folks, you need to come with me to the SUVs. You really should listen to Amber. She's knows what's best for you."

Mercury sighed dramatically. "Fine. I guess it would be easier if we had more supplies and a vehicle."

"Of course it would." Amber's voice came from behind them like she was herding them to the road.

The four followed Wes and Mitch to the SUVs.

"You can pass Mitch your backpacks. He'll put them in the rear for you. Damn difficult to sit comfortably with one on your back," said Wes.

"I'd prefer to keep mine," said Mercury.

Wes chuckled as he looked at Mercury's pack. "That's an awful big thing for a little lady. Just give it to Mitch. It'll make your life a lot easier."

Mercury caught Ford's eye and winked before she sighed again and said, "Okay, since you insist." She slipped it off her back, but instead of handing it to the man who stood near the rear of the SUV, Mercury swung it in a tight half circle and hit Wes squarely in his chest, knocking him backward into the road and off his feet.

At the same time Ford pulled something out of his coat pocket and with a flick of his wrist clicked it open. He lunged forward to the front left tire of the nearest SUV and stabbed it with the switchblade before he shouted.

"Run!"

Ford raced through the intersection and darted off the road to the left, where there was a long stretch of scrub and rocks. Mercury was on his heels, with Stella and Karen behind her.

Amber shrieked in rage. "Get them!"

The engine of one of the SUV's roared to life.

"We need to run north!" Ford told the women as they dodged around boulders, brambles and skeletal junipers. "That way it'll be harder for us to miss the creek."

The lights of the SUV flared behind them as the vehicle left the road and bumped crazily over the uneven terrain. Its headlights flashed up and down while it crashed over brush and sped after them.

"Should we split up?" Mercury called. She'd raced ahead of Ford and the others and had to circle back while the SUV gained on them—though they'd been zigzagging from clumps of trees and bushes to avoid its headlights.

"No!" Stella shouted.

"Mercury! Go ahead of us and find a way to get off a shot into that thing's engine," Ford said.

"Will do!" Mercury turned her back to her friends and raced ahead—shocked by how effortless it was to pull away from them. Her arms pumped rhythmically as she dodged scrub and hurtled over rocks.

Mercury had run what she guessed to be the length of a couple football fields when she slid to a halt at a two-lane road, on the other side of which she could hear Willow Creek bubbling over rocks. She spun around. At least one hundred yards behind her she saw the lights of the SUV. They illuminated Ford and Karen. Stella had pulled away from them, but Ford had his arm through Karen's and was almost carrying the older woman.

Mercury didn't hesitate. She took the .38 from the holster and flipped off the safety. Then she jogged forward as her father's voice echoed from her memory. *"Acorn, you're a damn good shot, but even a good shot can't be very accurate with a .38 when you're trying to aim at something a hundred yards or so away—for that you need a hunting rifle, preferably with a scope."*

"Well, Dad, the Winchester isn't here, so let's hope my new abilities stretch my accuracy." Mercury took a wide-legged stance. She lifted the pistol in a two-handed grip, focused every sense she had on aiming for the middle of the headlights that, with each passing heartbeat, gained on her friends. Mercury drew in a deep breath, let it out, and then gently, like she was stroking a skittish kitten, she squeezed the trigger.

In the silent night, the shot was deafening—so much so that the ringing in her ears covered the sound of the engine clinking and sputtering, though she saw the SUV fishtail and come to a halt. Mercury holstered the gun, shoved it back into her pocket, and then sprinted toward her friends. She reached Stella first.

"The road's just ahead. The creek's on the other side of it!"

"Where are you going?" Stella cried as she raced past her.

"To get Karen! Go, Stella!"

Mercury's remarkable speed ate the distance to Ford and Karen.

"What are you doing?" Ford and Karen staggered to a halt as she reached them. Karen had a hand pressed into her side as she gasped for breath. Ford shouted at her as he gulped air. "Get out of here!"

"No, *you* get out of here! The road and creek are just ahead. Stella's almost there. Take this," Mercury slipped Ford's backpack from her shoulder and handed it to Ford. "Now, run! I'll get Karen!" She didn't wait for Ford to answer, but instead went to Karen.

"Just—leave—me!" she wheezed.

"Not a chance. You're not gonna like this, but we don't have a choice. Trust me?"

Karen nodded.

In one motion Mercury scooped Karen off her feet and hefted her over her shoulder like a sack of grain for her dad's horses. She turned, and she and Ford sprinted away side by side. Behind them there was the crack of a gun and the sound of a bullet whizzed past them.

"Shit! Faster!" Mercury said as she pulled ahead of Ford.

There was the sound of another gunshot—and a second bullet splintered a juniper to Mercury's left. Then she was on the road, with

Ford right behind her. Stella was standing just a few yards on the other side of the street.

"It's here! The creek!"

Mercury put Karen on her feet. "I don't think I can make it down the bank carrying you, sorry."

"It's—okay. I can—" Karen staggered and would've fallen had Mercury not stepped forward to catch her arm.

In that instant another shot cracked from behind them, closer this time. Mercury felt something punch her high in her back, below her right shoulder. She lurched forward. Stella's scream was echoed by Karen as she caught Mercury.

Then Ford was there. He lifted Mercury into his arms. "Get to the creek!" They ran across the road and joined Stella.

"Oh no! No!" Stella said.

Mercury lifted her head from Ford's shoulder. Her back felt hot and wet, but there was no pain, though her vision blurred crazily.

"Put me down. I can walk." Mercury thought she said the words in a normal voice, but all that escaped her mouth was an unintelligible whisper.

"Get down the bank!" Ford said.

"It's steep. And there are brambles everywhere," said Stella as she touched Mercury's face and smoothed her hair back. "It's okay, Acorn. You're gonna be okay."

"Where the fuck are they?" Amber's voice was shrill and entirely too close.

Mercury's blurry gaze lifted to see a lantern bobbing behind them like a specter.

"Doesn't matter. We have to get down there. Now," Ford said. Without waiting, he tightened his grip on Mercury and they dropped over the side of the steep bank. She moaned as she jostled against him. Brambles tore at his jeans and sliced his skin, but Ford kept going until he reached the rocky bank.

Karen slid down the incline behind them. Stella followed her more slowly—then she stopped about a third the way down, her focus on the ground.

"What are you doing?" Ford hissed.

Stella's gaze went to him. "Her blood—it's making the brambles grow."

Mercury blinked and managed to clear her vision enough to see that Stella stood in the middle of an expanding thicket of thorns. Then her best friend smiled fiercely. She bent and lifted a thick branch tipped by nasty-looking barbs. Quickly, Stella sliced across her arm, then shook it all around her so that blood rained on the brambles. In a voice filled with intent, Stella Carver commanded, *"Grow!"* Then she slid the rest of the way down the incline to them.

As Ford and her two friends rushed away along the creek, Mercury gazed over his shoulder at the incline, where huge, spiked plants were spreading all along the bank like water loosed from a dam.

GEMMA
JENKINS

CHAPTER

38

"MERCURY! DON'T YOU fucking dare die! Stay with me, Mercury Elizabeth Rhodes!

Mercury wanted to open her eyes and tell Stella to hush so she could sleep, but even that effort was too much. She'd just take a little nap. It felt good to relax—to give into the darkness and . . . Mercury screamed in pain as someone pressed fire into her back.

"Okay, hold the shirt on the wound. I'm going to try to wrap my belt around it to keep pressure on it. If we don't slow this bleeding we're going to lose her."

Mercury thought Ford sounded terrible. His voice was raw with emotion, and then she couldn't think about that as her body exploded in pain again. Her mind was a fog, and her vision had tunneled to shades of gray and black. And she was cold. So, so cold. Ford lifted her into his arms and continued to move forward.

Stella's voice was close beside her. "You hold on, Mercury Elizabeth! We are going to get you to Gemma before you fucking die."

Mercury tried to answer Stella, but it was impossible to formulate words. She could hear what they were saying, but they seemed far away from her—like Mercury had already drifted from their world toward another.

"Wake up!" Stella snapped. "I've lost everything. I'm not losing you too!"

"Please—don't—die!" Karen said between sobs.

Mercury slitted her eyes open. Her vision had gone from grays and blacks to preternaturally clear. The newly risen sun was painting the dove-colored clouds with fuchsia and peach, and Mercury realized it was raining softly, like the sky was crying. The pain in her back was there, but she was detached from it. She was still cold, though her teeth no longer chattered. Her breath wheezed. She coughed—and was shocked to see blood and spittle wet Ford's shirt, which was already plastered to his body with rain and sweat.

"We have to move faster," Ford panted. His chest heaved as he gulped air, though he kept jogging along the rocky edge of the creek.

Mercury couldn't speak. She was barely able to breathe.

"They're here!" Imani's shout echoed from ahead of them. "They're here!"

"Finally! Imani, start the truck! Get the kids into the bed—now! And tell Gemma to get out here!" Stella cried.

Imani's voice lent Ford a burst of speed, and Mercury had to close her eyes tightly and press her face to his shoulder as he jostled her so badly that her vision grayed again.

Ford staggered to the slab of cement as Gemma rushed up to them.

"No! Mercury!" Gemma cried.

Ford gently placed her on the concrete.

"What happened? What's this wound from?" Gemma spoke frantically.

"She's been shot," Stella said. "There's an exit wound. The bullet went through her."

"Imani! Get the first aid kit! Mercury, can you hear me?" Gemma felt for her pulse.

Mercury opened her eyes and tried to respond, but another cough overwhelmed her as blood sprayed from her mouth. The pain wasn't terrible—it was distant, like her body belonged to someone else, and she was just an observer. Her vision was strange, grayed all around the edges and remarkably clear in the center. She was cold—so, so cold. And more exhausted than she'd ever felt in her life.

"Shh, shh, it's going to be okay." Gemma's hands trembled as she untied the belt that held a balled-up shirt against Mercury's wound. "Oh God! It's bad!" The teenager looked up at Stella. "She's dying!"

Mercury felt a jolt of shock, but the soothing sense of detachment didn't allow the shock to progress to panic. All she could do was observe silently as she gasped for air that wouldn't come.

"Do *not* let her die!" Stella said.

Gemma lifted bloody hands beseechingly. "Then tell me how to save her! I'm not a doctor. There's no hospital here! She needs adult people who know what they're doing—not me!"

"Bullshit kid!" Stella dropped to her knees beside Gemma and took the girl's shoulders in her hands. "Do you believe that I know things?"

"Y-yes." Gemma wiped away tears, leaving scarlet streaks across her face.

"Then listen to me and believe me—you have more inside you than any surgeon or hospital or damn adult. Do not fucking think about it—*just save our Mercury!*" Stella gave Gemma's shoulders a shake before she released her and pointed at Mercury. "Now, Gemma. Save her *now*!"

Gemma turned back to Mercury and yanked the wadded-up shirt from the wound. Mercury gasped as pain engulfed her, and her vision went from gray to red.

Gemma moved quickly. She pressed both of her hands onto the wound, bowed her head, and closed her eyes. "Mercury, I want you to heal. I want the wound to stop bleeding. I want your lung to inflate. And then I want your flesh to knit together. I want to you live, Mercury. Live!"

Nearby, Karen's plea mixed with Gemma's. "Please, Lord Jesus, please help Gemma save our Mercury."

Together, Gemma and Mercury gasped. The teenager's body stiffened and her head snapped up and back. Gemma's mouth opened as a scream filled with unimagined pain tore through the girl. Her body trembled, but she kept her hands pressed against Mercury's wound.

Heat engulfed Mercury. It began under Gemma's hands and expanded until it felt as if her veins pumped lava, and she would explode into a ball of fire and blood and agony. Mercury sucked in a huge breath and released a scream that echoed Gemma's and seemed to go on and on and on forever.

And then as quickly as the inferno of pain had begun, it was gone. Mercury looked up to meet Gemma's gaze—shocked to see that her eyes glowed with the same neon emerald as the toxic fog. There was blood at the corners of her lips, which lifted as she smiled at Mercury. With a spasm-like motion, Gemma's hands twitched off Mercury's body, and the teenager's smile widened to show her bloody teeth.

"I did it." Gemma said before her jeweled eyes rolled and she slumped to the concrete beside Mercury.

"Good job, Gemma," Mercury managed to whisper before unconsciousness pulled her under as well.

The bouncing of the old truck woke Mercury. For a moment she was completely disorientated and wondered why the hell she'd fallen asleep in the back of her dad's hay bailing truck. Her eyes blinked open, and at first she didn't understand why there were a bunch of people in the back of Dad's truck with her.

Then Imani leaned over and smiled at her, and reality rushed back.

There's been an apocalypse.

She'd been shot.

She'd been dying.

Gemma had healed her.

Mercury turned her head to glance at the warm spot pressed against her left side, which she realized was Gemma—looking pale as she slept.

"Is she okay?" Mercury's voice croaked.

"Gemma's fine," Imani assured her. "She woke a little while ago, drank two bottles of water, ate an apple and some trail mix, and then went right back to sleep. How do you feel?"

Mercury cleared her throat, which felt like it was lined with sand. "Thirsty," she whispered roughly. "And hungry."

"I'm not surprised. You lost a lot of blood. Gemma said you'd need to eat and drink when you woke. I have water for you, and some bread and cheese. Hang on a sec, though. I need to let everyone know you're okay."

Behind Mercury, Imani crawled to the window of the camper shell that lined up with the rear window of the cab and knocked on it. "She's awake!"

Mercury propped herself up on her elbow so that she could turn and maybe give a cheery thumbs-up to Stella, but was trapped by three wide-eyed stares.

Mercury cleared her throat again. "Hi. Good to see y'all."

"Are you really alive?" Georgie said.

"Absolutely," said Mercury. Her gaze shifted to the little boy, whose eyes overflowed with tears. "I missed you Cayden."

The boy hiccupped a sob and nodded several times.

Mercury held her arms open. "I could use a hug."

Cayden started forward and then cringed back, crying harder.

"Hey, it's okay. I really do feel fine."

"I, uh, think all the blood scares him," Georgie said, and Cayden nodded vigorously again.

Mercury looked down at herself. Her "Notorious RBG" sweatshirt had been ripped open to expose her right shoulder. Just below her clavicle was an ugly pink scar, puckered in the middle. It looked like someone had tried to clean the blood off her arm and shoulder, but dried rust still streaked her skin, and the rest of her sweatshirt was stiff with blood.

"Don't worry, Cayden. I clean up real well. And as soon as I do, I'll need that hug, okay?"

Cayden wiped at his eyes and nodded again.

"Here's some water." Imani handed her a bottle of water, which Mercury chugged gratefully. "They're gonna pull over in a sec. I think they need to find a spot that's not too muddy. It's been raining all day."

Mercury wiped her mouth with the back of her hand and then touched what was left of her sweatshirt. "All day? How long have I been asleep?"

"Well, you guys showed up at dawn, and it's sometime in the early afternoon right now."

Mercury struggled to sit. Imani leaned forward to help her and then propped a backpack behind her. Hesitantly, she lifted her right shoulder. It felt stiff and sore, like she'd worked out too hard *and* then had flu-like aches in her shoulder joint. With her left hand she reached back to trace a smaller version of the exit wound scar.

Imani handed her a baggie filled with slices of apples and cheddar cheese. "Want some bread too? We ate all the sandwiches, but we still have some loaves of bread and a bunch of cans of beans and tuna and stuff like that."

"I'll eat this and then see if I'm still hungry," said Mercury around a mouthful of apple and cheese. She squinted to peer out the dingy side window of the camper shell. "Where are we?"

"East of Madras?" Imani shrugged. "Ford's been showing Stella how to cut across country. You would not believe the amazing canyons we've been winding around. It's like something out of the Wild West." She handed Mercury another bottle of water, which she drained in just a few chugs.

"Or a racist John Wayne movie?" Mercury asked.

Imani grinned at her. "Or that."

"Who's been getting the gates?" Mercury said.

"Ford," said Georgie. "He says his head hardly hurts."

"That's good." Mercury's gaze found Gemma again. "She's incredible."

Imani nodded. "That's for sure. You should've seen her shoulder right after she healed you. It looked awful—covered with nasty purple bruises the exact size of your bullet holes. Last time she woke up, it had faded to almost nothing. It's crazy."

The truck slowed and stopped, and in an instant the tailgate was wrenched open, and Stella's head appeared through the rain.

"You're alive for real?"

Mercury grinned. "For real."

"Jesus, you scared me," Stella said.

"And me," Ford said as he appeared beside her.

"Me, too," said Karen as she held her cardigan over her head to try to keep the rain from her.

"You look terrible, though. All pale and bloody and very zombie-like," said Stella.

Cayden gasped.

"Stella's just kidding," Mercury assured him hastily. "Aren't you?"

"Yeah, totally. Mercury is fine."

"Hey, uh, I just realized I need to pee. Really badly," said Mercury.

"It's dumping rain. Think you can wait until we find shelter?" Stella asked.

"Not a chance, and I need to take off these bloody clothes. Stella, if you help me outta here I think I can kill two birds with one stone."

"If you hurt yourself again I'm going to be really pissed." Gemma's voice had everyone grinning at her.

"My hero!" Mercury leaned over and kissed the teenager loudly in the middle of her furrowed forehead.

Gemma sat and studied Mercury's scars. "No blood. No nothing except raised, pink flesh. It's crazy. How do you feel?"

"Now that I've had some water and food—great." Mercury met her gaze and took the girl's hand in hers. "Thank you for saving my life."

Gemma's pale cheeks flushed pink. "No problem. But it hurt real bad, so try not to get almost dead again."

"I'll do my best," said Mercury. Then she crawled to the open tailgate and peered out. "Yep, it's really raining. And cold. And where the hell are we?"

"Just west of the John Day Fossil Beds and the Painted Hills," said Ford, who hadn't stopped smiling since Mercury had started speaking.

"Here, give me a hand." Mercury reached forward. Stella and Ford each took an arm and steadied her as she climbed from the bed of the truck.

From behind her Imani said, "Sis, are you sure you wanna get out now?"

"Totally," said Mercury. "But would you get into my backpack and grab me some dry clothes? And isn't there a towel or two back there somewhere?"

"What are you thinking?" Stella asked as she, Ford, and Karen stared through the rain at her.

"I'm thinking y'all should get back in the truck. I'm going to go over there somewhere"—she jerked her chin in the direction of a small grove of junipers off the side of the mud road they'd been following—"to pee, and then I'm gonna strip and let the rain wash this blood off of me. I mean, my hair's even crusted with it." She lifted a stiff strand of hair from the side of her face that was already tracking pink water down her skin.

"Fine, but I'm coming with you," said Stella.

"So am I," said Gemma, who climbed out of the truck after Mercury. She held up her hands to show that she, too, was blood-stained past her elbows. "You bled. A lot."

Ford was suddenly in front of Mercury, blocking the rain as he pulled her into a gentle hug. "You scared me, Bellota."

"I scared myself," she said against his chest.

He reluctantly let her loose and then smiled at Stella. "While you ladies are using the vast but primitive facilities, I'll fill the tank with the rest of the gas we siphoned into that container."

"Thanks, Ford," said Stella.

"Mercury, do you want to change places with me in the cab, or do you need to lie down again?" Karen asked as she cringed from the rain under her soaked cardigan.

"I can sit just fine. As long as Gemma gives me the green light, I'll trade with you," said Mercury.

"You can trade with her," said Gemma. "But I'm gonna need more sleep."

"I'll help Imani find dry clothes for you," said Karen as she crawled into the bed of the truck. "Mercury?"

Mercury turned to look at Karen.

"I saw it again."

"It?" Mercury asked.

"Another light or glow or whatever. When Gemma healed you. This one was green, and it covered both of you."

"What is she talking about?" asked Stella.

"Only that it seems the green fog did change something about Karen," said Mercury. "But I think I should let Karen tell you guys. It's her thing—not mine." Mercury headed to the cluster of junipers just a few yards away, with Stella and Gemma following.

First, Mercury kicked off her cowboy boots and socks, peeled off her jeans and put them near the base of the biggest juniper so they wouldn't get soaked. Then she tiptoed behind the trees, squatted and peed for what seemed like forever as rain continued to wash pink water from her hair. When she was done, Mercury returned to where Stella and Gemma were standing in the middle of the circle of junipers.

"Aren't you freezing?" Stella asked as she rubbed her arms and shivered beneath the largest of the junipers, which provided some shelter from the rain.

"Yep, but I'm also bloody and gross. So, here goes nothing!" Mercury pulled her sweatshirt off and unhooked her blood-soaked bra. She stepped delicately out of her panties, and then walked from the ring of sheltering trees into the open. She squeezed rain and blood from her hair and then Mercury spread her arms wide and tilted her head back as the cold water cascaded down her naked skin. She laughed joyfully while she embraced the torrents of rain. "Skyclad is the best!"

"What the hell," Gemma said. "Me too!" The teenager got naked and then, shivering, joined Mercury in the rain.

Mercury was turning in a slow circle, arms still outspread, as she called to Stella, "Come on! Join us!"

"Uh, hell no. I didn't get as bloody as you two, so I'm going to stay semi-dry."

Gemma had begun twirling in a circle in time with Mercury. "Stella doesn't seem like a party pooper."

"That's because she *usually* doesn't poop on parties," said Mercury.

"I can hear you two, and I'm not pooping on anything!" Then Stella was naked, too, shivering and twirling beside them in the rain with her arms outstretched, embracing joy with her friends.

As Mercury twirled faster and faster, she felt as if the cold rain washed away her old life and baptized the new chance Gemma had given her to live another life—one that would be like nothing she'd ever imagined—filled with undiscovered miracles and limitless adventure. With that baptismal, some of her grief from those she'd lost was diluted as well. Mercury would never forget her family and her friends, but she also understood that by fully embracing the future, she would be accepting a new family, making new friends. Her thoughts shifted to Ford, and silently she added, *And a new lover.*

"Holy shit!" Stella said. "Mercury, Gemma, look!"

They stopped dancing to see that Stella was staring at the ground beneath their bare feet. Mercury looked down. Everywhere the rain had washed blood from their bodies wildflowers sprouted. Yellow and purple and orange buds burst into full bloom. The wind caused them to sway, so that it appeared as if they, too, were dancing in the rain.

CHAPTER

39

MERCURY FELT DRY and warm and incredibly happy as the truck bumped along a trail that looked like it had been made for and by deer. She sat between Ford and Stella in the cab, swathed in one of Karen's cardigans from her seemingly never-ending supply. Her "Rogers High School" sweatshirt wasn't exactly clean, and her boyfriend jeans definitely needed a wash, but Mercury was more than content as she nibbled on a cheese sandwich and sipped water while she stared at the ruggedly beautiful scenery.

"So, y'all don't think anyone followed us from Madras?" Mercury asked.

"Nope," Stella said. "As soon as we got you and Gemma into the back of the truck, we took off. I didn't even turn on the truck's headlights. With Ford's help, we've avoided any real roads and have not seen one living person since Madras."

"Do either of you know where we're going? It can't be long until sunset, right?"

"All I know is that we need to keep going east until we find it," said Stella.

"But what's *it*?" Mercury asked.

"I'm hoping Stella will know *it* when she sees *it*," said Ford.

His arm rested easily along the seat behind her and it felt right, *natural*, for Mercury to lean against his warmth.

"I have a feeling we'll all know it when we see it," said Stella. "Hey, is that a road up ahead?"

Ford sat up straighter as he studied the area in front of the truck. Then he smiled. "It's Bear Creek Road!" His voice was tinged with excitement. "It means we're crossing into the John Day Fossil Beds National Monument and the Painted Hills Preservation lands."

"And that's a good thing?" Mercury asked.

Ford nodded enthusiastically. "It's a *great* thing. I've hiked this area many times. It's considered one of Oregon's seven wonders, known for its remote beauty."

Stella allowed her gaze to leave the path for a moment. "Remote?"

"Yeah! There's only one real road that cuts through the national preserve. And only one little town within miles of here. No one can build on this land. Hell, the state doesn't even allow vehicles into the hills. There are a limited number of hiking paths that people can follow, with controlled access to them. Anything else is strictly prohibited."

Stella steered the truck up onto a two-lane road, where she shifted into neutral and stopped. "So, people don't live here?"

"Nope," said Ford.

"But it's the high desert, right?" Stella asked.

"It is," said Ford.

Stella's fingers drummed on the steering wheel. "That means little water and extremes in temperature, correct?"

"For most of the high desert, correct. But on the eastern edge of the preserve, there's a tributary of the John Day River that serves as runoff for the hills. Bridge Creek! That's what it's called. It doesn't go dry."

Stella's lips curled up. "That's it. That's where we're going."

Mercury's heartbeat quickened. "Like, for good?"

Stella nodded. "We're supposed to be here. For good. But we have to be near water, because even though our blood makes things grow, nothing lives long without water."

"We'll also need to figure out some serious shelter," said Ford. "It's chilly and wet right now, but that'll end by mid-spring. In summer, temperatures during the day can reach upward of one hundred degrees, and at night it can get really cold."

"Which serves as a deterrent for people—especially assholes like Eva Cruz or Alvin fucking Rutland," said Stella.

Mercury studied her friend. "You really think we could make a life here?"

"Once we find shelter, I know we can," said Stella. "Ford, do I follow this road or keep cutting cross-country?"

"Follow the road." Ford pointed to the right. "That's the only way we'll know how many people were stuck out here when the bombs hit. Plus, we can syphon gas and see if anyone survived."

"And might have formed a creepy militant group we need to avoid," added Mercury.

"No one who can't grow stuff with their blood would want to settle in the high desert," said Ford. "It's a tough choice, especially when people could settle by a major river, like the Snake or in the Columbia River Valley or any of the more fertile regions of Oregon that have easy irrigation and a better climate."

"Well, should we consider that?" Mercury said.

Stella shook her head. "My gut says being away from people is a good idea, and after Madras I believe that even more."

"Okay then. Let's look for something that can shelter us," said Mercury.

"But only after we get to Bridge Creek," added Stella.

They followed Bear Creek Road east as it wound through terrain that became more and more fantastical. As the sun dropped lower and lower into the horizon behind them, the rain turned to drizzle and then finally stopped completely.

"It's insanely beautiful!" Stella said as she braked so that they could stare out at the Painted Hills.

Mercury couldn't take her eyes from the land. Gently rounded hills surrounded them, and as the setting sun illuminated the valley, its rays captured the colors in those hills and, like a spotlight, revealed layers of ochre and magenta, jade and golden amber, deep purple and startling flaxen. Folds in the slopes of the hills made them look like a couture designer had thrown enormous capes over the rounded hummocks that hung there, waiting for one of the old gods or goddesses to pick them up and use them to swathe their magnificent shoulders.

In the valley between the colorful hill mounds cedars, junipers and clumps of several different wild grasses were interspersed with yellow wildflowers and squatty bushes. Mercury thought she recognized sagebrush and even young bluegrass, which made her feel a wave of homesickness for Oklahoma's Tallgrass Prairie.

"Oh my Goddess!" Mercury smacked her forehead. "I read about these hills. I can't believe I forgot. The paper reported a study geologists did on the colorful clay. It's a biologically active substance that can be used as, um . . ." She tapped her chin as she accessed her memory. "Fertilizer, cosmetics—and I even remember a mention of using it in the production of wine."

"Now you're talking!" Stella put the truck into gear and started forward again.

"I'd forgotten how beautiful it is," said Ford. "The first time I hiked out here I imagined that I'd been beamed to a different planet."

"I can totally understand that," said Stella.

"This *is* our place! It's like being surrounded by earth magick!" Mercury's voice was filled with excitement. "Stella, are you seeing all of this?"

"When I can look away from the road I am, but these sinkholes are frightening. Gotta keep my eyes on where we're going." As Stella spoke, she braked and then steered the truck off the road to avoid a clay-lined hole that had opened in the broken asphalt.

"I'd like to have a little chat with all of those seismologists who wrote the textbooks my geology professors swore by in college." Mercury's gaze was riveted by the landscape. "Over and over they said earthquakes can't tear open the earth. We've definitely seen that they were wrong about that. Also, I'm surprised that these are the first sinkholes I've seen."

"I thought earthquakes didn't cause sinkholes," said Ford.

"Scientists would say they aren't caused by quakes. Quakes only allow underground pockets already hidden in the earth to become visible—or something like that." Mercury shrugged. "Honestly, I think we're going to observe a bunch of geological features that weren't predicted."

"But these hills have always been this beautiful?" Stella asked.

Ford grinned. "For hundreds of thousands of years, yes."

"Ooh! That's something else I remember from the article." Mercury said. "This used to be the floor of the ocean. Then it was a tropical forest. You can see that in the green and purple striations. Apparently, the fossils they've discovered here are amazing."

"I love it when you talk all science-y," said Stella.

"As do I." Ford grinned at Mercury.

The narrow road took a northern turn, and shortly after that Mercury pointed off to their right. "Look!"

"It's Bridge Creek!" Ford said.

"I'm leaving the road," Stella said. "We don't want to settle anywhere near a traditional highway, or even a road as remote as this one."

"Makes sense," said Ford. "Go to the left so that we're sure we remain inside the preserve. That way we know we won't be running into any houses or little towns."

"Didn't you say there's one town not far from here?" Mercury asked.

"Yeah, I'll need to check out that map in the glove box, but Mitchell shouldn't be too far southeast of here. And by too far I mean we could drive there to see if we can find some supplies, but it's distant enough that we don't have to worry about people stumbling on our camp."

Stella guided the truck with white-knuckle concentration along the creek. After they'd driven for about another hour, to their left the gentle mounds of the colorful Painted Hills changed to taller, jagged peaks that had a predominately greenish-gray tint. Suddenly Stella braked.

"Holy fucking shit! That's it. That's where we settle." Stella put the truck into neutral, engaged the emergency brake, and then left the cab without even shutting the door behind her.

"Let's go!" Mercury slid past the steering wheel and hurried to catch Stella as Ford quickly exited the passenger side. Mercury heard the tailgate open and knew the rest of their group—their *family*—was piling out of the bed to join them.

"There." Stella lifted her arm and pointed.

At first the shadows cast by the setting sun were distracting, and Mercury couldn't see what Stella meant. And then she gasped in happy surprise. The slope of the craggy hill in front of them—the one whose base gently kissed the bank of Bridge Creek—was split open to expose the mouth of a huge cave. Glimmers of light could be seen within the cave, which meant it provided shelter but would also allow the smoke of much-needed campfires to escape.

"It's incredible," Imani said. "So, so beautiful."

"I've never seen anything like this land." Karen spoke reverently as she touched her crucifix, closed her eyes, and mouthed a silent prayer of thanks.

"It's so pretty!" Georgie stood between her brothers with her arms draped over their shoulders.

"I hiked the Painted Hills with my parents," Gemma said. "But this wasn't here before. I'm sure of it."

"So am I," said Ford. "I've backpacked through here many times. This cave, or at least the exposure of it, is new."

"And new means no one knows about it," said Mercury. She met Stella's gaze. "It's our place. I can feel it, too."

"This is it?" Imani's voice was bright with excitement. "Are we done traveling? Have we found it?"

Stella turned to face them. Her cheeks were wet with tears, but the light of her smile put the setting sun to shame. "It won't be easy, but it will be perfect. We'll make our homes on cliffsides from the living clay that surrounds us, like the Pueblos did in Mesa Verde."

Imani bounced on her toes. "We know how to do that! Remember that workshop we met in?"

Stella grinned. "I've never been happier that teachers learn a bunch of stuff people think of as useless. We'll use all of it—all of the things we've learned from years of teaching. We will build in harmony with the earth. That is also how we will live, and it will be unimaginably beautiful. We make our new life here. We are done traveling."

"Teachers for the win!" Mercury fisted her hand over her head.

"Teachers for the win!" The group echoed her cheer.

It didn't take long for the truck to reach the cave. Stella parked so that the headlights illuminated the entrance, though Ford and Gemma quickly made three circular stone areas in the hard clay floor of the cave. Everyone collected brush and dry juniper branches, and within minutes they had cheerful fires burning. They discovered that there were two easy entrances to the cave and that from one of them a mountain stream tumbled clear and cold into the creek—which made Stella squeal like a preteen at a boy band concert.

There was a sense of relief that permeated everything they did that night. It didn't take Ford long to use the tarps from the truck and his own camping supplies to create a tentlike structure within the cave, so as the night lengthened and the temperature dropped, the little group was snuggly sheltered.

Stella took charge of dinner, and somehow she made canned chili, rice, and the rest of the fresh veggies into a delicious meal. The children ate until their stomachs were full, and then Imani took the one lantern they had and led them to an area well outside the cave that Ford had designated as where he would dig their latrines. The kids put on their pajamas—something they'd refused to do for the two nights Stella, Mercury, Ford, and Karen had been in Madras—and the three of them fell instantly and soundly asleep.

Stella produced two bottles of rich cabernet sauvignon, which she opened and began sharing.

"Did you say that town's name is Mitchell?" Stella asked Ford as she handed him a bottle of cabernet.

"I did," he said and sipped the wine.

"Do you think we can find some stemware there? We're starting the world over, but there's no reason for us to be barbarous."

Ford chuckled. "I remember a few little stores. A couple restaurants, B&Bs, and such. We should be able to find something. Hey, how much wine do you have anyway?"

Stella's brow arched. "Well, I lined each of the four sides of the bed of the truck with bubble wrap before firmly packing wine bottles, then more bubble wrap, then our suitcases, groceries, and supplies against them so they would not break. There were sixty-eight bottles in total, and that doesn't count the three I put in my backpack. One we drank in Madras, and these are the other two."

Ford whistled in appreciation, which made Stella grin.

"I also absconded with two bottles of top-shelf tequila and three of twenty-five-year-old Macallan Scotch."

"Wow!" Ford said.

"And we have reefer," Gemma added. "*Lots* of reefer—including seeds."

Ford stared at her.

"What? It's medicinal," said Gemma.

"Truth," said Mercury. "Shall we smoke some?"

"Hell yes, sis!" said Imani. "But only if Stella says we're not gonna be in any danger tonight. I can deal with some shit a little tipsy. High, I'm good for nothing except giggles and a nap."

Stella sipped wine from the bottle before answering. "We are perfectly safe, and this is the first time I've felt like that since the night before the fucking apocalypse."

"Yaaasss," said Imani. "Gemma, if you give me a bag of bud and those papers I know Stella stashed away somewhere—"

"Both are in my suitcase," said Stella.

"I'll roll a couple joints," finished Imani.

"I'm on it." Gemma disappeared into the rear part of their temporary shelter where suitcases lined the cave wall.

"Do you think it's okay for her to smoke marijuana?" Karen asked as Imani passed her a wine bottle.

"I think Gemma can decide that for herself," said Mercury.

Karen opened her mouth. Closed it. And then nodded. "I think you're right about that."

"I almost forgot," Stella said. "What were you saying to Mercury back there in the rain about seeing something again?"

Karen looked at Mercury. "You didn't tell them?"

"I thought it was your place to do that," Mercury said.

"Tell us what?" Gemma returned and tossed a baggie of weed and papers to Imani.

"That the green fog did something to me, too," Karen said slowly. She took a long drink of wine, wiped her mouth, and then blurted. "I can see things now."

"Um, they need details," Mercury prompted.

Karen sighed and nodded. The hand that wasn't clutching the bottle of wine picked at the hem of her cardigan. "Okay, remember before we got to Madras when Mercury siphoned gas and then peed in the rain?"

Everyone nodded.

"She'd found a dead baby goat on the road and she did a quick little, um . . ." Karen looked at Mercury for help.

"I just said a simple prayer of release for its spirit and envisioned the little creature crossing over to the Goddess's Summerlands."

"Yes, that," Karen said. "Well, I saw it. The baby goat's spirit trotting through a glowing portal."

"Holy shit!" Stella said.

"And then at the park last night, when Mercury and Ford were alone by the firepit, I saw something else." Karen looked beseechingly at Mercury again.

"It was Ostara yesterday." Mercury explained. "Ford and I did a mini-ritual, and toward the end of it, we pretended that we'd written blessings on prayer paper, lit them, and tossed them into the air."

"Ooh, just like what we'd do at your Rituals back home," said Stella. "It's my favorite part."

"In case y'all don't know, prayer paper bursts into flame, floats up in the air, and extinguishes in just a few seconds," Mercury added.

"That sounds cool," said Gemma.

Mercury grinned at her. "It is. It's also what Karen saw."

Karen nodded. "Yes, even though they didn't have any prayer paper." She drew a deep breath and continued. "And it happened two more times. One was when Gemma was healing Mercury. Both of them glowed green—the same color as the fog."

"Oh! Sorry to interrupt, but that just reminded me," Mercury said. "Gemma, your eyes were green after you healed me."

Gemma pointed to her eyes. "They're always green."

Mercury grinned. "No, not your normal greenish eyes. They were emerald—just like the fog."

"Huh," said Gemma.

"When was the second time?" Stella asked Karen.

"It was while Mercury and Gemma and Stella were dancing in the rain." Karen's eyes widened and she hastily added, "I wasn't, like the kids would say, creeping on them. I was just watching the rain. Then something bright caught my eye. I could barely see the three of you through the trees, but as you twirled and danced, green light glowed all around your feet."

"But the wildflowers were yellow and purple and orange, not green," said Gemma.

Mercury smiled at Karen, "She wasn't seeing the flowers. She was seeing whatever it is that gives us the ability to make them grow."

Stella clapped her hands and grinned. "Mercury's correct. Ladies and gentleman, Karen has been changed by the green fog. She can see the energy of the spirit realm. That's really all our spirits, our souls, are—energy. Congrats, Karen."

"But my blood doesn't make anything grow," Karen said.

"Well, it didn't," said Gemma. The teenager got up and went to the neat pile of clean dishes they'd stowed in a natural ledge of the curving cave wall and grabbed a knife. Then she took an apple from a brown bag full of them and returned to Karen. "Here ya go. Test your blood now and let's see what happens."

Karen handed her the wine bottle and shakily cut herself below her thumb. She smeared some blood on the apple and then held her hand out to Gemma. "I'll take the wine again, please."

They didn't speak as they passed around two bottles of the excellent cabernet and stared at the apple.

Nothing happened.

Karen blew out a long breath. "Well, it seems I still can't make things grow."

"But it's undeniable that you're seeing spirit energy," said Stella.

"I just don't understand." Karen looked at them helplessly.

"None of us really do," said Mercury.

"There are no rules to follow for what's happening," said Ford. "I think all we can do is to accept that we don't know the extent of how and why any of you have changed."

Stella nodded. "Or at least not yet we don't."

"Oh Lord." Karen looked dazed. "What do I do now?"

"About what?" Mercury asked.

Karen's face was red and blotchy. She pointed at herself and grimaced. "This! Who I am now!"

Stella met Karen's panicked gaze. "You have the same choice the rest of us have. You can accept the changes or let them frighten and repulse you, so you'll be miserable for the rest of your life."

"Not to mention the fact that you'll never reach your full potential," added Ford.

Gemma sighed, "I sure hope there's another choice."

Mercury sipped from the bottle of wine before she nodded and said, "Oh, there definitely is." She turned to face Karen. "You can accept yourself for who you truly are, without judgment—and appreciate your uniqueness—and also practice being kind to yourself and others for the rest of your life."

Karen nodded and then slowly said, "I can see the spirit world."

"Here," Imani handed Karen a tightly rolled joint. "This'll help."

"Help what?" Karen asked.

"Help it all seem a little less scary," said Imani.

Karen studied the joint. "I've never smoked marijuana."

"Now's a good time to start," said Mercury.

"You could be right about that," Karen said. "Show me what to do."

As Mercury carried the lantern outside with her to the temporary restrooms, she was still giggling to herself about how absolutely hilarious Reefer Karen had been. She'd kept them laughing with anecdotes from her classroom that proved she'd had a sense of humor long before Mercury, or anyone else at Will Rogers High School, had realized it. Then, mid-story, the history teacher announced, *I shall go night-night now. Night-night!* She tumbled backward, hugged her backpack like a pillow, and within seconds began to snore softly.

Mercury quickly used the very rough facilities and then hurried back to the cave. The rainclouds had been blown away by a chilly northern wind to reveal a spectacular waning moon that was still almost full. The ebony sky was completely clear. It exposed a blanket of glitter that entranced Mercury. Just outside the entrance to the cave, she extinguished the lantern, leaned against the rough rock, and stared above her. She gasped as an enormous shooting star blazed to its death.

"You okay?" Ford's deep voice made her jump.

"Oh my Goddess, you scared me!" Mercury fanned her face, not sure if the wine, the weed or the fright he'd given her had made her cheeks so hot.

"Sorry 'bout that." His white smile flashed in the darkness. "I heard you gasp and, well, I guess I'm not over what happened this morning."

"Yeah, I'm not sure why I'm not more freaked out about it," Mercury said. "Maybe it'll hit me later."

"I hope not." Ford spoke so earnestly it made Mercury grin.

There was a movement several yards from them, and the moonlight illuminated the silhouette of a woman by the creek. She stood perfectly still on a little rise in the land. Her back was to them as she stared into the distance.

"Who's that?" Mercury asked.

"Imani," Ford said. "She went out just after you did."

"She didn't go to the bathroom area with me. I wonder if I should take the lantern to her."

"I don't think so. Gemma said she's been doing that every night."

"Doing what?" Mercury asked.

"Just staring. Gemma says she goes out by herself, turns to the southwest and stays like that—sometimes for hours. Do you have any idea why?"

"She's facing San Diego, where she had two kids—babies really—and a husband she loved very much. She's looking toward them."

"Damn. That's tough," Ford's voice was rough with emotion. "I didn't know."

"Imani acts like she's okay, but she's not," Mercury said softly. "I hope someday she will be, though."

"So do I."

They stood side by side in silence until Mercury realized why Ford must have been outside the cave.

"Oh, did you come out here for the lantern?" Mercury lifted the dark lamp.

"No, I came out here so I could say goodnight to you before you went to bed."

Mercury lowered the lantern and looked up at him. "You couldn't say goodnight to me inside?"

"No," Ford said softly. "Not like this." He stepped closer to her and reached out to cup her face between his hands. Then he bent and gently pressed his lips to hers. The kiss wasn't filled with passion; it was filled with promise. He whispered against her lips, "*Buenas noches, Bellota.* I am very glad you didn't die." He took the lantern from her suddenly limp grasp. "And I do appreciate this lantern. *Gracias.*"

As Mercury watched him disappear into the darkness, her fingers lightly touched her lips.

C H A P T E R

40

"Mercury! Wake up!"

"You've got to come outside and watch the sunrise!"

Mercury cracked her eyelids open just enough to see Gemma, Georgie, and the twins staring at her like she was a package under the tree on Christmas morning.

"The sun is just rising?" she asked as she reached for the bottle of water she'd remembered to fill and put beside her sleeping bag.

"Yeah, you won't believe the colors!" said Georgie.

Cayden nodded and put his little hand in hers, tugging gently.

"Okay, okay!" She smiled at the boy. "I'm coming." Mercury pulled on her jeans and then her boots and followed the kids, who were almost dancing with excitement.

As soon as she exited the cave, she understood why. Sometime during the night it had rained, and the rising sun cast rays the yellow of bright, perfect daffodils on the Painted Hills, changing their colors from the rich tones they'd witnessed the evening before to a brilliant watercolor pallet of coral and butter and moss green.

"Totally worth getting up early for, right Acorn?" Stella said as she joined her at the mouth of the cave.

"Totally," Mercury agreed.

"Oh, good! You're awake." Ford's smile was warm and intimate and sent little shivers of delicious anticipation down Mercury's spine.

"I am, and our new home is breathtaking," said Mercury.

"Just wait until we scavenge supplies from Mitchell," said Ford. "Did you know Imani has a minor in engineering?"

"Huh? I had zero clue," said Mercury.

Imani nodded as she walked up the gentle incline from the creek. "Yeah, that's right, I'm smart, and an engineering minor means that I can definitely help us figure out how to tuck adobe homes into the side of these cliffs."

"That's fantastic, Imani!" Mercury said.

"What's also fantastic is that we've arrived at the perfect time of year," Imani said. "As Ford explained while you were getting your beauty sleep, we're leaving the rainy season and have a couple months before it's stupid hot during the day. That should give us time to get a sizeable shelter ready for coming summer weather extremes."

"And also give us time to plant crops," said Stella.

"*And* round up some goats and chickens!" Gemma added as Georgie nodded and clapped.

"But our first step is checking out Mitchell," said Ford. "Stella, I've been thinking about what might happen if there are a lot of survivors there. We'll need to barter. Do you think it'd be okay to offer those bottles of twenty-five year old Macallan in exchange for supplies?"

"It would break my heart a little, but that does sound like a good idea," said Stella.

"If no one disagrees, I'd like to make that first town run sooner rather than later," said Ford.

"Oh, we need to go today—now, actually," said Stella.

"Okay, who all's going?" Imani asked.

Stella crossed her arms over her chest as she considered. "Ford is the only one of us who's been to Mitchell, so he needs to go."

"I've been, but I don't remember much about it except that I had a salmon sandwich from some little restaurant and then got super sick and puked all the way home," said Gemma.

"I would rather remain here," said Karen.

"Actually, so would I," Imani said. "And I could use Gemma's help with setting up a shelter over the latrine. I got soaked last night when I went to pee, It would be really nice if we could get a cover done by dark."

"Any kind of cover over the latrine would be dreamy," said Stella.

"Well, I'd like to go to town," said Mercury. "I've already started a mental list of necessities."

"Add to that list straw, if you can find it," said Imani.

"Straw?" Mercury's raised her brow.

Imani nodded. "Yeah, it's key to adobe brick making. Sand would be good too, but I have a feeling the clay from those colorful hills may not need the help."

"I've been thinking the same thing," said Stella.

"I'm really glad you two know what you're talking about," said Mercury.

"We absolutely do." Stella and Imani exchanged self-satisfied grins.

"I'm glad to hear it too, and look forward to you two explaining the process. Cliff dwellings—that was definitely not on my apocalypse bingo card," said Ford.

"You have an apocalypse bingo card?" Mercury asked.

He smiled. "I do now. And I finished unloading the truck a little while ago," said Ford. "So there's plenty of room in the bed to pile stuff, especially if we take off that camper shell."

"How about we get that shell off while Mercury eats something?" Stella said. "Then the three of us can be on our way to Mitchell."

"Are you sure it's safe?" Karen picked at the frayed hem of her cardigan.

Everyone turned to Stella, who cocked her head to the side in the inner listening pose they'd become accustomed to. Then she shrugged. "I'm not getting anything specific except a feeling that we definitely need to go there."

"Well, good," Gemma said. "If no one's gonna almost die again, then I for sure want to stay here and help Imani."

"The children and I will gather firewood while you're gone," said Karen. Then she hastily added, "But we'll be careful not to roam too far from the cave, and we'll definitely keep an eye out for green fog, right boys?"

The twins nodded.

"Okay, it's a plan!" said Stella. "Acorn, shove leftovers from last night into your face, make your morning toilette, and then let's go!"

"Ooh! I can't wait! I'm starting to like this hunting-and-gathering stuff." Mercury hurried back into the cave as she mentally added to her list of necessities.

They checked the map to plot the best path to Mitchell, and because the town was only about twenty miles away, the three decided to follow the regular roads rather than cut cross-country.

Bridge Creek Road fed into highway 26, which went straight through the heart of Mitchell. The section of 26 between the Painted Hills and Mitchell was riddled with sinkholes—so many that Stella drove most of the way on the shoulder of the road or the easements on either side of the highway.

They saw not one living person, though they were able to syphon enough gas to fill their tank and the spare containers they carried in the bed.

"I thought there would be more vehicles," Stella said. "Twenty-six is a major highway out here, isn't it?"

"Yeah, for sure," said Ford. "But this is a sparsely populated area, and the weather did report that the winter storm that hit a couple days ago was going to be a bad one. That seems to have kept hikers and campers to a minimum—at least between Mitchell and the Painted Hills." Ford pointed at the green road sign that had fallen across the highway. "Says Mitchell is one mile away. We should see it as we drive over this ridge and down into the valley."

"Are you sure we're far enough away from this town? If we hadn't stopped to siphon gas, it would've only taken about two hours to get here." Mercury chewed her lip.

"That's a Stella question," Ford said.

Stella moved her shoulders. "I can only tell you what my gut knows, which is what I said yesterday—the Painted Hills are our new home. That hasn't changed."

"I have an idea that will help our isolation and safety," said Ford. "If we can find a tree saw or an axe, I can cut down some junipers and cedars and create road blocks into the Painted Hills. I think it would also be a good idea to bring down that bridge over the creek."

"Yeah, we definitely need to do those things," said Stella. "As well as cover the path the truck makes from the road to our cave. Actually, covering the tracks won't be enough. We need to limit the use of the truck anywhere near a road so that we don't draw attention to ourselves."

"And we have to remember to try to reach Jenny and tell her we've found a place to stay," said Mercury.

"Imani and I already tried to do that this morning," said Ford. "We couldn't reach her, but Imani said we should drive the truck up as high as we can in the hills. That might help the signal stretch to Timberline."

"That's a good idea," said Mercury.

They were silent as the truck topped the incline and the town of Mitchell stretched before them.

"Uh, this is a town?" Mercury said.

"Yep, to about one hundred and twenty-five people," said Ford.

"Shit," Stella said as she braked the truck. "It's a valley. This is not going to be cool. At all."

"What are those black things on the street and in front of the—" Mercury began, and then she understood and echoed Stella. "Shit!"

"They're crows on bodies. Aw, man." Ford shook his head. "A lot of bodies."

Vehicles, mostly trucks and old SUVs clogged the two-lane that went through town. Around the vehicles, in the street and on the sidewalks that butted up to the parking spaces that lined the highway, were dead people. Many of them were deflated sacks of skin and clothes, but some—the women—had remained intact so that it was obvious they'd died sometime after the flattened men. Mostly it seemed they died from injuries that happened either after or during the earthquakes.

Stella steered the truck slowly around vehicles as clouds of dark birds lifted from their feast. She tried not to run over the remains of anyone, but had little choice. The three of them cringed and shuddered as the truck's wheels squished along the street.

"Do you see anyone alive?" Mercury's voice was hushed.

"I don't think there is anyone left alive," said Ford. "Look at this. Nothing's been moved—except by those carrion birds. It looks like the entire town was wiped out."

"Mitchell is in a valley," Stella said. "It must have been completely filled with the green fog, and until the storm blew through two days later, chances are the fog just sat here."

Ford nodded. "It's like Warm Springs. Remember, I told you I could see the fog was still there, even days after the bombs."

"Yeah, that town was in a low valley too," said Stella.

"But *no one* lived? *No one* was like us, able to survive the fog and change because of it?" Mercury turned her gaze from the bloated bodies of two women who had died with their arms around each other.

"They were exposed too long?" Stella stopped the truck in the middle of the road and look at Mercury. "This is proof that *we* can't even continue to expose ourselves to that stuff."

"That makes sense," Ford said. "It's logical that the human body can only change so much before it quits being able to adapt. We know it kills men, whether right away or after a few days, it still kills us. You ladies have to stay away from it too—until or unless we can figure out how much exposure becomes deadly."

Mercury shivered. "I'm not volunteering for that scientific study."

"Yeah, me neither," said Stella. "This is going to be gruesome, but let's get as much stuff loaded as quickly as we can and then get the hell out of here."

"I'm all for that." Mercury redid the ponytail she'd hastily pulled her hair up into before they left the Painted Hills. "I really do not like dead things."

"Just remember that they can't hurt you, Acorn, but I'm with ya. I don't like them either. Makes me feel like someone's watching us." Stella let the truck creep forward again. "Okay, jackpot! Up there on the left side of the street, next to that little post office, is the Wheeler County Trading Company—and I do believe that sign also says groceries, sporting goods, and hardware."

"It does! And across the street is the Feed 'n' Farm." Ford pointed. "There should be garden seed in there and tools, like the shovels and picks we need to dig the latrine. Oh, and also Imani's straw and sand."

"Maybe they'll have some chickies?" Mercury said hopefully, then her shoulders sagged. "But it's been six days since the apocalypse. They're probably dead chickies by now."

"I'll check," said Ford. "Stella, if you stop in the middle of the street between the two stores, I'll take the Feed 'n' Farm—"

"And we'll take the grocery," Mercury finished for him.

"I'll turn the truck around so that we can get out of here fast. We've seen how the green fog can creep into low places without any warning," said Stella.

"Are your spidey senses tingling?" Mercury asked.

"We need to be here. I know that. But I'm also thoroughly creeped out—so much so that I can't tell if it's my intuition screaming to hurry and get the fuck out, or just regular ol' common sense."

"Either way, let's be fast," said Ford.

"One more thing." Stella looked from Mercury to Ford. "We need to be quiet."

Mercury's stomach heaved. "I thought everyone was dead."

Stella nodded. "I honestly believe everyone who was in this town when the fog rolled in was killed. So, maybe it's just respectful not to make a bunch of noise in what amounts to a tomb."

"That's fine with me," Mercury said.

"Yeah, I have nothing to say to the dead," added Ford.

Stella turned the truck and parked it in the middle of the street between the two stores. She left it running, with the emergency brake engaged, as the three of them got out. Ford opened the tailgate and then they split up.

Mercury and Stella walked so close together that their arms brushed as they stepped up from the curb to the sidewalk and headed to the open front door of the Wheeler County Trading Company. Just inside there were three putrid, flattened bodies. Stella strode to the nearby wall—the only one not decorated with the stuffed and mounted heads of stags—and pulled down a US flag, a Confederate flag, and the state flag of Oregon. She draped the Confederate flag over the three bodies.

"That's the best use of that stupid flag I've ever seen," said Mercury.

"Yep," Stella agreed. "Stay here in the front of the store while I take a sweep around and cover up anyone else."

"Thanks." Mercury grabbed two handheld shopping baskets and headed to a nearby shelf that held analgesics, Band-Aids, cough medicines, and other over-the-counter pharmaceuticals. "I'll fill up baskets with this stuff and start running them to the truck."

The women worked quickly and quietly. They avoided the coolers. Nothing that needed refrigeration was still viable. But Mercury was impressed by the amount of canned goods, dried goods, and housewares the store carried. In the hardware section, there were lots of pots and pans, as well as several axes and some decent-sized saws.

"Oh Goddess, yes!" Mercury held up a copy of *Stillhouse Lake* by Rachel Caine. "I just found the book section! There's everything over here from mysteries to young adult novels, and even some picture books."

From across the store Stella said, "That's fantastic! We can read aloud to the kids at bedtime."

"And after that we can read aloud to each other. I'm an excellent reader-alouder! I can do all the voices." Mercury piled more books into a basket. "Yes! I just found books on the local area—the Painted Hills and the John Day Fossil Beds. There are actually some paper maps over here too."

"Grab them!"

After she'd raided the bookshelves, Mercury made her way to the rear of the store, where she discovered a glass cabinet that held a dozen hunting rifles; drawers under them were filled with ammunition.

"I hope we never need to use these," said Mercury as she stacked the ammo in a cardboard box that said "Pringles Original" on the side of it.

"I hope we don't either, but be sure you take every weapon you can find to the truck, as well as all the ammo. The last thing we need is to leave stuff here assholes like Rutland or Eva Cruz could get their hands on—and then come after us, or anyone else," Stella said as she quickly made decisions about what food staples and cookware they should take with them.

"I'm taking a bunch of these fishing poles and equipment," said Mercury. "But I'll also leave a few in case someone comes through here and needs them." She kept loading shopping baskets. "Hey, there are a bunch of waterproof coats and boots and other hunting clothes back here. I'll take enough for us, but I'm going to leave some of them too."

"Agreed. It's good karma," said Stella.

"I could see a family of survivors finding this little town and wanting to settle here," said Mercury as she continued to load baskets. "Maybe there are some homes nearby that aren't stuck down in this valley. They wouldn't have to build shelters, and I'll bet there're generators here and at least some propane tanks—which reminds me. We need to grab lighters and matches and charcoal. Oh, and I saw a couple boxes back there by the waders that said 'Webber' on them."

"Grills would be amazing," said Stella. "But no one should settle here. At least not as long as there's green fog. This place is ringed by hills. It's not safe. At all."

A tremor of fear fingered its way down Mercury's spine. "Hey, I just got a 'someone-walked-over-my-grave' feeling. Are we almost done here?"

"Yeah. You haul this stuff out to the truck. And when you see Ford, would you ask him to come in here and help me carry those barrels of rice and flour and such?"

"Girlfriend, please. I can carry one under each of my arms. Are you forgetting about my super strength?"

Stella peered around an aisle at Mercury. "Actually, I did. Grab those barrels, woman, and let's get outta here ASAP."

Mercury focused her vision on a narrow path to and from the truck to the store. When she looked around at all, it was only to check for flashes of green—not to glance at the birds that had returned to their feast, or the rotting skin sacks that used to be townspeople.

As she hefted the barrels of dry goods into the bed of the truck, Ford came out of the feed store, grinning like a boy who'd snuck cookies from a jar without getting caught. He was carrying a wire crate that contained—

"Chickies!" The word exploded from Mercury's mouth before she could stop herself. "Shit!" she whispered. "That was too loud. But oh my Goddess, they're alive!"

"They are. Well, these are. Don't go in there. You won't like the—"

Her upraised hand stopped him. "Only tell me about alive things."

"Well then, I can tell you that there are a dozen chicks alive in this cage, and inside the store there are also about half a dozen ducklings and four really cute rabbits."

"Oh, Ford! That's fantastic! The kids will be so excited."

"I'll be excited too, when they start laying eggs. I can make a mean frittata." Ford carefully put the cage in the bed. "Now all we need are some goats and horses."

"Goats are easy. They eat anything. But horses? They take grass and hay and tending to live," said Mercury as she reached her finger between the wires of the cage and stroked the yellow down of the nearest chick, who chirped at her.

"Well, good thing there's lots of seed inside that feed store, including hay and grass, and I happen to know several ladies who have a way with growing things. Can you ride?" Ford asked her.

"I'm from Oklahoma. I think it's a requirement. Yes, I can ride. I was raised with horses. That's why I know they need to graze and have hay and grain to supplement that grazing."

"But if they have those things they're self-sustaining—unlike that truck. We'll eventually run out of gas to syphon, and before that it may just stop working," Ford said.

Mercury's brow raised. "Huh. I honestly hadn't even thought about that. I guess I'm too used to going to a gas station to fill up and buying a new car when my old one gives out. But you're right. We need to see the big picture."

"How about as soon as things get settled in the hills, you and I make some day runs to find livestock?"

"I'd like that," Mercury smiled up at him.

"Me too, Bellota. Very much." He returned her smile as he pointed to a corner of the bed of the truck. "Check out what I found."

Mercury gasped. "Ford! That's a boom box!"

"Yep, even older than the one in Madras, but it's battery powered. I also found a stack of CDs." He met and held her gaze. "'Strawberry Wine' is on one of them."

Mercury's stomach was filled with fluttering butterflies. "Are we going to dance again?"

"I'm counting on it."

"Hey, did y'all hear that?" Stella dragged two baskets loaded with groceries to the truck and stopped as she stared off into the distance.

"I didn't hear anything," Ford whispered.

"Hear what?" Mercury asked softly.

Stella shook her head. "I don't know. I don't hear it now, but I could've sworn it was an engine. So, you two need to stop making goo-goo eyes at each other and get this truck loaded. I'm ready to leave this graveyard." Stella glanced in the bed and her frown changed to a brilliant smile. "Ooh! Chickens!" Then she clamped a hand over her mouth.

"I know," Mercury whispered. "I did the same thing. Okay, come on, y'all. Let's get this done! Uh, Ford, did you put those big metal troughs in here for the goats and horses we don't have yet?" She pointed to the troughs that were already filled with bales of straw, bags of sand, and several boxes of seeds.

Ford grinned. “No, Bellota. Livestock can drink from the creek. One of those troughs is to keep water in for cooking. The other I thought you ladies would like to use for baths. I also found a bunch of metal buckets so you could warm water and then dump it in the trough.” He disappeared back into the feed store.

“Damn, Acorn, I *really* like your man.”

“I really do too,” said Mercury.

They worked quickly and quietly. Soon Ford was securing the pile of supplies with bailing twine. The baby chickens and ducks made happy little sounds as Ford gave them and the rabbits grain and water for the trip, and then covered their cages.

“I think that’s a pretty good first haul,” said Ford as he finished knotting the last tie-down.

“Yeah, it was particularly cool to find all those sleeping bags and tents,” said Mercury.

“Don’t forget the coffee!” said Stella.

“*Never* forget the coffee,” agreed Ford. His dark brows lifted to his hairline.

“We also found a bunch of old grapes in the grocery part of the store. And they aren’t seedless!” Mercury grinned victoriously. When Ford didn’t appear to get it, Stella spoke up.

“Ford, grapes equal wine, which thrills me a lot more than coffee.”

“Oh, *now* I understand,” said Ford.

“I’m also thrilled about the stash of soap and shampoo I discovered,” said Stella. “But there wasn’t one piece of stemware to be found, though I did grab plenty of plastic cups and plates and silverware that’ll probably outlive all of us.”

“Hey, I think there’s a little pub around here somewhere. It’s attached to a small brewery. Tiger something,” Ford said. “I’ll bet they have wineglasses.”

“Do not tease me,” Stella said.

Ford grinned. “Look down the street there. Doesn’t that sign say Tiger Town Brewing Company?”

Stella spun around and then made a happy little squeak. “It does! Okay, how about if I grab just a few wineglasses and stuff them into the bed of the truck?”

“Sounds good to me,” said Mercury. “I’d hate to contemplate life without stemware.”

Ford hid his laugh with a cough.

Stella's brow arched up. "You jest, but you'll thank me when we're sipping an excellent red from real wineglasses tonight." She studied the road between them and the brewery. "Backing down there is not possible. Too many vehicles blocking the way. I'm just going to go there real quick, grab some glasses, and then we can leave."

"Mercury, you should go with Stella. You know she'll want help carrying those glasses," Ford said. "I need to take a restroom break before we leave anyway."

"Okey-dokey. We'll BRB," said Mercury as she and Stella walked briskly down the street, averting their eyes from the crow-covered mounds that littered the area.

They opened the door to the brewery, and both women stepped back, gagging.

"Holy shit! That's disgusting!" Mercury said as she tried not to puke. "Ugh! How could the bar have been packed early Sunday morning?"

Stella waved her hand in front of her nose to try and chase away the fetid stench. "Right? So damn gross. Okay, you stay out here. I'll run in—grab glasses—try not to look at anything or anyone—and run back out."

"No, if you go in, I go in too. On three. One, two, three!" Mercury pulled the door open and something came rushing at them—yipping, whining, and crying. "Fuck!" Mercury stumbled back, wishing she'd taken the gun out of the glove box and put it in her pocket. And then she realized what the thing was, and joy chased away her fear. "Hey, there! Who are you?"

The pit bull wiggled and whined as she circled Mercury. Her tail wagged so fast that it blurred.

"It's okay. It's okay. We've got you now." Mercury crouched down so the dog could lean against her. She had on a collar with the name "Khaleesi" engraved on a heart-shaped metal tag. "Hello, Khaleesi. Have you been stuck in there all this time?"

"That's what the smell was—dog poop and pee mixed with dead bodies." Stella bent and offered her hand to Khaleesi to sniff. "Poor girl. What a nightmare for you."

"She's pathetically skinny." Mercury ran her hand down the dog's back, feeling her spine and her ribs. "And her nose is cracked. I'll bet she needs water really badly."

"Wait out here with her. There has to be water in there somewhere. I'll get some and bring it out. Looks like we need to grab a leash and some bags of kibble from that feed store too." Stella grinned at Mercury. "You just found your dog. Now all I have to do is conjure my cat, and we'll be set."

Mercury had to blink back tears as Khaleesi leaned into her and gazed adoringly up into her face. "She's the same color as Kong—gray and white. She looks young too, probably barely a year old." Impulsively, she put her arms around the pitty and hugged her, which set off Khaleesi's blurring tail wags again.

"She's perfect for you—for us—and the kids are going to adore her," Stella said. "Okay, going back in." She drew a deep breath and rushed into the pub.

Khaleesi leaned against Mercury and whined softly.

"It's okay—she's coming back."

And Stella did, gasping and retching. But she had a big, wooden salad bowl filled with water, which she set in front of Khaleesi, who instantly began to lap it up. "Watch her so that she doesn't drink too fast and puke," said Stella. "There's a whole row of wineglasses hanging behind the bar. I gotta step over the remains of a bartender to get to them, but then I'll snatch and run." She drew in another big breath and ducked back into the pub.

"Stella is dedicated to her stemware," Mercury told Khaleesi. "You'll figure that out for yourself after you're around for a little while."

Stella reemerged in a foul cloud, but she was clutching a bussing tub to her bosom that was filled with tea towels wrapped around a dozen or so wineglasses that clanked musically together.

"Shit, I'm gonna—" Stella turned and puked off the side of the sidewalk. She gagged, dry-heaved, and then spat twice. "Fucking hell, that's disgusting!" Stella shuddered, which sent the stemware to music again. "I wouldn't even go back in there to rescue the bottles of booze and mediocre wine just sitting around behind the bar."

Still petting Khaleesi, Mercury looked up at her best friend. "You say that now, but I have a feeling you'll change your mind when we run out of wine."

"Maybe by then the stench will have faded." Stella turned to spit again.

"If you're done puking, can we go?" Mercury said, but her attention turned from Stella to Khaleesi, who had suddenly stopped lapping up water. The pitty's body had gone rigid under her hand. She was staring past Stella. A low, warning growl came from deep in her chest. "What is it, girl?" Mercury followed Khaleesi's gaze to see a sickening wave of green rolling its way up the highway toward them. "Fucking fog!"

Stella whirled around and gasped. "Go! Now."

"Come on, Khaleesi!" Mercury and Stella hurried down the stairs and back to the road, where they sprinted to the truck, with Khaleesi running beside them.

Ford was emerging from the side of the feed store. He saw the dog and a smile filled his face.

"Green fog!" Mercury shouted. "Grab some dog supplies and let's get the hell outta here!"

"On it!" Ford yelled and ran into the feed store.

"Don't break the glasses. Don't break the glasses. Don't break the glasses." Stella spoke the litany like a prayer as they raced for the truck. "I'm going to shove this bin in the back!"

Mercury opened the passenger door while Stella ran to the rear of the truck and pulled the tailgate down. "Come on, Khaleesi! Get in!" Just like she'd been listening to Mercury her whole life, the pit bull jumped into the cab.

Ford raced from the feed store with huge bags of kibble over each shoulder and a long leather leash hanging like a tie around his neck. Mercury heard him load the dog food into the truck and then shove the tailgate closed. He and Stella jogged around to the cab—and then they stopped like they'd run into an invisible wall.

Mercury frowned at them and opened her mouth to ask what was wrong when a deep, sarcastic voice came from behind her.

"Well, now, I've been looking for this truck everywhere. Imagine running into you girls again. Isn't that just a spot of good luck—for me, that is. Definitely not for you."

Mercury turned to see Alvin Rutland, an assault rifle gripped tightly in his hand, step from the narrow alley that ran between the Wheeler County Trading Company and the post office.

CHAPTER

41

From the cab of the truck, Khaleesi growled low in her throat.

"Whose mutt is that?"

Mercury ignored his question. "We were just leaving. And we don't want any trouble."

Al laughed humorlessly. "Guess you shoulda thought about that when you drove off and left me stranded in the middle of the highway the day all hell broke loose. Oh, and again when you broke the knee of one of my men, killed another, and tried to fucking kill me!" His sallow face flushed red as his anger boiled over. "It's way too late for you to pretend to be all sweet and innocent. I know the truth about you bitches."

Mercury studied Al as he spoke. His resemblance to the handsome, entitled man who had tried to commandeer their truck six days before was so slight that had he not spoken, she wouldn't have recognized him. Even a few days before, when he'd chased them through the blizzard, she didn't think he'd looked this terrible. He was gaunt—emaciated actually. Dark circles bruised the skin under his bloodshot blue eyes. His skin had a sickly, jaundiced tinge. The red-stained stubble under his nose had turned into a scarlet mustache. The front of the orange hunter's coat he wore was rust from the blood that ceaselessly dribbled from his nose.

"We didn't strand you," Stella said.

"And you and your men attacked *us*," Mercury added. "We were only defending ourselves. We didn't want any trouble then—we still don't want any trouble."

"You cunts don't know what you want," Rutledge snarled at them.

"Hey, there's no reason for name-calling." Ford took a step forward and positioned himself between Stella and Rutland.

Al's eyes narrowed as his expression turned sly. "So, I guess the girls weren't too good for *you*, huh? Why's that? What's so great about you?" His sarcastic laughter echoed in the dead town. "Other than the fact that some bitches prefer dark meat to white."

Ford's body went very still. "What is it you want?"

"Same thing I wanted the day the world went to shit. That truck. Only now I think I'd also like a taste of your girls. I've found that an apocalypse makes women act different. Some are just not as accommodating as they used to be. Tell ya what—what's your name?"

"Oxford Xavier Diaz," Ford spoke in an emotionless voice.

"Ooh, fancy. Tell ya what, Señor Diaz," Rutledge added a bad Mexican accent to Ford's name. "I'll share with you. My men and I have taken over a town off 216—made it a damn fine place to build a new world. Help me tie these girls up and shove them in the back, and then we can take this truck, that's already been loaded for me, cross country to where my men are sucking the gas out of stalled vehicles for our motorcycles. It's genius that we snagged a bunch of Harleys from some dead assholes. Makes it easy to cut cross-country to see what else we can forage. Damn convenient that my bike blew a tire just down the road from here, or you and the girls woulda heard me coming. What do you say?"

Ford's posture changed. He slouched and shrugged. "Sure." As he spoke, he turned his head so that he could meet Mercury's gaze—and winked at her.

Had she not been terrified and so fucking angry she could hardly see straight, Mercury would've laughed. Ford hadn't needed to wink. Mercury didn't doubt him for a moment. He was playing a part with an end game that would somehow get them away from Al Rutland.

Mercury would play her part too, but as she did, the green fog drifted ever closer to them.

"What the hell is wrong with you?" Mercury shouted at Ford.

"That one's feisty. And a pretty decent shot for a girl." Rutledge chuckled.

"Yeah, well, I just met these women yesterday." Ford waved dismissively at Mercury. "They've basically been using me as a pack mule ever since, and I haven't gotten much in return except a meal and a cold bed."

"Let's change that then." Rutland smiled, showing rusty blood crusted between his white teeth. "There's gotta be some duct tape in that store there." He jerked his head toward the Trading Company. "My AK and I'll keep an eye on the girls while you go get us some."

"I don't need to go in there." Ford smiled and started to move across the front of the truck toward Mercury. "They've got some duct tape right there in the glove box."

Rutland raised the assault rifle and pointed it at Ford. "Do you think I'm stupid?"

Ford lifted his hands and froze. "No. I didn't say that."

"You didn't have to. I know what's in that glove box. That little bitch right there used it to threaten to shoot out my knees the first time we met." Rutland took a couple steps closer to the truck. "I think you're being disingenuous with me, *señor*." He sneered the word. "And that's a shame because there aren't a lot of men left. But, change in plans. Say goodbye, señor."

"Wait!" Mercury raised her hands and stepped forward. "There's no reason anyone has to get hurt. We'll go with you."

"Now that's touching. She's your girl, isn't she?" Rutland asked Ford, though he kept speaking without giving him a chance to respond. "Which means she will be a fucking burr in my side after I shoot you, and if I don't shoot you and just take her with me, you'll come looking for her, which will also be a burr in my side." He breathed out a long-suffering sigh. "So, I'm gonna take care of both of you, which leaves me with the old girl there." Rutland shrugged and lifted his lip at Stella. "And that's a shame because I like young hens better than old, tough ones. Anyway, I'm tired of talking now so—" He turned the AK-47 on Mercury.

"You say women are different since the bombs. Have you noticed that the green fog has *literally* changed some of us?" Stella's voice sounded calm, like she was asking Al about the weather.

His brow furrowed. Al sniffed and wiped his nose on the back of his blood-stained hand. "What are you talking about?"

Stella smiled. "Exactly what I said. The green fog has changed some of us. For example, I know things I didn't before—things that are going to happen—things that always come true. And I know something about you, Alvin Rutland."

When Stella didn't continue, his lips twisted in irritation. "What do you think you know about me?"

"That you're a dead man walking. That bloody nose of yours is going to kill you if nothing else ends your life before it. I know that for sure. So, do you really want to meet your god, or whatever you believe in, with their deaths on your conscience?"

Al's face flushed red again, and then he threw his head back and laughed. "Oh, girly, that's a good one!" Then his laughter slid away, and his expression went flat. "But you've saved me another burr. Might as well go first, and your friends will join you." Rutland turned the rifle on Stella. "Say bye-bye."

Ford exploded forward as he shouted, "Mercury, get the gun!"

Rutland squeezed the trigger of the automatic rifle just before Ford reached him. The machinegun blast tore through Ford's chest, but his momentum carried him into Rutland. Ford hit him low, like a professional linebacker. Legs pumping, Oxford Xavier Diaz lifted Rutland, and the two of them flew backward together into the wave of green fog.

"No!" Mercury screamed as she wrenched open the passenger door, popped the glove box and pulled out the .38. She flipped off the safety and raced into the green fog just as Al was pushing Ford off of him and raising the assault rifle again. Mercury fired the pistol, and kept firing it as she strode forward. Later, she remembered that she'd been screaming the entire time. Then, during that moment, she heard nothing except the thunder of her own heartbeat as Rutland's body convulsed and fell backward.

Mercury shoved the pistol into her jacket pocket and reached down into the fog, grabbed Ford under his arms, and pulled him up and out of the lapping green. She carried him as she sprinted back to the truck. Stella was already behind the wheel. Mercury jumped into the cab, pulling Ford with her. "Get us out of here!" She yelled as Khaleesi whimpered and pressed against Mercury's side.

Stella floored the truck and they raced from Mitchell up 26 and into the mountains above the fog.

"Ford! Ford! Can you hear me? Wake up, Ford! Wake up!" He lay across Mercury's lap. Blood poured from holes punched through Ford's chest, front and back. If felt to Mercury as if she would drown in his blood—that it would fill the cab and turn her entire world red. "Hurry, Stella! We have to get him to Gemma! Hurry!"

"I am! I am!" Stella sobbed as the truck sped along the highway, tires screaming while she dodged sinkholes and stalled vehicles. Stella shrugged out of her sweater and tossed it to Mercury. "Use this to try to stop the bleeding."

Mercury pressed the sweater to Ford's chest. He drew in a shallow breath and his eyes opened.

"Ford! It's okay. You're gonna be okay! Stella will get us to Gemma. She'll fix you, just like she did me!" Mercury hugged him to her, cradling him in her arms like he was a child. "So you have to hold on. Please hold on!"

"Gemma cannot save a dead man." He rasped the words as blood bubbled between his lips, from his nose and ears and dribbled onto his beard.

"No! Don't you dare give up!"

"I breathed in the fog. It—it broke me. I can feel it . . . worse than the bullets."

"No!" Mercury sobbed.

Ford lifted his hand and touched her cheek. "Bellota, I would have liked to have made a new world with you."

He breathed in a rattling breath, let it out slowly, and then Oxford Xavier Diaz breathed no more.

CHAPTER

42

LED BY MERCURY, the women bathed and prepared Ford's body for burial in silence. Their sadness was reflected in the tears that washed freely down their cheeks, and their affection for him was clear in every compassionate touch. After his body was clean, dressed in the new clothes he'd worn at the festival, and lovingly wrapped in a soft blanket, they buried Ford just before sunset, near the creek, in a grove of cedar trees.

While they'd been preparing Ford's body and digging his grave, Mercury had thought about what kind of ceremony he would've liked. She considered and discarded rites from Pagan funerals she'd attended, finally deciding to speak from her heart.

Everyone wore what they considered their best clothes. Mercury smiled through her tears as she pulled on the beautiful dress she'd been wearing when Ford had waltzed her around the firepit. She asked their little group to circle around Ford's newly dug—and filled—grave.

"Please face east and then turn with me as I call the elements," Mercury said. With her friends—her family—she faced east and invoked, "Air, I call you to this Rite of Passage." Then Mercury led the group clockwise to the south and called, "Fire, I call you to this Rite of Passage." She continued to the west. "Water, I call you to this Rite of Passage." And, finally, north to invoke, "Earth, I call you to this Rite of Passage."

Then Mercury spoke the words that lifted from her heart.

"Those of us who believe in the Olde Ways know that when a person dies, it is only their shell that we lose—that the soul, the spirit, will return again in a newborn body to live another life. This is a tenet of our Pagan faith that has been taught since long before recorded words."

Mercury walked the circle of her friends, filling the wineglass they each held, as she continued, "O gracious Lady of the Earth, She who gives our worn bodies rest—I do invoke your presence. O powerful Lord of the Forests, He who embodies all that is wild and male in this land—I do invoke your presence. We thank thee for protecting and guiding Oxford Xavier Dias to the golden portal of the Summerlands beyond our own, and we ask that Ford knows the love and well-wishes we hold for him within our hearts."

Mercury completed the circle and moved to the center of the grave as she filled her own wineglass and then put the bottle down. She lifted her glass, and her friends lifted theirs in response. "I propose a toast—to the gracious and lovely Goddess of the Earth. Blessed be!"

"Blessed be!" Everyone echoed before they drank.

Mercury raised her glass again and the others followed her. "I propose a toast—to the strong and laughing God of the Forest. Blessed be!"

"Blessed be!" Again everyone drank with her.

Mercury raised her glass one last time. "And also I propose a final toast—to our beloved friend, Ford, who will be well missed, and who now revels in the infinite beauty and magick of the Summerlands. Blessed be!"

"Blessed be!"

"Mercury, would it be okay with you if I offered a prayer?" Karen asked softly.

Mercury smiled through her tears. "Yes, I'm sure Ford would like that."

They bowed their heads while Karen spoke a simple Christian prayer over the new grave. Then, with her adult friends, Mercury drained the last of the wine and the kids poured theirs over the grave as an offering to the Goddess of the Earth and God of the Forest. Then slowly, somberly, the group returned to the cave.

Karen walked beside Mercury and took her hand. "The light began when you called to the elements. It was green. You glowed in it.

Then, as your Rite of Passage progressed, the green went from your body into the earth, and it spread out into the Painted Hills. It changed color so that, for just a moment, the hills were lit by a soft glow that reminded me of my grandmother's porch light." Karen squeezed her hand before she released it. "I thought it was important that you knew."

"Thank you," Mercury said softly. "Thank you, Karen. I appreciate knowing that. And thank you for your prayer."

Dinner was a sad, silent affair. The small group was exhausted, and not long after full dark, Mercury was sitting with Khaleesi and Stella, staring into the fire, as everyone else had quietly gone to their beds. The dog never left Mercury's side, but shadowed her everywhere, providing comfort as only the love of a canine can.

Mercury didn't notice Stella was crying until her friend sniffled and wiped at her nose.

"Here." She handed Stella one of the tissues she'd carried to the grave in her pocket.

"Thanks." Stella blew her nose, and then a sob tore loose from her, and she buried her face in her hands and wept.

Mercury scooted over closer to Stella so she should could put her arm around her friend's shaking shoulders.

"I know. I can't believe he's gone. And I can't believe I only knew him for a few days. It feels like he took part of me with him," said Mercury softly as she wiped tears from her cheeks.

"I'm so sorry." Stella continued to sob into her hands. "So fucking sorry!"

"Honey, it wasn't your fault."

Stella looked up at Mercury. "Why the hell didn't I know he was in danger? I asked! Before we left I asked if we'd be okay—if we should take Gemma. All I got from my useless fucking intuition was that we needed to go to Mitchell and that it would be fine. But it wasn't fine. Why the hell didn't I know to bring Gemma?"

"I don't think she could've saved him," Mercury said. "Ford said it himself. The green fog broke something inside him. It wasn't your fault," she repeated. "You know Ford wouldn't want you to blame yourself."

"What the hell good is my intuition if it's faulty? It didn't fucking work today."

"Maybe Ford was fated to die; maybe, despite your new intuition, you can't change fate. Remember when we first met him? You said then that had we not been going to Madras and stopped when and where we did, he would've died. Maybe, no matter what, there was nothing we could've done about it, and that's why you didn't know it was going to happen."

"This has messed me up, Mercury." Stella shook her head. "I don't know how to be me after what happened today."

"It's like what we told Karen last night. You have to accept yourself—and that means flaws and all." Mercury sighed and stood. Instantly, Khaleesi was on her feet beside her. "I'm going to go to pee and then try to sleep."

Stella looked up at her. "I love you."

"I love you too." Mercury bent and kissed her best friend on her tear-damp cheek before walking slowly from the cave.

It was another clear, cold night. The sky was so alight with stars that Mercury didn't need the lantern. First, she headed to the truck, where she retrieved the boom box that she'd already loaded with the correct CD. Then she picked her way back to the newly dug mound of earth under which Ford rested.

Khaleesi lay at the edge of the dirt as Mercury turned on the boom box. She kept the volume low, pulled off her boots and walked to the center of the grave. She dug her feet into the freshly turned earth and breathed deeply of the scents of the clay and cedar, sagebrush and juniper that surrounded her. From her pocket, she brought out Ford's switchblade, opened it, and pressed its razor-sharp edge to her palm, where, a lifetime ago, she had accidentally cut herself and first begun to learn about the changes that were happening to them.

As scarlet bled from her hand, Mercury began to hum the melody of "Strawberry Wine" along with Deana Carter's sweet voice. Slowly at first, and then with more joy as she relaxed into the tempo, Mercury waltzed over the earth while her blood softly rained all over Ford's grave.

She felt the change and didn't need to look, though after the song ended and she'd taken the last steps of the solitary waltz, Mercury did glance down. The top of the grave was covered with yellow wildflowers that tickled her toes and lent their sweet fragrance to the somber night.

"I would've liked to have made a new world with you too," she whispered to his grave. "I'll miss you, Oxford Xavier Diaz. A lot."

Mercury retrieved the boom box, and she and Khaleesi walked slowly, silently, back to the cave, but instead of going inside, they went to the little knoll on which Imani stood as she stared into the southwest.

Mercury didn't say anything at first. She just stood beside Imani in the silent, but attentive night. Mercury didn't look to the southwest. There was nothing there for her. Instead, she turned her gaze up, imagining that Ford might look up at the same star-filled sky from the Summerlands and, maybe, mourn with her for what they'd lost.

Imani gasped, which pulled Mercury's attention from the stars.

"What's wrong?" She whispered the question to her friend, not wanting to break the listening silence.

"He will come!" Imani said.

"Huh? Who's *he*?"

Imani turned her face, and her dark, expressive eyes glowed the emerald green of the fog.

"The Destroyer. Prepare or perish."

CHAPTER

43

STELLA WAS STILL awake and staring into the fire when Mercury, Khaleesi, and Imani returned to the cave.

"Get the weed. I need it," said Imani.

"I'm ahead of you." Stella lifted a smoking joint and handed it to Imani, who looked wan and dazed as she sat heavily beside her.

Mercury sat on the other side of Stella, and the young pitty quickly curled up beside her, careful to always be within touching distance of Mercury. "Imani just prophesized."

"What!" Stella's thick silver-blonde mane whipped around her shoulders as she turned from Mercury to stare at Imani.

Imani coughed out a cloud of marijuana-perfumed smoke and passed the joint to Mercury before she answered. "I don't know that it was a prophecy."

"Then what would you call it?" Mercury asked.

Imani moved a shoulder restlessly. "I don't know. I just said the words. I don't even know if they're true, let alone where they came from."

"What words? Would someone fill me the hell in?"

"I was looking to the southwest. Like I do every night," said Imani. "I knew when Mercury joined me, but I couldn't say hi or anything. It was like my ability to speak was frozen, and then, sure as hell, there was a thaw because words suddenly poured out of my mouth: *He will come. The Destroyer. Prepare or perish.* That was it. Nothing else came to me. Maybe, I dunno, maybe I was sorta delirious or in a trance or something. I, um, haven't said anything, but when I go out there and stare toward my babies, I can feel them. Through the earth. And I know that doesn't make any sense at all. So maybe what I said doesn't make any sense either. Maybe losing them has made me lose my mind too."

"You're definitely not losing your mind. Your eyes glowed green," said Mercury. "What you said makes sense, even if we don't understand it yet."

"Then we prepare," said Stella.

"For what?" Imani shouted and then quickly closed her mouth as the three women peered into the darkness of the cave behind them where everyone else was asleep. When no one stirred, she continued more quietly. "I don't know why I said what I said, and I also don't know what a Destroyer is. How do we prepare for something we have no clue about?" She sighed and reached across Stella so Mercury could pass her the joint.

"We build our network of homes. There." Stella pointed up. "Right away. As in we begin tomorrow. We build knowing that it has to be our sanctuary and our fortress." She looked from Mercury to Imani. "We aren't fragile or hysterical, stupid or inept. We're smart, strong, capable. We're survivors. Hell, *we're magical!* We can do this. We must do this."

"I know you're right." Mercury spoke slowly, like her words were heavy. "I know we have to go on. And pretty soon I'll probably even want to go on. But right now I'm defeated. I don't want to deal with any more apocalyptic shit. I just want to sleep and sleep and sleep."

Stella put her arm around her best friend. "It'll be better in the morning, and then maybe a little better the next morning—and so on and so on."

"Time dulls the pain," Imani said. "It doesn't stop it, but it does make it easier to bear."

Miserable, Mercury met Imani's gaze. "I'm sorry. I don't mean to compare my grief to yours. I only knew Ford for just a few days. That's nothing compared to—"

"Love doesn't have a time stamp." Imani interrupted her. "Allow yourself to grieve. It takes nothing away from my loss."

"Thank you," Mercury murmured. She reached across Stella and hugged Imani and then hugged Stella before standing. "I can't be awake any longer today. I just . . . I just want to sleep."

"Night-night, Acorn. Love you. Sweet dreams . . ." Stella's voice drifted after her as Mercury, with Khaleesi at her heels, made her way quietly to where she'd set up her sleeping bag, pillow, and blankets. The T-shirt she slept in was folded neatly on her pillow. She took off her boots and the beautiful dress that held such sweet memories, and pulled on her shirt. Then Mercury slipped inside her sleeping bag and fluffed her pillow, smoothing the soft material that covered it before she lay her heavy head down. Khaleesi let her get settled and then circled several times before curling up, pressed against her back.

Mercury hadn't been lying to Stella and Imani. She really wanted to do nothing but sleep, and within just a few breaths she willingly gave in to unconsciousness.

The dream began with warmth. It radiated from behind Mercury. Her sleeping body responded, leaning into the heat. Mercury sighed happily as the warmth that was at her back spread, enveloping her, cocooning her, comforting her. Mercury breathed deeply, relaxing into the delicious heat.

Dogs are so great, her dreaming mind thought. *We don't deserve them, but I'm really glad we have them.*

A deep chuckle tickled her ear. Something brushed against the bare skin on her neck, causing her to shiver.

I'm not sure whether I should be offended or flattered at being called a dog.

In her dream Mercury gasped at the familiar voice and tried to roll over, but his arms held her back tightly against him as he spooned her. *Ford?*

What do you think? Can Khaleesi do this? Warm lips followed the path of the shivering skin on her neck. *Or this?* Teeth gently caught her earlobe. *Well, perhaps biting you isn't the best way to show I'm not a dog.* He chuckled again, and his warm breath played across her skin.

Ford! Mercury reached back to touch him. He was solid and so, so real that it made her ache. *But you're not really here. You're just a dream.*

Does this feel like I'm just a dream? His lips found her neck again, and he kissed the smooth curve where it met her shoulder.

No, she said breathlessly as his kisses sent more heat throughout her body.

I'm real. He kissed her neck to punctuate his words. *I'm supposed to be here. I'm meant to be here. I'm destined to be here. I'll always be here. With you.*

I guess that's why I wanted to go to sleep so badly. I was going to conjure you into my dream.

Bellota, you didn't conjure me into your dream. You conjured me into your life.

He moved her thick hair and kissed the patch of skin peeking above her T-shirt and then something brushed softly over her skin, causing her to squirm.

His laugh was low and rich and sensuous. *You are ticklish. I wondered. I also wondered if you would taste as sweet as I imagined. You do, Bellota. You do.*

The butterfly wings tickle stopped when he shifted and dropped something on the pillow beside her face. It didn't matter that it was so dark that she couldn't see it. She could smell its sweet scent.

A flower from your grave. I—I thought you'd like it if I made them bloom for you.

I did. I do. I also like your dancing, though next time you waltz, it should be in my arms.

I wish I could dance with you again, but instead I got you killed. I'm so sorry, Ford. I didn't mean— She reached back to let her fingers sink into his thick, dark hair, but her words broke off as she felt something strange—a hard nub, like a protruding bone or the beginnings of a horn. *Wait—what the hell is that?*

Soon, Bellota, soon you'll be ready to understand. Until then, know that I will be near—always and forever. Always and forever . . .

The cold woke Mercury. She sat suddenly, shivering—and then her dream came flooding back to her, and she spun around to look behind her. Nothing. Khaleesi had moved to her feet and was blinking sleepily up at her.

"Sorry," Mercury whispered as she leaned to ruffle the dog's soft ears. "I didn't mean to wake you." Then she shivered again, only this time from lingering desire. "That was some dream. Wow. My imagination is definitely working on overdrive." Mercury sighed heavily as grief chased away Ford's dream presence. She pulled the sleeping bag up and then turned to fluff her pillow—and froze.

There, beside the imprint of her head, rested a single yellow wildflower.

ACKNOWLEDGMENTS

THANK YOU TO my awesome agent, Ginger Clark, for believing in this book as much as I do!

I've loved returning to my editor and friend Tara Gavin! We make a great team.

Speaking of teams—my team at Crooked Lane is exceptional! Special thank you to Madeline Rathle, Rebecca Nelson and Melissa Rechter.

A special thank you to Diana Gill, who helped me with the blueprint for this book.

I must acknowledge the faculty I taught for fifteen years with at Broken Arrow South Intermediate High School. Teachers are magick! My intent was to do us proud and to showcase our resiliency, intelligence, experience and humor—we're superheroes!

As always, a big MAMA LOVES YOU to my daughter, Kristin Cast, who talks me off many plot ledges and gives excellent writing advice. Mommy/baby!

DISCUSSION QUESTIONS

I WROTE THE FIRST book of this duology, *Into the Mist*, for the same reason I wrote the very first book I published, *Divine by Mistake*. I wrote *Divine by Mistake* because, even though I adore fantasy novels and have been reading them since I was nine years old (beginning with Tolkien!), I had a difficult time finding high fantasy that included characters to whom I could relate. So, I simply wrote a high fantasy novel and peopled it with relatable characters.

Same thing with *Into the Mist* and *Out of the Dawn!* I love getting lost in apocalypse novels! But I have a very difficult time finding apocalypse novels peopled with characters—*most especially women*—to whom I relate. Because of that I decided to write the novel I most wanted to read. Apocalypse fiction with a feminist focus, peopled with real women (teachers!) who react to extraordinary events as I would, my friends would, or my daughter would, and so on.

1. So, let's think about relatable characters. What makes a character relatable to you? What makes them unrelatable? To whom did you most relate from *Into the Mist*, and why?

2. The bombs that devastate the fictional world of *Into the Mist* are symbolic for the destruction the patriarchy has caused in our world over many generations. Discuss that symbolism and its many layers. How does the biological agent, the green mist, play into that symbolism?

3. Would you have left Timberline? Why or why not?

4. Stella and Mercury decide to keep the fact that they have a working vehicle hidden from the people at Timberline (at first), and then later the people in Madras. Was that wise or selfish?

5. The biological agent released by the bombs alters the DNA of some of the women who inhale it. The first and most obvious element of that change is that their blood causes plants to grow. I added this element as symbolism as well as a plot device. Discuss how it can be both.

6. The heroines in *Into the Mist* are determined to rebuild their society as a matriarchy. What does that mean to you? It's clear by the reaction of some of the men at Timberline that it's a rather shocking idea. Why are they shocked? Compare and contrast this to how a group of survivors would react if men took charge. How would their priorities differ? How would the new world they create differ?

7. In Madras, Mayor Cruz seems to have created a utopia—a sanctuary for survivors—but we discover that she has a much darker agenda. Yet she has attained quite a bit of power and has many followers who are more than willing to overlook her nefarious behavior in exchange for safety and security. Do you find that credible? Why or why not?

8. Pagan ideology and rituals are an important part of *Into the Mist*. Can you see the reflection of a matriarchal society in that ideology and those rituals? Imagine if your country was Pagan and matriarchal. How would that alter your world?

9. Karen is deeply Christian, although as her experiences change and her world expands, she begins to understand the value of alternative belief systems. Do you think her change is credible? How do you feel about her change? Do you believe she can still be Christian *and* embrace her new spiritual powers?

10. I created my core group of women to represent archetypes: the warrior, the seer, the mystic or wise woman, the healer, and the spiritualist. Identify which character you believe personifies which archetype, and why. Which archetype do you relate to and see in yourself the most?

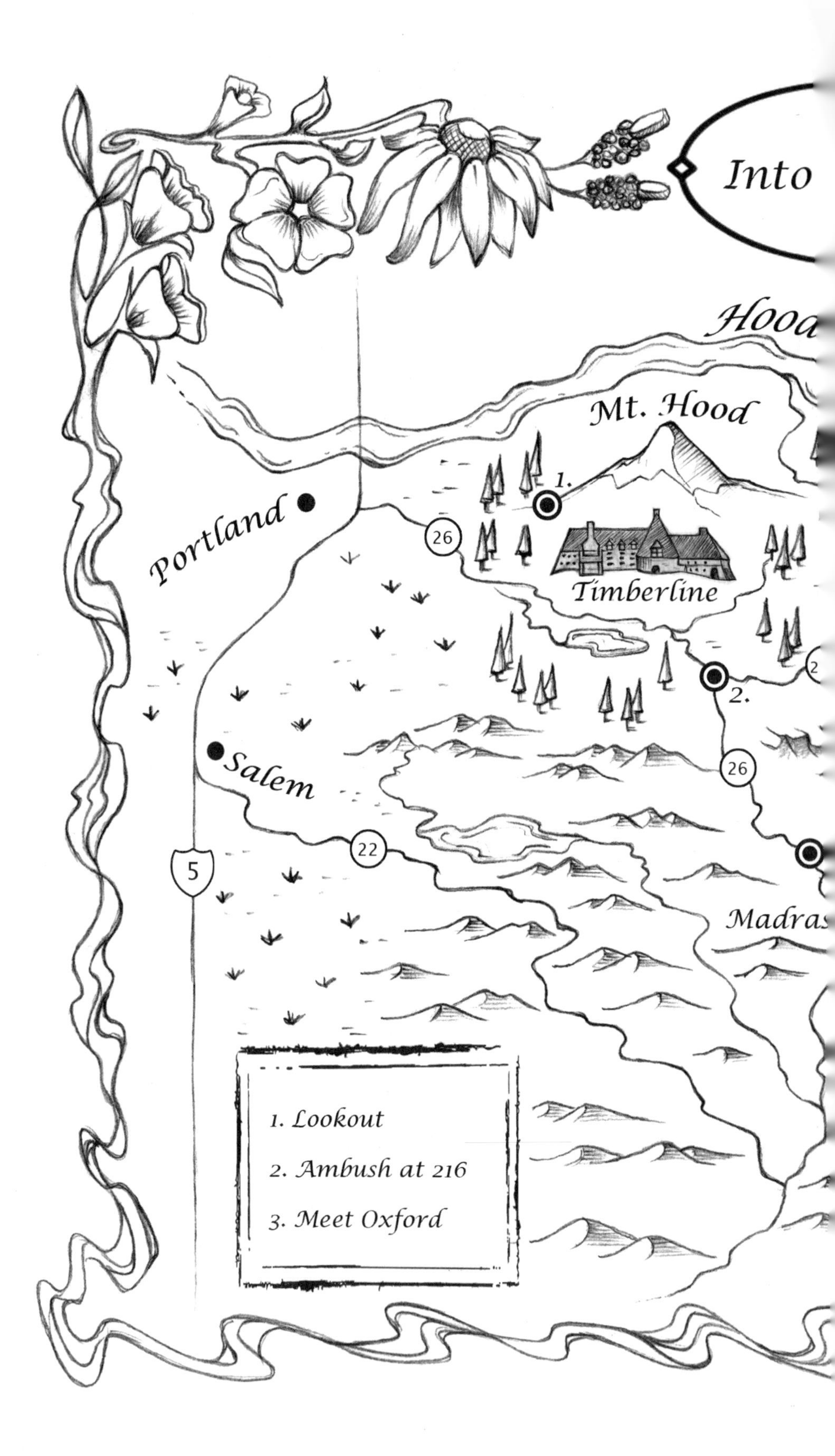
Into
Hood
Mt. Hood
1.
Portland
26
Timberline
2.
26
Salem
22
5
Madras
1. Lookout
2. Ambush at 216
3. Meet Oxford